AUSTIN S. BELANGER

The Champion of the Golden Queen

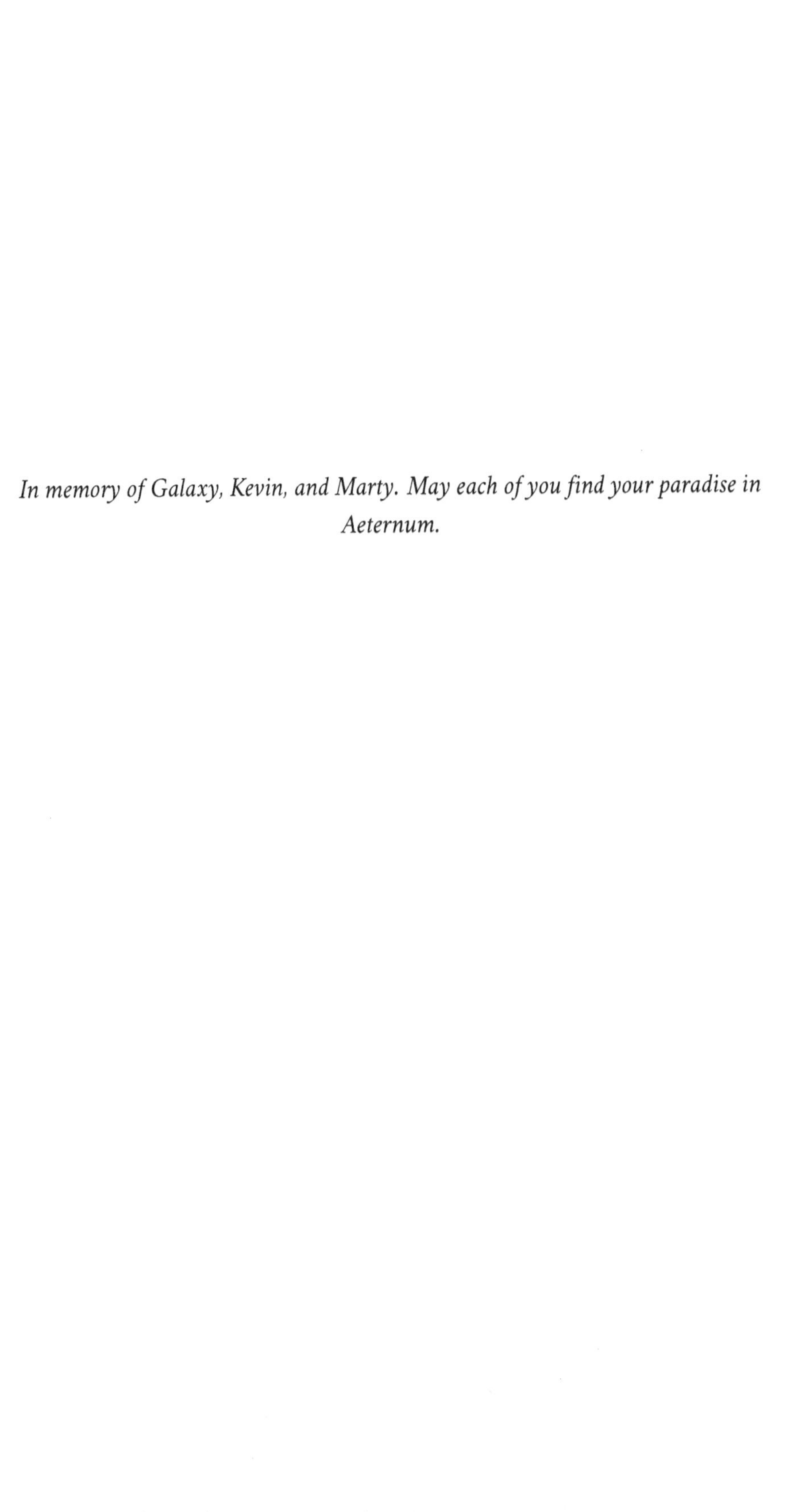

In memory of Galaxy, Kevin, and Marty. May each of you find your paradise in Aeternum.

Accept the things to which fate binds you, and love the people with whom fate brings you together, but do so with all your heart.

—Marcus Aurelius

Contents

Preface

The Goddess of Light stretched into the far reaches of Aeternum and woke her sleeping child.

"Hello, Mother," a surprised voice replied.

"I'm in need of you again, I'm afraid, my dearest child," Haya said with sadness in her voice.

"Will it be the same as the last time, Mother?" the voice asked with just a touch of excitement.

"That is not for us to know, young one. Now, go and begin your work on the Ert. Seek out your father in the darkness, and put fire to his followers' hearts," the Goddess whispered in the quietest of voices.

After hearing these words spoken, the embers of the Conflict that had laid dormant for centuries flared up, flying out of the heights of Aeternum to dwell in the hearts and minds of the mortals of the Ert. Haya knew the suffering her child would bring. She knew it from the first moment of creation, all those eons ago. But there was nothing she wouldn't do for her eternal love, and she was sure her efforts would bring him back to the light this time.

Acknowledgement

Nisha Martin—"Instigator"
Brad Pearson—Editing and writing coach
Naiha Raza—Cover art
Hillary Crawford—Editor, the final version

I

Part One

The Plans of the Goddess
"In the midst of darkness, light persists."
—Mahatma Gandhi

In the Beginning

I n the beginning, when Time was young and the fates were new, many things were decided on the whims of chance and chaos. Actions dictated reactions, shaping reality, as Time spun a tale without a certain course, as if it was one who stepped out into the darkness without seeing where it would land. Eons begat the millennia, and from these endless ages, the time of mortals; and in those many moments of chance, Haya, the Goddess of Life and Light, carved out the lands of the races she placed upon the Ert.

Before all that was, is, and is to come, there were two: Haya, the Goddess of Life and Light, and Haeldrun, her beloved. They lived in the great void that existed before time. Needing nothing, they were content to live in their own embrace, loving each other completely, fulfilling each other's needs, and maintaining the balance of the Universe.

But just as with every union, children soon accompanied the lovers within the void. First were the twin brothers, Runnir and Gunnir. They were identical Gods with identical temperaments, and each had an insatiable desire to best the other. The similar nature of the brothers sowed the first seeds of the Conflict within the void, but Haya couldn't see it through her newfound love for her children.

The peace and calm of the void were gone, shattered forever by the two new additions, who constantly competed for their parents' attention. There seemed to be no limit to the antics that these two were capable of, but Haya, loving life and light, embraced her two sons, hoping they would grow wiser with time. Despite the new changes she felt had come to the void, she had confidence that all was manageable.

These events continued for several eons, until Haya could no longer ignore the Conflict, so another addition to the family was born. Aluia, the Goddess of Peace and the Waters, joined the family of Gods in the void. Aluia was the opposite of her brothers. She was quiet and reserved, having a heart of empathy and a spirit of prophecy. Haya loved her daughter as a kindred soul, knowing that her early wisdom and compassion would balance out the mayhem that was her two older and less reserved brothers.

While Haya doted on her children, thinking she had doused the flame of the Conflict, Haeldrun harbored resentment, concealing his broken and jealous heart. Haya was "his" from the beginning, and he resented the division of her attention. He wanted his beloved all to himself. Haeldrun, feeling neglected and jealous, quietly tolerated the interruption of his wife's attention by his children, simply because the children were a part of him. In his vanity, Haeldrun saw his likeness looking back at him in the faces of his children, and this pleased him in some ways. This vain, distorted view kept peace within the family for a time. Still, the Conflict was smoldering and waiting for fuel, so it could burst into the flames it desired to become.

One day, as inevitable as it was, the brothers, Runnir and Gunnir, were arguing over whom was better at one thing or another. Gunnir felt bested by his brother. Not to be outdone, Gunnir, in his anger, reached into the blackness of the void and created a great stone, which he cast at his brother. In response, Runnir did the same, returning the gesture. Before any of the Gods could intervene, both brothers were in the middle of a maelstrom of flying debris and fire, creating great burning objects in the heavens and illuminating the darkness of the void for the first time.

The Conflict finally had all the fuel it needed. Aluia saw the commotion and wept for her brothers' violence, for she had seen this coming, but was powerless to stop it. Aluia's tears extinguished the flames on many of the heavenly objects, irrigating their surfaces with the first great rains and floods. Still, even in her great sadness, she could not stop all the flames that the Conflict had started. The result of this irrigation caused immense gardens to grow on many of the stones within the heavens, and the ones

Aluia couldn't put out continued to burn, bringing the first light the void had ever known. Haya was intrigued with the possibilities presented by this new turn of events. In contrast, Haeldrun was bored with the whole affair and did not like the light. Dejected, he went to sleep, taking a great nap.

While Haeldrun slept, the Conflict he had witnessed between his sons played in his dreams and molded his thoughts. Meanwhile, Haya resolved to create mortal beings in these gardens forged by Aluia's tears, and over time, she fell in love with the lives she had created. Haeldrun, awaking from his long slumber, and having been molded by the Conflict, was outraged. His love had created yet another distraction from her obligations to him, and he began to argue with her, demanding that she destroy the lives she had made. Haeldrun went on to insist that his love snuff out the new lights in the heavens.

The Goddess Mother was surprised by her love's anger and vehement behavior. She suddenly realized that the Conflict had shaped and molded her love into something unrecognizable, and it felt as if the center of her being had been torn from her. The Goddess thought about Haeldrun's demands for a long time, but then refused him, because she loved the light and the life she beheld, as it helped fill the new void in her being. Haeldrun, angered and jealous, left Aeternum and went on to create his own domain beyond the light. With Haeldrun leaving, the Conflict lost most of its fuel in Aeternum, but it still smoldered just below the surface.

Haeldrun loved the darkness, because he felt the light had stolen his love and mate. He blamed his immense pain on his love, and anyone who came between them. Without Haya's influence, the Conflict caused Haeldrun's true personality to emerge. His demeanor became the personification of evil, subtlety, and manipulation. The God created a world of darkness, in which to hide his hatred and malice. He named it the Underworld, creating spiritual beings he called Denir to be servants of darkness and their God's debauchery in his new domain. The Denir guard the gates of the Underworld, misdirecting any soul who becomes trapped there. Due to these sinister efforts, very few of those condemned to darkness find their way out of the Underworld catacombs to the gates of Aeternum. The Conflict thrived within this darkness, prodding events to his purposes, using his father and his minions to further his own goals.

After the departure of Haeldrun, Haya was sad, but she resolved to promote love and light within her new reality. Until that time, she had only created flora and fauna in several gardens of the cosmos. With her husband gone and her children almost grown, Haya was alone. So she decided to create people in one of the gardens that she named the Ert. No one is entirely sure why she made sentience within the Universe. Some think the Goddess was bored, while others attributed it to her loneliness. Others still, believe she had a need to nurture life and created her mortal children on the Ert. Many think she did this as an outreach to her estranged husband, using the Ert to spark his jealousy and compel him to come home. For whatever reason, she did it, and as soon as the Ert touched the Underworld, the Conflict entered it and tried to find a way to spread.

Before she created the mortals of the Ert, Haya started with the Treefolk. She placed them throughout the Ert. They lived for thousands of years in their copses and forests, prospering and multiplying without competition. There was no fuel for the Conflict, so he waited. Life was good, but boring, and Haya was not entirely satisfied with her creation, because she wanted variety and some excitement. Trees were excellent worshipers, but very tedious to observe regularly for thousands of years.

Haya then created the three mortal races of the Ert: Dwarves, Elves, and Humans. The Conflict smiled, becoming intrigued by the possibilities of three mortal races living side by side. The Goddess, in her great wisdom, knew the Conflict was coming, so she created the three mortal races, so they would need to interact peacefully with each other to prosper on the Ert.

The Goddess began her creation with the Dwarves. The Dwarves settled in the mountains to the East, and they named their home the Altyr. Many initially settled towns on the hillsides, but the Dwarves also created great cities below the Ert. In the beginning, the hill Dwarves provided food, drink, and textiles to those who chose to mine below the mountains, but over time, the usefulness of farmers eventually waned when the miners happened upon great treasures and golden riches. Soon, the hill Dwarves forsook their surface dwellings, letting their settlements fall into decay. Instead, they chose to join their kin below the mountain, taking up the mining trade, for it was much more fulfilling. The Dwarves claimed the mountains and all that was in them. They dug deep into the Ert, creating a subterranean world of stone. Their artisans fashioned many beautiful things from stone, gems, and ore.

Haeldrun, the God of the Underworld, seeing their fondness for shiny metal and stones, bestowed upon the Dwarves the skill to make their creations sparkle all the brighter. Mortals of the Ert coveted the Dwarven treasures and envied the skills with which they were made. Haeldrun used this newfound greed and envy to stir much strife among the future peoples of the Ert. Due to the efforts of the Underlord, many people would eventually perish in the pursuit of shiny baubles. Many others would spend their entire lives toiling beyond the reach of the sun, in search of riches located in the darkness below.

Possessing great treasures, but needing food and other goods, the Dwarves eventually made trade pacts with the humans to their West. The Dwarfish artisans provided treasure as payment for all the material needs of their people. Over time, prosperity and expansion caused the Dwarves to blossom, creating a great kingdom that rivaled even those of the largest of humans. Dwarves became content to stay private, under their mountains and out of the light, trading treasures with men, and their people grew strong, and their war hammers many.

The spirits of the Elves were joined with nature. From the beginning, they loved the open air and all things living, so Haya granted them the forests as their home. Elves were great hunters, but they grew much of their food and were content to eat of the fields and the forest. Still, at times, they were known to take a deer or two, or to fish within the streams when the crops were weak or if a religious feast demanded it. The Elves were a joyous people and celebrated the light and life, taking only what they needed from the Ert, always striving to preserve things in a symbiotic balance.

The first Elves built their homes among the trees and tilled the ground in great clearings. They strove to use only fallen trees for lumber, which impressed the watching Treefolk, who had minds of their own. One day, as the legend has it, Elfish holy women first spoke to the trees of the forest, at a place known as Torith, using a type of magic that Haya had taught them in their dreams. The Holy Mothers, also known as Tree-Talkers, befriended the Wood, asking it to create a large clearing where the Elfish people could plant their food. The trees, as is legend, honored their requests, because the forest saw their deeds and the respect the Elves had for all things living.

The Forest of Torith now consists of a thick ring of trees on the outside of the land of the Elves. It encircles a large clearing within its circle. Soon after its creation, the Elves took to building chiefly within the ring, hanging structures within large branches, and tilling the large clearing in the center of their lands. The trees, in turn, protected the Elves for their kindness, and the Elves respected and loved them back.

The Conflict saw this and became frustrated, for there was no fuel with which to work within the holy vales of Torith. Eventually, the Elves became entirely content with their new home, celebrating much in the woods and the center of their lands.

Haeldrun, in his darkness, despised the Elves for their love of the light and pitted them against their Dwarfish brethren to the South. Despite many petty conflicts, the Elves continued to be thankful to the light, marrying their kind, growing strong—and their longbows became many.

When humanity was young, it was given the largest portion of the Ert. In the beginning, men knew not that the Ert was finite, seeing land on the horizon in all directions, for as far as the eye could see. There was no need to fight over territory or resources; one simply moved farther away and claimed the new lands that were discovered. But eventually, through exploration and settlement, man found the edge of the lands of the Ert. The lands were encompassed in all directions by a great sea. In time, the new generations could not settle their lands freely, causing strife and desperation.

The new discord pleased the Conflict to no end. Future generations could no longer freely claim lands, for none were left to be had. This shortage began a time of landlords and tenants; greed and self-preservation provided all the fuel the Conflict would ever need to feed itself. Want for land brought about the need for new alliances against the threat of invasion from neighboring landowners. This distrust led to the formation of early tribes and clans, which would later grow into smaller nations, each led by ancient heroes.

Haeldrun, the father of darkness, knew men were easily corrupted over gain and vainglory. So the God used their fear and envy to stoke competition and strife among human men, as the Conflict had taught him to do. Eventually, bloody wars between the children of men established the great kingdoms of today; some on the side of the Light, and some on the side of the Dark, but most falling somewhere in between. The Conflict was pleased.

However, in the beginning, before greed and strife were known, men tilled the fields and chopped down trees—without the permission of the Treefolk—fashioning homes and fences against the wildlife. Those days saw plentiful crops, and for a time, man lived with his neighbor in peace, without a threat of violence or war; however, the Conflict burned within them constantly.

The Goddess knew from the beginning that the creation of humanity would be different. She knew Haeldrun would try to corrupt men, because men were emotional and unstable. So the Goddess sought balance by requiring that two forms of matter were used to fashion the souls of humankind—fire for the males, and water for the females. Men were not inherently evil, but Haya knew there would be times of foolishness and pride. Foreseeing that anger over injured pride or the thrill of an adventurous thing would often get the best of man, Haya tempered her creation with woman, who was fashioned from water.

Just as the water cools hot metal from a forge and can quench the angry flames of the Conflict, thus did Haya create woman to give man pause to think about what it is he sets off to do before he runs to do it. Haya created man and woman in the likeness of her bond with Haeldrun. It made the

Goddess happy that man and woman formed a perfect bond, resulting in equal halves of the same being. This creation enraged Haeldrun all the more. He truly despised mankind, because it reminded him of what was lost with Haya and his children. The God resolved to snuff out mankind's light and replace it with eternal darkness.

Haya placed mankind in the fields, and they eventually expanded to the shores, where they could farm, fish, and till the land. Despite the best efforts of the Goddess, Haeldrun deceived mortals into building great fortresses of stone or wood out of fear of their brethren. They insisted on protecting themselves with great armies, by anointing great heroes to lead their war bands.

The clans eventually grew strong and warred, each with their brethren, over pride, covetousness, or sometimes simple need. Men baptized their fields with the blood of their children and their brethren, as Haeldrun cheered from beneath the pyres of the dead. The fire of this constant conflict warmed Haeldrun's heart and forged it into something cold, hard, and unloving.

Aluia, the keeper of the waters, rained tears down upon the Ert when she saw the hate that had replaced the initial light of mankind, all due to the Conflict. Her tears caused heavy rains to fall upon the world. The young Goddess hoped her efforts would douse the flames of her brother, once and for all. Despite her sadness and disappointment, she eventually relented, prophesying that humanity still had a significant role to play in the events of eternity. So, Aluia thought on her visions and concluded that the goodness of humankind tended to outweigh their evil. She withdrew to Aeternum, comforted with her new hope, and the heavy rains ceased. Life continued and became even stronger on the Ert.

The Gods watched lazily at the world they had created, hoping for an entertaining series of events. Haya blessed, and Haeldrun schemed. Time continued down its random path, prodded by the whims of the Gods and the free will of mortal beings. The Conflict observed, looking for his chance to stir the chaos from time to time. Time wove its unending tale through the eternal winding paths of the mysterious intrigues of life and death.

Mortals were born and lived out their days under the sun. Generations passed into the haze of legend, remembrance, and song. Every moment from that first, unto this very one, brought this world to the point of now.

The sun continues to rise, and the great Gods provide for all upon the Ert. Yslandeth, the greatest of the kingdoms of man, stands as a friend of Elves and a beacon of truth among the kingdoms of men. Her King leads in righteous honor, and all prosper in the land, according to their station. But, as chaos has directed and the fates have decreed, one man and woman now step up to play their part in the cosmic play. As the pain has begun and the midwife is called, the time is at hand. It is a boy.

It's a boy

The account of this birth is not unlike any other. His mother was working at folding the Queen's linens and preparing for the afternoon meal, when suddenly, she was stopped in her tracks by the worst pain she had ever felt. She was reminded of a time when a horse had kicked her in her shin as a young one.

"That hurt badly, but I feel that I am dying this day! Wilda, please help me!" she cried to her mistress.

Wilda, who was directing the arrangement of the table settings in the royal dining hall, heard her cry. Fearing the worst, the head lady-in-waiting ran carefully to the laundry in her long linen dress.

"What is it, child?" she asked with obvious concern. "What is the matter?!"

"I hurt so badly that I cannot breathe, My Lady!" Arla exclaimed. "Am I dying?"

Tears now welled in Arla's young blue eyes as she doubled over in pain, gently hugging her well-rounded stomach. Then, as if on cue, her water broke, and Arla cried openly in embarrassment. Wilda comforted her while trying to hold back a laugh, as she realized that the only peril present was that a young woman was soon to become a mother. Remembering her terror at her first birth pains, she stifled her chuckle, hugged the young lady around the shoulders and reassured her that all was as it should be.

"Arla, my dear," she soothed, "it is your time to birth this child. Do not fear. All mothers who have come before you know this pain. I shall send for your husband and the midwives."

Wilda looked around at the gape-mouthed young girls who surrounded them, and sternly commanded, "You there! Stop standing there like a stone statue and get me some clean linen. And you! Get up and fetch the midwife in town. Tell her to make haste, for I think this child wishes to see the light, and soon! And you! Go to the guardhouse and have them fetch Durn the Constable, for he is the father, and he should be here! I am sure they can find someone else to pace the wall for a day!"

The three young preteen girls raced in all directions to their assignments. Linen was provided, and water was boiled. The midwife arrived within the hour, bringing strange-looking devices, herbs for pain, and books with magic spells or blessings, depending on who you asked. Wilda and the midwife moved Arla to a private room, and then Wilda left to inform the Queen of what was happening.

"I beg your pardon, Your Majesty," Wilda curtsied, "but I have news that the Queen should know."

"Rise, Wilda, you know I hate it when you bow to me. You have raised me half my life and have been such a friend. Please, stop!" the Queen smiled. "What news do you have, my oldest friend?"

"Well, My Queen, your handmaiden, Arla, who is with child, is in labor. We have prepared the servant's storeroom for her privacy, and the midwife has arrived."

"Wonderful news!" The Queen jumped up happily and nearly stumbled from her chair, prompting a flurry of attendants, and the glare of one guard stationed nearby.

"Cease with your fuss!" the Queen exclaimed. "We are fine. Let us inquire about the state of our maiden, shall we, Wilda?"

"As you wish, Your Majesty," replied the head lady-in-waiting, and she escorted the Queen to the servant's quarters, not far from where the hall was located.

Inside the room, Arla cried out, screaming and crying. Yet, among all that noise, a calmer voice encouraged with a "push now," and then, "relax, all is going well." One could also hear chanting and prayers said in low tones.

"We should not interrupt," the Queen asserted. "They are at a busy time. We do not want to be a distraction. Is there a room nearby where we can sit and wait?"

"Surely, Your Majesty." Wilda barked out a few orders to the girls in the area, and a table, some chairs, a tablecloth, and candles were brought into the common room for the servants. Many were uncomfortable, as the Queen was seated where commoners ate their noon meal, but the Queen did not care. The girls made the room as presentable as possible for their Queen. She acknowledged their efforts, but knew that only so much polish could be applied to the dingy plaster, and the light did little for a room without windows.

"Sit, all of you, and eat with us," the Queen said, "for this is a joyous occasion! A child will enter this world, Gods willing, and we will hold this little person in our arms! For we have seen in divinations, the coming times, and sense that this young one will somehow turn the tides when all is lost."

The Queen was well-known to the Elves, who appreciated her compassion and wisdom. From them, she learned the magic used for telling the future and healing. Her visions, however, were clouded and incomplete, because she was born of man, not Elf. Still, she saw things through the mist upon occasion. This vision was her strongest ever, and it reoccurred almost every day as Arla's due date had approached.

The girls did not know how to take the offer from the Queen, so she stood up and motioned to her lady and each of the girls, one by one, to sit down on the rough wooden benches and share in the refreshments they had provided. Wide-eyed, each young girl sat as straight as a pin, and Wilda glared at them, particularly the youngest one to the left, as she stared gape-mouthed at the Queen. The Queen covered her mouth and giggled, and told all of them to relax, but they did not get too comfortable, for they knew her station and where they stood in relation.

* * *

While the Queen ate with her maidens, her King arrived at the hall and was perplexed that no lunch had been prepared. He asked a guard who was present if he had seen the Queen, and the guard relayed the message that Arla was in labor and that the Queen insisted on being there. Rolling his eyes and sighing deeply, the King acknowledged the report and grabbed a servant who was passing by the area.

"Yes, Your Majesty, what is your wish?" the old man replied, his head bowed.

"Since our ladies and our Queen are preoccupied, and we are sure that she is not taking food at noon, per her physician's orders, we need a meal, fit for the Queen and several guests, delivered to the servants' common room."

"The s … servants' c … common room, My Liege?" the old man stammered, confused, furrowing his brow.

"Yes, you heard correctly. Apparently, Her Majesty is visiting, and we will need to go to her if we are to see our wife this day!" The King smiled and shook his head. *She is such a soft-heart,* he thought.

The servant departed, ordering his charges to their work, and the meal was prepared.

* * *

Meanwhile, while everyone prepared for a feast, Arla sweat and cursed, and then asked forgiveness. She prayed, asking to be spared, then cursed again, this time for her husband, who had not arrived, nor had been found by the guard. This caused Arla much stress and concerned the midwife, so she called one of her girls.

"Go to Wilda and tell her Durn has not come to his wife. Tell her that Arla is strong and that all goes well, but Durn needs to be here for his young wife, not walking the wall!" The midwife turned and said to Arla, "Wilda will fix him. He will be here in the flicker of a candle fire."

The girl found Wilda with the Queen and was caught off guard, seeing four ladies-in-waiting, sitting as equals at the Queen's table, sipping tea and eating hard biscuits. She bowed awkwardly and cleared her throat.

"Greetings, Your Majesty. I must have a word with Wilda, if you would permit it."

"Come in and stop bowing! Wilda, you have a visitor."

The lead lady-in-waiting was concerned that the midwife had sent her girl on an errand and stood. "What is wrong?" she asked, in a voice too loud for the room.

"All goes well with the birth, My Lady, but the maiden Arla's husband has not appeared from the wall."

"What!?" the Queen exclaimed, standing. "Where is the King!?"

"Here, My Lady," the King responded, arriving as if on cue. The midwife's girl wavered, nearly fainting from the surprise of the King. He steadied her, sitting her on a bench against the wall. "What is the problem, My Queen?"

"The problem is that men are always poised for war, but when life comes, they ne'er found!" The Queen was visibly upset, and the King consoled her.

"What can we do?" he asked.

"Summon Durn from the wall immediately … please? We're sorry, my love, but this is the moment of our recent dreams, and he is supposed to be here!"

"As you wish, my love," the King replied.

The King left the overcrowded common room as a caravan of food trays, drink containers, silverware, dishes, and two candelabras were brought into the space. He exited, thinking, *Thank God I am not in there right now!* and found the nearest guard.

"Guardsman!" the King shouted.

"Yes, Sire!" the guard responded, snapping to attention.

"If one needs to get the constable to the castle immediately, what is the quickest way to do so?" he asked the guard.

"Sire, one only needs to ring the tower bells three times, pause, and then repeat until he arrives."

"Outstanding. Go to the tower and tell the keeper that the King calls for the bells. Notify us upon the arrival of Durn the Constable."

"Yes, Sire!" The guardsman jogged off, his armor rattling.

Within minutes, the bells were ringing. What the young guard failed to tell the King was that not only would the constable be called, but this signal would also rouse the duty battalion to the courtyard. The duty battalion's five-hundred horsemen, one-thousand shield men, five-hundred spearmen, and two-hundred-fifty archers would fill the stone yard. The Commander of the day was Sir Ontak, the Bold, who was newly a Knight and at this time, only twenty-two years old.

The King returned to the common room, which was now filled with food and good cheer, and told the Queen what he had commanded. She smiled and giggled, covering her mouth, as was her habit, knowing that he knew not what he had done, but she knew in the end, she would have her way.

* * *

In the courtyard, bells rang, men shouted, and all hurried to form ranks. Sir Ontak, on horseback, was shouting orders to form the battalion, as was his duty.

"Form ranks! Form ranks! Shields upfront, spears behind, archers to the rear! Horsemen split into two groups and take the flanks! Do it now! Move your asses!" And move they did.

Out on the wall, on horseback patrol, Durn heard the bells. *I hope this is a drill,* he said to himself, as he spurred his horse to a gallop toward the yard. Arriving, Durn saw the duty battalion formed in perfect rows, silently standing at rest, awaiting further instructions. Not being in the army, but instead a civilian peacekeeper, Durn rode to the Commander and gave his report.

"All quiet on the wall, Sir Ontak," Durn reported.

He was acknowledged with a nod and a grunt from Ontak, and Durn rode to his section, where the police forces were gathered. No one knew what the matter was, but all were ready for anything.

The King heard all this commotion from where he sat in the servant quarters, not far from the courtyard. Rising, he excused himself, kissing his smiling lady's hand. Knowing that she only smiled like that when something was amiss concerned him. Reaching the balcony above the courtyard, the

King looked over the army in dismay. He turned, cursed, and then tried not to laugh, because more than a thousand men were standing ready for a battle, when there was no foe.

* * *

While the King looked at his army, Arla pushed one last time. With that last great push came the sound of a boy's healthy cries. The child was cleaned and given to the mother to feed. The boy was average for one of Yslandeth, and his skin was a healthy pink hew. His eyes looked as if they were tiny sapphires, and his hair was as golden as the dawn. Arla forgot her pain as she held him to her breast. She cried once more, but this time for joy, not pain.

The midwife emerged from the storeroom, informing the ladies in the common room that a healthy son had been born to Yslandeth. The Queen went immediately to the balcony, where she knew her husband would be awkwardly attempting to reason away his call to arms.

Arriving moments later, she heard the end of his exhortation to his men: "… So, men, we thank and praise you this day, for the readiness you showed and how quickly you formed for battle! More of these tests will be conducted in the future. Never forget that at any time, an emergency may arise! Yslandeth thanks you for your diligence in your duties."

"Durn! Durn!" the Queen reminded His Majesty frantically.

"Oh yes, yes," he said to his Queen. He turned to the men as they prepared to break ranks and return home. "The King has business with Durn the Constable. Durn, please come forth!"

Durn, shocked to hear his name, scurried and presented himself to the guards, and then bowed deeply to the King. "I am Durn, Your Majesty."

"Where, within the Underworld, have you been, Durn!?" the King asked with a smile. "We know that you were doing your job in the shires below. We have good tidings …"

The Queen cut off the King. "Let's go, man! You have missed the delivery of your son!"

"My son!?" the constable exclaimed, immediately recovering his bearings, as he realized with whom he spoke, adding, "Your Majesty."

"Yes, your son. Come, let's go see him!" Queen Falda smiled, and brought Durn and the King back to the room where Arla lay. The room was full of ladies and young girls, smiling at the new child who had been born. Arla finally saw her husband, and she smiled with delight, handing the newborn to her love.

With a tear in his eye, Durn declared, "My love for you is so strong, my Arla, and you are so young and pure. This child is born of that legacy. His perfection is unrivaled among my ancestors. He is the best that I have to offer. I will name him, Puryn, for he will stand just and strong for the Kingdom of Yslandeth and anyone in need."

After those words were spoken, Arla slept, and Puryn cried. Durn laughed with joy, as did the Queen, and the King quietly pondered the events of the day. An ordinary child had caused so much commotion, but if his Queen was right, the child might be anything but ordinary.

Heightened Tensions

In the elder days, when the clans and lesser nations were first founded, a great warrior led his clan to rout its enemies without mercy. This clan had many enemies, because their leader portrayed anyone outside of its fluid borders as a threat to the people's very existence. In this light, a great kingdom was founded.

After its first great hero conquered the lands and established the throne, the people called it Hodan. The primary profession of the Hodan was, by far, that of a warrior. In landmass, they were not the most prominent nation by any means, but still, they grew to one of the most powerful on all of the Ert. The people of Hodan were of the fiercest stock.

The Hodan religion officially worshiped Haya, but the people's Indigenous culture had a preference for her sons, Runnir and Gunnir. The twin Gods approved and, in turn, blessed the warrior nation with a fierceness of a kingdom five times its size. This gesture pleased Haeldrun, who exploited the fear of the nation to his advantage. As a result, the Conflict found a permanent home within the hearts of many who sat upon their throne.

The warrior culture permeated every facet of their daily lives. A duel or state execution often settled legal disputes and trials. If there was a lesser crime, the old rule of, "An ear for an ear, an eye for an eye, a son for a son," was common law. Even the throne, and all of its glory, rested on martial prowess. By law, upon the natural death of the King, there was no succession to his kin. It was custom that the finest warriors from every village would step forward to fight for the throne in a great tournament. The winner would be crowned King, and the losers were at the mercy of the new crown.

Many times, a lesser leader would eradicate his rivals by decree, but the wiser ones would employ their rivals as Generals and ministers, in service to the crown, making political gestures to the most powerful families, and thereby solidifying support for their reign.

In the case of a King dying of natural causes or in a battle against the enemy, the sitting Queen would be allowed to step down honorably. But if the King died due to a challenge, she and her family would become the winner's prize, to do with as they pleased.

The women and children in Hodan were expected to work in a trade and know how to fight. Despite this requirement, they were treated as second-class citizens in this male-dominated warrior culture. However, when young men became of fighting age and stood in the ranks, their social statuses changed. They became respected members of society by assuming the role of a warrior.

Women fighting, except in necessity or invasion, was frowned upon by the traditional hierarchy. It was considered an insult to men. In the view of the Hodan, women who fought without necessity were considered to be saying that the men defending the nation were not up to the task. This crime could be punishable by ten strokes from a rod, or sometimes even death, for repeat offenses. Still, in the end, the punishment depended upon the King.

Most Hodan were illiterate, instead learning a worthwhile trade from the age they could stand and hold a tool. Their industries included farming, ranching, lumber, and mining. They tried their hands at smithing and, by human standards, fared well at it. Still, once the Hodan made trade treaties with the Dwarves, their people mostly abandoned the art, relying heavily on the Dwarfish capital of Dornat al Ar for their weapons of war. Blacksmiths still existed, but were more apt to shoe horses, much like a farrier would, rather than fashion weapons of war.

Hodan, from the beginning, subdued many smaller clans, growing its size and strength, as was the way in those days. They eventually inherited the central plains and mid-eastern mountain ranges, absorbing their surrounding opponents and lands.

The nation prospered under the Dwarfish treaties and experienced a long period of expansion and economic growth. Hodan ate well. Trade remained unhindered with their allies, and the people were happy. However, King Swyk, the warrior of Yslandeth, knew from prior experience that this was when Hodan was the most dangerous.

Happiness and prosperity were not times for the Hodan to rest. Instead, their culture would use the wealth to strengthen its army and prepare for war, replenishing its weaponry and manpower along the way. This pleased Haeldrun and the Underworld to no end.

Swyk knew the Hodan riches were a means to an end, allowing them to gather more for themselves, while furthering the lore and glory of their warriors. The warrior from the South would seek to acquire more land or extort more treasure from his neighbors. Swyk knew it was just a matter of time.

* * *

Looking down at a map set upon a great table in his war room, King Swyk stood, thinking. The map was drawn on a great parchment, rolled out on top of a beautiful Elfish table, a gift from his friends in the forest.

He looked at the edges of the expertly carved wood top and pondered the intricate strokes of golden paint that adorned its surface. Then, looking at the depictions of the Gods of man and Elves, he remembered the meaning of the words written there in Elfish, as his wife had told him. They were an exhortation of brotherhood, and he remembered the words as this: "Peace be between Gods, men, and Elves! So may our leaders guide by their better selves."

Great lanterns hung by chains from the hall's ceiling, illuminating the parchment before him. The warrior was not in a good mood, as he imagined their flickering light as flames upon his lands. With a furrowed brow, the

King rested on his knuckles, fists on the table, looking down.

Swyk spoke. "So, you are sure of this?"

The merchant replied, "Yes, Your Majesty. I went down through Hodan, as you ordered, to sell my wares." The merchant looked around nervously.

Haeldrun fanned his fears.

"I saw their great fields, and they were practicing their tactics. Their numbers have grown another fifty-thousand, no, seventy-five-thousand men."

The King knew this man. He had spied for Yslan before and was not one to make up stories or exaggerate. Swyk sighed. "So, it is as we had imagined. The bastards did not fill their lust for blood during their last incursions. He will strike soon, but where?"

The warrior rearranged some of the pieces on the map. His oldest General gave his input after conferring with the others. "Your Majesty, may we suggest that quietly, over the next few weeks, we bolster our border defenses while sending a word of warning to our allies in the Kingdom of the Elves. My fears are that the Dwarves may have eyes on the Elfish wood again since their Hodan partners seem to be readying for another invasion of the Kingdoms of mankind."

Haeldrun scowled at the mention of Elves, envisioning Torith in flames. He smiled at his mental images.

The King agreed. "You are correct, as usual, our wisest advisor, Belrick. Send a rider now to the Elves, disguised as a merchant. No military riders. This messenger needs to go unseen by the Hodan observers, who are undoubtedly already within Yslan."

General Belrick, his body now old and well worn, snapped to attention, replying, "As you wish, Your Majesty." Then he turned smartly and exited the room.

The other Generals grimaced beneath their gray beards and shook their heads to themselves. The military hierarchy was getting too old for war. New blood was needed. Sir Ontak seemed a worthy candidate, but he was very young and hardly tested. More than one General closed his eyes quietly and murmured a prayer to Haya, asking her to provide worthy successors, so they could step aside and retire.

Haeldrun fed their fears again, and scowled after hearing them mutter his beloved's name.

The King praised the merchant and paid him handsomely, exhorting him to strengthen his walls and tend to his own family. The merchant bowed, thanking the King, and then turned, exiting quickly.

Yslandeth was the greatest nation on the Ert. It boasted the most lands and subjects. Yslan also had the greatest armies, supported by the superior longbow made by their allies, the Elves. The King could bring almost two-hundred-thousand reserve soldiers to bear within a week. An additional two-hundred-thousand regulars were trained and in full-time service, but even with these vastly superior numbers, King Swyk did not take the prowess of the Hodan lightly. He had seen it as a boy and fought it as a young man, during many skirmishes and lesser battles. He strove to avoid seeing that carnage again. Swyk knew that Hodan would spare no man, woman, or child in its quest for supremacy. When accounting for and allotting forces, the warrior would commonly calculate that one Hodan soldier may as well equal three of his own.

"Damn that man. When will enough be enough, and when will his envy cease?" the King asked as he paced.

Haeldrun grinned maliciously.

A rider was dispatched with a wagon and a small load of wine kegs to the Forest of Torith. About a week later, he arrived and gave his report to King Glorin, the Bright, of the Elves. The King welcomed the rider from Yslandeth as a great friend, opening his hall and calling for a grand celebration. During the glorious seven-course feast, the rider rose to speak to the Elfish King.

"Your Majesty, may you receive great blessings for the continued friendship between man and Elves. His Majesty, King Swyk of Yslandeth, does wish your people only prosperity, peace, and love." The rider paused.

The attendees cheered and clapped at this greeting, attentively looking at the visitor. Then, a nervous muttering began around the great hall as the listeners wondered what great news the rider brought.

Haya stood silently beside the Holy Mother in Torith. Haeldrun knew this and did not dare to appear. Besides Haya's presence, he hated the focus on the light within Torith.

"Pray attend, my brothers and sisters," the King said gently. "Be still and listen to the message that he has ridden a week to deliver!"

The rider stood nervously, clearing his throat. Then, reaching into his satchel, he opened a small leather scroll case and pulled out a sealed scroll. He broke the blue wax seal of Yslandeth. Opening the vellum, he gave his report from King Swyk.

My dear brother under the trees, we pray that Haya has blessed your people with peace and plenty and that your numbers grow daily. May your forest be filled with the sounds of laughter and children playing forever.

But my brother, we have cause to worry, for you and for our own people, for the vile power to the South does flourish, and our spies inform us that the days of peace for our people may be numbered. We can personally vouch for the reliability of our scout. He reports that the enemy has grown his military forces by fifty Legions of men. They are supplied with the finest blades and machines through alliances with those living beneath the Altyr.

The trade between our rivals has enriched both sides, and we fear that if Hodan is gearing for war, so too are the Dwarves. We simply wish to warn you all, our trusted allies. The peace that we love so dearly may be swiftly drawn asunder.

The evil of war seems to gather to our South, as our good man reads this epistle. Be well, old friend. May your kingdom last to the end of time. We remain your eternal allies and friends of the light.

We write this by our own hand.

Your friend in times, good or bad,

Swyk, the Warrior, King of Yslandeth, friend of Elf-kind.

The hall was quieted. The worried gasping of guests could be heard. Then, the murmuring started as a mild panic arose.

"Be still, my people!" said the King of Elves, in a much more powerful voice than he usually used. King Glorin stood in a glowing light, calming the fear in the room.

Haya infused Glorin with an aura of power and calmness.

As the light subsided, Glorin turned toward the mountains, looking at them through the great windows of his hall. He wore a concerned face. "So, the Dwarves wish to come out into the sun and sky again? They wish to kill our trees for their hearths or forges? What could we have that they do not already possess? Foolish Dwarves, you will receive blood for your greed and for your malice, death. Scribes!" The scribes came forward to record as the King commanded. "Write this message in the tongue of men."

The scribes handed the scroll to a younger Elf, who was the best at the common language of Etah, and the King spoke.

Oh, great friend of Elves, we thank you for your vigilance and warning. We shall not ignore your wise counsel. Know this day that I, King Glorin of the Elves, reaffirm Yslandeth as our friend and ally, in good times and bad. You can count on our bows and spears, no matter how this latest evil may play out.

Be blessed,

King Glorin, your brother in arms.

* * *

Haya frowned. She was displeased that the Elves were considering war, but she knew that Haeldrun's treachery left them no choice. The Goddess blessed her devoted, departing for Aeternum, and resolved to provide protection and light to those in need. After all, she, too, had her plans, but free will made things unpredictable. Haya hoped her plans took the unexpected into account, but she could feel the fires of the Conflict coming, and it saddened her.

Sealing the scroll with his signet on green wax, the King then handed it to the scribes, who placed the message within a woven scroll case and cast a locking spell upon its latch.

Looking to the rider from Yslandeth, the scribe warned, "If any open this scroll case, save King Swyk, the case will explode, causing great bodily harm to the opener, maybe death! The scroll will also disintegrate immediately. So please take the utmost care in delivering our message to Yslandeth."

* * *

The rider acknowledged the warning, bidding farewell to the court of King Glorin, and then he drove his wagon from the center of Torith back to his homeland with a load of Elfish linen. Hodan was none the wiser, and the rider arrived a week after leaving the forest, carefully taking the scroll case to the guard on duty.

"The King is the only person who can open that case," he warned. "The Elfish scribes cast magic upon that case, so if anyone dares to open it, save our King, they will cause it to explode and destroy the message within. Oh, and the Elves warned it would be no small explosion, so please, do not open that case, My Lord!"

The guard's eyes opened widely. Then, gingerly, he handed the case back to the rider and motioned for him to follow. The footman brought the rider to the King's chamber, where the courier bowed, addressing the King, "Your Majesty, I bring a message from King Glorin of the Elves."

"Hurry, man, hand it over!" the King forcefully exclaimed, motioning for him to advance.

The young man handed the case over to the King, who smiled when he saw the runes. Opening the case, the King yelled, "BOOM!" The rider nearly wet himself, falling to the floor, while the guard jumped back, looking for cover. The King chuckled loudly and said to the rider, "You were wise not to open this, or we would be wondering what had happened to you on the road, as you'd most likely have been blown to tatters. But excellent job! Guard, see that this man is escorted to the treasury and given one month's wages in gold. You are dismissed!"

The rider, thanking the King, bowed and exited the room. The guard did as he was ordered, and the rider left with a small bag of gold coins.

The King read the scroll in private and was encouraged. Later, his Queen joined him in their bed-chamber, and after seeing his smile, she was comforted. She kissed his face, brushing back his graying hair, as he laid down to rest in her embrace. She was encouraged for the future.

As the Queen closed her eyes and held him tight, she worried about her current visions and what they meant. She knew that the Elves would see harm, but she could not see the fate of her people, and this greatly disturbed her. Falda could not shake the feeling that she saw the end of her husband and the end of an age.

In accordance with her premonitions and visions, her convictions were reinforced that the boy, Puryn, had a significant part to play in the unfolding events, but she could not see how he fit in. He had scarcely seen his fifth birthday, when he began his learning at the towers with the Cleric Order of Haya. The Queen was determined to fashion her improbable savior as a holy man, vice a warrior, for she felt he would serve mankind best as a man of peace, not war. Looking to the heavens on more than one occasion, she pleaded for enlightenment, but received only silence.

Haya smiled at the woman's efforts, but shook her head and continued to push her agenda into reality. Sadly, the Goddess knew that this situation would call for violence, for the embers of the Conflict were burning too hot to quench them with anything less than blood. The boy would be no paragon of a peaceful era.

"We shall endure this also," she muttered to her King, slowing her breathing and finding sleep.

Swyk's eyes were wide open. He whispered to himself, "May it be as you see it, my love, but I am unsure. I fear this time may be different."

The King stared at the mural on his wall. It was an artist's rendition of the capital city of Empyr in Yslan. The high towers were gray against the blue sky, banners flowing proudly from their tops. The Great Wall was white against the forests and cliffs that separated Yslandeth from their foes to the South. Riders were depicted standing in vigilance atop it, protecting the lands to the North.

The city was painted with the sun's light behind it, giving it an appearance of the beacon of all that was good in the world. And so it had been since the formation of nations, but not without its own problems. Swyk was determined that Yslan would remain long after his reign had been welcomed into Aeternum. However, if that was to be, he knew there was work to be done.

Learning the Ways of Gods and Man

Puryn awoke to the tolling of the morning bell, and then uncovered, standing as he had been instructed at the foot of his bed in his nightclothes. In a few minutes, the headmaster would be by to give the morning prayer. The old man in the hat would then direct the morning cleanup of the living quarters and common areas, and then they would be served the morning meal.

Puryn's robe itched, but he stood stoically, awaiting his teacher. Looking around without moving his head, he viewed the dimly lit sleeping quarters. It was nicer than his home had been, but it was neither warmer in temperature, nor emotion. The towers were composed of gray stone, as were all of the rest of the compound's buildings. In fact, most of the government buildings of Yslandeth seemed to be made of the same gray, roughly-hewn stones, drawn many years ago from a quarry not far from the city. These buildings had stood the trials of the past, as had the Order of the monks who resided within the walls.

The Order was an academic and martial environment, where all things were centered on the cerebral. Emotion was a thing to be controlled. The boy was here to learn, and feelings were for another day. Thinking about that concept, Puryn wasn't sure how he felt about it, but then again, he didn't have much choice. The Queen thought this was the best course of action.

He was but five years old when ordered to begin learning the ways of the holy men in the tower at Empyr. All of the greatest minds of Yslandeth had gone here before him, and Puryn, Queen Falda's special concern, would be no different.

The young acolyte missed his mother and father. He missed playing in the sunshine and pretending to be a Knight. That, in fact, was part of the reason he was in this position in the first place. The Queen expressly forbade the training of Puryn in weaponry, because she felt the boy would better serve his people as a peaceful leader and savior. Falda would never elaborate on what she meant by that, but Puryn knew of her visions and that they were clouded.

Quietly, the young one wondered if his Queen really knew what was the best course of action, or if she was indeed guessing. He was only five, but he had a keen mind and the maturity of a young teenage boy. Since his birth, Puryn played with few children, being raised within the castle walls. He was the son of a respected constable and a young lady-in-waiting. Most of the lad's companions were older children, if not young adults. From their example, he learned to act like an adult, but secretly longed to play like the other children he could see below in the rough-housing common courtyards. However, he was always told that play was for another time.

"Step to it, boys," commanded the old man in the hat. "Make your beds, and let's get to the common areas. I expect this to be done within the hour."

The boys moaned, except for Puryn, who went about tucking in his bedding.

"That will be quite enough of that! Service to the Gods and Yslandeth is work. We must strive to maintain our living areas, as well as our bodies and minds! Get to it now, and stop with all of your complaints!" The old man stormed off. He was only half angry. He remembered being a child and being told to make his bed. He remembered rolling his eyes and protesting the orders of his elders. The old man bit back a smile while snickering as he turned to go. "Let's go!"

The boys cleaned the rooms within minutes. There were six boys in a room and five rooms within the dormitories. The rooms were segregated according to age, Puryn's being the youngest group. The boys had only been together about six months, but had already formed quite a decent little team. They assisted their slower roommates in completing their tasks, and then moved on to the common areas as instructed. The younger boys were sweaty, a little tired, and ready for breakfast within the hour.

"Time is up! How did we do, students?" asked the same old man in the hat.

To the old man's surprise, the youngest group had completed all of the tasks and was standing around awaiting further instructions. The older boys had finished right at the call to cease, and their efforts appeared dubious. The old man walked the rooms, inspecting the job that his charges had completed. He huffed and shook his head from time to time, pretending to be disappointed, but could not find fault with Puryn's team.

"You older boys are supposed to be setting the example. You should spend more time doing your assigned tasks, and less time fiddling around or talking about the milkmaid. The young ones embarrass you!" The old man turned to the younger team. "I find your efforts acceptable, and today, your group is awarded the morning meal prize."

The older boys moaned, and the old man dismissed their protests with a wave of his hand. "Don't complain to me. You will not see a reward for doing the bare minimum required. After almost six years, you should all know this! You are soon to be counted as men of Yslandeth. We cannot be mediocre, as we strive to preserve knowledge and our way of life."

The old man motioned for the boys to follow, and all of them exited the common hall to the dining hall. Instead of the gruel that the people of Yslandeth envisioned the monks eating, there was an excellent breakfast spread. Even the losing team was rewarded with fresh eggs, bread, pork, and juices or milk. The reward given to the winning team was a freshly cut melon. All of the boys ate their fill while cranky elders muttered about "excess and gluttony." The old man in the hat sat in the corner, sipping a cup of tea, enjoying the morning air, as it lazily breezed through the open window.

"Autumn is coming. We will need to gather wood and coal for the winter, and soon," he remembered. Then, he turned back to the thirty young men as they devoured the last of the morning meal. "All right, my boys, it is time to wash and get to school. Plates and utensils in their proper places. Let's do this quickly! Much to learn, and the day is short!"

The boys hurried to dump their dishes and silverware into the provided bins. Several servant boys came in from the kitchen to grab the loads and began washing. The students filed out in an orderly fashion, washed in provided basins,and dressed in clean tunics. The gray fabric was not soft, but far from the coarsest that Puryn had ever felt. The uniform was comfortable enough. It provided warmth for the coolness of the morning, but it was not so thick as to be too hot for the afternoons. The students grabbed their slates and chalk, proceeded to the main hall, and stood by their appointed seats.

The old man in the hat entered the room. The boys stood upright with eyes straight forward. There was no sound and no moving about.

"Good morning, class. May the love of Haya bless you with warmth, compassion, and the light of knowledge."

"May it be with you also," they all replied in unison, bowing slightly.

There was a sharp clatter of screeching desks and slates moving about, and then the room was silent once again. Then, finally, the old man exhorted the students to listen to and heed a story from the *Book of Lore*, which held all of the history and legends of Yslandeth. Puryn, who loved these stories, was looking forward to the first teaching period of the day. He had an uncanny memory and could quote almost every story out of the *Book of Lore*, verbatim, after a couple of years.

* * *

Years passed in a blur of repetition and learning. Every day seemed the same, as the routine never changed, but that became comforting for Puryn. The days consisted of a morning wake up, clean up, breakfast, washing, school until midday, lunch, physical training in the afternoon, afternoon chores, dinner, study, and finally sleep. A typical education was six years under the tutelage of the Order.

Puryn, at six months in, was already bored, but over the next five years, he would grow to love the towers and the routine nature of life. He had exhibited that he was exceptionally bright for a five-year-old boy from the very beginning. The Queen had seen to it that Puryn learned to read and write basic words before he ever attended the academy. She was always there, teaching, encouraging, and providing for his family. At times, Falda was there so much that the boy felt stifled, wanting to run away and play with other children. But that was for another time, as the Queen repeatedly told him. As a young boy, he wondered when.

* * *

After several years, Puryn no longer sought to play with the children. He was ten years old and only a few years from being considered a man. His play had become his studies—all of them—and he was good at all of them.

Physical fitness training within the Order was not what Puryn imagined it would be when he arrived as a young boy. Over his five years of attendance at the academy, he grew in status within the Order. However, deep in his heart, he still longed to learn the art of swordsmanship and horseback riding.

The Order had a rigorous training regimen involving strenuous stretching exercises, long distance cross-country running, and weight training. Still, they did no weapons training, save for a few staff drills. There were no horses to speak of. What the Order did do well was teach non-lethal hand-to-hand fighting. The Order was well-known, and the people of Yslandeth knew that one never wanted to find themselves in a fistfight with a monk from the towers.

Everything the Order did was to preserve knowledge and life. It would never condone killing, except in the most extreme of circumstances, like in order to save an innocent life, and only if no other alternative existed. Aggression or instigation of conflict was frowned upon and punished severely.

Puryn understood the Order's love for living things. He saw peace as the best option in most cases, but he did not understand the concept of willfully ignoring the reality of a need to prepare for war. He concluded this military thesis in his head, at the ripe old age of ten, one sunny afternoon, while practicing martial arts in the yard. That would prove to be the beginning of the end for him at the academy.

* * *

The old man in the hat, as the boys called him, was getting old and frail. His control of the boys was now a matter of respect for him as a man. In past years, the old man was known to dole out swift corporal punishment for wrongdoings. But, as Elig's days grew colder, the old man appreciated his time more. He loved his boys, seeing them much like the sons he never had, vice future leaders of Yslandeth.

Some days, he was too soft on them, and some of the other instructors saw this as a growing problem. The expectation was that Headmaster Elig, of the Order of Haya's Dawn, would soon retire, leaving Reti, his apprentice, to take over the reins of the academy. Reti had been groomed, having served under Master Elig for nearly twenty years. He approached thirty-five years old now; many knew it was Reti's time. Elig was tired, pushing sixty years old. The Order expected Reti to bring back the missing discipline as the old man softened in his twilight years.

One early afternoon, the sun showed on the West side of noontime, and all was the same as it always had been. As was his routine, the old man in the hat walked the grounds in the afternoon. The day was progressing normally, but things have a way of changing when least expected.

* * *

Athis, son of Verdin, was a malcontent of noble birth, who was put in the monastery by his father to learn self-control. Sir Verdin used special favors and influence to get his son admitted, expecting the routine and discipline would do his wild son some good. Verdin's son was a spoiled little tyrant, the son of a nobleman with connections. So, many monks were loath to impose too many sanctions upon him when he willfully misbehaved. Hypocritically, even those who lamented Master Elig's softness used a softened tone when it came to Athis.

Haeldrun owned this young soul and directed his dark young heart by constant whispers in the boy's ears. The young lad never failed to please.

The young noble, as usual, was disrupting the afternoon martial arts period. Despite the rules that the students would only go "half-speed," and that intentionally injuring a training partner was not allowed, Athis always did as he pleased. In addition, he habitually bullied the smaller students in the class, telling the others tales of how he was page to a brutal Knight, who taught him how to "really" fight. Compounding issues further, Athis was much larger than the average student, and with his last throw, he had just knocked the wind out of his third younger training partner, when Master Elig finally decided to step in.

"Who is this old man to question a noble-born son? To the Underworld with him!" Haeldrun whispered to Athis.

"Athis, what have you been told about hurting the others? You will see three lashes if you do that again!" Elig barked. Puryn watched from the other side of the yard.

"Will you take this scolding from a decrepit old man? You are the son of a noble Knight and trained to kill. Why should you listen to this doddering old fool?" Haeldrun hissed at the bully.

Athis became enraged and insulted. He turned to face his teacher with hate in his eyes. "Curse you, old man, and your weak teachings!" Athis replied in disgust. "My father and his men could run roughshod over this rabble, whose only skill seems to be slapping away at each other like quarreling women!"

Haeldrun chuckled, smelling death approaching.

"That is enough, young man. To the stocks with you!" Elig pointed to the stocks in the corner of the yard, but Athis refused to go. Instead, he cursed the old man, pulling out a small knife that he had pilfered from the eating hall.

Charging at Elig, knife in hand, the young attacker caught the old man off guard. Elig could not deflect the attack, and Athis succeeded in stabbing the old man between the ribs on his right side. Master Elig, now bleeding and in shock, was disoriented and unsure of what exactly had happened. He lay on the ground staring up at the sky.

Haeldrun and his minions rejoiced in their success. Another one of the light would soon be extinguished.

Puryn saw the knife from his vantage point and immediately began running toward the much bigger Athis, with as much ill-intent as he could muster. Despite years of trying to learn otherwise, he did not regret his feelings. He arrived late, after the knife had already found its mark. However, Puryn's blow still knocked Athis sideways and off of Master Elig's waist, causing the older boy to hit the ground with a crash. Athis scrambled to his feet, turning around with the knife still in his hand.

"Kill him!" Haeldrun prodded, chuckling, fully aware that Puryn was Haya's pet.

Puryn snapped expertly to his feet from off of his back, assuming a stance that no student with a fifth-year crimson belt should have known.

Haeldrun, amused, changed his tactics. "That pig has mortally wounded your teacher, boy; whatever shall you do about it?" Puryn's face changed.

Elig saw this maneuver and his eyes became as wide as dinner plates, as Puryn's demeanor changed drastically. The master knew what was about to happen. Puryn stood, at ten years old, in a perfect dragon stance, ready to pounce on a much larger, knife-wielding foe, and that foe had no idea of the pain that was coming his way.

Puryn, as was his personal philosophy, had prepared himself for the eventuality of war. Not subscribing completely to the monk credo of, "harm no living thing," Puryn had become an earnest student of martial arts. He kept his secret from anyone outside his circle. Every night, after everyone had nodded off to sleep, he would sneak off to the bathhouse to practice his forms.

During those private practice sessions, he considered the defensive movements he was taught. Then, he looked for ways to convert the rote motions to offensive and even potentially lethal techniques. One night, he was caught practicing by an older student named James, who immediately figured out what Puryn was doing. Rather than turn him in, the more senior student decided to practice with him. The result of Puryn's insight and proficiency, combined with the years of training James had beyond what Puryn had seen, produced serious advancements.

Haeldrun made sure to aid the two partners, by revealing uniquely brutal breakthroughs from time to time. The God was pleased with the results. The Underlord kept the two boys from being discovered for all those years in the bathhouse. The deadlier they were, the better they served his purposes, so he thought.

Elig wondered why he had never noticed Puryn's passion for the arts. He knew of several instances where Puryn was caught listening in on the higher master's training sessions, only to be caught and punished. But then, Elig realized that the boy would be back at it the next day.

Somewhere along the way, Master Elig thought, as he lay helplessly, *his red belt student had trained himself, to the black, right under their noses.* He feared Puryn might kill his first person, at this very moment. The old man sputtered to protest, but was unable to speak.

Haeldrun could only hope for the worst and prod the boy along.

Athis was returning to finish the job, when Puryn struck him with a fury. The young warrior slid effortlessly to the outside of the enemy's weapon-bearing hand, snapping his foe's knee with a crushing downward kick. As Athis fell, he shouted in pain. Next, Puryn grabbed the larger boy's arm, spinning his whole body over the top of his enemy, who now lay on the ground. He then locked the enemy's arm tight, performing a wrist and arm lock combination at an awkward angle. The smaller warrior then fully extended the technique, producing a loud snap. Puryn destroyed the arm at the wrist and elbow, and the knife left Athis's hand. As it sailed, the blade sliced Puryn's cheek below his left eye, leaving a nice, inch-long horizontal gash.

Everyone present expected Athis to scream out in pain after the loud crack of Puryn's execution. However, that scream was cut short as the defender, still grasping the ragged arm, dropped his entire weight in one fluid movement onto Athis's jaw, crushing his face. All the young nobleman was capable of from that point forward was spitting out teeth and crying in a mess of his own blood, snot, and spit. Puryn still saw red and was breathing rapidly, tasting the iron of his enemy's blood as it misted in the air in front of his face. Then, he geared up for a killing blow.

Haeldrun clapped privately from his vantage point.

Master Elig cringed and closed his eyes for a moment as he witnessed the entire scene, waiting for the grisly conclusion. Yet, as violent as Puryn's actions were, the old man could not help but feel proud of his little warrior, saving the innocent from attackers. He smiled briefly, but the smile was replaced with a furrowed brow when he realized how angry Puryn truly was.

"Kill him. He hurt your master!" Haeldrun prodded, smiling his razor-toothed grin.

Athis, now semi-conscious and barely recognizable from the grotesque purple swelling around his jaw and numerous facial fractures, groaned in pain. Instructors began running toward the two combatants now. It had only been seconds, but the damage was extensive. Students stood frozen in their tracks, staring in disbelief at the slight-figured warrior, who had just destroyed a foe almost twice his size—an attacker who was armed with a weapon, at that. The scene, to Puryn, was all adrenaline and anger now. Sounds of muffled cheers and protests filled the air.

Haya intervened, touching her chosen's shoulder gently, soothing his anger by reminding him of his injured master and his teachings.

The young boy began to tear up. Then, slowly, he began to settle his breathing, and his tunnel vision began to subside. Finally, realizing that the threat was no longer present, he released the tattered arm.

Haya smiled as Haeldrun scowled from the shadows.

The knife was now five feet away from both combatants, and Athis was unconscious. Puryn absent-mindedly realized that he was bleeding from a gash on his left cheek, but brushed it off, instead choosing to rush to Master Elig's side. There, Elig caressed the young boy's face and thanked him for his bravery. He commended Puryn's attention to his martial studies. Puryn stooped low at his master's beckoning.

"You are my favorite soul, my son," Elig whispered into Puryn's ear. "You must forgive this young fool. Do not allow anger and hatred to be your way. Remember: Chivalry, Honor, and Love. I fear you may soon see a tough road ahead, due to the decisions you made here today in your efforts to save this old man. But Haya knows your heart, and so do I. Mankind may not see it in the same light. Puryn, son of Durn, you are a young one, but your fire burns bright. Be sure to train it to burn in righteousness. Continue to protect the innocent, the old or young, ladies or those too weak or helpless to protect themselves. Do not be discouraged, for my time on this Ert may be ebbing away, but I shall proudly watch your story unfold as I sit above you in Aeternum, and introduce you to the other heroes before your arrival." Elig coughed a bit of crimson to his lips.

Haya knelt silently and invisibly by the master's side. Her hand was upon his shoulder. Several from the lineage of the master stood by the side of the Goddess, awaiting Elig's entrance to the afterlife.

Haeldrun slunk into the shadows and watched in disgust.

"Please don't go, master! I do not know what to do! Who will give me the answers, if not you? What will I do without you here to guide me?" He buried his young tear-stained and bloodied face in the old man's robe, weeping like the child he indeed was. The old man held him in his embrace until his end, and when he took his last breath, Puryn was there to feel his spirit leave and go to Aeternum. He openly wept for the man who he saw as has his second father. Through his sadness, he felt a burning need for revenge.

Springing to his feet, the young warrior shouted with rage. Puryn's vision was blurred by tears, but the fires of the Underworld now burned hot in his eyes, as he sought to end Athis where he lay. So furious was his gaze that one of the assistant instructors was startled and reached out to intervene.

Haeldrun grinned widely, "Yes! YES! Do it, boy! Avenge him now!"

"Don't do it, young master," the monk exhorted. "You are better than he is. Do not lower yourself or tarnish your master's legacy!"

Haeldrun cursed the monk's interference and left for his domain, knowing that his opportunity to corrupt the boy had passed. Haya had won this skirmish, but he still had his plans, and he knew she also did.

Puryn was stopped in his tracks by the monk's words, and the instructor took him under his arm, leading him to the healer's ward, where they cleaned his wounds and packed them with herbs and medicines. The young warrior cried silently in solitude as he saw the healers carry Athis in on a gurney.

The bully had been bound to his stretcher, hand and foot. He was conscious and in extreme pain. The young noble was unsure of why he had done what he had done, but knew it was too late now to take it back. Puryn's face was stone, but he could not help but feel great satisfaction at the pain he had inflicted on the worthless person before him. He only wished he had finished the job.

Secretly, the boy wished this murderer a painful death and an eternity lost in the caves of the Underworld. He hoped his enemy would never see the gates of Aeternum. Puryn's stare unnerved Athis, who closed his eyes and cowered in fear. Haeldrun was gone, and the older boy no longer felt invincible. The bully felt as if the whole ordeal was just a bad dream, but then the reality that he had just killed his master began to sink in. Athis wept silently. Puryn thought the tears were selfish and wished Athis more misery in the future.

* * *

The instructors thought it best to separate the two, leading Puryn back to his ward, where his roommates had completed the afternoon chores for him. They had also put a small bowl of food on his night table and placed a new set of fighting clothes on the bed. Puryn looked at the new tunic and was surprised to see that there was also a black belt on top of it near his pillow. Below everything, there was a small scroll with the symbol of the Order on it.

The scroll read:

To all who hear these greetings, be blessed. Know that by demonstration of martial prowess and physical ability, the Grand Master of the Order of Haya's Dawn, does award Puryn, son of Durn, the rank of Martial Master, 1st Degree, to be signified with a black belt to be worn at all times upon the fighting field and in training. All others of lesser ranks are to take heed of this warning and render the proper respect to his rank.

It was signed, "Reti, Headmaster of the Order of Haya's Dawn." The scroll had an ink symbol stamped below the master's name with additional characters. Puryn recognized the markings as a rank of the Order. Reti held the level of a Master, Senior, 5th rank of the same Order. Puryn's eyes opened wide at the realization. He had always thought Reti to be a sycophant, but he was accomplished of his own accord. After reading the scroll, Puryn looked up, realizing that all of his roommates had surrounded him in a silent and somber circle.

"Puryn," said Donick, the eldest in the room. "Master Reti said that I could take this from the scene." Donick held out an old hat and offered it to Puryn.

Puryn recognized it as Master Elig's and tried unsuccessfully to hold back his tears.

"I don't mean to bring you more pain, brother," Donick lamented. He looked at the floor in repentance.

"No, no, thank you all, brothers. I can't thank you all enough." Puryn wiped his tears and blew his nose with a handkerchief.

"We all loved that old man," Donick said, frowning. All of them removed their caps and then bowed to Puryn in a gesture of respect.

Puryn bowed back, puzzled. Then he began asking them to rise and stop all of the formality. "You are all my brothers; do not bow to me! I am the same as all of you!"

"You are a hero," Donick responded. "We will show you the honor and respect due your bravery."

A passing instructor on duty watched quietly at the door and was taken aback by the camaraderie he had just witnessed. "These are the future leaders of Yslandeth," he muttered to himself. "We will be in good hands, Elig. Sleep well, my friend." Then he cleared his throat.

Haya silently agreed with a melancholy smile on her face.

"Time for bed, gentlemen," the instructor gently remarked. The boys acknowledged as one, bidding the monk a good evening, and then they extinguished their candles and lanterns, one by one. There was not a dry eye in the dormitories that evening, and Puryn wept silently for the loss of his mentor and friend. He clutched an old hat to his chest, while he bit back the hatred he had in his heart for the one who still remained alive.

As Puryn closed his eyes, he tried to picture the glory and wonder of Aeternum, and although he couldn't quite grasp it through his sorrow, he heard a familiar voice in his head as he drifted off to sleep.

"You must forgive this young fool. Do not allow anger and hatred to be your way. Remember: Chivalry, Honor, and Love." The old man's words echoed in his mind as his eyelids finally closed.

There would be no dreams of armor, combat, or glory that night; there was only darkness and tears.

Repercussions and Politics

King Swyk sat listening to the official account of the investigation surrounding the death of Master Elig of the Order. Durn the Constable filled His Majesty in on the facts collected during his investigation into what had happened at the tower training yard. The conclusions were disputed by a nobleman, who stood out of view and listened with intent to Durn's version of the events.

"Go on, Durn, tell me the whole story," the King prompted.

"Yes, Your Majesty." Durn fumbled with his notes, before continuing his report. "At approximately the fourth hour of the afternoon, at the tower exercise yards, several witnesses have stated that the deceased, Master Elig, was verbally counseling a young man named Athis. The offense that led to this counseling was that Athis was allegedly beating the other boys excessively during training, and Master Elig sought to intervene. During that interaction, he reportedly told Athis to go to the stocks as punishment for being disrespectful and belligerent. Athis then allegedly produced a knife, taken from the eating hall, which he used to stab the headmaster in the right side of the chest, in the ribcage, which proved to be a fatal wound."

"Ah, Elig, you old fool. What were you thinking? You should have been on your guard." The King was visibly upset. Durn remembered the King telling stories of Elig being his teacher when he was a boy at the academy. Over the years, Elig had evolved from a teacher to a trusted friend and advisor.

"Why don't you finish the story, Durn," suggested a man in fine clothes, entering the chamber unannounced and without requesting permission.

He was the father of Athis, Sir Verdin, who was also known as "the Butcher," for he showed no mercy in battle.

Unseen by mortal eyes, Haeldrun had his hand upon Verdin's shoulder and was busily feeding thoughts and arguments into his ear.

Durn was visibly shaken by Verdin's presence. He knew Puryn's life might be hanging in the balance of how this report was received. Now an adversary had come to cast doubt and use his influence to silence the truth.

"Durn, tell us what happened next and who was involved!" Verdin exclaimed in a sarcastic tone.

"Well, Your Majesty and Sir Knight, the next event that occurred was an attempt to disarm Elig's attacker by use of the skills taught during the school's martial arts classes. The boy involved ..." Durn was interrupted again.

"Push him," Haeldrun urged in the shadows. "You are a nobleman and his superior! How dare this worm's spawn touch your son!"

"What was the boy's name, Durn!?" Verdin emphasized angrily. "Who assaulted one of noble birth within the city of Empyr? Who might that young man be, I wonder?"

Haeldrun chuckled quietly. He would have Haya's pet boy's head yet.

"Umm," Durn looked at the floor, trying to restrain his disgust for the man while looking for the right words to say.

"Umm? Umm? Your common son attacks my noble son, and all you can say is, 'Umm?'" Verdin paced like a prosecutor at a trial.

"With all due respect, Sir, your *noble* son," Durn sneered on the word noble, "mortally wounded the High Priest and Headmaster of the Order of Haya! My son, the *commoner*, stopped him from stabbing an old man on the ground. Have you no honor? You stand there, defending the indefensible action of your degenerate offspring with a straight face?!" Durn was fully aware that he had stepped over all lines of decorum.

Haeldrun's eyebrows rose. He was impressed by Durn's retort. He smiled, knowing that a stern rebuke was coming.

The King interjected. "Durn! Control yourself, man. Hold your tongue!"

"Exactly! Shut your common filthy mouth, Constable!" Verdin glared menacingly at Durn.

The King injected angrily. "Sir Verdin, you should choose your next few words wisely, for I have no use for your insults and slander. Durn is a man of integrity, and his son is a favorite of my Queen. But, on the other hand, your son, Athis, is a known brigand and menace to society. How many times has he been flogged for thievery and indecency with young ladies, including those who were molested against their will?"

Verdin cleared his throat forcefully. "I sent him there to improve his morals, not to be crippled by a common piece of trash. I demand retribution as a nobleman of Yslandeth. It is my right."

Durn was red-faced and livid. He would probably lose in a fistfight with this man, but just to punch his smug face once would make a beating worthwhile. The King mulled the request over. He knew the law, and it was clear. Despite the actions of Athis, who was a delinquent and a blight upon Yslan, the King would have to act according to tradition and law, in order to preserve the unity of the nobles, especially when war may be imminent with Hodan. He relented, against his will, and granted Sir Verdin a compromise.

Haeldrun reinforced the King's insecurity, whispering in his ear, "Remember the Hodan threat. You need these men. You cannot forsake your kingdom for one boy."

"Sir Verdin, seeing that your son murdered a man in a position of authority within our land, and seeing that he has a long track record of social deviance and violence, I will recommend to the elders of the temple that he is tried for murder and sedition. Now, on the matter of Puryn, son of Durn, and his actions, which caused great pain and suffering upon a nobleman of Yslan, it is true that he must be dealt with. Puryn will be removed from the temple at the end of this cycle, which ends in two weeks. If he can complete the final examinations with satisfactory grades, he will graduate as a member of the clergy. If not, he simply returns to his regular life as a common man." The King sipped from his wine glass, and Durn shifted his weight nervously from left to right.

"Your Majesty, I agree that the boy, Puryn, should lose his privileges and be expelled from the school. May I suggest that he is not afforded the opportunity to graduate? He should not be rewarded as a priest of peace and life when he clearly intended to end my son's. If it weren't for the intervention of several instructors in the area …" Verdin paused for effect. His smile was like that of a serpent. Durn fully expected a forked tongue to dart out and taste the air at any second. "… And, Your Majesty, I don't see how the boy is not put on trial for the assault of a nobleman. If my son goes to trial, he goes to trial. It is only fair, after all."

Durn was feeling ill. How could the attempt to save an old man's life be equated to taking a life? How could the King consider this to be just? It made no sense, unless you thought of things from the perspective of a privileged nobleman. They mattered, but the average person was just a place to rest their feet. Puryn had broken their code and stopped a spoiled bastard from doing as he willed, and now the bastard's father was quoting "justice" to punish he who did nothing wrong.

"Your Majesty, Puryn only sought to save the master. He did not plan the attack on this man's son. This man's son caused the action to be necessary. Please do not consider this argument!" Durn's eyes pleaded with the King.

"Durn, your judgment is clouded, being Puryn's father. I must abide by the law of our land, and it clearly states that any commoner assaulting a nobleman will be brought to trial in the temple. I have no choice in this. Justice will be impartial. Puryn will be tried by the council at the towers." The King could not look Durn in the eye.

"But … Your Majesty!" Durn protested.

"Shut your mouth, you worm," sneered Verdin, coming to within inches of Durn's face. "Be careful how you address the King. He is not your chum! He is your Sovereign, and you will obey him, do you understand?"

Haeldrun smiled widely at his victory.

The King said nothing at this point. Durn felt betrayed and looked at Swyk's face in dismay. He saw no emotion or tell-tale sign that the King had heard a word of his plea for mercy. Instead, Durn saw the reality of life under the banners of the gray-walled city. *You were just another soldier to them. You may think you are favored, but favor was held up by the whim of those who sat in power. When all was said and done, in their eyes, you were of little more worth than beasts of the field.*

"Durn, your son will be excommunicated from the Order, effective tomorrow morning. The trial will be held before the morning meal, and in the case of guilt, sentencing will be executed before noon. You are granted the day to attend to your family, but you are forbidden to meet privately with Puryn until after the proceedings are commenced. Do you understand these orders?" The King looked at Durn sternly, but felt as if his heart would break. He must do this for the nation. Verdin could very well sabotage the ranks, and Yslandeth needed troops who were ready for war.

"For the nation," Haeldrun whispered, chuckling softly.

"I do, Your Majesty. Thank you for the leave. May I be dismissed?" A single tear rolled down from Durn's eyes as he bowed to the King.

"Go," the King responded, waving him away as he slumped in his chair.

"You have ruled wisely, Your Majesty," Verdin offered.

The King turned angrily toward the nobleman. "Why, thank you for your approval, *My Lord*. Choose your next words very wisely, for seeking to blackmail or pressure the King into actions, against his will, is treason. You would not like to finish the proceedings of tomorrow with your head on a block, would you? I don't need the priests to command that event!"

Verdin's sneer disappeared, and his face paled as he bowed. "My apologies for offending, His Majesty. I meant no disrespect! With your permission, I will take my leave!"

"Get out of my sight. Do not return for at least a week, unless you are summoned. Do you understand me?" The King was not hiding his anger at this point.

"I do," Verdin stated as he backed out of the room and hurried down the hall and out of the chambers.

The King motioned for more wine. A servant filled his glass and began to pull the bottle back. "Leave it here," the King commanded. The servant bowed and fetched another.

New Management

The sun rose and filtered through the windows, as if nothing out of the ordinary had occurred. However, now everything was different. A new master meant a different tone to the way of life for those living under the roof at the school. Master Reti was making good on his policy of tightening control and discipline within the culture of the towers.

Haya was in the room, but unseen by those present. She watched the new master intently and was not entirely pleased with Reti's demeanor.

"Let's go, men," Reti barked. "Get moving and get to your tasks. The day is young, and much has to be accomplished."

One boy, in the bed adjacent to Puryn's, moaned a bit too loudly for the liking of the master and received a backhand for his troubles.

Haya made Reti's hand sting, as if it were temporarily on fire.

Reti yelped and rubbed his palm. "This is not a nursery filled with children. You are the future leaders of Yslandeth. Keep your complaints to yourself!" Master Reti glared at the boy, who covered a red hand mark on his left cheek. The boy's eyes teared up as he began to taste the iron flavor of blood in his mouth. One of the other instructors started to move toward the boy, but Reti glared at him.

"Will you defy your new master, brother?" Reti hissed. "This is what is wrong with this place. Everyone thinks they have a say in how things are done around here. We are training young girls, not men. Get to work, or breakfast will be a short one today. Puryn, to the front office … now!"

The young warrior was still in shock from the previous day's events and honestly did not care about the things that had just occurred. He was still numb. He felt a bit sad for the boy who had been struck, but Puryn had known Master Reti for a couple of years and did not trust, nor like the man. He was not Elig, that was for sure.

Puryn immediately made his way to the front office as ordered by the headmaster. There, he was greeted by two guards and his own father. His father looked ashen, as if he had just returned from a funeral. The boy wondered what the matter was. He stood and waited to be spoken to.

Haya stood beside Durn and held his hand without his knowledge. "It will be all right, Durn," she whispered to him.

"Puryn, son of Durn, by order of King Swyk, the warrior of Yslandeth, you are hereby excommunicated from the Order of the Brotherhood of the Goddess Haya. You are to collect your belongings and exit the premises by sundown today." Durn choked up and cleared his throat to continue. He wiped a tear from his eye as he saw his son's look of horror staring back at him.

Haya frowned, but knew that her plan was now fully in motion. Haeldrun was a selfish fool, consumed by jealousy, and he never saw beyond himself. Haya's nose wrinkled at the thought of the Underlord.

Durn continued. "Furthermore, you are charged with the assault of a nobleman. Being a commoner, that is a capital offense. You are ordered to stand before the council of the tower for trial. If convicted, the execution of the appropriate consequences for your crimes will be carried out."

Durn was a wreck at this point. One of the boys brought him a tankard of water, which made him cry a bit more. This was the only thing he could say to his son before the trial, and Verdin somehow had made sure that Durn would be the lone constable available to deliver the summons.

Master Reti responded. "We have received the order from the King and will put Puryn, son of Durn, in the stocks until such a time as the council can be assembled."

The guards led Puryn to the stocks in the martial arts section of the exercise yard and securely locked him within. The young man said nothing and just stared at the ground. Then his eyes meandered to the place where

Elig fell. He stared at that spot and frowned. His father tried to compose himself.

Angrily, Durn stared at Reti with eyes that could pierce steel. "The King has other orders," he spat. "Athis, son of Verdin, will also stand trial for the murder of Master Elig of the Order. This is also a capital offense. The King wished this to happen before the morning meal, but apparently, we are too late for that. So I suggest you move things along, seeing that the execution of punishment for these trials is to be executed by noon, under the command of the King."

"Easy my son," Haya cautioned Durn. "All will be well in the end."

"Gods help us! This gives us no time," Master Reti complained. He turned to his scribe. "Assemble the leaders in the hall. Bring in the remaining twenty-eight students to sit in witness of justice. It is the second hour of the morning. We have only four hours for two trials and punishment! Let's move!"

Durn looked at the stocks where Puryn was secured. Puryn was watching his father. Durn mouthed in an exaggerated fashion, "I love you."

"I love you, too!" Puryn yelled.

Haya smiled and hugged Durn from behind. "He is strong."

"Silence in the yards!" a random guard commanded.

Durn looked at his son, then stared down the guard, who could not look him directly in the eye.

The council gathered and discussed the situation before them. All of them had been a witness, first-hand, to the events in question, and none, save Reti, held Puryn the least bit culpable for his actions. In the eyes of four of five judges, Puryn would walk away unscathed, but the ultimate verdict was Reti's. The Headmaster had known Verdin since they were young. Verdin had gone the military route, but Reti's mother and father died young, leaving him to an orphanage at ten years old. Being of noble birth and without parents, he showed great academic promise. The orphan was adopted by Elig as his apprentice and began training twenty-five years before taking over the entire school. Elig was his teacher, but Verdin was a noble who the master knew personally.

Haeldrun worked that angle while Haya comforted Durn. "Verdin has power that could be used in a future time of need," he hissed into Reti's ear.

The headmaster had to come up with a good compromise, where all parties were punished "fairly," and the powers behind this farce were appeased. Politics and religion within the gray walls were familiar bedfellows.

At the third hour of the morning, the boys should have been washing and getting ready for classes, but instead, they were filing into their desks in the great hall. Placed at the front of the room was a great table covered in holy tapestries, candles, and incense burners. Behind the great table were five ornately carved and gilded wooden chairs. They appeared to be of Elfish design. One chair in the middle of the table overshadowed all the rest.

Puryn was brought in, bound hand and foot, and sat on a bench to the left of the room. Athis was wheeled in on a gurney, still healing from his wounds. He was seated to the right side of the room. As the council entered the chamber,the guards made an announcement.

"All rise! The Honorable Council of the Brotherhood of the Goddess Haya enters the room!"

The students, and everyone else present, stood quietly and waited for everyone to assume their designated positions. A scribe began feverishly scribbling notes down upon a parchment to the right of the table. The council sat as one. The students had never seen the monks dressed in such beautiful attire. The council wore robes of silk with velvet tunics over them. The colors were crimson over white, and each tunic bore the crest of the Goddess of Life—the rising sun behind a mountainous horizon.

Haya stood silently in the corner. No one was aware.

"Be seated," the guard commanded, and all sat quietly.

"We are pressed for time. The King has commanded these proceedings, and we are ordered to render judgment and carry out punishment by noon today." Reti looked around the room, pausing for emphasis. "Both of the accused stand charged with capital offenses, which may result in a sentence of death." Puryn stared stoically at Reti, so much so that Reti stammered, forcing him to clear his throat and look away from the tiny stare. Athis's face was fearful as he awaited the hand of justice.

Haya smiled at her little charge. "So stubborn and defiant," she pondered.

"Athis, son of Verdin, you stand accused of the murder of the High Priest and Headmaster of this very school—a school in which your father enrolled you to learn the basics of discipline and common decency. How does the accused plead?"

A lawyer for the defendant made excuses for Athis. His mother died young. His father didn't raise him in a loving home. Master Elig was too harsh and caused him emotional distress. Everything was the fault of another. Puryn was sickened by the display of legal wrangling, and the watching gallery of students rolled their collective eyes, randomly shouting out at the proceedings in anger and disgust.

"Order in this room! The next outburst will receive five lashes!" Reti bellowed.

However, Reti could not determine the source of the outbursts, because Haya was shielding the students from detection.

The room became silent once again. The council called a recess to debate the ruling on Athis after his lawyer finished his long litany of excuses. Within fifteen minutes, the council returned to the long table, ready with a sentence for Athis.

"All rise!"

Everyone in the room rose.

"Be seated."

"Athis, son of Verdin, I would request that you stand for sentencing, but under the advisement of your physician, I will not require it of you this one time. You are found not guilty of murder."

The gallery exploded into chaos. Master Reti called on the guards to restore order as the students angrily shouted obscenities toward the council. Finally, after five minutes, the room was returned to a semblance of decorum. Still, Reti knew that an all-out revolt boiled right below the surface.

Haya giggled sympathetically. She wondered what Elig had seen in this buffoon.

"As I was saying, before that totally inappropriate riot … not guilty of murder, but you are held guilty of manslaughter."

Angry whispers were exchanged between the boys. One could hear the occasional curse word, and Reti could not determine if the boys were referring to him, the council, or Athis, at this point.

"Silence!" the master commanded, but no one cared.

Haya shook her head in disgust at his petulant outbursts. This master had much to learn, but she reckoned that she had all the time in the world to teach him.

The man at the end of the table rose, opening a scroll and read. "Athis, son of Verdin, being that you have been convicted justly by this council of manslaughter, you are ordered confined in the tower prison for a period of two years, without parole. Furthermore, at such a time when you are able, you will be required to work, as directed, at heavy labor to pay for your keep and your crimes. May Haya forgive you and have mercy on your soul."

Haya decided to forgive Athis if he ever asked for forgiveness. However, she knew he was not sorry for his crimes yet; he was simply sad that he was convicted of the crimes.

The scribe was scribbling more furiously than ever. The guards took Athis into custody and escorted him to the tower prison, locking him out of sight. During this sentence, the only visitors allowed were doctors, the clergy, and family, unless granted special permission from the King himself. His lawyer shook his head and muttered something to the effect of, "Verdin will not be pleased," but Reti did not care. He was tenuously holding order in the room, and he did not want the populace of Empyr to get wind of the travesty that was happening in his court.

After the trial of Athis and subsequent execution of punishment, some order returned to the court, but now the council turned its focus to young Puryn. He was standing silently, bound hand and foot.

Haya stood behind him now, her two hands resting on his tiny shoulders.

Puryn was stoically looking at Reti, as if he spied a pig wallowing in its own filth within its sty. Reti could feel the boy's disdain and was not amused in the least. However, Puryn did not seem to care what his former master thought.

"Puryn, son of Durn, you stand accused of assaulting an Yslan nobleman. You are charged with this crime as a commoner. This is a capital offense. Unfortunately, it seems to be the theme of this day." Reti sighed audibly, looking with amusement at the twenty-eight young men who were almost daring him to sentence Puryn to any time. Reti was amused, but he knew a rebellion was brewing if he didn't get this right.

"We shall dispense with the formalities here, young man. All on this council saw what you did. We are ready to hand down a sentence. Have you anything to say for yourself?"

Durn watched, wincing. He hoped Puryn would not say something to make matters worse, but he was proud of the bearing of his young son under these extraordinary circumstances.

Puryn responded. "Every day, I sat here in this room and listened to the tales and the lore of my people. My master and my mentor, dare I say, my friend, read to me since I was a young boy, up until yesterday, when a murderer, who was just allowed to live, cut him down with a kitchen knife. This was done in front of all of you, who sit on this council."

Durn had never heard his son speak like this and was amazed at his ability.

Puryn continued. "One story in particular, which I remember was of the Ebony Queen, named Ramah the Beloved, who was not always a noblewoman. Some have even suggested that she was not even of this land! Yet she was chosen by a King and became noble. With that nobility, she did great things for the poor and aided those in need. This story tells me that not all things that are good and true need be born a noble."

"I fail to see what this has to do with the situation at hand," Reti droned.

"Master, as a student of this school, I came here a commoner, under the command of our Queen. She chose me to come here, because she felt, in some way, I have a future purpose by some divine design."

Haya looked at the boy curiously, smiling.

"I do not know if this is the case, but I have strived, by years of work and study, to be the best man I can be, in an attempt to honor the faith that Her Majesty places in me. I have learned, by Master Elig's teachings, to love life and preserve it. I simply saw my teacher in trouble and wished to protect him. I sought to stop the attack. That is all."

"Protect him? How? By twisting a classmate's arm almost completely off and smashing his skull to splinters? Where did you learn such things if you did not premeditate this violence? You learned these techniques in secret. I know this, because the teachings of this Order are only for defense!" Reti retorted.

"I simply reacted to protect someone who could not protect himself after he was ambushed by someone he trusted," Puryn said as a matter of fact.

The room agreed, murmuring, and the guards hushed them. Reti knew the boy was telling the truth, but he couldn't let him walk away without some sort of punishment. Society could not have commoners beating nobles every time a noble used his privilege to impose his will upon a commoner.

"Is that your statement?" Reti asked Puryn.

"It is, Master Reti."

"We will confer now."

Again, the council left the room, this time to cat-calls from the gallery. Everyone could hear the council members loudly arguing from inside the closed chamber. Someone called Reti a horse's ass, and the boys laughed loudly among themselves. Even a guard snorted, then composed himself. After thirty minutes of arguing to the point of almost brawling, the council returned to the courtroom. The monks were somewhat disheveled, and more than one council member appeared to be annoyed.

Haya was entertained.

"All rise."

They rose. The boys were not indulging the farce anymore. They wanted Puryn to go free. Even the sons of noblemen wanted this. The room was beginning to become warm, and the unwashed boys started to smell a bit from sweating.

"Puryn, son of Durn, stand." Puryn was already standing. Some of the boys laughed. Reti continued, ignoring the slight. "Seeing that there were extenuating circumstances, which lead to the assault on the nobleman, you are found guilty of assaulting a nobleman, third degree, which carries with it a sentence of ten lashes with a cane or whip. The sentence will be carried out within the hour." He slammed a gavel on the table and made haste for the nearest exit.

The room erupted, and the council quickly took their leave. The guards stood between the twenty-eight angry students, who were now throwing things at the five monks as they quickly exited the hall. Puryn was led to a stone courtyard in front of the Temple of Haya. There, he was bound to a post erected for just such an occasion. A plaque bore the inscription, "Here I pay for my sins. By these lashes, I am purified."

Many a ruffian or criminal had been scourged here in the past, but the Punisher did not remember a time when a ten-year-old boy, guilty only of protecting his beloved teacher, was strapped to his post. The Punisher was not happy with the day's events, but he was forced to do his duty.

Haeldrun goaded the man. "Beat him; he is a criminal." But the words fell on deaf ears, as the executioner looked at the young man standing stoically before him.

"Are you ready, boy?" the almost toothless face said with a cane, one-inch thick and five-feet long, in both of his hands.

Puryn thought about his actions and where he had ended up. He was at peace with his decisions. It was worth it. He would pay his price, heal, and then rise again. Athis would rot for two years and be disfigured for life, having limited use of that arm, until he was buried within the Ert. He could never forget, just as Puryn would always remember.

"I am, Sir. Haya, have mercy upon my soul."

She had already forgiven his violence. Haya stood by the post and witnessed his courage.

The Punisher drew the rod back over his shoulder. There was a loud crack across the boy's back. He yelled, "One!"

Puryn's classmates watched in horror as crimson stripes appeared on Puryn's back through the tunic shirt he wore. Puryn cried out in pain, standing his ground as best as could be expected.

"Two!"

Puryn was light-headed. Mercifully, the last word he remembered, until much later, was the echo of "Three!" And then he blacked out.

Moving Day

Queen Falda's entourage was entering Empyr's gates. The King could hear the trumpets sounding her arrival. He was not prepared to see her after the events of the past two days. Falda had gone off on one of her training excursions to Torith, in order to further develop her skills with Elfish magic. She was distressed that no matter how hard she tried, she could not see clearly, regarding the vision concerning Puryn and the future. She had been gone about two and a half weeks and was unaware that Elig was dead, or that anything of interest had happened at all.

"Greetings, my love!" she said, bursting into the King's chambers like a young girl returning from a long trip far from home. "Why are you so grave, my husband?"

The King turned from her and stared out of his window toward the tower courtyard. Puryn was no longer strapped to the post and was nowhere to be seen at the moment.

"What is wrong?" the Queen asked in a concerned, yet demanding tone. "What has happened?"

The King turned to her without making eye contact. She knew something was troubling him. The King took a deep breath.

"Please sit, Falda."

The Queen was worried now. He rarely used her name when speaking to her. Instead, he usually referred to her as "My Queen," "My Love," or "My Lady." Only when someone had died, or something awful happened, did her husband ask her to sit while calling her by her name.

"What has happened, My King?" the Queen asked, clutching her handkerchief in a ball within her left hand.

The King sighed deeply. "Much has occurred within the last few days, Falda, much. Some things have occurred that I am not particularly proud of, but before you hate me, know that I had the best intentions of the land at heart."

His excuses were falling on deaf ears, and he could see it plainly written upon her face.

"What did you do?" she asked sternly. "What has happened that is so disconcerting? Did Hodan do something?"

"No, nothing that grave, but still, grave it is, my love."

The Queen finally sat down. "Tell me."

"Two days ago, Athis, son of Verdin, attacked and killed Headmaster Elig of the Order …"

"My Gods! What!? Elig, No!" Falda wore a shocked expression and fumbled for her next words. "But he was so popular with the boys! He was so well respected. Why would that piece of dung do such a thing? Has he been dealt with? He had better have been dealt with!" The Queen stood angrily. "That little bastard! He deserves death for this!"

"Please, calm yourself, My Queen, for there is more." The King paced.

"More? My Gods, what else could have occurred!?" The Queen looked at the King's face and saw it plain, perhaps by Elfish intuition. "Puryn! Is he all right!? Is he safe!?"

"Yes, my love, he lives."

"Oh Gods, you had me so worried!" The Queen exhaled and relaxed a bit.

"But he was involved in the incident with Master Elig," the King said in a hushed tone.

"He did not help kill that old man!" the Queen defended angrily. She refused to hear anything more about his guilt in the matter. The King held his hands up, gesturing to calm his wife.

"No! He did no such thing. But apparently, Puryn learned a bit more than defensive hand-to-hand combat at the school. Some say that he took the basic learning and went a step further. On his own, he developed techniques of war. Quite impressive a feat, actually, for a young man of ten years. I should like to find out how he did that …," the King yammered on nervously.

"Get on with it! What did he do?" the Queen demanded, almost in tears at this point.

"Oh yes, I'm sorry, I digress. Puryn attacked Athis with his advanced fighting techniques, breaking his knife-wielding arm in two places, and crushing his jaw and face by blunt force."

"What?! The little smiling boy who I have loved from birth is a soldier after all!? Damn it to the Underworld! At least he gave Athis some of what he deserved." The Queen slammed her hand down on the arm of the chair.

"Well, there is a problem with that, My Lady. Athis is a son of noble birth, and Puryn is not. I had to send both boys before the council for trial this morning."

"You did what!?" The Queen opened her eyes wide, shaking her head in disbelief.

"Sir Verdin came to me as Durn gave me the report. I am told that poor Durn was the constable who had to arrest his own son. What a truly despicable day it was." The King frowned, looking out his window at the post in the courtyard.

"So that worm, Verdin, bends your ear, and you lose your mind?" The Queen was furious. "A boy defends an old man and goes to trial for it with a murderer by his side? What is wrong with you!?"

"Hold your tongue, woman. I am still King. You will respect that if you will not respect me as your husband. Verdin had a valid claim under the law. I had to uphold it. Puryn and Athis were both convicted of their crimes. Athis is confined to the tower prison for two years. Puryn…"

"Puryn what?!" the Queen shrieked angrily.

"Puryn received ten lashes at the post at midday." The King looked away, bracing for her response.

The Queen shrieked out in horror. "He's ten years old, for the love of the Gods. Who does that to a child!? May I have your leave, Your Majesty?" The Queen was now swallowing hard and had tears in her eyes. She was using a sarcastic tone, and the King heard it plainly.

"Yes. You may go. Hate me if you must, but I fear war is coming, and we shall need Verdin and his armies. I had no alternative."

"As you say. You had no alternative." The Queen bowed and walked away toward the towers, guards in tow behind her. She was livid.

* * *

Puryn could still move, but not without great effort and pain. After he had completed the execution of justice, the Punisher woke Puryn with some cold water. He felt so badly that he helped the boy to his room to gather his belongings and get ready to leave the school.

Master Reti watched them closely, but kept his distance. The master acted as if he believed that Puryn would steal the silverware, a book, or some other item. The boy had very little to take with him. He had Elig's cap, some journals, a slate, a bit of chalk, and his bedding. From a small trunk, he took out two complete sets of regular clothing that the school usually issued to graduating students. Reti knew that Puryn would have nothing to wear once he was not allowed to wear the uniform of the Order. The master was trying to make sure the boy just faded away quietly before anyone came looking for him.

Reti's strategy did not work, for coming up the walkway from the castle to the towers was none other than Queen Falda and her guardsmen. Reti cursed.

"Damn. Keep your story straight, Reti. Here she comes, and she is not pleased," the monk muttered under his breath.

As the Queen entered, one of the instructors called the school to order, exhorting the Queen's grace.

"Oh, shut up!" the Queen stated, and she swatted away at the priest. He scurried away with a confused look on his face, and then he remembered the trials. The monk went to his chambers to hide. "Where is Reti?" the

Queen bellowed.

Reti appeared as if he had emerged from an Elfish spell of hiding, materializing from the doorway to a back room. "Yes, Your Majesty. How may I be of assistance?"

"Where is Puryn, son of Durn? He had better be in good health," the Queen glared at the master.

"Your Majesty, Puryn has been excommunicated from the school for conduct unbecoming a monk, as the King has decreed. He was punished in the courtyard, according to custom, and released to collect his belongings."

"The King decreed? Oh, when I get back to that chamber …" The Queen trailed off in her thought, remembering where she was. "Where are Puryn's quarters, monk?"

Reti commanded Donick, who was in the area doing some of the afternoon chores, to escort Her Majesty to their dormitory. Donick acknowledged, bowed, and then led the Queen to the room.

The student entered first and called the room to attention. One other boy was cleaning in the area and stood still, as was the custom of the brotherhood when attending a person of rank. Puryn, weak, tired, and bloodied, was breathing with effort. The Punisher was assisting in packing Puryn's things while the boy changed his clothes. The Queen saw Puryn's stripes and burst into tears.

"You son of a whore!" she exclaimed, charging across the room and slapping furiously at the face of the man she knew as the Punisher. He dared not raise his hands, for fear of looking as if he was going to strike the Queen, and as a result, she quickly bloodied his nose. Puryn pushed himself between the Queen and a man who now looked as if he wanted to crawl under the Ert and die.

"Stop! Stop it, Your Majesty! He was only doing his job! He had no choice! Please, don't punish him!" the boy pleaded.

Haya was watching, impressed by the boy's heart.

The Queen froze in her tracks and stared at Puryn, who was now hugging the man, who had hours earlier beat him unconscious, by order of the temple council. He was shielding the Punisher from her blows and begging for his tormentor's life. The toothless old man picked the boy up by his armpits and gently sat him on the bed.

As Haya silently blessed the boy, the Queen could see Puryn bathed in a white glow. It dazzled her eyes for a moment, and then subsided as the old man addressed the boy.

"Master Puryn, you should not talk to Her Majesty that way! She only looks out for you. She loves you, boy."

The Queen blushed, embarrassed that the toothless man was defending her after her tirade.

"I know, Sir, but I could see that you took no joy in beating me today. I saw that it pained you to do your duty. I hold no ill will toward you. In fact, I forgive you for causing me this pain, for I know it was not you who commanded it." Puryn looked at his Queen, pleading for mercy.

The old man smiled his toothless grin, and said, "They were fools for putting you out of this place, Master Puryn. You have more heart than all of those peacocks will ever know. You have put into practice what they only know how to babble about."

Haya nodded in agreement with the old man's assessment.

The Queen was amazed by Puryn's compassion. She apologized to the Punisher, who refused to hear it, and told the Queen that it was not an issue. She smiled politely, but she was embarrassed at her outburst.

Puryn hoisted a small bag over his sore little shoulder and walked out of the main door to the towers, waving goodbye to all of his friends at the school as he went. He walked his way back down the road toward the castle, where he knew his mother would be waiting, folding linens or setting the table. He would see his father at the end of the day. Save for the burning stripes on his back that were now starting to crust over, and the fact of going through five years of training, only to get dropped from the school a year before graduating, it was not that bad of a day, all things considered.

He looked over his shoulder at the gray block towers and wondered how it felt to be Athis, locked away, alone for two years. He saw numerous little gray-robed figures waving in the windows as he turned to go. One of the instructors, the one who had stopped him from killing Athis, stood with a staff in his hand. He held his hand above his head, palm toward Puryn, bowing slightly, making a symbolic farewell usually reserved for a student who was being sent on a critical mission to a faraway land. Puryn returned the salute, bowing to his former martial arts teacher, who turned and went back inside the yards to teach the advanced classes. The boy knew he would miss this place and its routines.

"To the Underworld with Athis," Puryn muttered as he made his way back home.

"We shall work on that …," Haya promised, but the Conflict smiled.

"Watch your tongue, young man," the Queen scolded.

Haya giggled at the Queen's remark, remembering her speaking about Athis scarcely an hour earlier.

Puryn had forgotten she was there. "Yes, Ma'am," he replied.

The Queen smiled, and said, "Let's go see your mother!"

Falda brought the boy to the ladies-in-waiting, and they found Arla. She ran to where Puryn waited, knowing what had happened by the retelling of her husband. When she saw the boy, she cried. The blood from his stripes was starting to show again through his tunic.

"Oh, my poor baby! My poor son! What have they done to you? First, I send you there for learning and safety, but you are involved in violence! Then, to top it all off, you are convicted of hurting a nobleman who committed murder? While trying to save the man you looked up to? There is no justice, even in the temple!" She wanted to hold him, but restrained herself, because his back was a raw mess, and she did not want to hurt him further.

"It is fine, mother!" the boy said in an eerily cheery tone. "I have a new friend, the Punish … um, what is your real name, Sir?"

"Ottun, Master Puryn."

"This is my new friend, Ottun. He has helped me get home and aided me greatly!"

Arla looked at Ottun in disbelief. The old man stared back sheepishly. She knew he had beaten Puryn under orders and could see the man was distraught over the deed, but "helped" seemed like the wrong word when it came to what had happened to her son.

"Welcome, Ottun," Arla said awkwardly.

The Queen approached them. "Arla, my dear, I fear it may not be completely safe here for your family and, in particular, for Puryn. After Verdin was so easily able to influence my husband to his will, I fear a similar incident may happen in the future, or worse, if that swine seeks revenge directly. That Knight is a moldering piece of dung if I do say so."

Haeldrun stoked her anger toward King Swyk and her fears of Verdin in an effort to split the Kingdom of Yslandeth, removing Puryn from its influence. But, unbeknownst to the Underlord, Haya was counting on him to convince Falda to leave.

"What should we do, Your Majesty? We are unable to live anywhere in the kingdom where he cannot reach us," Arla said in a half-whispering voice.

"I have an idea. Let me speak with His Majesty. I will return." The Queen departed to find her husband. Falda saw the King looking at maps. He had been drinking.

"Your Majesty, may I speak with you?" the Queen asked officially.

"Of course, My Queen. What is your need?" the King dutifully replied.

"I fear for the safety of Durn, Arla, and the boy, Puryn. I would like to ask for your blessing to take them to the Forest of Torith to the Kingdom of the Elves."

Haeldrun sneered happily.

The King was looking down at the map. It stung a bit that his lady wished to leave on this trip so soon after returning from her last. He feared she may be so angry with his recent decisions that she may go and refuse ever to return.

"This is a wise observation, My Queen. Would you be gone long?" the King prodded.

"I would be gone for an extended period, visiting my friends, studying my arts, and protecting the boy while he heals. I figure that if man will not teach him the ways of life and honor in Yslandeth, perhaps the Elves may step into the role if I ask." She sat stiffly across the table from the King.

Haeldrun had not considered the Elves, and he was not pleased. The Underlord had hoped that Falda would run to Edenyag's libraries or Cinnog's Citadel, not the Elves, and their nature and light. The Goddess of Light smugly smiled from beyond her husband's view.

The King nodded, thinking she was a wise woman. His wife knew what she wanted as an outcome, and had devised an alternative plan to continue with Puryn's training in peaceful respect for life. Swyk was genuinely impressed. "I love this idea. I just do not love that I will not see you regularly, my love. I know you are angry with me, but I hope that with time, you will accept my visits to the forest and allow me to see you."

"Of course. Always, My King. I will be waiting for you to ride out," she lied.

The King thought things over and knew the Elves would not refuse her, because she was well-loved by the King of the Elves and respected as an honorary dignitary of Elf-kind.

Swyk wanted his wife to have some of the comforts of home. He took her hand gently and kissed it, holding it to his breastplate, which he was still wearing from earlier in the day. He scarcely remembered that warfare practice had ended hours ago and hadn't realized in his worry that he had forgotten to remove his armor.

"Take Durn as security ... and some guards. Arla should be your temporary head lady-in-waiting, and she will need a few of the young girls. Make sure to bring money and clothes, and ..."

The Queen looked at her love with compassion. She could see his genuine love for her. The concern for her well-being and happiness was evident, even as Swyk's eyes betrayed his reluctance to say goodbye. Falda forgave his politics. She pardoned his backroom compromises with noblemen of ill repute. She simply saw him as a sad man with too many things that needed doing before him.

"It is fine, my love." She touched his hand. "We will pack well. I will take a small contingent of servants and security. Durn, Arla, and Puryn will accompany me as my 'guests,' to alleviate any worry about Verdin and his minions. The Elves will have me, and they have good healers there. Puryn will be as good as new. Perhaps, you should send for one for the boy,

Athis. He may be scum, but he is still a person. Maybe he will find love and compassion while in the tower."

Haya applauded her change of attitude and thought about the rehabilitation of Athis. The Goddess had not given up on the boy.

The King responded softly, "I will suggest this to Verdin. I am sure he will find it a splendid idea. Thank you, My Lady."

"Goodnight. I will give the orders and go to bed. We will leave after morning prayers tomorrow. Will you be up long, husband?" she asked, holding her gaze into his eyes a bit longer than necessary. Then she turned to go to her chambers.

"If you will have me, I will join you very shortly," the King said.

"Always, My King. You are my husband and my true love. I would suggest that we spend the night together, seeing that this will be my last night here for some time. Don't be long." She smiled at him, and he returned the gesture.

After finishing his notes, he removed his armor. He washed and then went to her.

Back to the Elves

The Queen woke at around the second hour of the morning, to the sound of industry in the courtyard. There, she saw a caravan of four large, neatly packed carts, each drawn by four large draft horses. In the middle of the line was a very nicely made carriage used by Their Majesties when going on official state trips. If the King was alone on such a trip, he left the carriage at home and simply rode his horse with his contingent of guards. Asking the Queen to do the same was out of the question, not by her standards, but his. He not only wanted her to be comfortable, but also protected as well.

Haya added to their protection by blessing the caravan. She then returned to Aeternum to monitor her plans from her seat of power. Haeldrun had left the night prior, worried that his plans would be derailed by the meddling of the Elves. He sat in the darkness of the Underworld, anxious, working on ways to sabotage the influence of his wife's designs.

A few moments later, the Queen saw Durn, Arla, and little Puryn, finding room on one of the supply carts in which to sit. The Queen would have none of that! She called down loudly from the castle's third floor, "Durn! Get out of that cart and sit in my carriage! That is not a request!"

Durn looked around, but did not see where the voice was coming from, then Arla pointed up to the Queen and waved. The Queen smiled and waved back. They moved to the carriage. When Durn had settled Arla, he called Puryn to help him with the horses. The lad ran up next to his father.

"What can I do, Father?" Puryn asked with excitement. He had always wanted to ride a horse, and he was finally close to one. They were much bigger up close than when he watched from the tower windows. Durn smiled widely. He was glad to have his boy back.

"I just wanted to get you out from under your mother's wing for a second!" Durn joked.

Puryn laughed and flinched.

"Still hurts a lot, I will wager."

Puryn looked at the ground.

"Not your fault, boy. You did what a man worth his salt would do. I am proud to be called your father, and many call you a hero. The story is told nightly by the tavern fires in the villages. That may be why Her Majesty wants to get us out of the city for a while. Sir Verdin is a vindictive cur. The stories will soon reach his ears, if they have not already. He will not be pleased that people know the truth. We are not safe here."

"Where do we leave to, Father?" Puryn looked up inquisitively.

"The Queen says we go to the Elves—all the way to Torith! After all, she is well-known and loved there," Durn said with a wide grin.

"The Elves! Torith!" Even grimacing in pain, Puryn could barely contain himself. His eyes were wide open, and he looked like the boy he should have been, instead of the reserved monks he tried to emulate. He had never been outside of the capital city or the towers in his entire life. This was an adventure!

* * *

The Queen said her goodbyes and made her way to the King's war room, where she knew His Majesty was poring over maps and defenses as she was packing to leave. *Always a soldier,* she thought. *Maybe that is for the best, under these circumstances.* Verdin was in the room when she arrived.

"Your Majesty," the Knight hissed and bowed with exaggeration.

"My Lord, greetings. May I speak with His Majesty for a moment?" the Queen replied politely.

"Of course, I will take my leave until summoned again." The Knight nodded to the King. Then Verdin slithered out of the room. The Queen was sickened by his presence and glad to be rid of him for the time being.

"We are ready to depart, My King," she said in a somber tone.

The King embraced her openly. The ladies-in-waiting blushed, and some of the girls giggled. Then they were shooed away by the older ladies, giving Their Majesties their privacy.

"The city will lose much of its luster with your absence. I will miss your face. I will miss your smile. I will come as soon as possible to visit." The King was visibly saddened.

The Queen kissed his cheek and squeezed his hand. "It will not be long before our next reunion, my love. I will send word of our arrival when we get there safely."

"Be blessed, My Queen. I love you."

"And I love you, also."

* * *

Arla had prepared a basket of foodstuffs, drinks, and hygiene-related items in the carriage. She stowed them under the seats and in the side containment compartments, which really amounted to a couple of chests affixed to the front and rear of the carriage. She was ready to be a head lady-in-waiting. Several of the girls were seated with the provisions and equipment. They were given pillows at the Queen's order.

The guards rode up to the caravan. They were a small Queen's Guard detachment of twenty men. All were expert swordsmen, outfitted with the finest equipment, at the King's orders. Their horses were also the finest warhorses that His Majesty's Royal Cavalry could muster. They were quite a sight to see. The guards were a bit confused, however, that the constable had been made Captain of the Guard by the King. More than one guardsman thought they were much more qualified to lead a military detachment over a local sheriff.

"Sir, Queen's Guard Detachment, reporting as ordered," the senior guardsman saluted and stood ready with his men.

"Good morning, guards," Durn replied. "The King has put me in charge of this detachment as a courtesy, I fear," Durn admitted. "I shall rely upon each and every one of you to give me input as to our best course of action when the time arises. We shall drill and practice together, so we will work together as smoothly as the sun hands the day off to the moon."

The men were pleasantly surprised that a civilian appointee was not trying to assert himself and claim to have a better way of doing things than what they had been trained to do over the years. They nodded in approval.

"Sir, should we set a basic perimeter around the carriage to protect the Queen and her party?"

"That sounds like a great idea, Sergeant. Carry on." Durn turned and picked up an Elfish bow. He was an excellent shot and had won many awards as an archer in the kingdom.

The Sergeant noticed the awards that Durn wore on his belt. "Now I remember you, Sir. The archer. You have been top five in the kingdom for five years now. Am I correct?"

"Yes, Sergeant, you are correct," Durn modestly replied.

"It will be nice to have an archer on my side who can hit something for once!" The men laughed.

Durn smiled, but replied, "Well, hay bales and targets are one thing. I will see about a moving man when the time comes!"

The Queen arrived. Trumpets played to announce her arrival in the courtyard. She was annoyed with all of the fanfare, but went along with it anyway. Several servants assisted her into the carriage. Arla offered her Queen something to drink, but the Queen refused and thanked her. Durn tipped his hat and climbed onto the back-perch seat set on the backside of the carriage. It was more of a shelf with a strap and springs. He nocked an arrow and set the bow across his lap. The King appeared in the archway leading out of the main hall and waved goodbye. The Queen saw him and waved her silken handkerchief in the wind. It blew as if it was a silver banner. She wiped a tear from the corner of her eye.

"Arla," the Queen said in a low tone, "the King is not an evil man. Please know this!"

"I would never think such a thing, Your Majesty," Arla replied, shocked at the statement.

"There are forces in this kingdom…" She searched for the words. "Factions … laws … alliances. Sometimes, the King has to play the right angles to ensure solidarity. This thing with …," her face twisted a bit, "Verdin …" The Queen mumbled a few incomprehensible words.

Puryn blurted out, "Was that Elfish, Your Majesty?"

The Queen laughed, replying, "Yes, my boy, but not the Elfish that I hope you will be learning!"

"I get to learn Elfish!?" Puryn looked at his mother as if he had just received the blue ribbon at the farmer's fair.

Quizzically, Arla looked at the Queen.

"I suppose we will be there for some time, so why not?"

"Truly! Why not?" the Queen agreed.

There was a loud crack of a whip, and the front cart driver called his horses to duty. The carts squeaked a bit, clattering out of the portcullis and into the cobblestone city streets of Empyr proper. There were many people gathered, waving to the Queen as she left. She was well-liked, and it was always a big deal when she left for Torith.

It was now the fourth hour of the morning. Arla insisted that the Queen eat some bread and cheese, "at the least," citing her physician's orders. The Queen acted annoyed, but then smiled and took the food and drink. Puryn and Arla ate with Her Majesty, while Durn kept an eye out for brigands. The former constable was a good guardsman and was in constant contact, verbally and by hand signals, with the escorting guard. Every man was within eyesight of the other.

After a half-day of travel, when the hour was getting late, the caravan pulled to the side of the road, about a hundred measures from its edge, setting up a pavilion for the Queen and several smaller tents for servants and the girls. The drivers and their men would sleep in the carts. The guard was split into four shifts of five men each.

"Men, I don't expect trouble, but we never know. I don't need to remind you of the importance of vigilance. I do not want to insult your profession. I know you are all the best at what you do. We are approximately a week's ride from Torith, and the Queen and the girls will need their rest, so please go about your duties as quietly as possible."

"Yes, Sir," the Sergeant replied, and then he set the watches.

The drivers set a medium-sized fire in the center of the ring of tents and carts. They pulled out some provisions, including a small hanging iron pot filled with water. Then they boiled some meat and vegetables, making a simple stew. It smelled edible to the Queen, but she would stick with her cheese.

"Your Majesty," Arla said at the Queen's pavilion door.

"Come in, Arla. I am changing into traveling clothes. The King insists on me wearing all of this regalia, but it is such a bother to travel in. Can you help me with the latches on these necklaces, please?"

"Of course!" Arla hurried and helped the Queen dress in warmer night clothes and an overcoat, so she could join the others around the fire. The head lady-in-waiting had her girls set up the Queen's portable chair near the fire, as well as her footrest. Falda was pleased and sat down. Everyone rose when Her Majesty arrived and then sat. Many gathered, sat around the fire, drinking and telling stories or making idle conversation.

Puryn was off by himself, in the shade, sitting. The Queen thought it was sad and was ready to call him over, when she realized the boy was praying. He knelt, facing the setting sun while meditating. Falda decided to leave him alone.

Perhaps, despite all that has happened, he got the message, after all, she thought, and then comforted by the notion, she smiled.

Puryn stood, bowed toward the sunlight, and began exercising. He stretched, did several sets of calisthenics, and then started his martial arts forms. The Queen was intrigued. She had never watched a monk practice before. Puryn was as close as she had ever gotten to the arts.

Squatting into an uncomfortable position for most, the young monk slid gracefully from side to side, his hands, feet, head, and arms, all moving in a coordinated effort. Then, at random moments, the Queen was startled by the loud voice that erupted from Puryn as he barked, "HAI!" from his diaphragm. Then the boy proceeded to go in the opposite direction, doing the same thing he had done the first time, but in reverse.

To the Queen, it looked as if he was doing some bizarre courtly dance, but she knew of no dancing that could break an opponent's arm in two places and crush his face. She knew the dances meant something, but could not see the violence in Puryn's grace. Falda was impressed.

When Puryn had finished his routine, one of the cart-driver boys, probably about five years older than him and technically a man in Yslan, approached the young monk.

"What are you supposed to be doing, kid?" he mocked. "Are you a performer or something? Dancer?" He laughed.

Puryn answered, as a matter of fact, "No. I am nothing but a boy. I did not finish my training, so I have no title."

"So, you washed out of being a page, or what?" the elder boy taunted.

"Monk," Puryn dead-panned.

"Monk? Like from the towers, monk? Yeah, right!" the elder boy challenged.

"You don't have to believe me, but I speak the truth," Puryn stated and started to walk back to the fire.

The wagon boy grabbed the departing dancer's shoulder and spun him around. Puryn cried out in pain and was trying to control his anger.

"What is it that you need?" the younger boy replied, his hand absent-mindedly finding its way by muscle memory over the top of the older boy's hand.

"You need to pull your weight," the older boy bullied.

"Please, let go of my tunic," Puryn replied.

"I'll let go when I'm ready," he responded.

Puryn grabbed and turned the other boy's arm over at an awkward angle, sweeping his outer foot to the rear in a small semi-circle. The older boy cried out and found himself locked in a bent-over position, his arm was twisted unnaturally, and he was in great pain.

"I do not want to fight with you, My Lord," Puryn said calmly. He was sweating as his back started to burn from the exertion. Small patches of blood were starting to seep through his shirt. "May I offer you some of my dinner and a drink? I would like to start over and be friends, if that is permissible."

"Yes, yes, that is a grand idea," the older boy said, groaning.

Puryn released the hold. The other boy stood up, rubbing his wrist and shoulder.

"Wow, what did you just do? Was it some of that monk fighting?"

"I was dancing, My Lord. Yes. The monks taught me to dance, but a bit differently than in a ballroom." Puryn smiled and offered his hand to the older boy. The boy thought for a second and then risked it, shaking the younger boy's hand.

"I am Puryn, son of Durn."

"You're Puryn? You're the student who destroyed Athis? Oh, my Gods. I thought you were bigger! You're still a young one. Well, I know you can fight, that is for sure!" The older boy looked as if he had just met some great hero of old. He led his new friend to his father.

"Da, Da! Look who I found!" he exclaimed. "Oh," he said to Puryn, "I am Marhan, son of Thad."

"What is this ruckus, boy?" Thad asked in an annoyed tone. "What are you babbling on about?" A stocky, well-muscled, middle-aged man about five-foot, seven inches tall came around one of the carts with a tack hammer in his hand.

"This is Puryn, the hero of the stories at the tavern! He nearly twisted my arm off, proving it to me!"

"Well, well, now, you are not much to speak of in size, Puryn, but you look as if you may have a heart too big for that small body. But, you will grow into it, I'm sure," Thad joked.

Puryn felt his chest and did not think anything was wrong with the size of his heart. He was unsure what Marhan's father was going on about, but he smiled politely. They talked for a while around the fire, until Arla called

Puryn to bed. Durn collected his son and brought him back. Marhan and Puryn became good friends that night, and Marhan spoke of the encounter with his hero at every opportunity he was presented. Puryn thought it odd that an older boy was so impressed with someone such as himself.

The young monk didn't understand what the big fuss was all about. He won a fight with a school bully who had murdered a man he loved and who was his mentor. Others had protected those they loved, and no one reacted this way for them. The young boy did not realize how he was an inspiration to everyday folks concerning the nobility. He was too young, and his family was fortunate to have the protection of the royalty. He knew nothing of the daily struggle of the commoner. The boy had lived a sheltered life so far. Oppression and cruelty, until of late, were foreign concepts to him.

Puryn went to bed, but he was a bit disappointed with the trip so far. He wanted to see an Elf in person, and he had not met one yet. Unknown to him, they had met him hours ago with their reconnaissance patrols and had been tracking the group's movements for several miles. Once they had determined that the caravan was not Dwarfish and that one of the female passengers was, in fact, Queen Falda, the Green, they called off their stalking and plans of ambush, instead setting up their own covert protection where prying eyes could not see them.

The human guards had not a single indication that the Elves were there. The Elfish patrol used a well-known ability to blend with their surroundings in wooded and natural areas, casting a camouflage on themselves that only a trained eye could detect. As good as these guards were, they saw nothing but trees and fields for miles.

There were twelve Elfish long bowmen within one-hundred-fifty feet of the royal encampment. The stalkers were not trying too hard to stay hidden by Elfish standards. But still, to the Draj, this practice was essential to perfect their arts for when direr times came.

The Queen was stirred from her sleep by a strange noise. Puryn was snoring in the distance. Walking outside her tent, Falda looked around. She could plainly see the silver outline of her friends. Laughing, she stretched, waving toward the fields, saying in the Elfish tongue, "Goodnight, my friends. May the stars be ever watchful and guard your souls tonight." Then bowing, the Queen waved and went to bed.

The human guards thought their charge was drunk and shrugged it off as nothing new for the nobility. It was late. It was quiet. Life was good on the watch that night. There was nothing to report. The Elves in the fields shook their heads and set their own watch.

An Unexpected Escort

The Queen stirred from a restful sleep on the down mattress, on which she laid. Being "in the field," as her husband would tell it, was all hardship and woe, but she felt as if she was in the castle and nothing was amiss, except for canvas walls, where stone usually stood. She slipped on her overcoat and slippers and opened the tent flap to a beautiful sunrise. The sun broke above the Altyr Mountains, southeast of their position.

The air was crisp, and her every breath was visible as she smiled at the beautiful morning's greeting. The sky was a perfect purple that developed into a bright blue as the sun crested over the mountains. The Arondayre stood open and free. The grass was swaying in a gentle breeze. She imagined that the waves of the sea looked like this when one crossed on a ship to some faraway land. She looked out and saw the silver outlines on the edge of her sight and knew her watchers were still out there, holding their vigil.

As she enjoyed the scenery, a guard approached.

"Can I be of service, Your Majesty?" he asked, standing tall.

"Yes, please. I must use the privy and require an escort." The Queen was mildly embarrassed.

One of the girls was poking at the embers of last night's fire, trying to get it started to cook the morning meal. She snapped up and grabbed the toiletries. The Queen went off to a secluded area, where a specially made chair with a bucket under it was erected. There was a small tent set around the "throne," as the Queen jokingly called it. She entered, closing the flap, and proceeded to take care of her business, all the while talking to herself about all of the things she wanted to do when they arrived at Torith. The guard looked off into the distance, thinking about other employment opportunities he had turned down in the past.

"There, I am finished!" the Queen announced. She bowed jokingly, and the guard ignored the gesture. The Queen made a face and stuck her tongue out at the guard, who cracked a half-smile. The Queen was satisfied that she had made him lose his bearing.

"I will attend to the matter, Your Majesty." The girl bowed and went to her work, moving the bucket farther away from camp and then finding oil to use to burn the waste. She used sandalwood to mask the smell a bit. The Queen always hated using the privy in the field. As she washed her hands, she looked at the silver outlines again and thought to herself that it was not hospitable of her to leave them out there all night and now during the daytime.

"You there. Yes, you. I see you. Stop pretending you are not there!"

The guards reacted with surprise and surrounded the Queen.

"Gentlemen, relax. They are friends, not foes! See, they come. In fact, they have been here all night." The Queen winked at the Sergeant, who was horrified at the thought that they had not detected twelve Elfish bowmen, as they came out of hiding and approached the camp slowly.

"Hail, good Queen Falda," replied the leader in Elfish. "I hope the stars kept you comforted in your slumber."

"They did, good Sir. And did you have any troubles in the wood?" She smiled, knowing well that Elves are more comfortable outside in the wood than in their own homes.

"It was a wonderful evening. Thank you!" replied the Elf, bowing.

"Come! Come close to our fire and warm yourselves, friends," the Queen called to them, motioning for them to enter.

The guards moved and relaxed. The Elves greeted the guardsmen, officially explaining that they were an elite forward reconnaissance team sent to watch Dwarfish movements in the area. They had received reports, from Elfish hunters, of bands of Dwarves poaching trees from disputed lands—some reportedly, from clearly Elfish territory.

They were there to determine the validity of these claims, and when they saw the caravan, they sought to investigate it. The Elfish Captain then finished in the language Etah, which mankind used in common. "And then we recognized the Queen of Yslan and decided we would not interfere with your movements, but would stay out of sight and back your forces with our bows, in the case of Dwarfish hostilities."

"Thank you for your concern, Captain," the Queen smiled. "Please, come and eat."

The Elves dined with the human caravan. While the humans ate eggs, bacon, and toast with tea to drink, the Elves stuck to the oatmeal and fruits that were offered. They apologized to Queen Falda for any insult, and she shushed them, saying they were not doing anything disrespectful.

When breakfast was completed, it was only the second hour of the morning. By that time, the wagon drivers had taken down most of the encampment and efficiently packed it away under the tarps on the carts.

"Queen Falda," the Elfish Captain said, "would you be opposed to our company assisting in the security of your caravan unto Torith?"

The Queen looked at Durn and her men.

Durn shrugged. "The more, the merrier, Your Majesty. We could use more bows."

"Then it is settled. I accept, Sir. Thank you for your gracious offer of support." Falda bowed.

The Captain bowed lower. "It is no trouble, friend of Elves. You are important to many in my home. I am honored to be of service." He swept around, turning to his men. He barked out several orders in Elfish, and the men answered as one, sprinting off into the fields. The human guards could see them for a while, because they watched them run off, but within minutes, they were invisible again.

"How in the Underworld do they do that?" the Sergeant muttered in a frustrated tone.

"It has little to do with the Underworld, Sergeant, and more to do with hundreds of years of practice at camouflage and magic. We can learn these techniques if we work hard and have the time on the Ert." The Queen commended him for his honor, bravery, and attention to duty, leaving for her carriage, where the girls were packing the last of the items in the chests.

"Your Majesty, I have set out your clothes—the ones you prefer," Arla said.

"Wonderful!" the Queen replied, and she entered her pavilion to change. Within minutes, she emerged in a tunic and pants, much like a man would wear. The guards looked at her quizzically, then shrugged and returned to their duties. The girls smiled and wondered what she saw in pants.

"They are so freeing, ladies!" The Queen demonstrated, spinning like a girl. "No under dress, no frilly fuzzy things, no heavy overdress and layers of insanity to weigh you down—just two legs and a shirt. The Elfish women dress this way when working or not attending a formal gathering. I will be right at home there. You shall see!"

The girls accepted the explanation, because Elves or no, the Queen would do as she willed, and they would not be the ones to argue with her.

After the Queen exited her pavilion, the men were given the approval to tear it down and pack the Queen's items. It was done in minutes. Falda then looked around again, took a deep breath of fresh air, and entered the carriage. Arla, Durn, and Puryn joined her. Her Majesty looked at Puryn. He was miffed, because he had overslept and missed the Elves.

"You shall see them all in due time, my little friend. You needed your rest," the Queen said.

"I know," Puryn replied. "But they were bowmen!"

The Queen smiled and touched his face. "You are on an adventure, my little friend, and I understand your excitement, but don't discount all of the beauty that surrounds you at this moment." She pointed to Arondayre and the Altyr. Puryn gasped. He had never seen such a beautiful sight. The tops of the Altyr were white. It had snowed at higher elevations overnight.

The cart drivers cracked their whips and called out to the horses, which responded, and the caravan was again underway. The guards were dispersed in the same manner as the day prior. They were not only looking for aggressors, for now, they were trying to locate Elfish bowmen as a challenge. One guard would banter that he "had found one."Another guard would dispute the claim, laughing and accusing, "That was only a tree or a rock." Then all of them laughed, having made it a game.

Durn protested. "Gentlemen, may I remind you that we are on watch, and this is an open area. This is the Queen of Yslandeth, not common cargo! Please, refocus your attention on the task at hand."

The men, realizing that Durn was right, responded affirmatively, becoming the professional band again. They would play the Elf finding game later if they had the time.

Several miles later, on the dirt roadway, one of the Elves appeared, as if from thin air, running toward the Queen's carriage.

"Stop! Stop!" the Elf implored. "Something is ahead!"

"All hold! Assume defensive posture! Defend the Queen!" Durn shouted with authority.

Two of the carts were placed on the flanks of the carriage and one in front and in back. The guards encircled the caravan, drawing swords. Durn stood, an arrow nocked, scanning the horizon in three-hundred-sixty degrees. He saw some smoke from the trees slightly to the southeast, close to where the road would dip toward Torith. Some horse-drawn carts were moving up and down a path, heading toward the Altyr Mountains. The intruders appeared to be short humanoid beings. They were Dwarves, and they were poaching the trees.

Technically, the Dwarves were harvesting trees from a region that was generally accepted as a buffer zone between the Dwarf kingdom and the Elf kingdom. The Elves were not happy about the deforestation of the land or the fact that the Dwarves were moving ever so slowly toward Torith and its fringe forest lands. To the Elves, an encroachment there would be an act of war.

"What do they think they are doing?" the Queen asked.

"They do as they please, until someone addresses it. The Dwarves will do this sort of thing, then feign ignorance, and ask for forgiveness if confronted by a superior force. Unfortunately, over the past hundred or so years, Elves have been more interested in music, dance, and art, than learning to defend their lands. The Dwarves are emboldened by their perception of our weakness, coupled with the fact that the humans to your South feed their need for resources." The Elf stared at the destruction of the forest and sighed angrily. "Apparently, these little miners need more wood and coal for their forges. They stripped Altyr almost bare, and Hodan is asking a high price for lumber. The Dwarves will just take as much as they can from this forest, at the price of labor and a short transport. We have sent letters of opposition and concern, but they are answered by 'technical legality and a dismissive Dwarfish leadership.' I fear if things do not resolve soon, we will go to war. But to what end?"

"Do not fear, my friend," the Queen reassured. "My husband will not sit idly by and watch harm come to our brothers and sisters at Torith. He will not stand for this. All your King need do, is to send the courier." The Queen noticed Puryn's facial expression as he stared blankly at the Elfish bowman, feet from where he sat.

"Wow," he sighed absentmindedly.

The Elf nodded and smiled at Puryn, who was beside himself. Then the bowman bowed and bade the Queen farewell, rejoining his band. The patrol wrote down notes concerning location, size, operations, military posture, and forest damage, then rolled up their scrolls and packed them away.

The travelers now entered the thick forest, and the trees seemed more overgrown and angry than they had been in some time. The Elves noticed that thick underbrush had developed, and vines with thorns obstructed much of the free movement of Elf, Dwarf, or man through the trees off of the main road. The wood was apparently setting up the bulwark against the attackers. The Elves were concerned that the forest was on the defense. They noted their findings one last time.

The caravan entered the forest. It was cool, lush, and green. Some of the trees were starting to turn the colors of red, orange, and yellow. It was late in the season of Fortes, and the heat was waning and giving way to the coolness of Glorus, the harvest time. Falda figured in another week, the forest would be ablaze in color. Puryn would faint. She giggled at the thought of his face, covering her mouth. Then she looked to the South and smelled the smoke of the Dwarves and was saddened.

Several days and nights later, the caravan arrived, without incident, at the edge of the forest of Torith. There, waiting for them, was a large formation of bowmen and spears. A few horsemen rode about, calling out orders. In the fields surrounding Torith, Falda could see thousands of tents. They spanned around the entire circumference. The Elves were performing war games and getting ready to make a statement to the Dwarves. *Things are about to get dangerous,* Falda cursed to herself.

"From one fire to another." She closed her eyes, shaking her head angrily. "Durn, we must send word to His Majesty."

Durn acknowledged. "Guard!" The Sergeant rode up to Durn.

"Yes, Sir."

"Please dispatch a rider to Yslandeth and inform the King of the situation occurring on the border between the Elves and the Dwarves. It is of the utmost urgency that he knows of this."

"Yes, Sir," he replied. Then he wrote a message on a piece of parchment, rolling it up and handing it to his subordinate. "Take this to His Majesty. Do not rest until you are there. Send a rider back with his reply, or return yourself. Understood?"

"Yes, Sir!" He rode away at a gallop.

The horns of the Elves sounded as the caravan arrived. The vanguard of the King's forces rode out to greet them since they were about half a mile away.

"Your Majesty, back again so soon?!" the young Lord joked.

"I missed the wine, My Lord," the Queen bantered, then motioned for him to come close, and she embraced him with a big, long hug. "Narulas! How are you, my friend, and why are you in armor? What is the meaning of all of this? I leave for a few days, and you go to war?"

The Elf answered in his tongue. "Falda, friend of the Forest, we have enemies who seek to use the trees to further their own designs. Only baubles interest them, apparently, not living things or nature. We have asked them to stop, but they ignore us or simply refuse. There is a time to fight, and it may be now, but it has not come to that … yet."

"Well, let us hope that this can be resolved without conflict. War is such a hideous thing. The aftermath lingers for so many years," Falda frowned.

"Agreed. Come, let me take you to Uncle! He will be glad that you have come!" Narulas replied jovially.

The Queen commanded the caravan to follow Lord Narulas through the forest defensive forces into Torith proper. Once through, Puryn saw the great clearing he had read about. The crops were bulging and ready to pop. The Elves were gathering the harvest. Puryn saw houses at all levels of the trees. The shops, inns, and marketplaces—everything was suspended or built onto a large tree or branch. The boy was impressed by all of it. Everything here coexisted with nature. The Elves had found a balance that preserved the forest while providing food, water, and prosperity—all this, accomplished without the destruction found in human and Dwarfish societies. Some humans were becoming more conscious of their surroundings, but Dwarves did not understand or care.

The caravan was led to a row of houses given to Falda by the Elfish King. The wagon masters unloaded the carts and then set up the traveler's homes. The Guard set up camp on the grounds, nearby the Queen's house. The Queen was tired and went to bed early.

Durn could scarcely control Puryn, who wanted to run amuck, and explore everything he saw, all at once. Arla just stared at all of the beauty around her in wonder, laughing at her ten-year-old son. *Amazing,* she said to herself as she finished her duties.

The Queen released Arla for the day, so she returned to her family, who all ate a decent meal, and then sat in their new kitchen, taking in the scenery. Elves began playing music somewhere. There was drinking, eating, and laughter. Puryn lay on his bed and struggled to find rest, listening to the new sounds all around him. Then finally, sleep took him, and he dreamed.

The dream was not a happy one. Armored, he sat upon a horse, looking out over the field of Arondayre. He was covered in blood and surrounded by men he didn't know. The men of Hodan were there on his flanks. They all looked at him with blank stares as a great darkness closed around their position, blotting out the sun. He woke with a start and cried out.

"What is it, child?" Arla asked worriedly.

"Nothing, Mother, just a dream, a strange one. It must be from all of the excitement of the past few days!" Puryn wiped the sweat from his brow.

His mother tucked him in, and he protested, insisting that he was a grown man, or almost was. She shushed him, and he relented, allowing her to kiss him with a big, wet kiss on his forehead.

"Oh, Mother, eww!" He recoiled, wiping his forehead with his arm. He reached up and hugged her neck, and kissed her cheek. "Goodnight, Momma," he said to Arla.

She smiled, happier than she had been in five years. Her son was home and such a little man he had become. She was relieved that he still knew her and loved her. Arla was unsure of the future, but resolved to be happy at this current moment, for it was not a bad time right now. However, what is to come is never sure.

A New Perspective

It started low on the horizon and then crept silently up into the sky. Puryn was awake early with excitement, listening to the commotion around his new home while looking out of his window. He watched in awe as the rising orb of bright light crowned the snow-capped mountaintops with hues of silver and bright gold. Bright beams of light were cast between a few cumulus clouds that dared to mar the periwinkle sky. The breeze played with the treetops, swaying the large branches and ruffling the now-turning leaves. They appeared to Puryn much like red, yellow, and gold feathers. He saw this sea of color for as far as his eyes could focus, and gasped at its beauty.

A running river was heard off in the distance, and Puryn could hear the water moving quickly nearby. The white noise was a comforting background to the peaceful chirping of the remaining birds. Somewhere, a woodpecker was searching for breakfast, and with that, he got up to look for some of his own.

The boy recognized the familiar smell of a wood fire. He always loved the smell of burning wood, especially when there was a chill in the air and the Ert smelled of dampness and grass. Living within a monastery had its privileges, but the former monk could not remember what they were as he took in the sights around him.

Elves were busy with their lives. They were cooking, cleaning, making things, and selling them. The active nature of the market reminded him of home, but the homes of the Elves were so much more interesting. There were no walls to protect them, save for the ring of trees around the great clearing within the middle of the forest. Torith was a natural fortress.

"Puryn, sit," Arla demanded. Grabbing a wooden bowl, she filled it with oatmeal. Then, she drizzled a healthy portion of honey and cream on it, handing it to her son.

"Thank you, Mother," Puryn said absentmindedly, watching Elfish bow masters walking to the far-off corner of the clearing. It was quite a way away, but he could see the Elves shooting, and could barely make out the arrows flying toward their hay bale targets.

"Eat your breakfast and clean up, young man. The Queen has plans to take you to the Elves to ask them to continue your education." His mother was visibly upset about the proposition, but the Queen was the Queen, and she was merely a handmaiden. She had no right to say otherwise, so she held her tongue.

"But, Mother, I want to learn to ride horses and wield a sword like Father did when he became a man, not run around in robes and learn about flowers and trees!" Puryn sank into his chair. He stirred his bowl and looked at it with disappointment.

"I understand, my son, but we must do as we are told."

"Why? Why must I do as I am told? When do I get to do what I want to?" he protested loudly.

"When you are a man, young one, you will understand our station in this life. We are favored, yes, but not entirely free. We are bound in service, and in service, we shall stay." Arla sat and stirred the pot. She was frowning.

She did not mind serving the Queen, but she longed for the day when she would have her own say in how her family lived. It felt as if she was still a child and that the Queen had become her mother, running her household and making all of the decisions. Durn just followed orders. He never spoke up in any way.

"Are you finished? I will take your bowl, and you go out and wash." Arla looked at Puryn, who was fiddling around with his food, but had barely eaten five bites.

"I'm not hungry," he moaned, getting up from his chair and leaving to wash in the basin on his bed stand.

The Queen arrived shortly thereafter in tan Elfish leggings and blue tunic. She had on a strange-looking wide-brimmed hat that sat squarely on top of her head. Her hair was in two large braids on the sides of her head. Each hung below her shoulders. Arla rarely saw Falda's hair down and was surprised.

"Good morning, Your Majesty," Arla curtsied. "Would you like some oatmeal?"

"No, thank you, my dear. The girls took care of me this morning, as you had arranged," the Queen replied. "Is the boy ready to go?"

Arla was a bit anxious. "Are we sure this is the way, My Queen?"

"I see no other since that jackal, Verdin, sabotaged his chance at the towers. The Elves may prove to be better teachers still!" the Queen said emphatically.

"Of course," Arla said, agreeing half-heartedly.

Puryn heard the Queen and went to the kitchen. He was wearing a brown tunic and brown pants. He didn't want to go, but put on a happy face for his mother's sake. His mother hugged him, kissed his forehead, and said, "Behave for the Queen. I shall see you soon."

"Are you ready, young man?" the Queen asked, smiling. But then, she realized that something was wrong. "All right, let's have it. What is the matter here?"

Arla said nothing and looked at the floor, but not Puryn. The boy, at times, had no filter and said whatever was on his mind. This was one of those times.

"Your Majesty, I don't want to leave my parents again. I really appreciated the time in the towers, learning all of the things that I did. I was able to meet great people and great friends, but I missed my parents, and they missed me, also. I don't want to go to another academy, far from them for a long time." He realized he had said too much and shuffled his feet a bit, looking toward his mother, who was wincing a bit at his honesty.

The Queen was shocked. "Oh, my Gods! I did not realize how much I had put you all through. I knew that the towers would be a sacrifice, and I know the past week or so has been traumatizing, but everyone in Torith goes to school. That includes all of the children and young men and women. Oh, and they stay in their own homes in the evenings. So you won't be away from your mother and father again, my little friend. At least you won't be while you are here in Torith!"

"Oh, thank the Gods, not again," Arla sighed in relief.

The Queen smiled, waiting for enthusiasm to come back into the room, but Puryn blurted out, "But I want to ride horses and learn to sword fight! Will they teach me these things also?"

The Queen rolled her eyes. "What is it with man-children and sharpened metal objects? I suppose you may learn some of that."

Puryn hugged the Queen, who was surprised, but smiled and hugged him back with one arm while she held Arla's hand with the other. "We shall make this time a happy one. I will not ask much of you this trip, nor will I take your son away again, if danger does not demand it."

As the Queen looked at her, Arla was speechless and felt a knot in her throat. She knew the Queen meant every word.

"We must go, boy! Come along!" Falda left with her arm around Puryn.

Puryn's mother waved as they descended down a short rope ladder to the ground. The busy nature of the Elfish market was only eclipsed by the ease with which they interacted, haggled, and made their transactions. *Almost* every exchange was amicable, but two Elves were haggling over a price somewhere in the area. One man cursed in Elfish during the argument that ensued, calling the vendor "a horse's ass."

"I've heard that word before," Puryn remarked. "Didn't you say that one time when you were talking to that Elf bowman about what happened at the towers?"

"I did nothing of the sort," the Queen denied, looking at him sideways with one eye closed. Unfortunately, this one was too smart for his own good. "That man said something very uncivilized. You should not repeat it!" The Queen turned and glared at the swearing Elf, responding curtly in Elfish, "Watch your tongue, Sir. This boy is listening!"

The offender repented, "Oh dear, I apologize, Falda, many apologies!"

"It is fine, Feli. I forgive you ... this time!" She smiled at the Elf as he looked at her sheepishly.

The Queen and her charge made it to the schoolyard within an hour. They would have made it more quickly, had the Queen not been stopped by Elves, greeting her and waving to her all along the way. She was polite to them, even though she was in a rush. Puryn saw that even the ordinary people of Torith truly loved the Queen of Yslandeth. The boy smiled at the happy faces, and they rubbed his head, messing up his hair.

"Here is the door. I hope you will learn some of the language while here." The Queen paused at the entrance.

"I would love to do that!" Puryn replied with excitement. He was acting more like a boy, day by day, and that was all right with the Queen.

They entered a building on the ground with high, pointed wooden arches. An Elf of indeterminate age was seated inside at a beautiful dark wooden desk, writing with a quill on parchment. He had several things bubbling in various beakers on a table to his left, and was eating a small biscuit while he wrote his notes. He looked up in wonder and realized at once, it was Falda.

"Enter Falda, the Green. How may I be of assistance, Your Majesty?" The Elf bowed his head and then went back to munching on his biscuit while scribbling numbers down on his parchment, only half paying attention. Puryn was a bit irritated with his nonchalant demeanor. This was the Queen of Yslandeth. He was insulted for her, but the Queen acted as if she was the one who should bow to the seated Elf.

"I have a new student for you, Master Gulsbane, one of very high importance. This is Puryn, the one in my visions. I would ask the favor that you would train him as one of your own." She bowed. Puryn was confused, but followed his Queen's lead.

"I have no need for new students, Falda. I haven't finished with the ones I have now!" The Elf laughed, and Puryn could tell that this was no ordinary Elf. This Elf was someone special.

"Please, master," she said as she switched to Elfish. "He may be our only hope. I cannot see his fate clearly, but he leads us from oblivion … somehow. I hope to mold him as a man of peace, so he can bring peace to the land."

The elder Elf furrowed his brow and lit up a pipe. He smoked it for a minute, blowing out long plumes of smoke that filled up the tiny room. The smoke escaped out of the open windows. Puryn was still not amused. He coughed a bit and rubbed his eyes.

The elder Elf answered Falda in his native tongue. "What makes you so sure that he is supposed to be peaceful, Falda? Is this what you see, or is this what you want to see? Perhaps he is a warrior. You have told me that he wears armor in your visions and dreams. Why would a man of peace be armored and on a horse? I think you hope for peace, but know that he is destined for war. I will teach him. I will prepare him for the truth of what awaits him. If you do not wish me to do so, take him elsewhere. I will not teach him how to die."

The Queen heard these words and was shaken. She frowned and admitted to the master that she hoped for a peaceful end to the dreams and visions. Still, for a long time, Falda felt that the option of peace and tranquility was quickly fading away. There would be war, and little Puryn would be on the field somewhere. Finally, she gave in.

"Teach him as you see fit, wise master. Teach him the light arts and the dark, but please teach him. I trust only you." The Queen had tears in her eyes, and Puryn reached out and grabbed the Queen's hand. She turned to him and smiled. "He is such a good boy."

"Come here, boy," the Elf commanded in Elfish, motioning for Puryn to come forward. Confused, Puryn stepped forward and stood tall and squarely, as taught at the towers. "He is taught by Elig, I think," the Elf said to the Queen.

"Elig no longer lives, master. He has joined Aeternum."

The master turned to her sadly. "When?"

"Seven days, maybe eight. My mind is hazy," the Queen replied.

"He was a good friend and a good teacher," the Elf said sadly. He thought a minute about his departed friend and decided. "I will teach him."

The Queen was jubilant. "Thank you ever so much, Master Gulsbane. He will not disappoint you."

"I am sure he will be an excellent student … and with such high praise from you, my best student," he replied, sounding more like a father than a master.

The Queen blushed and turned to Puryn. She said in Etah, the common tongue, "Puryn, this is Master Gulsbane. I have known him since I was a maiden. He will be your teacher, as he is still my own to this day."

Puryn looked at the Queen in disbelief. "He is your teacher, My Queen?"

"Who do you think I learn from, boy?" she responded.

Puryn looked up at the Elf. He was more than a head taller than him and only slightly larger in build. Elves were slimmer folks. Puryn thought this Elf did not look old enough to be a master. The master looked to be in his late thirties to early forties to the boy.

The master looked at his skeptical expression and grinned. Then he started laughing loudly and slapped his own knee. "I have seen that face before somewhere, Falda," he said in Elfish.

"Master, please, use Etah. The boy has no idea what you are saying!" the Queen stated, smiling.

"He looks as if he sees me as another self-important horse's ass!" the master said, grinning.

Puryn cocked his head and repeated the phrase, "horse's ass" in Elfish. "I have heard this word several times. What does it mean?"

The Queen was flush with embarrassment and turned away, trying not to burst into laughter at the innocent question. However, the master took no measures to hide his amusement and laughed until wheezing.

Puryn didn't understand, but realized that he had said something funny. After both adults had composed themselves, the master answered Puryn's question.

"That is the phrase that translates to "horse's ass" in Etah, Puryn."

Puryn's eyes widened, and he looked back and forth at the Queen and the master, excusing himself and backing up.

"Have no worries, Puryn, my boy. I am a horse's ass upon occasion, and believe it or not, Falda can be one as well, when she is in one of her moods." The master made a funny face and looked at the Queen.

Trying not to be angry and staying focused, the Queen giggled, covering her mouth, as was her habit. "Shush, old man! This boy need not know all of my secrets." Her face had reddened. "I will leave him with you. Our houses are up on the elms beside the market."

"I know where you stay, my dear. I will send him home an hour before supper time," Gulsbane smiled.

"Thank you for all of your help, my teacher. Do as you see is wise. Prepare him to face the future well. I trust you with my life. I trust you with his." Falda turned away and bid farewell to Puryn. "See you tonight at mealtime! You will tell me everything!"

The boy waved goodbye, then turned and bowed to his new master.

"We do not bow here unless in a ceremony, young one. Please, feel less formal in our instructional setting. The only time I require formality is at some ritual or formal proceedings. I will let you know when those things occur and teach you the proper etiquette. We must teach you to speak a proper language first. Let us start with the alphabet and common letter combinations."

"Will I learn to ride a horse?" Puryn asked hopefully.

"Yes."

Puryn almost exploded with excitement. "How about sword fighting?"

"A bit, but that is not our forte. We fight with bows and spears, most of the time."

"That will do!" Puryn beamed.

"I am glad you approve, young one, but before one should learn to take a life, one must learn to heal one. So we will learn the healing arts also, as well as tracking and hiding in plain sight. But, of course, academics also." The master could see the air deflate from Puryn a bit with the word "academics." He laughed. "It's not all that bad, young one. Lore is actually quite interesting, as is mathematics."

"Lore!? I love lore! I know all of Yslan's lore!" Puryn was interested again.

"Wonderful! You will tell me what you have learned from Elig. He was my friend since he was your age …" He trailed off and choked back a tear. "How did it happen, child?"

Puryn retold the story and began to cry during the part where Elig lay on the ground dying. He told his new master what Elig had said about forgiveness, and Gulsbane smiled and looked upward to the sky. He knew that such a soul looked down upon them both, and this meeting was foretold by fate and chance. Elig watched, the master thought, and he was laughing. He envisioned Elig rubbing his hands together near a fire with a warm mug of mead, impatiently waiting for them to "get on with it."

When Puryn finished, he wiped his nose with a handkerchief. Then, he apologized for crying and stood straight and tall.

"I nearly killed that boy, and I am ashamed to admit that I do not regret it in the least." Puryn looked at the master, waiting for a scowl or a rebuke. He got none.

"Puryn, my son, know this—we are imperfect. We strive to live as close to the light as we possibly can, but when darkness threatens to kill the light, we have no time to waver. We must show evil no quarter. We stand and kill, if necessary, to defend love, decency, and freedom. You protected someone you loved, who could not rise and do for himself. If the roles were reversed, Puryn, Elig would have done the same, if not worse. He was not rebuking you as he died, boy. It was a warning not to let the hate fester in you. He was warning you not to abandon the light for the seduction of the darkness, for the darkness is a temptation, and men and Elves are weak. You did the honorable thing, young man. You learned your lessons well from Elig. Check your pride and anger. Forgive as best you can. Harbor no ill will. Continue to live in righteousness. Those are all you can do, young Puryn."

"Thank you, m … master," Puryn stammered, trying to compose himself. He would have a hard time calling anyone else master after Elig.

"If it is easier for you, Puryn, call me teacher. It is all right," he replied knowingly.

"Yes, teacher. Thank you for your wisdom and your kindness," Puryn replied calmly.

The master was impressed by his response and led him to a small desk, which was to be his. He gave him some Elfish children's books and some scrolls with letters and pronunciation on them. Puryn murdered the spelling and pronunciation of the letters and words. Gulsbane corrected him gently. Puryn tried again.

Back to square one again, thought Puryn as he learned his alphabet. *But I get to ride horses, Master Elig, and shoot bows!*

He daydreamed for a second, then forced himself back to his studies. He would learn this and become literate. He was smart, and he picked things up quickly.

Puryn was sure he would be a master horseman in no time. He would hit the mark like his father, in a matter of weeks! The boy was up for this new adventure, but he was in for a surprise. Proficiency came from practice, and practice could be hard work.

The afternoon horns were blowing. Master Gulsbane called to Puryn and said a traditional benediction and farewell to his student in Elfish. The new acolyte responded, "And may it be also with you." He wasn't sure, but felt it was an appropriate response. The Master smiled.

"Go home and eat, my boy. Come back early. You will be a fine student. I already like you."

Puryn ran home excited to tell everyone of his first day at "Elf school," as he called it. The Queen was there, waiting patiently. Arla had dinner ready. She rolled her eyes as Puryn scarcely ate again, while going on and on about his day. Still, Arla beamed, because she saw her son was happy. He hadn't smiled like that in days. She had begun to wonder if he was ever going to smile again.

Young hearts mend quickly, she thought. *I'm glad. He is too young for that kind of sadness.*

Durn kissed Arla's cheek and listened to his son try to say the Elfish alphabet. The Queen grimaced and then laughed. He would get it eventually.

A New Master

The moonlight still splashed a crooked crescent through the window. Puryn was up before the sun. He hurriedly washed and dressed and was in the kitchen, ready for breakfast. There he found his mother, a bit haggard, with a furrowed brow, shaking her head.

One minute you can't get the child to eat, the next, he's standing there looking at you like you're moving too slowly, she thought, yawning and stirring the morning oatmeal.

"What brings you here so early in the morn', young Master Puryn?" she asked in a slightly mocking tone. Then she closed one eye, acting as if she was actually waiting for an answer.

Puryn excitedly replied, "I'm ready to go to school! How long until I can go?"

Rolling her eyes and sighing, Arla said in a stern voice, "You will go nowhere before you eat a bowl of food, young man."

Puryn agreed and then waited impatiently for the mush to heat. His mother dressed it up with cream and honey again, as she had done yesterday. The boy ate voraciously, ignoring how hot the food was, chugging down a small wooden cup filled with fruit juice.

"I'm done," he declared, as he put his bowl in the washbasin. Arla shook her head. "Did you taste any of that?"

"Yes, it was wonderful, Mother! I must go. The teacher is waiting!" Puryn turned and hugged his mother and kissed her cheek. The Queen was sipping some tea in the open doorway, yawning. She wanted to see him off on his first real day of "Elf school."

"Good morning, my dawn," stated Puryn unsurely in Elfish. "May your sun be warm within you."

The Queen nodded and blinked, trying to decipher what he had meant to say, but admittedly didn't mind being called "his dawn." "Puryn, you need to practice, but not too bad," Falda responded in Elfish. "You will be fluent in no time, boy!"

Puryn understood "practice, fluent, boy." He got the gist of her words. He moaned. "I'm terrible at this, aren't I?"

"You've only been at it one day, my boy! I have been at it all of my adult life, and I still only understand about seventy-five percent of what I hear. Of course, reading is easier, once you figure out their letters."

Puryn felt a little better. He simply said, "Goodbye," in Elfish, then raced to his teacher's house, arriving winded and a bit sweaty. Gulsbane was at the same desk, sipping a hot cup of something brown. It smelled amazing. Puryn stood in the doorway and waited to be called in after knocking three times.

"Come in, son. Be seated at your desk. We shall start the morning with language and lore. Then a bit of arithmetic." He yawned, excused himself, and then sipped from his cup again. "Later, if we have time, perhaps we shall visit the stables or learn how to handle a bow at the range."

Puryn could barely contain himself. He sat down and pulled out his slate. The teacher helped him practice the alphabet and his penmanship. After an hour or so, the teacher switched to lore. He spoke of Elfish traditions and ceremonies.

Gulsbane spent an hour more on holy days and special celebrations created to honor not only heroes, but also the seasons and nature. The eager student stored these stories alongside those already residing in his heart. He really loved to hear the stories of old. They made him feel like he was there, experiencing the adventures first-hand. Master Gulsbane was a master storyteller, making the subject that much more exciting.

Around the fourth hour of the morning, about two hours before the noon meal, Master Gulsbane called for a break from all of the academic studies. He took his student outside for the physical fitness portion of the day.

There, the Elf led Puryn, one-on-one, in strength and endurance training. When the exercise portion was done, he began to show Puryn the martial arts of the Elves. Theirs was a system of submission holds and throws, not unlike what he had learned at the towers. The master was impressed by the skill Puryn already possessed, but cautioned him not to use deadly force unless it was entirely unavoidable.

"Do not kill out of anger, young one. Do not let your actions be driven by hate. Instead, perform your techniques without emotion. Deliver the blow correctly and with sufficient violence to end the encounter while doing the least damage to your opponent." The master stopped and made one exception. "Unless it is war, or you defend one who is defenseless. At these times, show an adversary no quarter."

Puryn was not expecting to hear that from the peace-loving Elves, especially a teacher the Queen trusted to teach him to be a "man of peace." He was not complaining. He had often thought peace was the best thing, but sometimes it would take violence to achieve the desired outcome.

Puryn simply replied, "Yes, teacher," bowing respectfully before going inside to change. The elder smiled and shook his head.

Monks and their bowing, Gulsbane thought to himself. After the noon meal, at the second hour of the afternoon, the master gave Puryn a choice. "It is late in the day. You have done well so far. Would you rather learn the horse or shoot the bow? I will give you a choice."

Puryn wanted both, but knew that there would be another day. So he replied, "May I shoot a bow, and then tomorrow work with horses?"

The master smiled at the request. "Would that there should be six more hours to the daylight, and we could do both! We shall see what the weather allows tomorrow, my student. Today, we shall learn the bow and perhaps shoot a few arrows for good measure."

Puryn was excited. He had never operated a real weapon before. Everything he had learned was staff fighting. To him, a staff was a glorified stick. He didn't want to swing a cudgel around—he wanted a sword. A bow would do in the meantime.

The two made their way back to a storage shed behind Gulsbane's house.

There, he pulled out two Elfish longbows. They were both bigger than Puryn was. The master then reached in and pulled out a long cylindrical satchel with a shoulder strap. He untied one end of the bag and slid out a beautiful dark wooden bow that was just about the perfect size for Puryn.

"This bow was one once used by another student of mine. She has since outgrown it, and I'm sure she would not mind if you take possession of it until such a time as you have grown a foot or two!"

Puryn took the bow in his hand gently. He was in awe of its sleek shape and smooth finish. It was a beautiful mahogany bow with intricate knotwork scrolling along the face of each limb. The string was made of some sort of silvery filament that Puryn could not identify.

The master showed him how to "step through" to string the bow. Next, he showed Puryn the parts of the weapon and the terms for the parts of the arrow. After the nomenclature was learned and each part's purpose, the master gave him the safety lecture.

"Always point your arrows downrange. Never point at anything you do not intend to shoot. Do not draw your string until ready to loose. Never loose an arrow with another person downrange of you." The master looked at Puryn with utmost sincerity while telling him these rules. "Do you understand what I have told you?"

"I do, Sir. This is not a toy. I understand." He looked down at the bow in his left hand with respect. He knew this instrument could kill a man with one well-placed shot. He did not want to be the one who accidentally let loose on some poor unsuspecting soul.

After the lecture was completed, Puryn packed his bow and quiver full of arrows. Then, the boy and his master made their way to the archery range. Once cleared to enter, the master moved him forward to the firing line. Of course, the young archer immediately wanted to shoot. But, instead, his master told him to wait. The teacher ordered his acolyte to listen to what was going on around him and learn the range commands, as they were yelled out in Elfish, to the line of experienced Elves nocking arrows on their strings, drawing, and loosing.

Some of the Elves present were deadly accurate with their bows. Within thirty minutes, the indoctrination was concluded, and the commands were learned. Puryn nervously took his position near a marker with a symbol that resembled the sun. He found a target downrange with the same character. The target was only thirty yards away, but Puryn thought it might as well be a mile away.

"Shooters take your positions," the range master commanded. Gulsbane nudged Puryn. The boy straddled the firing line, mimicking the other shooters.

"Nock and stand ready!" the range master declared loudly.

"Shooters may loose at their targets, at will." The range master raised one hand and then signaled downrange. The swish of arrows, strings, and reloading surrounded the new archer, and he was so engrossed in what was going on around him that he forgot to shoot his own arrows.

"Shoot, Puryn. Get a good, natural alignment." Puryn shifted to emulate the other, more experienced bowmen. "Good, that's it. Now nock an arrow." Once again, the boy copied the Elf next to him. "Hold the bow in the 'V' of your left hand. Cock your wrist slightly to the right so that …"

Twang! The bowstring slapped Puryn's right arm so hard, he let out a little yelp. He looked around, embarrassed, and then nocked another arrow. The first one went somewhere, but in his pain, Puryn had not a clue where. He was embarrassed, and his face was now beet red. The now determined archer cocked his wrist correctly the second time and drew back the bowstring to his nose and chin, like the Elf to his right, who was nocking out the red spot in the middle of his target with every shot. The boy loosed the arrow. It hit the very top of the left-hand corner of the hay bale. It missed the mark completely.

Gulsbane shrugged. *Second shot, and he hit the bale. Not too terrible, but much improvement to be had,* he thought, muttering to himself. "Puryn, step off of the line and come here."

Puryn did as he was told. His arm was sore and throbbing from where the string had struck, but he was not letting on. Gulsbane knew full well he was hiding his injury.

"You must not only find your aiming point, but you must also learn a fluid motion. Your motion must become consistent. This way, you will know that you are shooting the same way each time. Control your breathing. Breathe in, then half out, draw, aim, loose. Then breathe, relax and nock. Take your time, but don't hold the arrow on the string for more than five seconds. If you do, you will start to fatigue, and your shot will be influenced by your form."

"Yes, teacher." Puryn bowed instinctively. The master dismissed him and told him to relax. The novice rejoined the line of seasoned archers.

The boy assumed a good natural alignment, then drawing an arrow from his quiver, he nocked it. He breathed in deeply and imagined that he was aiming at the advancing Hodan hordes coming to raid Yslan. Exhaling half of his breath, he pulled the string back, ensuring that his wrist was bent in on his bow hand. He didn't want another forearm incident.

Then he looked at his mark and loosed. The arrow flew awkwardly as if his release was less than perfect. Still, the bolt righted itself halfway to its destination, striking cleanly in the two-point ring. He had actually hit the target. It was not even close to the bull's-eye, but it was on the canvas. Master Gulsbane clapped and nodded approvingly. Puryn beamed.

"There you go, boy. Now tighten it up, and you will see even better results. You will be proficient in time!" The master smiled for the first time all day. He really loved to shoot. In fact, he stood with a full Elfish longbow and entered the box where Puryn had just finished shooting his twenty arrows. For the day, Puryn had registered a three-point shot, a two and a one.

Puryn sat on the bench behind his new master. The master got in position and pulled an arrow out without looking at the quiver. Placing it on the string, he drew and released in one smooth motion. The arrow ripped through the air faster than anything Puryn had ever seen. Dead center. The next shot right next to it. Then again and again. The master fired twenty arrows in three minutes or so, hitting twenty, ten-point shots. Puryn's jaw dropped as he sat in amazement. His teacher knew what he was doing with a bow.

The range master called "hold," and all archers hung their bows on stands near their shooting box. They took their quivers and waited for the "all clear" to be called. "All clear" was eventually sounded, and they all went downrange to glean their arrows. Master Gulsbane pulled his twenty arrows, but complained that he broke one by hitting it with another shot.

"I meant to drop that shot an inch lower. Damn it," the master swore. "These are my favorite arrows. I will have to get Rothas to make me another score."

Puryn's collection took a bit longer. He found eighteen of his twenty arrows, but two were lost forever. The master muttered something about new shooters and range demons eating arrows, but Puryn was exhausted and simply looking at him in awe.

"Why do you stare at me so? Am I growing a second head?" the master teased.

"You hit twenty bull's-eyes in a row! That is incredible!" Puryn remarked loudly. A few of the other Elves smirked, then chuckled quietly to themselves. "What? What did I say?" Puryn asked, slightly embarrassed.

One of the Elves spoke to Puryn in Etah. "He is known as Master Gulsbane, Primaris Archeron."

"What is Primaros Archeerun?" Puryn asked as he murdered in Elfish. The Elf smiled patiently.

"Primaris Archeron in your tongue means Premier of the Archers. He is our Archery Champion." He turned to Gulsbane. "Ten years running now, eh, master?"

"Aye, ten years. You will beat me this year, Dahnivus. You practice too much!" the master quipped with his challenger.

The challenger laughed and saluted the master. Gulsbane smiled, bid the Elf farewell, and led Puryn back to his home. It was almost time to close up for the night when they arrived at the house.

"You did well today, young man. You hit the target three times on the first day. Tell Falda that, if you dare!" The master made a funny facial gesture as if he was pretending to be terrified. Puryn laughed and set his bow near his desk at the instruction of Gulsbane.

"I will tell her," Puryn promised.

"At your own peril, my young student. I will miss you," the master said, smiling with a fake ominous air about it. Then he lit his pipe.

* * *

Puryn collected his things to go. He bid farewell to his teacher and walked home, tired from a busy day. His left arm still stung, but he knew what to do now and why it was not wise to do it another way. He arrived home as Arla was setting the table. Falda was there assisting his mother with the cooking and arrangements. Puryn looked at the Queen with a puzzled expression.

"What? I can't put the silverware down?" Falda asked indignantly.

"Frankly, Your Majesty, you can do pretty much whatever you want to. It was just an odd sight for me!" Puryn responded.

"Oh, an odd sight, eh?" She hugged him and told him that he should clean up. "Get ready to eat. Your mother has slaved over the fire all day for this special meal in honor of your first full day."

Puryn washed, and when he pulled back his tunic sleeve, he saw the bruise from the bowstring for the first time. It had bled a tiny bit and was scabbed over nicely.

"Oh dear, Mother, is going to lose her mind," he muttered to himself. "Might as well let her see it now and get it over with."

Puryn paraded into the dining room like a miniature conquering hero. His mother gasped at the wound and fussed about it until Falda calmed her. "This is a normal bow string strike. I had these every day for a year!"

The Queen pulled out a bottle of liniment potion and rubbed it on the wound, as Arla had named it, saying some Elfish words. The boy's arm was warm for a second, and there was a faint green glow in the area where Falda had rubbed the herbal concoction. After that, the wound felt much better.

"Now, leave that alone, and it should almost be gone by tomorrow morning, maybe by lunchtime," Falda said with certainty. "Tell us all about your day!"

Puryn spoke at length about the lore part of his academic studies. He opened a scroll and told his mother and the Queen about gold Dragons that inhabited caves full of treasure, up in distant mountaintops, high in the clouds. He told stories of how the Dragons were friends of Elves and Dwarves, but how they had all become reclusive, as the years of gluttony and warmongering started, during the period of the clans of man and the warring states. Falda was pleased with how Puryn emphasized a sentiment of disgust when talking about those old warring days. She was happy that he hated death and mayhem, and instead loved peace and honor.

"Then we went to the range and shot arrows," Puryn concluded, sitting quietly.

"Well? How did you shoot?" Falda questioned with interest.

"Oh yes, Master Gulsbane told me to tell you that I scored a three, two, and a one in my first twenty arrows. Then he said something like 'nice knowing you,' and I was confused." Puryn looked at Falda expectantly.

"Oh, you little ..." She trailed off with a howl of laughter. "That old coot. I will tell him what for when I see him next. I ne'er found the target for three weeks of shooting." She squinted at Puryn. The boy's eyes were wide, and he was unsure whether he should have said anything. Falda smiled broadly and congratulated him. "Good job, boy. You will be beating your father in no time."

Durn was in a nearby, comfortable, padded chair snoring quietly after having several ales at dinner. He snorted and awoke. "What? What happened?" he blurted out in a stupor, startled.

"Nothing, dear, go back to sleep," Arla replied.

Durn mumbled and slipped back off to sleep.

"I should wash and get to bed," Puryn said sleepily. "It has been a long day, and tomorrow the teacher has told me that we may ride horses if the weather cooperates!" Puryn was visibly elated.

His mother moaned. "If a bow can do that, just think what a horse can do!"

The novice archer remembered the bowstring incident and resolved to listen to ALL of the instructions tomorrow, before embarking on this next big step in his education. There was no need for another mishap and a more significant wound to worry his mother.

* * *

He excused himself, kissed his mother, hugged the Queen, and quietly stepped around the chair containing his sleeping father, to avoid waking him. The lad washed quickly and dressed in his nightclothes.

Puryn fell asleep quickly, and as he slept, his dreams returned, but he was not terrified this time. In this vision, he was wearing a shining suit of chain mail and was mounted on a beautiful, armored white horse. He wore the livery of the King of Yslandeth and was surrounded by banners of various factions, friend and foe. The wind blew and a silver scarf, adorning his neck, fluttered in the strong breeze. The air around him smelled of wildflowers or rose petals, reminding him vaguely of something he couldn't quite grasp, but still missed with a sorrow.

The men of all nations looked up at him. He could see his own reflection in the armor of the man nearest to him. His reflection showed him as a grown man. As he began to speak, Puryn woke from his vision with a start and in a cold sweat. An uneasy feeling gripped his young heart. He felt as if he was witnessing his own death and the deaths of all who surrounded him. A cold shiver ran down his spine. Reciting a quick prayer to Haya, he asked the Goddess to dispel the evil and let him sleep in peace.

Haya heard his prayers and smiled upon his request.

Puryn slept soundly for the rest of the evening, waking at the sun's rising, ready for his second day of Elf school.

"Good morning, Haya!" Puryn said in a subdued voice. "Thank you for your assistance with those dreams. I will strive to protect and respect all living things this day."

Haya smiled from Aeternum, blessing the boy.

The boy pulled back his covers and prepared for breakfast. He was eager to ride a horse. Unfortunately, Arla was not so enthusiastic about the proposition. Durn hushed her, telling his wife that by Puryn's age, he had his own horse.

The young lad finished his breakfast, listened to his father's tales, and said goodbye to everyone at the breakfast table.

"Have a great sunlight! See you when the foot returns tonight," he said in Elfish.

The Queen snorted in the other room. "We will work on that tonight!" she yelled happily, chuckling at his attempt to speak Elfish.

Puryn scratched his head, wondering what he had actually said. He wasn't sure he wanted to know, so he went to school.

Herbs, Potions, and Horses

In fact, weeks passed before Puryn ever saw the saddle. Instead, the boy focused on learning every subject sent his way. Upon arrival at school one morning, the student discovered that his master had a different routine planned out for the day. The boy sat in his usual chair, expecting the daily routine, but instead, the first hour was simply a cursory review of the previous day's lessons. The acolyte was a bit confused by what the hurry was all about.

"Puryn, I have decided today we will do some alchemy and herbalist studies."

Puryn sprang to the fires and bubbling potions that his master had going on his own personal workbench, but Gulsbane redirected him to a wooden counter top on the other side of the room. There, the boy saw a small metal rack with several jars labeled in Elfish, which held liquids of various colors and smells.

"Come here and learn," the master prodded. "You will learn to make a healing liniment today."

Puryn watched his teacher mix several pungent-smelling plants in a crucible, then Gulsbane grabbed a beaker and added some green fluid, and a splash of a yellow oil of some sort, stirring vigorously, while repeatedly chanting several Elfish words.

"Life, health, and healing," his teacher invoked. Puryn saw the mixture glow slightly as Gulsbane stirred. The teacher finished his batch, cooling it and pouring it into a small flask. He labeled it with the symbol for health.

"Now you do it," the master said plainly. The young student grabbed the same flowers and plants, and clumsily ground them in the crucible.

"When you add the essences to the herbs, be careful not to spill them," the teacher warned. "If the wrong substance is mixed with wood or soil, the stench can be overpowering."

Puryn stirred even more carefully, adding the oils and liquids to his herbs as his master had. He tried to chant, but nothing happened.

"Stop for a moment," Gulsbane commanded gently. "You must focus on the power of Nature and Life around you. When you call out these power words, you must be connected to the source of their power. Close your eyes, Puryn, listen to the forest—its birds, trees, the river. Connect to it with your spirit. You should feel peaceful in this meditation. You should feel invigorated."

Puryn tried, but he was embarrassed. The master insisted that he do it again. The boy tried again. After several tries, he decided to ignore his embarrassment. Focusing, Puryn heard the song of Life around him and became grounded in the moment. He woke from the meditation to his own voice chanting, "Life, health, and healing," in perfect Elfish. He was still stirring the potion. As it glowed slightly, Puryn gasped. His teacher smiled.

"Good. That should be it. Let me see it here, lad," the master commanded, motioning for the mixture. He smelled the concoction, stuck his fingertip in it, and rubbed it on a small cut that he had on his left hand. There was a slight green glow and the wound scabbed over immediately.

"Good job. It works. You are a natural, as usual!" Gulsbane rolled his eyes. "Put it carefully in a flask. We are going to the stables today. I hope we shall not need these potions by day's end!"

Puryn poured the concoction into a small flask and etched the symbol for "health" on the container. The master nodded in approval. Puryn smiled and put it in a pouch on his belt. Then, they left for the stables across the large clearing on the opposite side. Thankfully, the boy thought, the range shot in the opposite direction from the stables. The student looked around and realized that this place was well planned out. It was an efficient use of limited space.

Gulsbane walked into the stables and spoke Elfish to the young stable boy, who ran from stall to stall, brushing, feeding, and watering the horses. The boy nodded and went inside. After about fifteen minutes, he returned, walking out two smaller, muscular specimens of Elfish warhorses. They were built for speed and agility.

"Puryn, this is Haystorm. She is a good mare. You should be safe riding her and getting used to the reins." The master handed the reins to Puryn.

The new rider looked up at the animal. She was a beautiful white horse with dark brown patches. She had a bit of brown on the front of her head. The mare was looking at Puryn expectantly.

"Put your foot in here and pull yourself up. Then swing your leg over." The master effortlessly mounted his horse.

Puryn tried to grasp the saddle and reins properly, but slipped, falling in the dirt. The horse whinnied and scratched at the ground. The boy looked up at the mare and felt as if she was laughing at him. He scowled in embarrassment. Getting up, he dusted his tunic off and tried again. This time, he faltered, but was able to lie down on the saddle and kick his leg awkwardly over the top of the horse. His feet were in the stirrups, and he was now seated in the saddle. The novice felt ten feet tall. He was pretty close.

"Puryn, lift your reins and goad the horse gently at first. Gauge how much force you'll need to get the horse to comply with your commands. Remember, these horses were trained from birth by Elfish trainers and riders. They are more in tune with their riders than the horses that men usually ride. I think she senses your worry and fear. Just relax."

Haystorm turned her head and looked at Puryn. *The funny-looking Elf was sure clumsy,* the horse thought, as she reached down and bit off a clump of grass, munching it as she waited for something to happen. Puryn kicked with the goads lightly and muttered something to the effect of, "Come on horse," in Elfish. The horse automatically strolled toward Master Gulsbane. The master shook his head.

"Take charge, Puryn, or she will just mill about as she pleases, eating grass. Talk to her and use the bit to steer her."

"Yes, teacher," the boy said nervously. Puryn looked at the horse and said in broken Elfish, "Look, horse, I mean Haystorm, I really like you, and you are very wonderful. I have always wanted to learn to ride, and this is my first day in a saddle. Would you work with me, please?"

The horse did not understand Puryn's words, but recognized the familiar sounds and settled down, listening attentively. Puryn kicked the goads a bit harder this time, feeling bad. The horse did not seem to mind and trotted off at a leisurely pace. Puryn pulled the reins to the left and right in the flat open field. The horse responded in kind, and he was off and trotting around. The boy was having a grand time, but he was still a bit intimidated. Then, the master called him over.

"Puryn, we shall now trot a small obstacle course to learn how to control the horse in tighter spaces and over different terrains and man-made features."

Puryn could see a small bridge, several yards of cobblestone, a sandy road, and some packed dirt. There were also low hurdles to jump over. He was a bit nervous, but excited at the same time. His teacher ran the course as if he could do it in his sleep. His horse responded gracefully and floated over the obstacles. The boy had been riding Haystorm for two hours and felt a bit more confident, but he was unsure how he would fare on the course.

"Do it now," his teacher commanded.

"Come on, Haystorm," Puryn goaded the horse, speaking in Elfish. "Let's show the teacher what we can do!"

The horse galloped toward the sand road. Quickly, the mare cleared the first medium, and her novice rider slowed her to a steady trot on the cobblestones, fearing damage to her hooves. Next, the horse crossed the wooden bridge without incident. Puryn felt overconfident and began to get a bit cocky.

"Good girl! We did it!" Puryn exclaimed, accidentally jamming the goad into the horse's flanks. Haystorm took this as a queue to run. Puryn was pulling her reins to the right to turn around. Instead, Haystorm kicked and spun to the right, taking off toward the bridge at full gallop. Her rider was thrown ten feet to the left onto the hard-packed ground. Puryn used his martial arts training to tuck his head and roll out of some of the impact, but he still absorbed a solid blow as he hit the ground. The young man sat wheezing, his breath knocked out of him, as Gulsbane hastily trotted over.

"Are you all right, my student?" the master inquired with a concerned look.

"I am," Puryn coughed. "I must rest for a moment, teacher."

"Take a moment then. I will go collect the horse."

The master galloped over, grabbing the reins and taking control of Haystorm, who was eating tufts of grass in the middle of the training field. He rode back to where his student was now sitting cross-legged, doing breathing exercises, while getting his wind back slowly.

"Your mother will not be pleased, I fear," the master said, raising an eyebrow.

"She's a mother, master. She is never pleased when adventure exists and where danger may follow!" Puryn smiled, rubbing his ribs.

"We shall take a look at you when we return to the room," the master said, handing the reins to Puryn.

"I am fine, girl," Puryn said to Haystorm. "Sorry about the goads. I'm new."

Haystorm stuck her head down in Puryn's chest and nuzzled him a bit. The boy found a carrot he saved for a snack in his pouch. He gave it to the horse. She took it greedily, and the new rider mounted her once again.

"Whoa, easy now, Haystorm," the young rider cautioned. Then the novice rode his horse to the stables and turned her over to the stable boy. The master paid the boy a copper coin, and he led the horses away.

Puryn walked with Gulsbane back to the house where they met each day. The master removed his student's tunic and checked for broken bones. The elder Elf found none, but his acolyte did have a nasty set of bruised ribs. Gulsbane rubbed Puryn's potion on the bruise, chanting the exact words used when the brew was created. The injured boy recoiled and complained a bit, but the area warmed and tingled, much like when the Queen had done the same to his bow arm. Then, the injury felt a bit better.

"It doesn't hurt as much, teacher," Puryn said in amazement.

"Good, then it is working!" Gulsbane responded. "We will read some for the rest of the day. You have had enough adventure for one afternoon."

The day ended two hours later. The pair did no martial arts that afternoon. Puryn was happy that they skipped it for the day. The boy was worried his mother would overreact when she saw this new injury, but the aspiring warrior was determined to learn how to ride and fight.

"One lesson at a time. Learn one thing, at least, each day," the master said.

"Today, I learned that falling off of a horse hurts. So I will not turn the horse while goading her to accelerate … at least not until I know how to do so while remaining in the saddle." Puryn finished muttering to himself, read a couple of assigned tales on scrolls, and packed it in for the day.

The student bid his teacher farewell and limped, ever so slightly, back to his home in the trees. The boy couldn't wait to try to ride again. He hoped it would become a regular event.

Within the hour, the acolyte arrived at his home near the elms, limping gingerly into the kitchen. His mother saw this feeble attempt to cover his injury, shaking her head angrily. "What happened to you now, young man?" she shouted.

"I fell off of a horse," Puryn replied dead-panning, rolling his eyes.

"You fell off of a horse!? Are you all right?"

"Yes, Mother. Master checked me and performed some healing on my sore ribs. I am completely fine! Please, calm down!" Puryn was a bit annoyed and embarrassed at all of the fuss his mother was making.

"Well, that's great. I'm glad you didn't break your neck, young man! Go wash for dinner." Arla glowered over him, daring him to sass her again.

"Yes, Mother."

Puryn washed, frowning. He feared he would be forbidden from returning to riding lessons. But, when he was done, he saw his father in the dining room.

"So, did I hear you telling your mother that you fell off of a horse today, eh, boy?" His father stifled a grin.

"Yes, Father. Then I hit the ground and attempted to roll out of it. I was partially successful, but still bruised my ribs. Master healed me. I should be good in a day or two." Puryn looked over his shoulder. He continued in a hushed tone. "Mother was not amused."

"Well, you're becoming a man, Puryn. She still sees you as a little boy. Sometimes men do dangerous things, when little boys need protection. I see you growing up. You will be a man soon, but don't be foolhardy and get yourself hurt or killed by rough-housing or being disobedient to your teacher. You should always get right back up on that horse and figure it out. It is what a man does. It is what you should do. Don't *you* worry. I will handle your mother. She is such a hen."

Puryn was relieved to have a parent on his side. "Father, will you teach me the sword?"

"Of course I will, but you must learn your skills from the Elves first, before I start you on another path. You have too much to master as it is!"

"Thanks, Da," the boy smiled and sat down at the table.

At dinner, Puryn told the story of the horse. The Queen listened intently. Her visions returned to her as she envisioned Puryn on the white horse, but still, she was unsure of how everything would play out. So she kept it to herself. Puryn could sense that something was wrong, but said nothing. When his story was finished, the young man said his goodnights and went to bed.

Falda remained up, drank a bit of Yslan wine that she had stored, and thought about her visions. Things seemed to be moving faster and were getting progressively more violent. She knew Puryn saw something as well when he dreamed. Many nights, the boy would toss and turn and call out in his sleep. She was unsure what he saw.

"You see the things I do, young one. I would wager a hefty sum," Falda muttered to herself.

The Queen finished her goblet and snuffed out the candle, before going to bed. She prayed for a dreamless sleep. She had not slept well in weeks.

Coming of Age

The days turned into weeks, and the weeks, into months. Months became years, and in peace, the boy grew.

Puryn lived for five years among the strictest of human monks, learning their ways and perfecting his martial arts prowess, despite the continued efforts of the Queen to fashion him into a holy man of peace.

The Gods and fate saw fit to place the boy at a crossroads, where he was forced to flee his home and become a stranger in a foreign land. There, he assimilated into his new home and adapted, learning the ways of the Elfish hunter, healer, and warrior. Many would expect that with all of this training, he was ready for anything.

Truth be told, he *was* ready for most things, but he was not prepared for *her*. One day, much like all of the others, Gulsbane and Puryn practiced horseback riding and combat skills. Looking off to the side, Puryn was uncharacteristically distracted for a moment by a young lady of exceptional beauty and grace. Gulsbane responded by knocking his now fifteen-year-old armored charge off his horse and into the fodder on the ground within the fighting arena.

The rider hit the ground with a thud. "Oof! Oh, that hurt," he said absent-mindedly, lying on his back without even attempting to get to his feet, his eyes never leaving their target.

Gulsbane craned his neck around, shielding his eyes against the sun to get a better look at what was so interesting. There, he saw Princess Adasser, the youngest daughter of King Glorin of the Elves. The Princess was wearing a white layered gossamer dress and head covering. On top of the covering was a small tiara made of woven branches and laurels.

Gulsbane sighed, and barked at Puryn, "Are you paying attention, boy, or daydreaming!? The enemy will not care if you are distracted! He will run you through and watch you die a gruesome and painful death!" Then realizing that the Princess might hear his rebuke, the master lowered his voice. He whispered, "You do realize that she is a Princess, right? That is one who you should decide to forget, young man!" The master laughed aloud and held his hand out to his student, barking in Elfish, "Get up. You don't want her to see you lying there like a horse's ass!"

"Yes, yes! As usual, my teacher, you are correct," the embarrassed young man replied, scrambling to regain his dignity.

The Princess intently watched the human, who was getting up from the ground, as his teacher gave him some pointers. The young warrior had removed his helmet, and she could see his shoulder-length mane of blond hair tied back out of his face. He was tall for his age, but muscular and fair, with beautiful blue eyes.

She thought to herself, *So innocent, they are. They speak of hope and a pure heart.* She was intrigued, but continued on to the shop, to which she was traveling, in order to do some window shopping with her ladies-in-waiting. She looked over her shoulder again, seeing the young man as he remounted his horse.

Now, when comparing the races of the Ert, one is wise to remember that Elves age differently than men. The maturity of mankind is often developed far before that of the Elf, when physical attributes are the only things considered. Puryn was fifteen (fifteen-and-a-half, if you asked him to his face). Adasser was a young eighty years old in the reckoning of Elf-kind. The young Princess only looked a year or two older than Puryn. Still, she already possessed wisdom beyond his human years, having lived a much longer life.

Despite her comparatively longer life, she also exhibited the maturity level of a teenage human girl. Elves knew more, experienced more, and may have more knowledge of nature and magic, but the race "grew up" to adulthood much slower than the short-lived human race. Consequently, she still desired to have fun, loved beautiful things, and was interested in boys. This folly irked the King in many ways, but he had endured her older sister's antics and knew he would survive Adasser's.

The average Elf lives to one-thousand years old—a human, a mere sixty years, on average. Elves have more time to play under the sun, while mankind was doomed to grow old, much too soon. Due to this disparity, romances between Elves and humans often did not work out. It was hard on the Elf when losing a partner at a young age and then living without them for many, many years to come.

However, being young, Adasser was not concerned with the future. She was intrigued and attracted to this beautiful young soul. He was more than a pretty face and muscles, and she wanted, more than anything else, to know more about him. She would wait until he was declared "a man" before pursuing her prize, if her father would not forbid it.

The scheming Princess looked through the shop window and felt his aura from afar. She knew he was someone she needed to meet. It was no accident that she saw him here today, or that he saw her in her favorite dress. She had long watched his routines in secret and decided to reveal herself subtly to her interest. She could wait. She would let him mature a bit more and revisit her interest. She had time.

Puryn was smitten. As the two walked back to the schoolhouse, the young man incessantly hounded his master concerning details of the Princess. Like a Dwarfish machine, he kept the questions coming. "How old is she? What is she like? Does she like human men? Can I meet her? What do I say to her? Oh, my Gods, what if I look like a horse's ass? Master, what do I do?"

Gulsbane beseeched the heavens, muttering something to the effect of, "Why me?" and then looked at the pathetic, love-stricken boy before him. "First thing's first. You must prove yourself worthy to court a Princess. You are not trying to run off with a milkmaid, boy!"

The statement stung. Puryn looked down at the ground, realizing his shortcomings. "I'll never be good enough, will I, master?" He looked at his muddy ragged boots, and his heart sank in his belly.

The master softened his tone, his brow furrowed. He knew the Princess would be lucky to have a Prince such as this one, but he also knew the King. "Now, don't get ahead of yourself, young man." He lifted Puryn's chin and stared him in the face. "You know who you are, don't you?"

"I'm a failed monk and a charity case among the Elves," Puryn stated in a sad, defeated tone. "I'm no one, Sir."

"You are wrong, my young student." The master stood straight and tall, stating assertively, "You are soon-to-be counted as a man of Yslan. I have no doubt that you would have been a monk, had events unfolded differently. You adapt to your situation and master all things thrown at you, and I have yet to see you run from a challenge or a foe. You are approaching mastery of nature-magic, archery, horsemanship, lore, and culture. You seek to go further and become a Knight among men. So far, you have turned everything that has obstructed your path into a learning experience."

Puryn listened, but was not convinced. "But I will never be an Elf, and I will never be a Lord. I will never be good enough for her."

"Do not dismiss the possibility of the unexpected, young one," Gulsbane replied emphatically. "You have proven that the Gods apparently love you. I will look upon your future deeds proudly, knowing that I taught you for a time."

Haya smiled with confidence. She knew she had chosen well.

"I hope never to disappoint you, my teacher. You have been a great mentor and friend." Puryn extended his hand. The master took it and smiled, shaking hands in the custom of men. They led their horses to the stables and then went off to the range to shoot the daily course of arrows. Puryn scored fifteen bull's-eyes out of twenty. His master was perfect, as usual.

The young warrior returned to his home a bit more cheerful than in the afternoon. He went inside, put his worn, loaned armor on his armor stand, and then washed. Then, after changing his linen tunic and pants for a clean set, he headed down to the kitchen, hoping for a snack. Puryn was surprised to see the Queen and his parents seated at the table. He looked at each of them quizzically. They all had looks of dire seriousness on their faces.

The tired student stood, worried, thinking, *What have I done now?*

"Puryn, sit here," Falda commanded in a serious tone.

"Yes, Your Majesty," the boy replied, pulling out a chair. The Queen was holding a scroll, on which the wax seal had been broken. It appeared to be the seal of Master Gulsbane.

"Puryn, this was delivered by courier this morning." She held up the missive. "It's from our teacher," she said, looking at it intently. "It is a solemn document." Durn and Arla looked almost afraid as they maintained a steely resolve on their faces.

Puryn sat wondering what this could be about and why his master would send a letter home to his parents. The young man searched his memory for offenses. He thought he had been doing well and that the master was pleased. Now, a gnawing doubt rose in his throat. Queen Falda raised the scroll, unrolled it, and translated the Elfish to Etah.

To all who read this missive, greetings. I greet you with the hope that you are all blessed by the Gods with health, prosperity, and love. I have trained young Puryn, son of Durn, for over five years now and have concluded, after many observations and tests, that this young man is an adept apprentice and skilled warrior. Therefore, as is with the traditions of my line, I command, as Grand-Master of the Order of the Silver Tear, that said Puryn stands to be tested to join the ranks of the Elfish Draj. Testing will commence on the first day of Sana, on the day of his passing from a child unto a man.

Signed,

Gulsbane, Grand Master of the Order of the Silver Tear.

Puryn sat in disbelief. Was he ready to be tested? He thought there would always be more to learn, but his master was willing to let him go out on his own. He was humbled and numb.

"How can this be, my dawn?" he asked, in perfect Elfish to the Queen. He meant every word, for she was the one who had saved him and lifted him to this station, and he knew it. She loved him like a son and almost cried whenever he called her that.

She replied in Elfish. "You speak the tongue, you heal those in need, you use the magics as if you've studied them as long as I, you know all of the stories of old by heart, and you fight as if you were ten years older. What else is there for you here, my favorite boy?"

"I will not fail. I will miss the master. Will we leave this place, My Queen?" Puryn asked in a concerned tone.

"Perhaps, but not immediately. There is much to complete before we head back to Yslandeth. I am hoping that my King will still have me." Falda looked wistfully into the horizon, hoping he still loved her.

"The King waits for your return, Your Majesty. I have no doubt." He hugged her around the shoulders and kissed her cheek. "We all love you."

Falda dried a tear from her eye and said in Etah, "Tomorrow, you must accept the challenge. Then, in six months, you will test out. You will not fail!"

Durn was extremely proud of his son. *Puryn was odd, though,* thought Durn. *He never really was a boy. Instead, he was constantly training for a higher purpose and never just played without a reason or design.*

Durn knew the next logical step would be to Squire Puryn to a Knight. He hoped the King would pair him with a fair man, vice a tyrant, but the choice was sometimes a political match-up.

Despite who inherited the boy, Puryn would devour his teachings, mastering the sword, as he had done everything else. Durn had no doubts. As a father, he wondered when his son would get to be his own man. The old constable hoped his lad would find his happiness in this world, but wondered if it would ever happen. The Gods always seemed to have need of him. It was almost unfair, but his boy seemed to thrive on these challenges.

Puryn excused himself, hugging the Queen, kissing his mother, and saying goodnight to his father. He went to his room and tried to sleep, but the excitement of being admitted into the Elite forces of the Elfish Guard kept him awake. The Draj were known throughout the kingdoms as the forward reconnaissance and shock troops of Torith. Only the top ten percent of all trainees and students were candidates for the honor.

It was very unusual for a human to be considered for promotion. Puryn knew this was his chance to shine. He hoped Adasser would hear of it when he became a Protector of the Forest. The young warrior was determined to pass all of the tests before him and show his love who he really was. If he could impress the Princess with victory, he knew he would make his master proud.

* * *

As Durn poked at the logs with a metal rod, the fireplace quietly crackled. Arla cleared the dishes while the Queen quickly wiped down the tables. Durn sat in his chair and lit his pipe. The Queen, completing her task, sat at the table, pretending to read a small book, but was really staying in the area to hear what Durn was obviously thinking about near the fire.

"Puryn wants to be a Knight," Durn said plainly. "I should return to Yslandeth and petition His Majesty to attach him to a suitable Knight. I just pray the King picks a fair and skilled warrior."

"Durn, my love, do you really think that is necessary? The boy will be a trained monk and Elf warrior in a few months! What more does he need to master?" Arla swept the floor and tried to dismiss the conversation as foolish talk.

"You must understand, wife. A human Knight fights with the sword. It is our custom and our code of chivalry that demands it. Puryn has shown an uncanny knack for doing the honorable and chivalrous thing. But, if he is to be a true leader of men, not just a member of the Elf community, it is imperative that he is mentored by a Knight of Yslandeth. He must become a Squire."

"Damn it all to the Underworld with all of this talk!" Arla exclaimed. "I will never see this boy again if he is attached to a Knight. I have enjoyed these past few years living as a family. Did you not enjoy your time here, living in peace, husband? Would you trade it now on a dream of glory for your son? What if he sees action against Hodan? What then? Will we bury him in a potter's field next to the other poor who die for 'noble' causes?"

Arla was frantic. She had swallowed about enough of all of this. She wanted her baby back. Time was running out for her. Soon, the boy would grow and marry. Then, he would leave, and she would be without children in her house. She was not interested in that proposition.

"Arla, he is almost sixteen years old! He will be conscripted into the reserves, regardless of your protests."

Arla interrupted. "At least the reserves are not in fealty to a Knight. They can come home after they drill. They do not live away from home, nor do they leave the city, unless there is serious conflict …"

Durn interrupted in turn. "And they get rudimentary training. I have witnessed what Hodan and Dwarfish forces do to the reserves in battle. The casualty rate is one in three on average—if against Hodan, one in two, most of them dying from their wounds days later. Would you have our son trained to be fodder, or would you have him trained by the best?"

Arla teared up. She knew the only answer. Durn was right, although she hated to admit it. "Fine! Ride to Yslan. Talk to the King. I have had enough of all of this. I am going to bed."

The Queen stood to comfort Arla, but she would have none of it. Falda stepped aside, allowing Arla to storm out of the room, sobbing. Falda felt terrible for her. She lamented the fact that Puryn was never allowed to be just a child or son.

The Queen closed her book, looking up sadly. "I had hoped for a priest to lead the people out of darkness. But, apparently, I will have to settle for a champion or a defender of the Light. Either way, Haya knows what is best, and I will comfort myself with that knowledge. Sleep well, Durn."

"And you as well, Your Majesty," Durn said as he stood.

When the Queen departed the room, Durn sat before the fire, puffing gently on his pipe and thinking of the future.

"I must ensure that Puryn is attached to an honorable man," a tired Durn remarked. He snuffed the pipe, scraped out the tobacco, and threw the remains into the fireplace. Then, closing the fire screen, he thought, *I will keep confidence that Haya will sway the King to do what is suitable for Puryn.*

Durn extinguished the lanterns and headed to bed. He wondered if he'd be sleeping on the mat near the mattress.

Beneath the Altyr

Emissaries from Torith and Yslandeth stood quietly at the gates, under a diplomatic banner, bearing scrolls from their respective Kings. Bogrol, son of Bathir, King of the Dwarves and the Kingdom of Dornat al Ar, pondered his next move carefully. He knew Yslan would back the Elves in any conflict with the Dwarfish forces, because his people had long allied with Hodan, the sworn adversaries of the Yslandeth. King Swyk would never hear his grievances against the Elves, as long as Dornat al Ar stood allied with King Jabir. That was a dream. Peace was going to be short-lived, but Bogrol could stall, and that was his plan.

Haeldrun rejoiced at the thought.

Hodan was essential to the economy and security of the Dwarf Kingdom. The Dwarfish Monarchy knew the only reason their armies and people were well-fed was that Dornat al Ar supplied Hodan with finely made weaponry and armor. Every now and then, upon a whim of one of the Hodan King's concubines, Bogrol would see his jewelry masters put out a load of baubles. Still, mostly, his forges churned out weapons and materials for war.

The Dwarf pondered this reality for almost a decade, while providing these goods to the Hodan. Now, the King regretted the decision, knowing those blades could make still Dwarfish hearts just as quickly as they could extinguish the life of an Elf or human. Hodan was a problem, but he had no solution. The Dwarves had not dwelled above ground in over a century, and all those who knew how to farm were too old or long gone. He was too proud to ask the Elves for any assistance.

Dornat al Ar was stuck in a difficult position. They needed wood to feed their forges. They required the forges to make the weapons. They needed the weapons to quiet the Hodan and provide food and other goods for the people. Many times, the King had thought to send emissaries to Yslan, but the hostile posture of Yslandeth toward the Dwarves kept him from acting. The last thing he needed was to be shut out by King Swyk, while alienating his only strong ally, the Hodan. There was no good answer, only bad ones.

Haeldrun fed his fears, ensuring the status quo was maintained.

"Centurion!" the King bellowed.

"Sire!" responded a soldier dressed in gilded armor.

"Escort our guests to the grand hall, and see to it that they are taken care of. Spare no luxury. Entertain them until I arrive."

"As you wish, My King." The soldier snapped to attention, his armor jingling ever so slightly. Then, grabbing the hilt of his sword, he left the well-lit throne room and proceeded to the gate.

Bogrol sat alone, save for a servant or two and his guard, thinking about his predicament. He was unhappy and felt Hodan would draw them into war. It seemed inevitable.

At the gate, the two emissaries and their entourages waited impatiently. The Yslan diplomat was a short, fat man with a sour disposition. It was odd that such a wise King would send such an angry little man to debate and negotiate with an adversary.

The Elf looked at the familiar face before him and raised an eyebrow in disapproval. The human huffed and opened a small book, acting as if he read it, but instead, he looked back at the Elf with disdain. Soon after, a Dwarf dressed in golden armor appeared and spoke to the sentries on duty.

"By order of the King, open the gate and let them pass." He motioned to the men on the wall, and they lowered their crossbows. "You and your entourage will stay close to my guards and me," he stated firmly. "Any deviation from our directions may result in your death. Do you understand?"

The human twisted his face and was about to blurt out something inappropriate, when the Elf interceded. "Thank you, Centurion. We understand and will comply with your orders." The human glared at the Elf. The Elf looked at him, once again, with an eyebrow raised.

A wagon was arriving at the city gates for use by the guests of Dornat al Ar. As it approached closer, it was apparent that this was no ordinary war wagon, but instead a wooden carriage fit for members of royalty. The thing measured twenty feet long and twelve feet wide. It was ornately carved and covered in gold and silver. One dozen Dwarfish draft horses pulled the coach, allowing it to move swiftly down the road. The diplomats saw the gilded ornamentation reflecting the illumination of the cavernous city passages. The Elf marveled at the workmanship. Even the haughty human gasped at the beauty before him.

The Dwarfish escort smiled and nodded.

"To the meeting hall. Ensure that our guests are given every comfort. These are the words of the King." The Centurion bowed to the diplomats, who returned the gesture and boarded the carriage. The Dwarf Commander then turned about smartly and left the foreign bureaucrats and their attendants with a team of six Dwarves, who escorted them through wonderfully carved cavernous passageways to a meeting with the waiting King of the Dwarves.

The human looked out of the carriage, marveling at how everything was done with such precision. The floor was hewn from granite and bedrock, but it was so smooth and level that it appeared to be polished marble. Immense pillars in the styles of Yslan and Hodan ran from the streets and grounds to the ceiling, hundreds of feet above them. They were underground, and the sun did not reach where they stood, but it was not dark. It was quite the opposite.

Large subterranean fires were channeled into windows cut into the city's walls. These fires glowed brightly from the core of the world itself and reflected off of everything within the eye's view. The Dwarves, fond of metals, had gilded the walls of their city in gold, silver, mythral, and jewels. To ride down these streets as a human was to feel as if you were living within the treasury at Yslandeth. Still, the Dwarves they encountered on the streets saw nothing but the norm and went about their business as if nothing special was about them.

About an hour later, and several miles from the gates, the carriage was stopped before two huge doors, clad in mythral and white gold. Diamonds, rubies, and emeralds lined its hinges, and the handles appeared to be polished gold. The guard worked two immense knockers, pounding furiously until a small door opened ten feet above them. The Elf and the human could not see where the door ended, and the little hatch began.

"Open in the name of the King. We have brought his visitors!" the guard declared.

"As you command, Sir!" a deep voice said from ten feet above. Then the sound of machinery was heard. Gears turned somewhere, and there was a loud click. The guard pushed the large door with one hand, and it glided open without a creak. Everything was precision.

"Please, come in," motioned a steward. The emissaries entered and sat at a large wooden table covered in polished silver and encrusted with semi-precious stones. The chairs matched. The human and Elf sat, noticing that the chairs were a bit lower than they had anticipated. Neither said a thing. Shortly thereafter, the servants brought wine and assorted food and refreshments. A bard played a stringed instrument in the corner and sang quietly. Ironically, he sang an ode to the First War of the Clans, where all the races of the Ert fought each other, and many had perished.

Appropriate, thought the Elf, and he turned to the human, who had no idea what the Dwarf was singing. So they ate and drank, awaiting the King.

Bogrol made his way to the hall and entered with the usual fanfare. Horns were blowing, and drums were beating. Then, a crescendo of pomp and circumstance ushered the Dwarf King to his chair. The emissaries stood, bowing respectfully. When the din had subsided, the King seated himself on the opposite side of the table with his council.

"Greetings, esteemed guests. I am honored to have the emissaries of Yslandeth and Torith within my mountain. What brings you to my glorious kingdom, friends?" Bogrol switched his gaze nervously between both of the emissaries.

The Elf spoke first, as the human was swallowing some wine. "Your

Majesty, I have been sent by King Glorin of the Forest to negotiate terms for the withdrawal of Dwarfish lumber operations from our southeastern borders. We wish peace between our kingdoms and fear that Dwarfish operations are moving dangerously close to the Elfish territory."

"I assure you and all of my neighbors to the North that we have not breached the territories of the Elves. We are in open territory, operating within the buffer established years ago by our wise ancestors. We only harvest trees away from Torith."

"This is not so, Your Majesty," sneered the human. "Yslan scouts have reported that your Dwarf lumberjacks have stripped the trees on a path over the Altyr to the Plains of Arondayre! This is in direct violation of treaties with Yslandeth and is virtually a declaration of war on Torith!" The human's face was red. He had no couth, and this was visibly irritating the otherwise stoic Elf.

Sighing, the Elf continued, trying to limit the damage that had just been done. "Your Majesty, although my colleague is correct that the Elfish Kingdom is concerned with the proximity of your troops and lumber operations, we, as a nation, have not considered this an overt act of war, but perhaps a misunderstanding?"

The King's face softened, and he rethought his response to the rude human. "Perhaps, it is my friend, perhaps it is. I will order the withdrawal of our troops and lumber operations. I will decree that wood harvesting will be restricted to the foothills of the Altyr and no farther. Will this suffice to stay hostilities between our two proud nations?"

"It will, Your Majesty. If it is your willing desire to compromise, my King has authorized me to offer a treaty stating as much." The Elf pulled a scroll from his satchel and handed it to the King's council. It was written in Dwarfish, Elfish, and Etah. King Swyk had signed for Yslandeth and King Glorin for Torith. The last binding signature required was King Bogrol's. After a short deliberation with his council, the Dwarfish King signed the treaty and shook hands with the Elf. Bogrol stood, thinking the meeting had concluded, when the human opened his mouth again.

"Pardon me, Your Majesty, but I must address a pressing issue concerning the treaty between Yslandeth and Dornat al Ar! King Swyk of Yslandeth bids you health and prosperity. Still, he wishes to discuss a situation that seems to be festering below the surface of the pleasantries shown here today."

King Bogrol was not pleased and unsure of where this was going. A guard stepped forward. The King waved him off. For a moment, the smarmy look on the human's face was replaced by fear, as he thought that the guard was going to run him through.

"What nefarious activity do you accuse my noble people of now, Yslandeth?" The King spoke forcefully, and his words burned as if acid dripped from his angry lips.

"King Swyk has had scouts …," the human started smugly.

"Spies, you mean …," the King interjected, tapping a ring on the table.

The human cleared his throat. "Scouts, Your Majesty, not spies. He also has merchant reports of a growing military threat in Hodan. Their military might grows, because of the trade deals you have made with our enemies."

"Hodan is a respectful ally and friend of Dornat al Ar. I resent your accusations! What have they done, save building a defense against the coming onslaught of Yslan armies?! Who in this whole land has as many armies as Yslandeth does? None! And you speak to me of a building threat? If Hodan is a threat, then what shall I call Yslandeth? Impending doom to all other nations?"

The human was caught a bit off guard by Bogrol's retort. Clearly, the reports of the Dwarf King being a drunkard and a weak imbecile were greatly misstated. Someone's head might roll for this, and he was now trying to ensure that it wouldn't be his own.

"Well, Your Majesty, Yslandeth has been invaded multiple times by the aggressive Hodan over the ages. We were the only thing standing in the way of their total domination of the continent in the last conflict. We are concerned that in their prosperity, their trade with your people has increased their military power to a point where no nation is safe," the human argued.

"Yslandeth does not dictate to the world. All shall live as they please under their own governments and in their own kingdoms! Who are you to lecture sovereigns of other lands? Yslandeth is not our keeper! We shall reserve the right to self-determination and alliance. I reject your accusations with vehemence. You speak of what you do not know, and slander our longtime allies!" The King pounded a fist on the table.

"Then what of the talk of subversives weakening the kingdoms of Sudenyag and Edenyag? Eden has become a surrogate to Hodan, incapable of resistance for fear of invasion, and Suden has become a puppet state. Hodan is building its armies with a purpose. That purpose is to dominate the entire known world. Will Dwarves be shown quarter when all other races are put down?" The human looked genuinely concerned.

One of the council members hissed. "Who are you to question Suden or Eden? Perhaps they sought protection from the overbearing eyes of Yslan?"

"Who, may I ask, are you?" the human sneered toward the robed figured, who was obscured by a hood.

"I am the emissary of Suden. You are correct to be concerned. We have allied with the Hodan. We will not be dictated to by the Yslan court as to which nations we can or cannot trade with. Hodan and the Offlanders from the sea are our bread and wine! Who are you to judge, living behind the great stone wall, within a nation that knows no true poverty?Hypocrites!"

The human was caught off guard. Even the Elf was surprised. They had no intelligence that stated emissaries of the other nations would attend this summit. This meeting had just become a much bigger affair. The Elf was uncomfortable with the situation.

The Elf interjected. "Please, gentlemen, we are here to discuss a way forward that does not involve war. So please, tone down your rhetoric and posturing. There is no need for hostility. Where people talk, there is always hope of a solution without violence."

King Bogrol nodded. He knew that war threatened his food supplies and his access to other essential goods. He wanted to avoid it if it were at all possible. "Yslandeth," said the King calmly, "means well. I know this, but the constant meddling in other kingdoms' affairs is not only insulting, but also bothersome. We seek to be treated as equals, not underlings who need the attention of a master or a father. We know what we do, and we seek to be self-determinate. Yslan must recognize that it is not the law of all lands. Yslandeth must stop its interference and spying. This, above all else, is what wars are sparked by. Hodan is autonomous—even if I agreed with your King, I could not demand that they disarm. It is their right to prepare for war if they feel threatened, and Yslandeth threatens us all with its grand armies and its logistics. Who is the true aggressor here, My Lord?"

The King had a point, and the emissary from Yslandeth wrote down all of the Dwarfish King's objections. Then, humbly and honestly, the human spoke. "Yslandeth is not your enemy, Your Majesty. I hear your protests. I will take them to my King. He is a just man, and he will hear me out. I can only hope that he finds a middle ground where we can all live peacefully. I wish for you and your lands to prosper and see peace eternally!"

The King was taken aback. The human seemed to be a decent fellow after all. Perhaps his posturing was a façade to defend against the appearance of weakness. He did not know, but Bogrol felt as if the truth was uttered here by this man.

"And also with Yslandeth, My Lord. Safe passage home." The King bowed.

Everyone stood as the King exited the room. The Elf spoke with the emissary from Sudenyag as the other quiet figure with him stealthily worked his way to the human emissary. The quiet one removed his hood.

"I am from Edenyag. Take this." He then shook the human's hand, depositing a tiny, sealed scroll into the emissary's hand. "Please ensure that your King is given the whole story, My Lord. Safe journeys."

The Edenyag emissary turned and left. The Yslan emissary put his hands in his sleeves, keeping the small scroll out of view of anyone. Then, quietly, he deposited it into his satchel and fastened the bag shut. He told no one of its existence, not even the Elf, with whom he had arrived.

Shortly thereafter, the guard contingent returned with the beautiful carriage. Through wondrous caverns, the Elf and human rode with their entourages. Finally, both emissaries arrived at the front gate without incident and were allowed to leave freely. The guard saluted the departing emissaries as they went on horseback back to their places of origin.

"Be safe, Nestor," the human waved to the Elf.

"You as well, Willun. Say hello to King Swyk for me! I will give your greetings to Glorin!" the Elf waved back. Despite their feigned animosity, the two had been on many diplomatic missions together. Although they had gotten on each other's nerves from time to time, they genuinely liked each other, when all was said and done.

The two rode together for a bit, splitting up at Raven's Pass, the Elf traveling to the East, and the human to the West. The sun was high in the sky. It was only noon, but it had already been a long day. Under the mountain, it was always daytime and always night. Those who actually lived there were never sure of the time.

The two riders yawned and traveled toward their homes.

Grace Under Fire

The smoke from the southeastern corner of Torith told her everything she needed to know. There was fire in the woods and in the city. Adasser shuddered to think of the destruction of her beloved forest.

It had been almost a year since the summit between her father's people and the emissaries from the South and the West. Since then, Hodan had forced Edenyag into compliance with its new Southern Alliance, and Sudenyag hid behind its Hodan masters to their North. Cinnog remained free, but no one knew for how long. Yslandeth was deploying her troops throughout the Ert, and the Elves were under siege from the Dwarves and Hodan from their South.

"My Lady, the King orders you to leave the palace at once and to meet him in the courtyard." The lady-in-waiting was visibly nervous as she heard muffled explosions, shouting, and crashing objects in the distance. "We must flee the city, My Lady. We must go!"

"Not yet," Adasser snapped angrily. She was waiting for him. He was Draj. He would come.

The fires burned on the horizon, and machinery could be heard tearing through the woods. Cries in Elfish were heard from every quarter as the men, women, and children fled North to the mountains of Oron Falmarindi on the shore. There, an ancient forest would allow cover for the people to hide and wait for deliverance from Yslandeth.

The mountain's rocky, sheer cliffs fell straight into the sea, and there was only a single passage that led up to the plateau, where the Elves planned to wait for reinforcements. The Draj were fighting valiantly, inflicting heavy casualties upon Dwarves and Hodan alike, but they were outnumbered three-to-one and took heavy losses of their own. So they had retreated to within the forest tree wall.

As if from thin air, he appeared silently in the doorway. There, clad in Elfish mail, with a bow strung over his back and a short-glaive in his hand, was her love. Puryn stepped forward, removing his helmet. Adasser stood expectantly.

"Your Highness," Puryn said, bowing. "You must flee. It is dire in the wood. They come for all of you! I shall not watch you perish!" His face was deadly serious, and she could see the worry lines furrowed on his brow.

So much on such a young soul's back, the Princess thought to herself.

"Hush, my dearest soul," she replied, taking his hand gently. "I needed to see your face one more time before I left. One never knows when goodbyes are forever." Her eyes teared up as she brought his hand to her heart. She kissed the back of his mailed hand.

"I will live to see you again, my heart," replied the young warrior in Elfish. "I will walk with you again beneath the moonlight, under the stars, within your tree line. This I swear, or I will not live to speak of it again."

"Be still! Do not throw your life away playing the hero, for I'd rather walk elsewhere, beneath a new moon, with you by my side, than ere stand on this ground again, alone." She kissed his hand again, and he brought her other hand to his lips.

Hurrying her, the warrior escorted the Princess to the courtyard. A visibly upset King was pacing and cursing up a storm.

"Where in the Underworld is that girl!? I have an idea. Damn that boy!"

Finally, King Glorin saw his daughter's approach.

The King leered angrily at Adasser, who turned again to Puryn. Her sullen gaze gripped the young man's soul, but her tearing eyes betrayed her stoicism. Bowing, he kissed her hand and said goodbye. He saw her as if she was in a mist, his head swimming, as a knot formed in his throat. She boarded the carriage, and the royal family made its way through the fleeing refugees, traveling northward to the mountains. He watched her fade into the distance as a silent tear rolled beneath his eyes. An older Elf patted him on the back and said something unintelligible. Puryn cleared his throat and pulled himself together.

Turning his gaze to his unit, he saw the Draj now forming ranks to see how many remained. Puryn could see Master Gulsbane running the infirmary, which was overflowing with wounded. Queen Falda had remained in Torith, along with Puryn's mother and father. Falda and Arla helped with the wounded, while Durn created more with the militiamen. Puryn had never seen his father in combat. However, he was impressed with his skills with the sword and on horseback. Indeed, there was more to his Da than an old fiddling constable. He would ask him later if they were so lucky.

Puryn rejoined his ranks. His Commander looked around aimlessly. He seemed visibly shaken. He was war-worn, and his thoughts were foggy and disoriented. Nevertheless, he was trying to remain composed and was failing badly.

"I have lost so many men," he muttered. He looked at the ground, defeated and tired. "What is the use? Perhaps we should surrender. Maybe they will let us live!?"

The Draj, beaten and demoralized, began to feel similarly. Several looked as if they intended to bolt and run with the refugees. Puryn was indignant. He stepped forward, pushing the trembling Commander, who appeared to be only two years older than he was, out of the way, and stood in front of the formation.

"Stop!" Puryn raged in Elfish. "All of you who call yourself Draj! I am Draj, and you are my brothers and sisters! How dare you pity yourselves and think for your own well-being! Why do you feel defeated when we still stand in our homeland? Who has told you that you have lost? Is the enemy here? No! I tell you that they still fight in the forest and our people still live! Our King and his family still live! We swore an oath to Torith and to the King! We must give them time to escape and regroup. We must fight, for there is no other option for the Draj! Your honor depends upon it! And the honor of your family! So pick up your weapons and take heart, my brethren, my sisters! We have won if the people remain! These buildings can be rebuilt, and trees will regrow, but the souls of those we love will never come this way again. They are treasures that cannot be replaced. So I say that we kill every invader! Soak the Ert in their blood! Fill the skies with their cries for mercy! Burn their corpses and send their camp women wailing back to Hodan in ashes and sackcloth!" Puryn was beside himself and did not know where the words came from.

Runnir and Gunnir stood by, looking down with approval from Aeternum. They blessed the Elfish warriors with strength and courage. They were impressed by Puryn's devotion to duty, and watched intently to see what he would do.

The newly self-appointed Draj Commander could see Gulsbane smoking his pipe against the post of the infirmary. He thought he could make out a smile on the old goat's face. Had he heard his student's words? Master Gulsbane stood at attention and saluted young Puryn, then smartly turned about and reentered his post to heal those in need. The young Draj smiled.

The formation was silent. Puryn's thoughts returned to eighteen months before this moment, when he stood on this same field and won his position in the Draj. The King rolled his eyes in the stands as Adasser smiled and clapped at the boy's every victory. The Draj's face reddened, remembering how embarrassed he was when she overtly cheered and even whistled when he won the archery championship! The young man remembered her flowing gossamer gown and how she "accidentally" dropped her handkerchief over the railing where Puryn was seated on horseback, awaiting his turn for the equestrian portion of the tests. She smiled when he picked it up, and the light seemed to concentrate aroundher lovely face.

When he became a member of the Draj, he became almost acceptable in the eyes of Elfish society. He swore to defend the Elfish Kingdom as an outsider, and had learned their ways and made them his own. Puryn was generally accepted by the public, but that did not make him a favored suitor with the King. The people did not know that part.

The days that followed his passage to manhood found that Adasser sent her ladies to his home, inviting him to secret meetings in random locations. The meetings were nothing salacious or untoward! There was always a lady-in-waiting present. The young couple simply went on long walks, talking under the moonlight, with the occasional embrace or kiss.

He was almost seventeen years old now and had secretly courted the Princess for nearly twelve months. Glorin disapproved, because he feared Adasser would be widowed at a young age, but his daughter was young and rebellious. The King knew she would do as she willed, regardless of his objections, so he chose to do nothing. Soon, there was a rumor among the Elves of the Princess's betrothal to a human. Snickers came from the mouths of traditionalists, in the corners of the court, and sometimes in the marketplaces and the temples. Still, Adasser did not care, nor did Puryn—for he loved her, and she loved him.

The formation stood at attention in front of Puryn. No one challenged his claim to command, for all knew who his lady was, and no one wished to incur the wrath of the crown. The former Commander sheepishly fell into ranks, grabbing a bow.

"Fall in! Shields to the front, poles to the rear! Do we have any horsemen left?" He looked around. There were none to be found. "Damn those Hodan dogs! Forward! March!"

The unit of approximately two-hundred-fifty Elfish men and women stepped off smartly. Puryn directed his unit to the point where the Dwarfish forces were cutting through the tree wall.

"Stay in the general area! Fall out!" The remaining Draj sat down. Food and water were passed around. Archers inventoried and then divided up their arrows evenly. Some tended to minor wounds, while others cleaned their weapons or napped.

* * *

On the outside of the tree line, the Dwarfish machines were chewing up trees as fast as possible. The Dwarfish engineers figured they would be through the wall within three or four hours. They could see the clearing through cracks in the forest wall, but the trees were too tightly entangled to pass through or even shoot an arrow through.

"Sir," a Dwarfish Centurion stated, saluting. "Is that an Elfish unit on the other side of the trees? Are they mad?"

"Why are they mad, fool? They are defending their homeland. What choice do they have?" the disgusted Dwarfish Commander replied. Secretly, the Commander thought this incursion into Elfish territory was an overreach, however, he also knew his place. The King commanded it. That is what he kept telling himself, even though he knew that Hodan was behind the attack. Bogrol was a puppet in this whole mess. The Dwarf scowled. "They are honorable foes. They stand for their people, as we do for ours. Do not insult their bravery!" The Centurion looked at the ground, acknowledging, and walked away.

"Soon, we will be inside of Torith," the Commander lamented. "But for what end? What do we need so badly that we attack our neighbors without real cause? Pride will be the end of us all." The Commander stared at the Elves on the other side of the thinning tree wall. With every minute, the Dwarfish machines edged closer to their goal. Watching the destruction of the forest, the Commander remembered the reason for the campaign.

A year ago, after the summit in Dornat al Ar, the Elfish King Glorin felt as if the southern border of his kingdom was in jeopardy. So he sent a scouting party South to spy upon the Dwarfish logging operations and to assess any Hodan forces within the immediate vicinity.

The King's nephew, Narulas, was chosen to lead this expedition, but being a new leader, he mistakenly led his men too far South into the territory of the Dwarves. A cooperative Hodan and Dwarfish patrol spotted the intruders and engaged them, killing several of the scouts, including Glorin's nephew. This sparked an immediate escalation of hostilities and was Hodan's real purpose for the attack on the small scout team. King Glorin sent swift and deadly retaliation. The Elves razed several lumber operations and camps directly inside Dwarfish territories, killing scores of Dwarves and, ultimately, some of their families.

This was the moment that Hodan was waiting for. They declared war "in the name of the Alliance," claiming to come to Dornat al Ar's aid in dealing with the "Elfish atrocities." This forced the Dwarfish King's hand. He knew that Hodan wanted nothing less than total domination of the Elf Kingdom, and they would use any excuse to wage their war.

Foolishly, the Elves gave them the excuse they desired. Hodan knew Yslandeth was busy on the West coast, thwarting Hodan's attempts to subjugate Cinnog. Yslan deployed much of its military to reinforce its wall. It also sent Legions to the common borders between Hodan and its homeland. King Jabir of Hodan knew that Yslan could not effectively wage war on three fronts. So he counted on Swyk to leave the Elves to fight alone. So far, so good.

* * *

In Yslandeth, King Swyk called his champion, Sir Ontak, to lead a cavalry advance over the open plains toward Raven's Pass, in an effort to flank the superior numbers of Hodan troops and Dwarfish Legionnaires near the Plains of Arondayre. Ontak had only five-thousand men—one-thousand horsemen with lances and swords, one-thousand archers with longbows, two-thousand shieldmen with swords and mace, and one-thousand pole arms. The King figured the enemy had three times that amount.

"Ontak," the King said as he looked at the Knight.

"Yes, Your Majesty," the Knight said as he stood tall.

"The Queen is in Torith with our friends. The Elves are our allies, and they flee. We cannot stand for this aggression any longer. You must succeed in giving them support. Cinnog is going poorly, but I worry more for the Elves." The King looked away ashen, thinking of his wife and the family who left Yslan years ago for the safety of the wood.

"I will not fail, Your Majesty," Ontak replied confidently. "Or I shall never walk into this court again under my own power." He saluted the King and bowed.

The King returned the salute. "May Haya hear my words and protect you and all we love. You are my friend and the champion of Yslan. May our forefathers fight along with you, at your side."

* * *

Sir Ontak had been on the road for a week now. His men were uncomfortable, cold, hungry, and angry. It was raining when they cleared the pass and saw the Hodan horde on the western flank of the Dwarves. The Dwarves used their machines to tear into the forest, and they were almost through. Ontak called his Commanders to the front.

"You know the drill, gentlemen. We are outnumbered, and we may be outmatched, but since when has that mattered to any of you champions of Yslandeth? We shall kill as many of these bastards as Haya will allow, then we shall kill a few more for Runnir and Gunnir. We must make them bleed until they retreat to their nests like the snakes they are. The Queen and her party depend upon us. We must not fail! Make them bleed. Make their women wail and lament. Make their mothers wish they had never borne them! We are Yslan! We go to get our Queen. If we save the Elves, so be it."

All of the Commanders nodded, grunting in unison. Then, they joined hands in the group's center and prayed to Haya for glory in battle. Next, they asked Runnir and Gunnir to rain fire down from the heavens on their foes, and as their prayers concluded, lightning streaked down as if it had answered their requests. The Commander of the archers chuckled and raised a fist in the air.

"Nock one now! Ready your bows, gents! Wet the tips of your arrows with the blood of our enemies!" A loud roar of angry Yslan archers rang out.

Ontak shook his head. "So much for the element of surprise." He smiled and mounted his horse. "Shields to the front. Cavalry to the flanks. Poles behind the shields. Archers to the rear. Hunter teams on me!" The unit formed in seconds. "Forward, march!"

The unit marched until it was in longbow range. "Halt! Archers ready!" The archers drew. "Fire at will. Volleys on the Commander's order!" Arrows filled the air. Entire ranks of Hodan and Dwarves fell where they stood, but their comrades were shifting their focus and regrouping. Finally, Yslan's Commanders shouted, "Stand by for incoming!" Shields were lifted and interlocked. Most enemy arrows bounced off harmlessly, but a few found their marks, leaving the shield wall to adjust, stepping over their dead momentarily.

"Forward at a walk!" The unit moved forward as one. Archers remained behind, raining death from afar. The Hodan bows could not reach the Yslan archers, wielding Elfish longbows. Hodan's dead and dying were bleeding the field red as the Yslan forces closed on them. They then did what every Hodan unit does—they charged.

The Yslan Commanders shouted, "Brace for impact. Repel!"

There was an Ert shattering crash with countless screams on either side, with commands lost in the din of metal impacting metal. Hodan fought like rabid animals, trapped in a corner, chewing their way to freedom. Yslan suffered significant losses, but had cut the Hodan down at a rate of two-to-one.

It is a good day to die, thought Ontak, as he crushed another attacker's skull with his sword edge. *Yslan fought well!*

On the other side, the Hodan Commander was concerned. The damn Yslanders were not going quietly. They were destroying his forces, and his King would not be pleased with the steep loss of warriors or the expense and destruction of weapons and supplies. He calculated that the Dwarves could handle the incursion into Torith, recalling much of his cohort to his position on the hill. This would give him some tactical advantage, and he knew that if Yslan attacked on foot, Hodan still had the numbers on the field. So his men rallied to their Commander, forming a square.

Ontak saw the retreat as a chance to engage the Dwarves directly on the wall of Torith, but looking that way, he was keenly aware of a medium-sized Suden unit between his position and the wall. He had lost at least a third of his forces, but the cavalry seemed largely intact.

"Squire!" Ontak bellowed.

"Yes, Sir!" the young warrior responded, riding up rapidly.

"Take five-hundred horsemen and make the Suden women cry. Kill them all. Don't charge in headlong like a fool, my student, but instead ride in like the wind, then strike fast and ride out. Small bites until they are devoured."

"Yes, My Knight!" the Squire responded, saluting. Then, he formed his unit into a column of twos. The Yslan cavalry, armed with horsemen's spears, attacked the Suden with devastating effect.

The Suden army was not a battle-hardened unit, nor did it possess any allegiance to the fight. Sudenyag was there for show, and had no idea they would actually be tasked to fight. So the unit folded like parchment. Sudenyag broke ranks, and its men began running toward the Altyr Mountains. Those who deserted were cut down by the Yslan horsemen.

"Suden dung. I will remember this treachery and report it to the King if I live to see Hodan again." The Hodan Commander looked over with concern at the Yslan archers, and knew he could not advance without a barrage of arrows. Nevertheless, he held the hill, and on the rise, his bows were more effective. His enemy had the open field and he the higher ground. It was a stalemate. The Hodan leader decided to allow the Dwarves to handle Yslan.

Ontak advanced to the Dwarfish lines as they finally broke through the tree line. He could hear the screams in Elfish on the other side of the wall as the Dwarves poured into the breach. The Knight feared he was too late, but then he saw them. The Draj had formed a square in the breach and were killing the siege weapons operators before they could use their machines on the shield wall. "Huzzah, Draj!" Ontak exclaimed. Yslan echoed his sentiment.

A loud cheer of "Huzzah, Draj!" filled the air from two-thousand voices outside the tree line. The Dwarves turned in horror to see the Yslandeth Legion had sealed off their only retreat.

"Dwarfish warriors, stand fast! Push toward Torith—they are weaker on that front! Push toward the city!" The Dwarfish Commander knew they were all done for if he didn't get his unit out of that passage.

* * *

Inside the wall, in the Draj square, Puryn was directing the defense of the breach. Then he heard a strange war cry. He thought he heard "Huzzah, Draj!" coming from the Dwarfish side of the battle. Climbing up on the back of a wagon, he shouted to his snipers in the trees behind him. "What in the Underworld was that?"

The sniper responded. "I am not sure, Sir, but if I see correctly through the dust, I think I see the standard of Yslan behind the Dwarves!"

Puryn's head swam. He was giddy. "They came! They came! I knew they'd come!" He danced in a small circle, pumping his fist into the air. "Stand tall, Draj, our brothers from Yslan have come to our aid! We shall win this battle, and it shall be talked of for eternity!" Light danced on the edge of his blade. Knowing they sought to harm her, he resolved to end them all or die trying. Yslandeth had granted him an opportunity to make the Dwarves pay, and dearly.

The Draj cheered, "Huzzah, Yslan, huzzah!"

"Form the shield wall! Pikes behind! Archers to the rear! We are the anvil! They are the hammer! Be strong! We shall win this battle for our families and friends!"

Puryn grabbed a bow and started shooting until his arrows were spent. The Draj shield wall stopped the Dwarves in their tracks, and they never did set foot within Torith proper. Instead, Yslan drove a killing wedge into the Dwarves from the rear. The Dwarves fought valiantly in close quarters, but had no room to maneuver. It became a war of attrition, and Yslan killed their enemy very rapidly and with extreme violence. The slaughter continued until the Dwarfish Commander called hold and hoisted a white flag.

When the mayhem ceased and the dust settled, the surviving Dwarves were rounded up and captured as prisoners of war. Later, it was determined that the Dwarves had lost approximately seventy-five percent of their forces in the attempt to invade Torith. Likewise, Ontak had inflicted a death toll of fifty-percent of the Hodan forces, and the Suden were annihilated. This was an embarrassing defeat for the Southern Alliance, and a glorious victory for the Yslan Alliance.

Ontak made his way over to the slightly built Draj Commander. He had expected to greet an Elf, but was surprised to see a young man remove his helmet and present his hand. "Who may you be, My Lord?" the Knight asked.

"Sir, I am Puryn, son of Durn, Commander of the Draj by battlefield commission."

"Well, Puryn, son of Durn, you have made a fine mess of these Dwarfish fellows. I commend you for your tactics." Ontak smiled and put his hands on his hips. He laughed heartily and clapped the young warrior on the back. "I seem to remember a Puryn who left in search of peaceful teachings, but here you are, the warrior. The Queen must be livid!"

"Sir, Haya has a funny sense of humor. I fear that she has left me to the warring brothers, Runnir and Gunnir!" Puryn drank from a water skin handed to him by one of the medics, who happened by.

"You have made your master proud this day, young warrior. I will see you again soon. I am sure of it!" The Knight turned and exhorted his men with coarse jokes and raucous humor. He said something about Elfish women not being as hairy as Dwarfish women, and then went on about a girl he used to know. His men laughed, seemingly shrugging off the horror of battle while eating their rations. Then, they set up the watch, as if it was just another day, like all of the rest.

Puryn thought, *It most likely is a regular day for these fellows.* And the young warrior shuddered at the thought of constant combat. Looking at the blood on his hands, he realized he had several wounds of his own. So, the new Commander made his rounds, visiting his remaining Draj, and then made his way to the infirmary.

Ontak sent a messenger to King Swyk in Yslandeth, reporting their victory and the enemy withdrawal. Then, his demeanor changed drastically. No more joking or laughing, as he solemnly numbered the losses and compiled a list of the dead through the evening musters held by his remaining

Commanders.

There, Ontak sighed as he learned that his victory had cost the lives of more than half of his men; less than two-thousand remained of five. Still, he felt fortunate that the Hodan Commander was as incompetent as he was a coward. Any other day, against that number of Hodan, it would have meant the certain destruction of his unit. It wouldn't always be that *easy* if losing sixty-percent of your men could ever be called easy. Ontak took a long swig from a whiskey flask his Lieutenant handed him. He then handed it to his Squire.

"Good job, boy. Glad you are still with me." Ontak took the flask back. The Squire smiled sheepishly and nodded.

"Is there anything else you need of me, Sir? If not, I wish to tend to the men of our unit." The Squire looked over at the injured. The medics had already started laying blankets over those who had died while awaiting care.

"No, son. Thank you. Do as you have spoken." The Squire turned away and went to work.

Ontak drank more, watching the young Draj Commander he had met earlier. The young Elfish leader walked the ranks and shook the hands of his men. He hugged some of them as if they were his blood. He shared their food and drink and ordered the injured to see Queen Falda at the aid station. All these things he did in the Elfish tongue, impressing Sir Ontak even more.

After a while, Puryn formed up the remaining healthy warriors of his unit and had them post a small watch in town, policing against looters. A more significant Elfish force comprised of conscripts was sent to augment the Yslan forces stationed at the breach in the forest. Torith was mending itself, but it would be days until the first tree line was thick enough to keep out a bear.

* * *

Upon the clearing, on top of the plateau, at Oron Falmarindi, King Glorin, Queen Hansu, their daughters, and the remaining survivors of Torith made camp. The camp had only one approach, so the King positioned his archers and horsemen on the steep trail. The Elves hid on the mountain, witnessing the fire and noise below in Torith. They were unaware of the victory. To the King, it seemed pretty quiet, considering what was going on.

Adasser was beside herself with worry. She sat quietly crying. Gazing at the reflection in her mirror, she brushed her hair. She saw his eyes staring back at her through her tears and felt alone. Not knowing if his soul was among the living was the worst thing she had ever felt in her eighty-or-so years on the Ert. She covered her head in a scarf and sobbed.

"I know why you cry, daughter," Hansu said as she hugged her daughter from behind. "It is a burden of all women to watch as their men go off to fight and possibly die. You experience this pain at too young an age, my dear. He is human. He will die and leave you to live alone for years to come. Are you prepared for this?"

"I know, Mother," sighed Adasser, "but I cannot bear to think of a moment without him beside me! His touch melts my heart, his voice cheers me when I hear it, and when I look upon him, I see the future generations of my line. I love him,Mother. I cannot help who my heart has chosen. He is all I could ask for, and a short time with him is better than eternity with another." Adasser's tears flowed freely now. "He cannot be dead. His light is too strong. He is too good to die that way."

Hansu dabbed her daughter's tears, and replied, "All men and Elf die. We must make the time we have count, no matter how short it is. I shall speak with your father, Adasser, but he's a stubborn old fool. He loves you, girl, and only wishes you happiness. He is afraid you will be an old dowager in a tower when your love departs this world!" She rolled her eyes. "He can be so dramatic and stubborn! I will work on him, but you must be wise, my daughter!"

Adasser hugged her mother. "Thank you so much. I love you, Mother. I knew you would understand."

"Now, lie on the mats and get some sleep, Adasser! We will find out what is going on when the light comes. It is pointless to wear yourself out worrying! Yslan will not abandon us. You shall see! They will come. They always have, and we have always been there for them when they are in need."

She kissed her daughter on the forehead and put a blanket over her. Adasser sat awake and imagined where Puryn was. Then she muttered a quick prayer and closed her eyes. Tears wet her pillow as she saw his face in her dreams.

Hansu padded to where Glorin was seated. "Send a scout, now. She needs to know, husband."

"Know what, wife?" the King asked, playing stupid as he ate his ration.

The Queen stood angrily. "Now that is enough, you pompous ass! That boy is down there fighting for our people, not his! He loves your daughter, and she loves him. You should come to grips with this already and deal with it!" Hansu was angry, and her King sighed with annoyance at her badgering.

"Fine!" Glorin declared with exasperation. He looked around hurriedly. "Soldier, come here!"

"Yes, Your Majesty?"

"I need you to scout down to Torith and bring back word of what is happening there!"

"Yes, Your Majesty."

"Take several guards with you and do not be seen by the enemy, do you understand!?" Glorin emphasized his words.

"Yes, Your Majesty." The guard then went over to his Commander and relayed what the King had commanded. The Commander formed a scout team and sent them on their way. It was late, but there was a full moon. The Elves would pass silently and unnoticed to Torith and be back by morning.

"Are you satisfied, woman?" Glorin asked sarcastically.

"Yes, I am," Hansu said with an attitude. "You should prepare to Knight a few Draj if they still live, Your Eminence," the Queen quipped mockingly. "There is a good chance that a young human warrior will be an Elfish Knight by morning, if justice is served." She looked at her husband.

Glorin hadn't considered the possibility. He was not amused by the notion of making an Elfish nobleman out of a human.

"Good night, My King. For your daughter's sake, please stop being a stubborn horse's ass. You are not going to win this fight. The women of this family are far too obstinate. You do remember this?"

"I do. How I do remember, how could one ever forget! I will endeavor to improve my wretched person, Your Majesty," the King said, raising his hands while trying not to chuckle. "Good night, my love, you old witch!" He winked at his wife and smiled.

Hansu smiled and kissed him on the cheek, then went to bed.

King Glorin sat up with a sword in his hand. He was old and past his prime, but he would not sleep while his men were at war. Secretly, he hoped the boy had made it. He waited up for the scouts to return.

Securing the Forest

Puryn was eating a bit of his breakfast ration and speaking to Sir Ontak when a commotion began at the northern edge of the perimeter, along the route the refugees had used for their escape. A Draj patrol spotted movement in the trees and challenged the intrusion.

"Halt! Who goes there?" the patrol leader commanded. "Show yourself, or prepare to die!"

"Hold your arrows, brother!" a voice answered from within the trees. Puryn knew it had to be an Elf, for the trees would have no other pass through them, especially after what had just occurred the day prior. There was an awkward silence as twenty bows, and five spears advanced on the voice. Then a white rag on the end of an Elfish longbow was produced, and the patrol leader began to laugh.

"You live, you sorry bastards! Come out, now! All of you!" Twelve Elfish scouts appeared from within the tree line as if from thin air. Puryn saw this and rushed to the scene.

"You there! Who are they?" Puryn demanded of the patrol leader.

"Commander, they are scouts. They are Draj." He then saluted Puryn and stood smartly at attention.

"At ease, my friend." Puryn turned to the leader of the scout team. "Do you have word of Their Majesties and the refugees?"

"Yes, Commander," the leader said with a puzzled face. He did not understand how Puryn had assumed command, but went with it anyway. "The King sent us to see what had become of all of you. Where are the Draj?" The leader of the scouts looked around expectantly.

Puryn replied in a somber tone, "There. There is what remains. One-hundred-fifty maybe two-hundred soldiers of thousands."

A look of horror spread across the scout leader's face. "My Gods, what happened?"

Puryn said plainly, with a hint of sorrow, "The Dwarves came with thousands. They brought with them thousands of Hodan and Suden. We fought them, thinning their numbers greatly in the open fields, but our cavalry was cut down by Dwarfish crossbows, so we had to reform within the ring. The Dwarves pursued, and we set our survivors inside the breach, ready to die in defense of the kingdom, but then Yslan came, pushed back the Hodan, and routed the Suden. Then, my brethren from Yslandeth sealed the breach, and we soaked the forest in Dwarfish blood." Puryn wiped a tear from his eyes. "The Dwarfish Commander was forced to surrender. We have the prisoners of war in the corrals, surrounded by Draj and Yslan forces. They are not going anywhere. Sir Ontak has sent word to King Swyk in Yslan. Until now, we worried that there was no word from all of you."

The scout looked around and saw that Torith was in shambles. The order was restored and the borders secured, but most buildings were destroyed by a fire that had raged unchecked for almost two days. The worst of it had died down now. The trees cut all hanging structures free from themselves, withdrawing a safe distance from the smoldering remains of what was once the Elfish capital. The palace was the only structure untouched. Puryn suspected the forest had something to do with that, but he could not be sure.

The leader turned to Puryn. "Sir, I must reform my unit and return to His Majesty to report on the situation, by his orders."

"Understood. Please be careful, and if I may ask one personal question, brother ..." Puryn's eyes betrayed him to the Elf.

The scout smiled broadly and grasped Puryn's arm. "She lives, my brother. She is well. She awaits your return, and from what I hear from the voices near the royal encampment, she is giving her father fits concerning you. I am glad, for all of our sakes that you still remain among the living!" Puryn hugged the scout, who then laughed with Puryn. The Elf was taken aback by the gesture.

"Be well, brother," the Elf said, saluting.

"You as well, my brother," the young Commander responded, and the scout team faded into the forest the same way it had appeared.

Puryn approached his patrol leader and commended him for his vigilance, then directed him to form the remains of the warriors. He needed to pass information and organize reclamation efforts before the city could recover.

The Sergeant jogged off and began shouting, "Fall in, fall in! All warriors and Draj, fall in immediately!"

There was massive chaos and dust for a minute or two, but then a small rectangle of Elfish men and women stood proudly at attention, but looking very worn out and beaten. Puryn marched smartly to the front of the formation and saluted the Sergeant who was standing at attention and awaiting his arrival. The leader returned his salute. "All formed and ready, sir!"

"Post!" Puryn barked. The leader marched to his position, and the young Draj took command.

"At ease, all of you! I am proud to call you my brothers and sisters. You are the survivors. You are the heroes who remain! I have just been contacted by a scout team from the refugee encampment. The royal family lives, as do thousands of your families and friends! This is due to your bravery on the field these past days, and the unwavering support of our allies from Yslandeth!" Puryn nodded to Sir Ontak, who bowed partially with a smile. The humans cheered and raised their weapons. "It has now fallen on us to rebuild! We must salvage what we can, reinforce our defenses against counter-attack, and make Torith our home again! Their Majesties will return to a city, not a pile of rubble! I know the Elfish people can count on all of you to rebuild while we stand to defend! I am proud to be Draj. We have shown the enemy what Elves are made of. They will not test us again soon!"

Ontak was impressed with the boy's optimism, but the Knight knew Hodan was still a formidable force, capable of attacking within a week or two. He figured that the Hodan Commander he defeated on the field would be replaced, and the new Commander would come back to clear Hodan's honor. The messenger who Ontak sent was instructed to tell King Swyk as much, even though Ontak knew he was only stating the obvious to His Majesty. Swyk would have already thought of this, and Ontak hoped he would send reinforcements as soon as possible.

There was suddenly a great commotion at the breach in the forest wall. Yslan forces were clamoring to respond to something advancing across the Arondayre. Ontak and Puryn ran to the gap in the trees and saw a large contingent of wagons. They were driven by Dwarves. One rode out ahead of the caravan. It was a female Dwarf, an elder in robes. Puryn knew she must be a Priestess. She carried a white flag on a long pole. The Yslan archers drew and readied to fire.

"Hold your fire," Ontak commanded. "Stand down, but stand ready, boys!"

The army parted and allowed Ontak to advance to the front. One archer took aim at the approaching Dwarf as a precaution. "Hold there, Dwarf. What is it you seek here?"

The robed Dwarf responded solemnly, without anger or malice. "Oh great Commander of the Yslan armies, I greet you. I come to you in peace to make a grand request of your most chivalrous person."

"Speak, Priestess," Ontak responded harshly. "What would Dornat al Ar dare to ask of Yslan at this time in history?" Ontak squinted and looked at the woman with a faint expression of disdain, which she picked up on immediately.

"I understand your mistrust," she said, showing her hands. "I bear no weapons, nor do any of my charges. I simply request access to the breach, so we may collect our dead and make arrangements for their souls to pass unto Aeternum. May they see the peace in death they did not find in life." She was crying.

Ontak saw her tears and heard her words. His heart was stirred, but he willed himself to be stoic. Puryn watched from afar, and his brow furrowed, hoping Ontak would grant the request to remove the bodies. Ontak did. "We will inspect your carts and every Dwarf before entering the sacred forest. Anyone carrying as much as a butter knife will be put to death on the spot."

Ontak stifled a chuckle as he witnessed several Dwarves in the convoy jettison their feasting gear for fear of being executed for a steak knife. Then Ontak let them in, one cart at a time. Finally, he turned and went over to Puryn, who was watching in awe at the respect both sides showed, as the Dwarfish priesthood removed the fallen Dwarves and placed them on their carts.

Ontak turned to the younger Draj warrior. "My young friend, we will clean up the field. I will need to take men to the killing fields beyond the forest wall. I will collect our dead, but I will leave the Suden and Hodan to rot in the sun."

Then Sir Ontak relented. "No, as much as that would please me, the disease would be too much of a risk to the city. I will have my men gather oil and wood. We will make great pyres to the Gods of all men on the field this day. If there are any Elfish holy people left, I will leave the Elves to them."

"Thank you, sir, for your compassion and consideration," Puryn responded. "I will see who is left and ask them to tend to the dead also. We have so many ..." The young man trailed off, as he began to realize the carnage that stood before him. He was watching as approximately twenty-thousand souls were collected and disposed of. Religious people fretted over hurried rituals, but in the end, every man, woman, Dwarf, and Elf who fell were of the same fate—dead.

After locating a handful of elder women who spoke to the trees and a couple masters, including Master Gulsbane, Puryn assigned a contingent of ten Draj and fifty civilians to the task of collecting the fallen Elves. They were overwhelmed. The Elfish losses were approximated at around eight-thousand. Puryn held his face in his hands and realized that what he had left was all there was to defend his new home. The inadequacy of two-hundred Draj against thousands of Hodan hit him like a punch from a hill giant. He was glad that Yslan did not appear to be leaving anytime soon.

Several days passed, and the teams removed the dead and burned them in great pyres. Women and children who were unable to escape the conflict to Oron Falmarindi assisted in the cleanup operations, often finding a father, a brother, or a son amid the carnage. Among the smoke and smell of burning flesh, there was the constant sound of tears and wailing.

War was losing its luster for Puryn, and he found his sleep came with difficulty. He longed for his Adasser's kiss and embrace. He needed her words to encourage him. She could always calm his troubled mind. But, alas, she was not here, and it had been almost a week since the scout patrol had left to report back to the King.

Within another week, the bodies were managed. The Dwarves had long collected their thousands and burned them at the foot of the Altyr Mountains, outside the main doors to Dornat al Ar. Puryn imagined there would be similar scenes of wailing and misery there. He was downcast and depressed as he walked the charred streets of Torith. The teams of Elfish survivors had cleaned up most of the debris, and some minor rebuilding was taking place, but it would be months, if not years, before the area was back to normal.

* * *

Upon the mountain at Oron Falmarindi, King Glorin received the scout report and breathed a sigh of relief. Adasser nearly exploded with joy when the riders reported that Puryn had not only survived, but was also in command of the Draj forces who saved Torith from the Dwarves. She taunted her father, referring to her Puryn as, "The Savior and Champion of Torith."

The Queen giggled whenever her daughter said those words, for it brought the most delicious twist of annoyance to her husband's face, but secretly, the King was pleased the boy had survived. He was proud of his daughter's choice, but he would never admit it to the women.

The people gathered in a large clearing at the calling of the heralds and criers to hear their King address them. "Good Elves of Torith! I greet you this wonderful, brisk morning on the mountains of Oron Falmarindi! We have made it!" The crowd cheered, waiting for the King's next words. "The Draj suffered unimaginably against vastly superior numbers, but held the city! Yslan reinforces us and our people ready the city for our return."

The people cheered loudly, responding with a traditional Elfish blessing: "Glory to the Draj! Saviors of the Elves! Blessed be their mothers forever! May the line of heroes never end!"

The King's voice wavered as he continued. "My friends, my family. Our Draj heroes fell in vast numbers. I fear only a few remain. I call for a moment of reflection by all. Please remember any man or woman serving who you may know personally. Pray for their safety or for their souls to enter Aeternum. Reports state that scarcely two-hundred-fifty remain."

There was a collective gasp, and then the crowd began murmuring. Cries of anguish were heard in every quarter from mothers whose sons and daughters were down on the killing fields in Torith.

The King's guard Commander shouted forcefully. "Pray attend to His Majesty! Pray attend!" The crowd quieted down, except for those who openly cried and sobbed, wondering if their loved ones were no longer among the living.

The King shifted nervously in his robes. He looked at his Queen, whose eyes were red, and he faced the crowd. "We shall pack up and leave this place immediately. We shall travel back to our home in Torith, mend our forest, and rebuild our lives. You will all have your answers when you return to your homes. The scribes have been compiling a list of the causalities, but they had to begin with the funeral pyres and rites some days ago. The birds and the rats were already working on the enemy, and they did not want the same to happen to our heroes!" The King lied. He knew it was because of the stench and disease, but the little fib would give some comfort to the parents of those departed. He did not think the Gods would mind.

In fact, Haya did not.

The people packed up their backpacks, carts, and wagons. They carried everything back down the mountain trails to the forest's edge. It drizzled as they arrived, and the trees opened to the Elves as they approached. The refugees passed through the woods without incident, disappearing into the thickets and appearing on the other side without effort. Puryn's troops were surprised and elated.

"Sir! Sir! They are home! They are home! The people are returning," the watchman yelled.

Puryn turned to see crowds of people entering Torith from the North. They were carrying their life's belongings on their backs, and many had looks of horror on their faces, as they viewed the damage to the city. Others kissed the ground and thanked the Gods for being home.

Master Gulsbane set up the casualty registry and records office, while Puryn's folks and Falda tended to the mess. Gulsbane had an exhaustive list of the Elfish dead, and had set up an office under a canvas tent for families to come and inquire about their warrior's fate. Many knew the answer before they entered, looking around at the meager forces who remained after the battle for Torith. Many tears were shed that day, and for many more to come.

Puryn waited impatiently for the King's convoy to arrive. They came in dead last with great pomp and circumstance as expected. Horns blared, and heralds proclaimed the coming of the royal family. The war-weary Draj Commander watched the spectacle, searching intently for Adasser.

He found his love within the din. She was on a white horse with brown patches. Immediately, Puryn smiled, recognizing his horse as it broke with the procession, making a beeline for his person. Adasser had chosen Haystorm to ride to the mountains, because she knew the mare was Puryn's. And not because her love technically owned the mare, but because the ornery girl hated anyone else riding her. Haystorm knew Adasser loved her boy, which was good enough for her. The horse stopped in front of Puryn, lowering her head, nuzzling his chest. Puryn smiled broadly, pet the horse, and helped his love out of her saddle. Adasser kissed her love with force and passion. The Queen fanned herself and raised an eyebrow. The King's mouth gaped open. He was mortified.

"Close your mouth, Your Eminence," giggled the Queen. "You are making a scene!" She slapped his hand playfully. "Why do you not kiss me that way anymore?"

"Wha … What?" the King stammered, then he saw his wife's facial expression. He wasn't going to win this argument. He smiled. "I will kiss you that way tonight if you are not careful, woman!"

"Promises, promises …" The Queen rolled her eyes and laughed.

The King chuckled. "These two will be the death of me," he said.

"On the contrary, Your Majesty," replied the Queen. "The Champion and Savior of Torith …," the Queen emphasized the title, as the King squinted as if in pain, "… may be the only reason we are still alive."

Glorin nodded. "You are right, My Queen. I will pray for my daughter's happiness and worry about the future when it comes. First, we must make this common boy fit to wed a Princess of Torith. I know the way to make this so."

The King directed his carriage driver to ride over to where Adasser now hugged Puryn, her legs wrapped around his back. Puryn looked at her like a wounded puppy as she cried all over his face. The King sighed, then cleared his throat forcefully.

"You two! Stop it!" he commanded. Adasser dropped off of Puryn, and the boy was frozen in immediate fear. "If you cannot contain yourselves, and you persist in defying me concerning this common Draj soldier, you leave me no choice, daughter."

Puryn swallowed hard and prepared for judgment. He thought to himself, *It's been an interesting life.* Then he looked at the ashen-faced, terrified Adasser. *But totally worth it.*

"Father! Please!" Adasser begged, envisioning what was about to happen.

"Silence, girl." You could have heard a cricket eating grass in the open area of Torith, as close to ten-thousand Elves stopped to witness what they thought would be an execution. And then the King continued. "Puryn, son of Durn …" The King stared at Puryn with eyes that the boy imagined contained fire and brimstone. "It has been said that you are 'The Savior and Champion of Torith.' Is this so?"

Random voices affirmed the claim. Puryn's eyes darted around to see who answered.

"Speak, boy, since you would dare to defy my words!"

Puryn frowned and then stood at attention. He looked at Adasser, regaining his resolve. Near the infirmary, he could see Queen Falda beside his mother and father, watching anxiously. Puryn spoke clearly, with confidence. "Your Majesty, eight-thousand Elves bear the titles of Saviors and Champions of Torith. I simply did my job and held my ground. My Liege, I did not seek to disobey your wishes, but I cannot deny my love for Princess Adasser. If it means my death, then so be it. I cannot live without her."

The Queen audibly sighed and let out an, "Awwww ..." Then she whispered to the King and her older daughter, pointing at Puryn, who was now visibly concerned that the Queen was pointing at him. Adasser was frozen in place, speechless, and fearing the worst was about to happen.

The King replied. "So you, a commoner, dare to touch a Princess of Torith? You know that you can never wed this woman as you are, don't you?"

Puryn closed his eyes and lowered his head, remembering how he had never thought he would be good enough for her. But, now the King's words were making it so.

The King continued. "I do not accept your excuses and modesty concerning your conduct on the battlefield. I have ears, boy! The people murmur ... 'he takes command when the courage of others fails ...,' '... he stands in the breach with one-hundred-fifty Elves against ten-thousand enemies ...,' and '... he puts his men before himself...' These are not the deeds of a common Draj."

Puryn was still looking at the ground with a knot in his throat. He was not a Lord and could not have her. Despite the commendations, he heard only condemnation from the King. He was awaiting his sentence.

The King continued. "Look at me, Puryn, son of Durn."

The bruised hero looked the King in the eye.

The King said in a gravely serious tone, "I see you, hero. I know your heart and my daughter resides in it, and she alone. On this night, before I sleep, you will clean your filthy self and put on clean garments. You will bring your master, parents, and Queen Falda to the throne room for court, an hour after the evening meal. There, I will remedy your inadequacies. I will make you the last remaining Draj-Manot and grant you the title of a Lord of Torith. This is for your gallantry, bravery, sacrifice, and service to the crown, but this is also an elevation to allow for a lawful courtship of Adasser. Be forewarned, hero. I am the King, and I wield supreme power in this land! I will not forget, and I will hunt you down if you ever hurt or disgrace my daughter. I will stick your corpse on a post for all to watch as the birds eat your flesh. Do you understand?"

Puryn's eyes were huge, and his mouth was wide open. He could not speak.

"Do you understand, boy!?"

"Ye … ye … yes, Your Majesty." Puryn felt lightheaded and needed to sit down.

Adasser was bouncing up and down, clapping madly, to her father's displeasure. He rolled his eyes and finished his speech. "Do not be late, Champion. Do you understand?"

"Yes, Your Majesty."

Haya grinned widely. Haeldrun cursed, storming off to the Underworld, departing stealthily from his hiding place in the shadows.

"Driver, take us to the infirmary! Adasser, you may openly remain with your suitor, but remember your decorum and decency, young lady!"

"Yes, Father!" She beamed at him. "I love you, Da!"

The King waved his hand at her, pretending to be put off, but he smiled and looked at his child. She was the happiest he had ever seen her.

The Queen also smiled, and said, "And tonight, I will kiss you as she does him, you old soft-heart. I knew you had it in you, you old goat!"

"Hush now, you old witch," the King whispered as his Queen hugged his arm. She noticed he had misty eyes. This was the man she had married five-hundred years ago, when she was a foolish young girl, as her baby, Adasser, was now for Puryn.

The driver turned to his duties, smiling. He loved his job. These two people were very entertaining. They were a cute couple, even if they were the rulers of the land. He rode to the infirmary whistling a happy tune.

"What are you so cheerful for, driver?" the King asked.

"Nothing, in particular, Your Majesty. It's just a wonderful afternoon back in the forest!"

Haya agreed with the driver, smiling as she departed for Aeternum.

The Spoils of War

The stunned warrior watched as Their Majesties rode away in their carriage. He was dumbfounded and turned around to see a jubilant Adasser with her hands over her head, dancing in a small circle.

"He accepted you! He accepted you, my love. Finally!" the Princess smiled broadly. Puryn was stunned by how beautiful she looked when she exhibited pure joy.

"I must go wash and change, My Lady," Puryn said. "I am filthy, and the King ordered me to get myself in order. I still reek of battle."

"I do not care," said Adasser in a playful, coy manner, then she kissed him again and caught a whiff of what her love meant. "Oh dear, you do smell awful!" She giggled. "Go, go clean yourself, and I will meet you later. Guard!"

A guard approached. "Yes, Your Highness?"

"Please escort me to the palace," the Princess said happily.

The guard could not help but smile at her enthusiasm. "Of course, Your Highness." The guard, an older Elf, then turned to Puryn. "Good afternoon, sir. Be well, my brother."

Puryn was caught off guard. "And you also, brother," he responded, bowing.

"You shall never bow to me, hero." The old man smiled, standing at attention.

Adasser was astounded by the respect shown by the elder Elf. She was touched and put her hand on the older warrior's shoulder. "We must let him prepare for the evening. We should go."

"Of course, Your Highness, my apologies."

"None necessary. You honor me by honoring him. Thank you," Adasser said seriously and hugged the guard. Then, he walked her to the palace.

Puryn watched and then ran toward the infirmary, where the King had just departed. Arla was there and frantic. "Boy! Did you hear the King? Get those filthy chains off of you. I am warming a bath and found some soap! You must cleanse the filth of death from you. Oh, and I hear you have a new lady in your life. Officially, that is."

His mother had a particular inflection to her voice on the last part of the statement, which made Puryn blush. Everyone knew they were together every night, even though Puryn and Adasser thought they had hidden it well. Queen Falda sat in the corner of the room, snickering and nodding. Puryn's face reddened further.

"He faces ten-thousand enemies, gets tackled in public by a Princess, is chewed out by a King, and now he hides?" Durn chided. The room erupted in laughter.

The family left for what remained of their home. When they arrived, they saw the damage was significant, but their house still stood, and that was more than most had to return to.

Puryn sighed and scurried off to a back room, where he disrobed and washed in a large basin made from a barrel. He hid underwater when his mother entered with clean clothing. Queen Falda had produced a fine woolen cloak and a beautiful, hand-stitched, full-length tunic and undergarments. The tunic was Yslan blue and white, with hand-embroidered golden Dragons on each shoulder. The Queen had known he would be Knighted, just not where or when. So she kept the garments with her, hoping she guessed the age closely and that everything would fit. They would be a tiny bit large, but he would look presentable.

A messenger arrived while Puryn was dressing, bearing fine, high-Elfish boots. A note found with them stated, "A gift from Her Highness, Adasser of Torith, on this auspicious day. I love you."

Arla sighed and smiled. Durn chuckled, mumbling something about Puryn "dressing for the ball." Queen Falda sat alone, sipping a bit of wine that she had stashed, contemplating the events. She had seen these things, but he was still too young. However, he was an amazing young man, and she was incredibly proud of her surrogate son.

"Hurry up, boy, and come eat a bite before we have to go!" Arla commanded.

Puryn entered the room groomed and dressed better than he'd ever been dressed in his life. His mother dropped the plate and cried. "Oh my Gods, my baby! You are a man! Look at you!" She caressed his cheek as tears rolled down hers. "Where did my little monk go?"

Puryn hugged his mother and reassured her. "He is here, Mother, but he has seen much in a short time. He has grown strong, due to a great family and wonderful friends." Puryn looked at his ruined home. The burned walls were barely upright. They were living in ruins, but were thankful for what they had. He sighed at their predicament, but was still living on cloud nine. The young man looked at his Queen. She smiled at him.

"Come, son, it is time to go," Durn stated thoughtfully. "Never keep a King waiting. Trust me on this!"

"Of course, Father." Puryn stood. Falda, Arla, and Durn prepared to walk to the palace a few miles up the road, when a carriage arrived with a driver looking for Puryn.

"Excuse me, gentles, but is Puryn, the Hero, here? I have been sent to carry his family and him to the palace by order of the Princess. Your Majesty, good evening!" He bowed to Falda.

"He is here, driver," Falda answered.

"I am honored, sir." The driver bowed and opened the door for Puryn, who bore a look of confusion. He was not used to being treated with such honor. He was uncomfortable.

"Thank you for your kindness," the humble warrior replied. Then he helped Queen Falda into the carriage as his father guided his mother to her seat. Durn then assisted his son, getting all of the flowing garments into the door before closing it behind him and sitting down himself.

The ride was short, and the family arrived at the palace within thirty minutes. There was a huge crowd outside the palace portcullis. They stood, almost in a military formation, crowding closer to the passageway, as Puryn and his family stepped off the carriage.

"There he is! The Savior of the Elves! Huzzah!" a voice screamed from somewhere.

"Defender of the trees!" another bellowed.

"He who defeated ten-thousand Dwarves!"

Then the crowd started cheering. "Huzzah, Huzzah, Huzzah!"

Puryn looked at the crowd and was overwhelmed. He hurried into the palace antechamber to constant cheers. When he waved upon entering, the crowd erupted in what sounded like a war cry. The hair on Puryn's neck stood up. Then he felt his father's hand on his shoulder.

"We need to go. Now!" Durn commanded.

"Right. Did you see that, Father?" Puryn asked as if a small boy.

"Yes, I did. I remember when Ontak defeated the Hodan horde at the Citadel in Cinnog. A very similar scene. People need to believe in something, my son. Whether or not you feel worthy, they see you as a God right now. Do not let that go to your head! Be humble, put the people first, and they will love you for it. Be a smug tyrant, and they will soon turn on you. Remember these words."

"I will, Da. Thank you. I am so nervous!" Puryn was shaking and trying to compose himself.

Durn laughed. "You make me laugh, boy. How can you stand before thousands, in the face of your own death, and shrug it off, but tremble when people gather to praise you? Enjoy this, but do not get a big head!"

Haya smirked as she listened to Durn's wisdom. Puryn was still an innocent boy at heart, and she loved that about him. He was humble when others would have been egotistical and full of pride. She could work with this young one.

"It was easy, Father. She, I mean, Adasser needed to live. I had to give her a chance to flee. I wasn't thinking of myself. I didn't matter." Puryn looked as if this truth was self-evident, even to the casual observer.

"Spoken like a true hero, my son." Durn grabbed his son's forearms and shook him squarely. He looked Puryn square in the eyes. "This is your time. This is your hour! You have done well. Do not question your ability. You will be recognized for who you already are, not made a Lord or Knight. The King is simply putting on your regalia. I am the proudest that a father could be."

Puryn looked around at everyone. Falda, Arla, and Durn all had their hands on their boy, bowing in prayer to Haya. They asked for her wisdom, strength, and continued honor. Puryn and his family hugged and then entered the court hall. A herald announced their entrance.

Haya blessed the family, as they prayed and watched, as her plan unfolded—much to Haeldrun's dismay.

"Pray attend! Here doth enter the court hall of His Royal Majesty Glorin—Queen Falda, the Green; one Puryn, son of Durn; and his parents, Durn and Arla, of Yslan."

Everyone in the room stood as the King began. "All, be seated and comfortable. My friends, please approach the thrones and assume your positions at the front."

The room was filled with government ministers, legal clerks, religious leaders, and Lords and Ladies throughout Torith. There were three lavish seats in front of the thrones—two were on one side for Arla and Durn and one on the other side for Falda. Pillows were strewn upon the floor surrounding the area, and two bearing the mark of Torith were located in front of the thrones.

The most prominent thrones were in the middle of the setting. Queen Hansu, the Gracious, sat on the left of King Glorin. To the left of the Elfish Queen sat her two daughters: Princess Adenya, the elder sister, and Princess Adasser, the younger. All of them were dressed in their finest garments, with the formal gold and jeweled crowns upon their heads. Puryn stood between his mother, father, and Falda, and before the royal family. He could see Adasser in the light of the braziers. She looked like a Goddess. She stared at him intently. His love was eerily serious, a face Puryn was not accustomed to.

"Come forth, Puryn, of the Draj!" the King's herald bellowed.

Puryn marched to within inches of the pillows before the thrones, saluted, and bowed low. He paused and then stood straight.

The King spoke in Elfish. "Puryn, son of Durn. I have called you before my court to recognize the man and friend of the Elf who you are. No, not a friend, but a brother. I watched you come to my city, six years and some months ago. I watched as you trained without rest, learning our ways, our language, and our combat arts. I watched as you excelled at everything, compelling me to induct you into the elite Draj of the Elves. But, you did not stop there. As an exemplary soldier, when some lost heart, you took command and organized the defense of our kingdom. You held the breach until help arrived and ensured summary destruction of the invading enemy. In essence, you saved the Elves by your leadership and your devotion. Furthermore, you took no care for your own life, admitting that you were prepared to die, in order to give those you do not even know a chance to live. Do I have a witness to these feats?"

"Yes, Your Majesty." Puryn looked to see Sir Ontak speaking.

"Speak, old friend. Tell us your tale," the King responded.

"I rode to reinforce the Elfish border, arriving too late to bolster the defenses. I was forced to engage three armies on the fields of Arondayre. All three were already attacking Torith, and this young man's Draj forces had culled the herd nicely before withdrawing to a more defensible position. By reports, the Draj were surrounded by thousands of Suden, Dwarfish, and Hodan. They were able to soften their lines to the point that Yslan was able to push the advantage when we arrived. Even then, when I saw the Dwarves pouring into the breach toward Torith proper, I lost hope, thinking the Elves were defeated. However, lo and behold, the Draj stood firm, led by this young man, and his stubborn devotion to honor and duty. They held as the anvil, and we crushed as the hammer. Without this leader, the Dwarves would have razed Torith and killed all who remained. I have no doubt." The crowd murmured quietly.

"Pray attend!" the King's herald hushed.

"Thank you, Sir Ontak, Champion of Yslandeth. Your words are well taken and appreciated." The King nodded. Ontak bowed, took a step back, then turned, pacing away smartly.

"The King needs one more witness!" the herald shouted.

"Your Majesty, I have words to speak on this man's behalf." It was a young Draj in dress uniform. He wore the rank of Commander.

"Come forward, Commander," the King ordered. The young Draj walked forward and saluted his King. He bowed and paused, then stood straight.

"I am Draj Commander Feli. I was on the breach that morning with this man, Puryn, son of Durn. I lost heart and panicked." Puryn grabbed his arm, trying to stop his confession, but the Elf continued. "No, brother, the truth must be known. I must tell what happened." Puryn frowned and then nodded, releasing the Commander's arm. "When I froze in the face of that unconquerable force, Puryn stood up and challenged me. When I could not move or speak, he took command and organized the defenses. After defeating the enemy, he tended to the men and to their needs, sending the injured to the infirmary for treatment. He did not eat until all had food. He did not sleep without posting a guard and a patrol to control looting. He organized working parties to tend to the dead and clean up the city's debris. He showed his mettle in battle and his leadership in its aftermath. He is a Draj-Manot, Your Majesty, if I have ever thought I would meet one. I apologize for approaching you, but I thought you should know the truth, My King."

"Thank you, Commander. Dismissed." The King eyed Puryn more intently. This was no ordinary human. He was destined for greatness.

The King rose from his throne. "Let it be known that Sir Ontak, of Yslan, and Draj Commander Feli speak favorably of Puryn, son of Durn. Moreover, let it be known that the heroism and honor of said Puryn have been established by two witnesses, and this man's conduct has been without reproach. Are there any with a grievance against this man? If so, speak now."

There was utter silence. Adasser smirked under her veil. She was trying to contain her glee. Her man was about to kneel and be recognized for who she already knew he was. Hansu's gaze drifted to Adasser. The Queen could see the love in her daughter's eyes, and she smiled. Hansu was a happy mother. She was soon to gain a son, she assumed.

The King looked at his herald. The herald commanded, "Puryn, son of

Durn, hero of the Draj, kneel. Bring forth the Spear of the Sun!"

An individual wearing a hooded robe approached the assembly of people. He stopped to the right of the King and handed him the Spear of the Sun. Glorin put the spearhead to Puryn's throat. Arla gasped, but Durn put his hand on her shoulder reassuringly. Durn whispered, "Relax, woman." The King winked at Arla, and she sighed nervously.

"Puryn, son of Durn, I lied to you the other day. I did not realize that a Draj-Manot still lived, and as is the custom of the Elves, he and he alone is worthy of reading this oath to you. Before all who hear this greeting, I will declare you a Lord of Torith, a nobleman, and a brother of Elves. All who live in this kingdom, do I charge to render proper honor and respect to this rank. You are entitled to lands and charges as you see fit, with the approval of the crown. Rise, Lord Puryn." The King removed the spear from Puryn's throat as the warrior stood, and the court cheered. A lady-in-waiting put a laurel of flowers on the new Lord's head and a golden torq around his neck, signifying his new rank. Then the King turned to Puryn's father and mother. "Durn, Arla … stand."

Durn stood puzzled, and Arla leaned against her husband. She was not used to the attention and was utterly embarrassed.

"Because you have been such a great inspiration to this young Lord, and because you have raised such a son of Torith, I also declare you both, Durn and Arla, of Yslan, a Lord and Lady of Torith, to rank as such from this point forward. I charge all of Torith to recognize these titles and to render proper honor, respect, and obedience, as appropriate." The lady-in-waiting put laurels and torqs on Durn and Arla, before bowing and exiting the ceremony. The King turned to the robed, mysterious figure. "Draj-Manot, Master of Nature, and my brother, always, I defer to you for the rest of this ceremony."

The King bowed slightly, the Draj-Manot bowed deeply, pausing, and then standing straight. He took possession of the Spear of the Sun and turned toward Puryn. He lowered his hood. There stood Gulsbane, Puryn's teacher from the beginning of his time in Torith. The young Lord smiled, knowing that his master had always had an air about him, yet he had never once let on.

Gulsbane spoke. "Young Lord Puryn, warrior and hero of the Draj, His Majesty doth call you before him for a most noble honor. Through honor, chivalry, duty, and selflessness, you have proven yourself worthy of being considered for this title of Draj-Manot." Gulsbane stopped and looked at Puryn, speaking plainly. "Are you ready, my boy?"

Puryn smiled. "I am, Master Gulsbane, and you never cease to show me new things."

Gulsbane chuckled. "Then put your hand on the shaft of the spear, and swear by it these things that I read unto thee." The room was silent as the master continued.

"You are the heart of the people. You are the soul of the Elf. You stand for justice and mercy. Never will you sit idly by when injustice or corruption is in your midst, and the weak shall never fear oppression in your shadow. You shall ride into battle, whether the odds are in your favor or death calls to you from the other side. Never shall you back down from a fight, nor will a challenge go unanswered.

"You will keep your faith in your Gods. You will protect the sacred forest. You will stand for truth, even if it means your death. You will protect the innocent, the women, and the children, as well as those incapable of standing up for themselves. You are charged with maintaining your honor at all times on the battlefield, taking only the advantage necessary to defeat the enemy. You will not suffer your charges to break the code of chivalry, no matter the conduct of your foe. You will provide comfort and shelter to refugees of all sides when you have the means. Do you understand this oath and accept its conditions?"

"I do," Puryn stated clearly, kneeling.

The Elfish Queen was fixed on Adasser, who had tears streaming down her face beneath her sheer veil. The Queen began to tear up. The King stood stoically and watched his first Draj-Manot created. Gulsbane had won that honor one-hundred-and-ten years before the King was born, during the last King's reign.

Gulsbane responded. "Present your shield hand, Draj." Puryn put out his right hand. Gulsbane slashed his own hand, and then he slashed Puryn's. It was a very superficial cut. Then he pressed their hands together. "With this exchange, we are blood, my brother. Arise, Draj-Manot of Torith."

Puryn stood, and the King and Gulsbane turned him around to face the court. The King instructed the herald. "This Lord will be known with the title Protector of the Elves. Add it."

"Yes, Your Majesty," the herald said in a hushed tone, making a notation in the logs.

The herald shouted, "Torith! Behold your new Draj-Manot, Lord Puryn, Protector of the Elves! Three cheers for Lord Puryn!"

"Huzzah! Huzzah! Huzzah!" the crowd shouted.

There was raucous applause. Queen Falda hugged Puryn. "Go to her, you fool!" She smiled, goading him toward Adasser, who was sitting on her throne.

Puryn knelt on one knee and took Adasser's hand. "I love you."

"And I you, My Lord. Will you come and visit later?" Adasser smiled.

"I will. We shall walk beneath the stars, as we did before all of this ever happened." Puryn kissed her hand, and then she was whisked off by her ladies-in-waiting to some other required appearance. The younger girls giggled at the hand-kissing. Puryn waved at them, and then they twittered all the more.

The King was waiting for Puryn to be done with Adasser.

"Lord Puryn," the King said calmly. "Do you wish to ask to court my daughter formally?"

"If it pleases the King, yes. I wish to court Princess Adasser," Puryn responded.

"It pleases me, son. If you ask for her hand in marriage someday, I will be hard-pressed to give you a hard time." The King shook Puryn's hand, then pulled him close and hugged him. "You are a good choice. She has chosen well, boy. Live long and smile with her many days!"

The young Lord was beside himself. Arla now bawled inconsolably. She could not believe her baby was a man. Durn hugged his wife and gently comforted her. He was the proudest father Yslandeth had ever seen.

Falda sat back and reclined in a soft seat, sipping Elfish wine. She prayed quietly to herself, *Not bad, Haya, not bad! Thank you for your blessings! Please protect my beloved young man and those he loves. I am beside myself with joy! Your kindness is abundant. My thanks to you, My Goddess, for all of these things!*

Haya whispered, "You are welcome, friend of the Light."

Puryn sat down and sipped ale for the first time. It was bitter, but not that bad.

Sir Ontak sat beside the new Lord. "May I, My Lord?" He smiled.

Puryn nodded and swallowed.

"Go slowly, my friend. The first is easy; the second kicks!" the Knight joked. He continued, "Well done, young one, well done. King Swyk will be proud!"

Puryn had almost forgotten he was Yslan. He had spent six-plus years as a refugee from Sir Verdin, due to the events at the monastery, and had become accustomed to Elfish culture and life. The new Lord was unsure how he would fare if he ventured back to Yslandeth and the capital Empyr. He wasn't used to large populations of humans. Humans could be brash, mean, and, many times, rude. Puryn liked Elves. They were more of a family. If he ever had to leave, the warrior decided he would have to find a way to bring Torith with him. For now, he would just bask in the glow of the night. He would drink a tankard of ale and then meet Adasser under the moon. Today was a perfect day.

Lady Arla danced with Lord Durn as Queen Falda drank too much wine and fell asleep in her comfy chair. The minstrels played a quiet, but lively tune. Those in the court hall were having a grand time socializing, eating, and drinking. Sir Ontak excused himself and asked to dance with an Elfish lady. Puryn slowly left the hall, trying to disappear without further fanfare, but was stopped and congratulated at least twenty times before reaching the door. He impatiently waited to see Adasser, but graciously spoke with each person as he made his way out of the door. The crowd outside had dispersed, and it was a beautiful, clear evening. The moon hung low over the Altyr.

After a short walk, he saw her in the moonlight, beside their well. She was a vision in the moonbeams. Her dress captured the light, and she glowed as if she was afire. They kissed, holding each other for hours, dancing at times to Adasser's humming, laughing carelessly in the commonplace. He was so relieved she was safe, and she was thankful he was alive.

Off in the distance, out of view, a stealthy Elf watched over them as a chaperone at the King's request. The Elf sat quietly, feeling like a Peeping Tom, but the King was insistent. Finally, the spy sighed and made himself comfortable in the brush. These two weren't going anywhere tonight. They were just happy to be together. He envied them.

The Aftermath and Mending Fences

So, Torith found peace by the scribes' reckoning on the twenty-third day of the month of Volen. By then, it was winter, and the crops had been in the barns and silos for three months. The war had extensively damaged the food stores by fire and bombardment, but as always, the Elves made do by scavenging and hunting in the forest to meet their needs. Times were tough, and making ends meet was difficult, but as hard as it was, the Elves were thankful for their chances.

Yslandeth remained within the forest for two years, allowing Torith to rebuild its defenses, but even with two years to conscript, Torith scarcely fielded five-hundred-seventy-five warriors. During this restoration, the Elves captured wild horses that had migrated across the Arondayre, from where the Gods only knew. The Elves broke and trained an additional fifty steeds for their cavalry, but those additions were far from the number they had lost in battle.

Infrastructure was rebuilt quickly. The trees gave up lumber as needed, and many prominent landmarks were restored with ease. The temple, storehouses, marketplaces, and schoolhouses all stood within a year. By the third season, Torith was nearly back to its old self, except it sorely needed warriors. The markets were full of food and wares, and as Elfish society began to have hope, Yslan looked to its home, recalling its forces to the Great White Wall.

All kingdoms had suffered a similar fate, burying a generation of heroes and living with the scraps of what was left from the carnage. All nations told similar stories and recovered in their own time, according to their ability.

Sudenyag was the exception. Against all protest and counsel, they continued to trade with the people called the Offlanders, who came to their southern ports by great ships. King Swyk, of Yslandeth, sent many threatening missives to the Suden King, but King Yanat il Arnar, the Extravagant, was a pompous and proud man who ruled with cruelty and subterfuge. Being a liar and a coward, he used anyone and anything to promote his own advancement and wealth. Ignoring the protests of Swyk, he cited the autonomy of his kingdom and its rights to self-determination. He knew Swyk could not move on Sudenyag, so he ignored his threats.

Out of sheer necessity, Hodan broke its ties with all of its allies. The losses of this war were catastrophic for their economy. Sudenyag had proven to be a liability, vice an ally. In addition, the Dwarves were a drain on food and resources since Hodan no longer needed to buy weaponry and armor.

Hodan looked inward and hoarded its remaining resources. The people of the warrior nation remained vigilant and hostile with Yslandeth for many years after many other nations had laid down their arms.

Shortly after the cessation of battle, Cinnog and Edenyag declared peace with Hodan, allowing the defeated army to concentrate on the Yslan border North of their lands. This new standoff hurt both nations, but Yslandeth could bear the drain of resources much better than the isolated Hodan. The people of Hodan starved, living in burned-out homes or within holes in the Ert, but they were proud, and many still clung to a foolish dream of a glorious victory.

Edenyag expelled the Hodan and Suden from its borders by the use of a hastily formed citizen army supported by Yslan forces. Hodan had invaded the eastern kingdom during the war, killing many of the citizen-soldiers of Edenyag. Still, the heroic people of Eden kept answering the call to service by willingly taking up the places of their fallen comrades.

When Yslan finally reinforced the Eden army, the fields were covered in the blood of the scribes. The killing fields are still known to this day as Scribat Ternut Sangras, or "The blood of the Scribe's Stand." Eden's King Cathir, known as the Enlightened, had a monument erected many years later in remembrance of their fallen brothers and sisters. When peace was declared, Edenyag adopted mandatory conscription, seeking out Yslandeth to train its forces. Eden resolved to be ready for the next incursion.

The final grim total of the dead of all factions was estimated in the hundreds of thousands of warriors, and no army retained an advantage or gain after the war was completed. Estimated civilian casualties ranged from one-hundred-thousand to half a million souls.

The Dwarves were decimated by conflict and loss of trade. The kingdom under the mountain starved without Hodan trade and the knowledge of farming it needed to grow its own food. King Bogrol tasked his wisest scribes to inhabit the long-abandoned hillside villages, in an effort to grow food, but inexperience at farming provided a meager crop with which to feed thousands of hungry mouths. King Bogrol of the Dwarves was desperate.

Sensing the situation was becoming dire to the southeast, King Glorin of the Elves decided to dispatch his emissary, Lord Puryn, Draj-Manot, and Protector of the Elves. He sent his man with a hand-picked entourage with a diplomatic mission to sue for peace with the King of the Dwarves.

Dornat al Ar warmly received the emissaries of Torith, and Puryn was allowed to deliver King Glorin's demands directly to the Dwarfish King. To Puryn's surprise, King Bogrol, the Warrior, was very receptive to Glorin's words and penned a personal message to the King of the Elves. It read:

Glorin, great King within the trees, hear my words. I stand beneath my mountain, a sorrowful old fool who was driven to do things I regret through the goading and actions of allies I did not want. But I do not seek to make excuses or shift the blame for my actions. Instead, I apologize to you and the Elfish people for the invasion of your lands, the deaths of your people, and the destruction of your sacred forest. If only I could take it all back and start again.

My people starve. Our alliances are dead, and we cannot grow food. The winter is again soon upon us, and most of our supplies ebb low. I fear that many more Dwarves will die under the mountain, due to hunger and disease, than by the sword. I beseech thee for your forgiveness and offer my head as payment for peace and aid. This I do swear by my honor and my life.

Sincerely,

King Bogrol, the Warrior.

Bogrol then ordered four cartloads of silver, gold, and gems to be loaded, sending them back with Puryn as reparations. A note was enclosed in the chests, stating: *I now know that one cannot eat gold and treasure, but perhaps you can pay for supplies and rebuild with these gifts.*

It is written that when Puryn and his band returned to Glorin with Bogrol's letter, Glorin was driven to tears. He thought long and hard, deciding that enough death had occurred. The Elfish King resolved to make amends with his neighbors to the South. Taking supplies received as aid from Yslandeth, Glorin divided the food into a large shipment in several wagons. He sent a wagon train back to Dornat al Ar with Puryn, and his response to the King of the Dwarves was:

Bogrol, my worthy neighbor, we have all been led by folly to the commission of heinous misdeeds. I accept your gracious apologies and offer my own for isolated actions that were unbecoming of my armies. So long have I sought an avenue of approach, in order to seek peace and unity with my neighbors to the South, but I was hindered by the specter of Hodan, looming over the mountain! Now that the shade has been removed, we can speak plainly as friends and equals.

Indeed, both armies fought valiantly to a stalemate on the fields of Arondayre. I consider your honor intact, and I hope you consider mine in the same light. I offer my hand in friendship and in peace. I wish an everlasting alliance without the compulsion of war. I withdraw my complaints of lumbering on our borders with your assurances that we will both ensure that new trees are planted to replace those removed. In good faith, I send enough food to feed ten thousand for a month and one-hundred farmers to assist in preparing your fields for the planting season.

I am sure our new friendship will be awkward, but we can coexist in this valley in peace if you take my hand in friendship. May we reforge the alliances of old, when our races were both young on the Ert, and the Dragons protected us from the evils of foolishness and malice.

Sincerely,

Glorin, King of the Elves.

Puryn rode with his cohort South toward the Dwarfish Kingdom. The band passed the dwindling Yslan outposts that dotted the countryside along the way. When the caravan arrived at Dornat al Ar, the guard at the city gates cheered at the sight of the carts and Elves. Puryn was puzzled at their reception, still harboring a grudge against the kingdom under the mountain. Nevertheless, the Draj resolved to respect his King's wishes and put aside his own feelings of malice and distrust for the time being.

The Dwarfish guard escorted the food to their storehouses, traveling through droves of starving Dwarves, who were on the verge of rioting. Puryn, seeing the faces of the children, and the tears of those who begged for scraps, was ashamed for his hatred.

When all was in order, the Draj-Manot delivered a sealed scroll to King Bogrol, who cheered, raising his fist in the air after reading it. The Dwarfish Queen cried in relief as a new alliance of Elf and Dwarf was formed—one that had not existed for more than ten-thousand years. The Dwarfish horns bellowed out in unison, as the captured standards of Torith were flown on equal standing with those of Dornat al Ar. Puryn smiled and bowed to the King of the Dwarves respectfully.

* * *

Over time, on the hillsides, the hill Dwarf villages were rebuilt, and Elves helped restore the Dwarfish farmers' self-sufficiency. By spring, the mountain was green with vegetables and saplings. Elves and Dwarves freely traveled between the two kingdoms, and the trees eventually forgave the trespasses of the Dwarves, allowing them to pass as freely as an Elf.

In Torith, Puryn watched as the Eden scribes rode away, waving to them. Things were returning to normal, slowly across the Ert. Eden was collecting the firsthand accounts of war and documenting the battles for addition to the volumes of the history of the Ert.

Over the two years since the final battles, Torith had regained much of its splendor. The new alliance between Dwarf and Elf held without coercion.

The Dwarves had their own forest of saplings on the mountainside, and their farmers eventually learned the art of growing food quickly and plentifully.

Soon, their reliance on Hodan was but a bad memory, and the Dwarves stood on their own with the Elves, like a family. Many Dwarves lived within Torith now, and Elves lived in Dornat al Ar. The exchange of cultures benefited both, and their bonds grew stronger.

Finally, Yslandeth's King decided to call his few remaining forces home. King Swyk sent a messenger with four scrolls to Torith.

One was written to Queen Falda, one to King Glorin, one to Sir Ontak, and the final one was addressed to Puryn. They were all marked private and sealed with Swyk's signet. King Glorin was notified that Yslandeth intended to pull its forces out of Torith and Dornat al Ar by week's end. Swyk cited the new Dwarfish-Elfish alliance as an unintended, but stupendous development. He congratulated Glorin on his diplomatic skills and reaffirmed his devotion to their own alliance.

To Ontak, Swyk simply sent his orders. "Collect all of the men, and march for home on the day of Fredis." Ontak began the arrangements immediately.

Falda received her scroll nervously. She had been gone from Yslandeth for many years now. On occasion, she had visited with her husband, but she feared that her obsession with visions and the boy might have been too much for her marriage. The Queen opened the message hesitantly. She was angry with her husband when she left, almost nine years prior, but that anger had long since passed. She was his wife, and she still loved him, and there would never be another. She feared Swyk would tell her to remain in Torith, releasing her from her vows. Her scroll read:

My Dearest Falda,

I hope you are well after all that has occurred. I apologize for not being able to leave my post and tend to your well-being, but Hodan is being Hodan, and the threat remains real at the Wall. Be that as it may, I am deadly sorrowful without you here by my side. Have I not paid enough penance? Has this separation not been enough? Please, will you not come home to Yslan and your husband? I do not command you to do so, as is my right. My love, I simply wish to declare to you that there is no other, and there has been none, from the day you departed. My dearest Falda, life grows colder with every passing moment you are not here with me. Please bring the sunshine back to my heart.

All of my love,

Swyk.

Falda's face was blank. She smelled the scroll, hoping his scent was upon it, and cried silently. She would return to him. Puryn was a man who would find his way in the world now. Haya had a habit of providing the best of circumstances for his benefit. She wiped her tears away, sought out Sir Ontak, and informed him of her decision to return to Yslandeth. Ontak acknowledged, bowing to the Queen. She returned to her home in the trees, and packed the remainder of her belongings.

Puryn's scroll had the official Yslandeth military insignia on it. It was sealed in wax with the King's own signet ring. Puryn cracked the wax and read the short note.

Greetings Champion,

I, King Swyk, do commend you on your achievements while residing within the borders of Torith. You have learned your lessons well, climbing to status and renown. Most importantly, you have proven yourself a worthy and honorable man upon the battlefield. I am proud you are of Yslan stock. I would like to invite you to return to your homeland, Lord of Torith. I will recognize your titles and give you the same here, granting you lands near Empyr, if you so choose to return home. If not, I will not hold it against you. There is nothing dishonorable concerning the realm of the Elves. They are a just and trusted ally. Just let it be known that Hodan still threatens our people, and I need men such as you to rebuild our kingdom and protect our borders from their hordes. Please consider my offer.

Sincerely,

Swyk, King of Yslan.

Adasser walked into the room where Puryn read the scroll. She did not know why his face looked so long. "What is it, my love? Not bad news again!?" Adasser asked, worried.

"Not bad news, at least not evil, but not what I was looking for!" Puryn tossed the scroll on his desk. He was in deep thought.

Adasser picked up the scroll and read it. She gasped. "My Gods, you will not go without me!"

Puryn smiled. "Not a chance, My Princess!" He smiled and put his hand on her cheek.

"Promise me!" she demanded frantically.

"I promise, my love! Yslandeth rejected me, yet some small part of me misses my home. But in reality, Torith has embraced me and is truly my home! So what in the Underworld am I to do, Adasser?" Puryn paced. "Damn these politics and games. How do I ask Glorin?"

"How do you ask Glorin what, Puryn?" the King asked, entering the chamber.

"Your Majesty, my apologies for my insolence!" Puryn averted his eyes, bowing.

"Calm down, boy, and speak plainly. What does Swyk want of you?" Glorin's brow furrowed, awaiting an answer. "Stand up."

"He wishes my return to Yslandeth and offers me titles and lands." Puryn looked at Adasser. "But I am not sure I want to return there."

Glorin thought for a moment about the possibility of Puryn leaving. The Draj and his army were nonexistent. Puryn was not necessary to lead the meager Draj forces while Yslandeth was dealing with a swelling force of Hodan on the Great White Wall.

"Have you pondered where you would be most beneficial to the Elves and man, young Puryn?" the King asked.

"I am not sure what you mean, Sire. I wish to serve Torith and protect my family here!" Puryn protested.

"Think tactically, strategically, if you will. Sir Ontak speaks to Swyk regularly. No doubt he and others who monitor the situation know of your abilities and your reputation for getting the dirty jobs done. Whether it be slaughtering the invading enemy with meager troops, disposing of the bodies, or rebuilding the temple, you are there organizing, working, and leading. Men like you are worth their weight in gold, son. If I had an army to lead, I would implore you to stay, but in reality, the only army standing between the conquest of Elf and Dwarf is Yslandeth. There you should ply your trade. Your trade is the death of the enemies of the light. You should go, get your titles, and take your lands. Raise up a human Draj of your own. I am sure it will become a feared bedtime story for elderly Hodan women to tell their brats around the fire!"

Puryn panicked and looked at Adasser. Her face was saddened, and her lips frowned in an exaggerated manner. Puryn looked back at the King, who had a look of expectancy on his face. "Say it, boy. Just go ahead and say it." The King raised his eyebrows, pursed his lips, and shook his head.

Puryn kneeled on one knee. "My Liege, I pray that you will not be offended by my forwardness, but I plead for permission to ask your daughter, Adasser, for her hand in marriage."

Queen Hansu of the Elves entered the room, acting as if she had not been listening outside the door. Adasser looked at her suspiciously. "What did you say, boy?" the Queen shrieked.

"He wants Adasser, Hansu. He wants to marry her." The King looked at Hansu, who turned away from the view of the young couple. She was trying to contain her giggle.

Then she buried her face in the King's chest and wailed. "My baby! He wants my baby!"

"See what you've done?" the King scolded. "There, there, my dear!"

The Queen then twirled around quickly and got right in Puryn's face, much to his alarm. "What in the Underworld took you so long?! You'd think humans lived one-thousand years, Puryn, for Haya's sake!"

Puryn slowly grasped that he was being toyed with, subduing his smile. Adasser hugged him tightly from the back. "Yes, I will marry you. Yes, a thousand times, yes!" She kissed his neck and ran over to her father and mother. They hugged as a trio.

"I wonder where we will live, husband," Adasser said, stressing the word husband.

Puryn didn't care. He would live with her under a tree or within one. He would build her a home she would be proud of and lead his people with dignity and honor. He hugged his new fiancé, shook the hand of his soon-to-be father-in-law, and hugged his soon-to-be mother-in-law.

"I will bill you the dowry," the King said, laughing loudly. "A joke, my boy, a joke! Relax, you are the reason I have everything I own. You owe me nothing, boy, except to love her and treat her as your Queen."

"Always, until my final breath, Father," Puryn replied.

"I know you will … I know you will," the King replied, smiling at the word "father."

Puryn kissed Adasser, then ran out of the door to find his parents and Queen Falda. When they heard the news, the Queen cheered for him.

Durn caught his wife, Arla, who fainted, and was last heard saying, "My baby, my baby!" She woke to Puryn's hug, and she hugged him back, harder than she'd ever squeezed him before. He was all grown up, and they were all going home.

The Joining of the Hearts

The King ordered only the best for his baby girl. The rebuilt halls were decked in the finest white linen and silk banners. Candelabras were placed throughout the royal court hall, and a carpet of the deepest red was unrolled from the door to the thrones. In front of the thrones was a small alabaster podium for the High Priestess to perform the ceremony.

Several score worked, running to and fro, setting the stage for the wedding between the Hero of Torith and Princess Adasser. Everything had to be right; the Queen would have it no other way.

Hansu just looked on, smiling. She ordered the flower arrangements and directed their placement, decorating the hall as it was years ago when she was the young Princess betrothed to a young Prince. Reminiscing quietly, Hansu daydreamed of the old days when life was less complicated. She was pleased. Things were coming together nicely for the ceremony later that night.

* * *

Durn, Arla, and Falda were back at their house. Queen Falda talked to a couple of Elfish seamstresses, who were putting the finishing touches on Puryn's garments for his wedding. The Queen was very excited, not only to be witnessing the union of two who loved each other beyond doubt, but also for her journey back to Yslandeth. She longed for her homeland now, thinking more and more about Swyk and her lost time with him.

"Make sure the seams are even, and watch the edges on the trim, please," the Queen instructed in Elfish. The woman nodded, and the robes were removed from Puryn. Unfortunately, it was already approaching midday, and time was short. "Please, put a rush on this," the Queen stated emphatically.

"Yes, Your Majesty. It is our top priority." They took their leave to complete the task. Falda looked at Puryn, who was all smiles and totally naïve as to what was to come after years of marriage. His face was almost comical—a boyish man-child with scarcely a beard on his chin, grinning with a silly smile of a boy at Winterfest—but the Queen saw more. In his eyes, she saw a genuine love for his Lady that warmed her heart. Falda was a bit jealous of their new love, but brushed it off. *I had my time,* she reasoned with herself.

* * *

Adasser was with her mother, Hansu, who was fretting over the veil of her wedding dress. She did not like that it wasn't gauzy enough. It was also too concealing, and did not make allowances for the strategic hints of Adasser's features to show through.

She turned to the seamstress in charge. "This will not do. Can you fashion something out of gossamer? The silk is too heavy. My baby should float down the aisle, not look like she has a curtain on her face!" Queen Hansu glared at Glorin, who was audibly chuckling at her dismay, while sitting in the corner and sipping a goblet of wine.

"Mother! It's fine!" Adasser was red with embarrassment.

"No, it is not. Marriage is special. Second rate will not do. You did not settle for just any man, did you?" The Queen raised an eyebrow inquisitively.

"Why no! Never! He's the one I want. There is no other!" Adasser responded in a defensive tone.

The Queen smiled. "Then we shall make you look as you should for your husband. I will not allow this bucket to sit upon a Princess's head." Annoyed, the Queen turned to the seamstress. "Take this away and make it in gossamer, or something light and flowing."

"As you wish, Your Majesty," responded the embarrassed seamstress, grabbing the headpiece and scurrying back to the sewing room.

The dress was perfect. It looked as if it was constructed of moonlight and silk, flowing gently over Adasser's figure. It complimented her in every way. The headdress would also, or Hansu would have someone's head.

The afternoon passed, and the Elves began to gather in their town center, eagerly anticipating the arrival of the royal couple, even though the actual ceremony was not to occur for several hours.

The commoners made their own party in the square. Some brought firewood and braziers, while others brought food and drink. The place was filled with singing, drinking, and laughing. The entire forest was in attendance, except for the Draj, who sat in defensive positions, standing against an attack that most knew was not coming. At least the Elves hoped for no new aggression in the near future.

* * *

Puryn dressed in his tailored robes, and Adasser's headdress was finally completed, to the approval of Queen Hansu. Then, both young lovers boarded their respective carriages and were transported separately to the royal court hall. The pair were seated in opposing side rooms adjacent to the hall before the ceremony.

All was finally ready, and the people in the gallery took their places. Attendance was mandatory for all nobles of the Kingdom of the Elves. The King of the Dwarves was also present with his Queen and their young son. Humans from the towers were present to represent Yslandeth, but

King Swyk sent a letter of apology for not attending personally, due to the situation on his southern border. He asked that Queen Falda be considered the envoy of Yslan. She was warmly accepted and sat in a place of honor for royalty, wearing the crown and regalia of Yslandeth.

In over nine years, it was the first time that the crown had sat upon Falda's head. It felt awkward and uncomfortable, but she was proud to represent her people at this auspicious event. She again looked like the Queen of old, vice the Elfish student she had taken to being over her stay at Torith.

The horns were sounded. The heralds called out, and all were bid to be seated and comfortable. The King stood and walked forward to the Priestess, who backed away from the podium, yielding the floor to the His Majesty.

"Kings and Queens, Lords and Ladies, and all who hear my voice this night … be filled with cheer and gladness, for tonight we celebrate the union of a hero and a Princess, both of whom are dear to my heart. I would ask that each of you remember your own joining to your spouse—the love and the excitement of a new life together, the trials and tribulations, and the triumphs. These two embark on this same journey of their own, and we are witnesses to their bond and their vows." The King stepped back, asking several legal questions regarding the legitimacy of the union under Elfish law.

He faced his legal scribes, and the head scribe responded. "Your Majesty, Puryn, son of Durn, is a Lord of the Elfish people, a holder of the position of Draj-Manot, and a veteran of wars with the Elfish people. Therefore, by the requirements of Elfish law, he fulfills all legal requirements of a willing marriage to an Elfish Princess, which from what I am told, Princess Adasser is not opposed."

"She is not!" the King laughed, and the crowd chuckled, then settled down to quiet once again.

"Then by the laws of Torith, I see no reason why these two should not be joined, save the King forbid it." The scribe closed a dusty book, more for show than he'd been actually reading it, for this part was all a formality, and everyone knew it.

"I wholeheartedly endorse this union," the King responded. Queen Hansu blew her nose into a handkerchief. The King smiled at his Queen, who was dabbing her eyes, as he took his place beside her.

The Priestess walked up to the podium and said an invocation in Old Elfish. It was a strange dialect, long forgotten. Many responded, reflexively, not really knowing what was said, responding, "And with you also." After the crowd responded, the music started up again. This time, flutes and harps played a quiet, soothing tune. Finally, the doors to the side rooms were opened.

"That's our cue, boy. Let's go!" Durn commanded in a whisper. Puryn sprang to his feet nervously and stood by his father. They walked out to the central aisle, side by side. On the other side, Adasser was led by her ladies-in-waiting and her sister.

"There he is," the girls twittered, but Adasser's eyes were already fixed on him. He looked so handsome and scared. She smiled behind her veil, though no one could see. The parties bowed to each other, then turned in unison toward the crown, walking solemnly as one toward the appointed area before the thrones. Puryn looked at Adasser from the corner of his left eye. She looked incredible. They arrived before the small altar in front of the podium.

"Who gives this man to Torith?" the Priestess asked calmly.

"I do," Durn replied. The Priestess bowed slightly. Durn stepped back, returning to where Arla was seated in the front row.

"Who gives this woman to Torith?" the Priestess asked calmly.

"I do." The Priestess bowed slightly to Queen Hansu, who sat back on her throne.

"Do you, Puryn, and you, Adasser, stand here tonight of your own free will and decision?" the Priestess asked the two standing alone before her.

"We do," the pair replied in unison while looking at each other.

"Then we shall proceed!" the Priestess declared emphatically.

The crowd cheered and clapped, then tapered off, allowing the Priestess to speak and the ceremony to continue. "Today is a sacred day beneath the stars and the moon. Haya watches from behind the sky at the vows you take tonight. Let us all understand that love is not to be taken lightly or trifled with, for love is what saves the soul in the darkest days, and love is what brings life to this world when hate would see it all extinguished. Therefore, I charge all here who are involved in this night to revere the promises made here, and consider them a promise to death and beyond. Do you two agree?"

"We do," the couple responded.

Haya smiled from behind her Priestess. The bond of mortal love was one of her favorite things.

"Lord Puryn, son of Durn, the Draj-Manot, and Protector of the Elves, do you love Adasser and wish her to be your wife, through all this world gives you and takes away, through joy and peril, and happiness and death? Do you swear to protect, honor, and hold her in the highest regard, not as your possession, but as your equal, your friend and your partner, in this journey ahead?"

Puryn's eyes went steely gray. The King cocked his head in curiosity, wondering if he was changing his mind at the last minute. Then Puryn replied. "Holy Mother of the Trees, I am not worthy of this Princess, but I swear that if she will have me, I will do all of these things and more, to my final breath."

Tears now ran freely down both Hansu's and Adasser's cheeks. The King breathed a sigh of relief and then smiled, thinking, *She chose wisely. Good for her.*

The Priestess turned to the misty-eyed Adasser, who cleared her throat and waited her turn.

"Princess Adasser, Tree-Speaker, and Friend of the Forest, do you accept the oath of this man and wish to become his wife and partner in this life? Do you swear to honor him and support him through the trials that surely come to all who marry? Will you bear him children and be the voice of compassion when needed? Will you carry forward the oath of the Friend of the Forest?"

Adasser breathed deeply. "I do, and I will fulfill all of these duties, and any others, as required. I love you, Puryn, son of Durn. I always have."

"Then, as the High Priestess of the Forest, I decree from this moment forward that Prince Puryn and Princess Adasser are now joined in holy matrimony. Let those who seek to damage or dissolve these bonds be cursed. May Haya bless this union with love, happiness, prosperity, children, and peace from this moment forward. May your love endure forever. You may remove her veil, Your Highness, and kiss your wife."

Puryn looked at the Priestess with a puzzled expression, then realized that he was now a Prince by marriage. His eyes opened wide. The Priestess smiled warmly, looking at Puryn as if he was an overwhelmed child.

Puryn turned to Adasser and untied the lace of her veil. She was a vision of beauty, wrapped in gossamer and silk. Puryn gently wiped away her tears with his fingers and cradled her face with one hand. She began to cry again, and he kissed her. The music played again, and the crowd cheered, but Puryn and Adasser heard nothing but their own heartbeats. She hugged him tightly.

After the two had rejoined reality at their hall, they turned and walked down the aisle to the adoration of the people in attendance. As is the tradition of the Elves, the people threw wildflower petals at the bride and groom, covering their path in flower petals. Puryn and Adasser left the hall to an awaiting carriage that took them to their reception. The driver carefully navigated thousands of cheering of Elves, who were now well into their own partying in the square. There was no fuss, just a genuine feeling of happiness and revelry, everywhere within the Forest.

Haya was overjoyed with this display of peace and unity. She would never admit it, but the Elves were her favorite.

The reception was a fine party, including good food, music, and dancing. The bride and groom were given many rich gifts of treasure and goods by the nobles and royalty in attendance. At the King's request, a large chest was brought into the hall, and the presents were locked away for safekeeping.

As the hour grew late, the King turned to Puryn. "You should really leave with your wife. I wouldn't spend my wedding night in a room full of stuffy old Lords."

Puryn blushed. "We will take our leave then, Sire. Thank you for all you have done. Thank you for accepting me into your family."

"She chose well, son. You will do right by her. I want some grandchildren. You better get busy, boy!" The King smiled widely, because Puryn's face was redder than he had ever seen. *He is so young,* the King thought. "Get out of here, boy, and go be with your wife!" the King motioned with his hands.

Puryn stood and said good evening to his new family, escorting his wife to the waiting carriage. Some raucous whistles and laughter broke out, and the King pretended to be offended, but then broke into a fit of laughter himself.

The carriage rode away to a reserved house in the trees, a place where the two could truly be alone for the first time in their lives. Puryn was nervous. He had never been with a woman, and this was "the" woman to him. He did not know what to do. Adasser sensed his worry.

He carried her over the threshold and placed her on the bed, kissing her gently. She rose gracefully, looking like an angel in her white, flowing dress. Puryn did not know the dress was all she was wearing. She pulled a string, and the dress opened and fell to the floor. There she stood, nude before him.

He had imagined this sight so many times in the past, but none of his visions compared to her true beauty—she was perfect in every way. She grabbed his hand and bade him stand up, kissing him. She worked the lacing on his tunic, pulling it off of him, over his head. Then he removed his undergarments. She was impressed by his physique, touching a few scars on his chest, but then Puryn turned to move a sheet from the top of the bed, and she saw them—the stripes from last days at the towers. Adasser covered her mouth and whimpered at the sight of the savagery that had been laid upon his back. She hugged him in tears for his past suffering. She never knew.

Puryn turned to face her. They were nude, awkward, and overly excited. Neither of them knew exactly what they should do, but they knew how it was done.

He looked her in the eyes. "That was a lifetime ago. They cannot hurt me anymore, my love." She pushed him gently back onto the bed, and they made love for the first time, guiding each other, enjoying their moment in bliss. After several hours, they fell asleep in each other's arms until daybreak.

* * *

The sun peaked through the drawn blinds—it was at least the second hour of the morning. The sound of horse-drawn carts and people on their daily travels was audible from the room where the couple slept. Puryn was up first. He dressed quietly and found a porter off about fifty feet from the door.

"Excuse me, but may I have some food and drink delivered to our quarters?" Puryn asked the Elf.

"As you wish, Your Highness. The usual fare?" he asked.

"Yes, whatever the Princess likes," Puryn responded.

"Of course, right away." The porter left on horseback.

Puryn returned to the room and caressed his wife's shoulders as she lay naked under the sheet. He was thinking about how wonderful his wedding night had been. The porter returned shortly with a breakfast of pastries, fruit juices, and tea. He knocked at the door, and the Princess woke, covering herself and hiding in the bed.

"I've got this," Puryn said as he kissed her on top of the head. Then he went to the door. "Please leave it here. The Princess is not ready for visitors."

"Understood, Your Highness. Have a wonderful day."

"You as well! Thank you," Puryn responded, taking the food into their room.

Adasser smiled, because he had thought to bring her all of her favorites. Puryn ate the food and drank some tea. Adasser's smile was like light to him, and he could not live without it. Shortly after they ate, she dragged him back into bed, and they made love one more time.

"We may be on the road many days, my love," Adasser justified. "I am not sure of the next time we shall be alone!" She smiled, and Puryn did not object in any way. Adasser laughed.

When they were finished, they cleaned up and made themselves presentable. Each dressed in new clothes and put away their wedding garments. Then, the couple left their honeymoon house, returning to the palace by carriage. Today was a traveling day, and the destination was Yslandeth.

Sir Ontak had arrived the night prior with a contingent of one-hundred men to escort a Queen, a Princess, a Prince, a Lord, and a Lady to Yslandeth. He was taking no chances with this group of charges.

King Glorin gave Queen Falda a new carriage to replace her old one, because it was destroyed by fire during the Battle of Torith. He gave the travelers a second to accommodate their numbers. Both of the royal carriages were made of the finest woods, expertly carved, and ornately decorated with gold foil and gems. Each had room for six and a platform on the back for any luggage. Glorin made sure to include an extra chest with gold and gems to assist the new couple in establishing their own lands. He had a good idea of what Swyk planned, and Glorin knew the lands his children inherited would be challenging for a couple of young, new leaders.

"Puryn, I wished this day would never come," Queen Hansu lamented, "but if she had to leave, at least I have entrusted her to a Champion and an honorable man. Son, please protect my baby."

"With my life, My Queen," Puryn responded. Adasser hugged his arm tightly.

"Thank you, Mother and Father, for everything. I will miss you both. We will visit often if we can, right, Puryn?" She looked at her husband.

"Of course, my love. Every chance we get. I will miss everything about this place every day I am not here." Puryn looked around wistfully.

"Remember, she is in your care now, boy. You are the man who I have trusted to protect her. I don't think I could have chosen better. Do not prove me foolish!" King Glorin extended his hand, shaking hands with Puryn. "There remains one more who wishes to see you off."

Master Gulsbane walked up to the carriage and held out his hand. Puryn grabbed his forearm, as did Gulsbane his, which was the custom of the Draj. Then Gulsbane pulled Puryn closer and hugged him. "Be blessed and forever under the protection of Haya, my friend … no, my brother."

Puryn bowed. "You will always be my teacher, friend, and brother. I will always seek to make you proud."

Gulsbane bowed, and said, "Go forth and spread the light, My Prince."

"I will. How could I not, with her by my side?" Puryn replied.

"How could you not, indeed!" Gulsbane bowed and walked away, smiling. "Until your next visit, Highness!"

The carriages were loaded. Falda, Durn, and Arla decided to sit in the Queen's carriage to allow the two lovebirds time alone on the journey. They needed to enjoy each other's company and figure out the rest of their lives together. It would be a week, at least, until they were close to Empyr. This would be a perfect time for them to talk about their expectations and dreams, and how to incorporate their ideas into an effective rule. They were very young, but both were wise beyond their years, except in the realm of marriage and relationships.

After an hour and several goodbyes, the caravan headed out of Torith into the Arondayre. Puryn froze, staring off into the horizon, as if remembering something disturbing. Adasser could feel him tense and sensed his heart racing as sweat formed on his forehead.

"Are you all right, husband?" Adasser asked in a worried tone.

Puryn snapped out of his trance. "I am fine, my love. I apologize. Bad memories."

Adasser kissed his cheek. "Only good ones from now on, my love. The bad is in the past."

Puryn hoped she was right, but for many months after the war was over, he still heard the screams of those who were dying in his dreams. He still smelled the burning homes and corpses, and saw the faces of the crying children pulling on their parents' lifeless bodies in the streets. The horror visited him less and less, but when it did, he never knew when it would happen or for how long.

These episodes left him in a bad mood for days. However, looking around,

Puryn realized he was now married to his only true love, riding in a carriage made for a King, and on his way back to his homeland to inherit titles and lands. Life was good at the moment, and there was no downside to this. He resolved to create another Torith with his love, except his Torith would be filled with people of all races, working together and prospering.

He hugged his new wife as the horrors faded. He was thankful to be alive.

A Hero Goes Home

Sir Ontak's cohort waited impatiently for the pleasantries to be dispensed, the goodbyes to be said, the hugs to be hugged, and the tears to be shed. He rolled his eyes and sighed, but kept his inner commentary to himself. After all, there were three royals and two nobles in these carriages. He really didn't want to anger his charges. Nothing good came of ticking off Queen Falda—this he knew too well.

Finally, the Elfish royalty stepped back from the carriages. The Queen of the Elves blew her nose and dabbed at her tears as she waved goodbye to her daughter and her new son-in-law. Ontak took that as a queue to get the show on the road.

"Platoon!" Ontak projected from the saddle. "Forward! March!" And they were off. Twenty-five bowmen, twenty-five foot soldiers and fifty horsemen surrounded the two carriages and two wagons laden with supplies, servants, and personal effects.

It was a formidable sight—a caravan surrounded by horsemen with spears bearing silken banners of the King of Yslandeth. A sea of blue and white fluttered forward in the breeze to the thunderous hooves of fifty warhorses trotting aggressively in sync. Ontak looked at his formation. The men were perfectly aligned. Several archers were beside each wagon, and four were positioned directly on the carriages, atop the platforms and roofs.

Puryn looked around uncomfortably. He was not used to being protected. He would much rather have been on horseback in the wall of defenses. Adasser smiled wide, reading his thoughts.

"Relax, husband, you are a Prince now. They will protect you for once!"

she goaded.

"This is not a position for a man," Puryn brooded. "Swyk rides out in front of his men in many battles, and I sit here, a pompous horse's ass, while the others protect me."

"Excuse me, My Prince, but I have been protected my whole life by men such as these! Am I, too, a pompous horse's ass?" The Elfish woman responded with irritation. Puryn knew he had hit a chord with her, because she had switched to Elfish without realizing it.

"No, no, my love! You are a woman. It is perfectly acceptable to rely on the protection of others." Puryn stopped—he bit off his sentence, thinking better of it, but only after it had escaped his lips.

Adasser began cursing in Elfish and threw a pillow at her husband. "You think I am helpless?! Am I a burden to be borne? I will show you someday what I can do!" Adasser looked around at her surroundings and muttered to herself. Puryn was beside himself and didn't know how to respond.

"I'm sorry?" Puryn smiled sheepishly.

"Save your apologies!" Adasser hissed in Elfish. Puryn kissed her cheek awkwardly and looked out a window. The Princess was annoyed and looked out the other one, shaking her head.

Falda watched the two and giggled, then covered her mouth, as was her habit. Durn looked up. "What is it, My Queen?"

"Oh nothing, Durn. It seems the newlyweds are arguing. I think Puryn stepped into something he didn't expect." The Queen giggled harder. "She is very annoyed. He looks like someone has shot his dog with an arrow."

Durn craned his head over to look, but could not see anything due to one of the archers. Nevertheless, he was sure the lovebirds would work it out.

Arla prayed for her son. First, she asked the Goddess to grant her son "the sense Haya gave a horse." Then, she joked with Falda about, "Puryn not carrying on like his father." Durn laughed. The wagon train had only scarcely gone a mile out of Torith, and the drama already had begun.

Ontak took the families through the open plains of Arondayre, West toward the Raven's Pass, and North of the Altyr Mountains. Off in the distance, on the mountain range, the travelers could see the progress the new hill Dwarves had made in farming and reforestation. Green was slowly replacing the charred and broken landscape. War was being erased by nature. Renewal truly had begun outside the walls surrounding the cities.

By the end of the first day of travel, the caravan had made good time. They arrived within a day's ride to the opening of the Raven's Pass, which ran southeast of the capital of Empyr. It would be at least another four or five days ride, but Sir Ontak's superior navigational skills, in conjunction with the excellent weather, had cut off at least one day of travel. The Queen was pleased.

"Outstanding job, Sir Ontak. I will tell the King of your proficiency and efficient use of manpower. You are truly an asset to our kingdom." Sir Ontak took the Queen's hand and helped her down from the carriage. A group of soldiers set a place for her to sit as they set up camp. Instinctively, Puryn grabbed a hammer and began unloading canvas tents with the men. The soldiers were puzzled at the assistance.

"Your Highness, please. We have this," a young Squire insisted. "Go to your wife!" He smiled at Puryn. Puryn looked at him with a peculiar face.

"I would much rather drive stakes at this moment. I am none too popular with My Lady at the moment. I, um, said the wrong thing." He winked and grabbed a hammer.

"Right, right. Well, if you insist, Your Highness. I will protest no further, but please let the Knight know that I tried?" the Squire begged.

"Yes, of course! I will get to work. I am not used to this watching business!" Puryn grinned and began setting stakes.

Falda shook her head. "I will never get that boy to act like a Prince," she sighed. "Just as well. Most Princes I know are asses!"

Durn chuckled and went over to his son. "Boy, you have men for that now. You have to lead, but you can't be doing everything yourself. Find a balance. You must separate from the men and be their Prince. I know this flies in the face of everything you have done for years, but you are not a common soldier anymore. You are their High Commander now, right below the King himself. Generals and Lords do not set up tents, let alone Princes!" He looked over at the soldier setting the corners of the pavilion.

"Footman, please relieve the Prince of his hammer immediately."

"Yes, My Lord." The soldier took the hammer, bowed, and ran off to complete his tasks.

"But, Father," Puryn protested.

"No buts! You must adjust, my son. Besides, there are things that need your immediate attention. They need tending. This is your responsibility, not driving stakes." Durn looked at Adasser, who was sitting alone, except for the two archers, who stood by her side. She was somber, hurt, and knitting something in the late afternoon's waning light. Puryn walked over to her.

"Adasser, I am sorry to have hurt you. I did not mean you were helpless. I meant you were more precious than I. I only meant that I am not worthy to be protected. I should be actively protecting you. These men are for you, in my eyes, not for me. What I would give to don my armor and to ride with my weapon. It is there where I feel I serve you best, my love. I desire to serve and honor you. You deserve never to worry; your mind should never wonder for your safety and security. I feel useless in these robes, riding in a carriage like someone I am not." Puryn touched her shoulder gently. "Do you forgive my boorish nature? I am a man. We are known to be fools."

Adasser stifled a smile. "You are a buffoon and a horse's ass," she replied in Elfish. "But I still love you, and I accept your explanation and apology. I just want you to realize that I am not a porcelain doll to be put in a cabinet and protected from the world. I am an Elfish woman, a Princess, and a tree-talker. It is something I have really never spoken to you about." She looked at him with a worried look. "I will show you that it is not a problem, once we get to our lands, my love. I promise."

"I could not care less. If you were a tree, My Princess, I would still love you." Puryn smiled at her, and she looked into his big blue eyes, stroking back his blond curls from his face. She could not be angry with him for long. He was too beautiful in her eyes, and his heart was always in the right place. She reached up and hugged Puryn tightly.

Falda saw the hug and quietly applauded. "Hooray, that's over!" she said to the group around the fire she was starting. Arla perked up.

"They're good again?" she asked Falda.

"She's hugging him, and there is no yelling, so I think it's all blown over!" Falda grinned and struck the flint and steel on the kindling. At first, the fire smoldered, but Falda expertly coaxed it into a proper campfire within minutes.

* * *

Ontak set the guard, food was prepared, and the party retired for the night. According to the guard report, there were no incidents of note over the evening. The soldiers broke camp in the morning, the fires were extinguished, and the party moved on.

Three days of the same elapsed, except there were no more marital quarrels. The caravan reached the gates of Empyr without incident, and in record time. Ontak had taken five days to traverse a seven-day, open wilderness trek. The Queen was very impressed, as was King Swyk. The travelers rode into the courtyard, and the King of Yslandeth was informed by the guards on duty.

Ontak called out to the unit as he entered the courtyard. "Platoon! Halt! Fall out! Stay in the area. Unit leaders, on me." Several young Squires rode up to Sir Ontak. "All right, gentlemen, organize your men. I need the wagons unloaded and delivered to the proper locations. Set everything for the Prince and Princess aside, as I don't anticipate that they will reside here for very long. The rest of you, get the horses to the stables and have them tended to. When that is completed, come back to me and report in. The evening meal will go when we are done with our duties. Do we understand these orders?"

"Yes, sir!" the five answered in unison. Then they broke off and attended to their duties. King Swyk appeared in the courtyard with several scribes, a few young men, and Master Reti, who was still the headmaster of Puryn's old order.

"Puryn! Good to see you, lad!" Swyk said enthusiastically. "You are much bigger than I remember!"

"Yes, Your Majesty, I have grown a few years since our last words. I have missed you and this place. How are you?" Puryn tried not to sneer at Master Reti as he looked down the line of people who were there to greet the new Prince and Princess of Torith. However, the tension was not lost on Reti, who was visibly nervous concerning their reunion. "Master Reti, how goes the monastery? I am sure it is as excellent as I remember it," Puryn said graciously and diplomatically.

Adasser was pleasantly surprised. She remembered hearing Puryn growl, more than once, that he would love to split the pompous ass's head with an ax. She saw the fear on Reti's face and was happy it was he who was afraid this time.

"We are well, and things are still very strenuous with the order, as you well know, Your Highness. We do the best we can with what we are provided." Reti made excuses and related platitudes. Puryn looked at the young men standing with the scribes and could not shake the feeling that they were familiar to him somehow. From his estimation, they were all within two or three years of his age.

King Swyk interrupted. "Puryn, we have some formalities to attend to. Please, step this way, and we will dispense with the legalities and get back to our reunion. Is this your lovely wife?" King Swyk bowed to the Elfish Princess, and she bowed back.

"Yes, Your Majesty, this is my lovely Princess Adasser, daughter of Glorin and Hansu." Puryn stated her lineage with pride. King Swyk smiled at her pedigree.

"Well, welcome to our kingdom, Your Highness," King Swyk offered.

"I am honored to be counted as a member of your house," Adasser responded, bowing.

The King smiled nervously. He saw Queen Falda sitting alone, a ways off from the formal gathering, waiting patiently for her time alone with the King. Their eyes met, and the King stammered. "S … scribe, come forth and make the proclamations and grant the titles per my decree."

"As you command, Sire." The scribe stepped forward. He was wearing a very formal and expensive-looking robe. His hat looked ridiculous on his head. Adasser turned away, stifling a giggle, as the chief legal scribe began to read. "Know now, Yslandeth, by decree of King Swyk, Sovereign of the land, that Puryn, son of Durn, is made a greater landed noble of the realm. He is bestowed the title of Baron and will, from this day forward, be entitled to the title of Excellency. Adasser, Elfish Princess of Torith, by right of marriage, will retain the same rank as Baroness, and also the title of Excellency. These titles give the bearers direct access to the King and his court, and entitle the bearers to be granted lands within the kingdom." The scribe stopped, stamping several scrolls with the signet of the King, and Swyk signed them each by his own hand. "The lands bestowed upon Baron Puryn, of Yslandeth, are the Forest of Erynseere to the southwest of Empyr proper. Its borders are the lands between Kelti, Korin, and Empyr, with the southern border against the Kingdom of Hodan. So, by decree of King Swyk, this land shall be in possession of Baron Puryn and Baroness Adasser and is willable to their line, in perpetuity." The scribe then stamped the deeds, and the King signed them by his own hand.

Then the King looked at Puryn. "I know you are a great warrior and hero of renown within the trees of Torith. I have heard of your prowess and honor from my most faithful, Ontak. Will you be Knighted in Yslandeth? Will you swear fealty as a man of the King? Will you come to our kingdom's defense at my call?"

Puryn looked at Adasser, who simply nodded, knowing that arguing about this was a lost battle. "I will, Your Majesty, and would be honored to accept the Knighthood of my homeland."

"Then kneel, hero, and receive your commission." The King called for his sword. Ontak held it in front of the kneeling hero who had his hand upon its blade. "Puryn, son of Durn, hero of the Elves, and Baron of Yslandeth, do you kneel here, willing to take the title of Knight of Yslan, with all of the responsibilities and obligations that come with the position?"

"I do," Puryn solemnly responded.

"Then repeat this oath:

"I, Puryn, son of Durn, do swear on my honor and my life, to respect the crown of Yslandeth, protect the people, and always uphold the code of chivalry, no matter the circumstance. I swear to defend women, children, and those too weak or unable to defend themselves against all threats of aggression or harm. I promise to be just and fair in the administration of justice in the King's name, and with this oath, I swear fealty to the King of Yslandeth. This is a binding oath until death. It is not reversible, except by the death of one of the parties present, you or me. These things do I swear. So, say I, Puryn, son of Durn, Baron of Yslandeth."

Puryn repeated the oath, and his face became stone, realizing that he had just enlisted into another army and could never return to the service of Glorin. However, Glorin knew this, and Puryn was certain when his father-in-law sent him here, the old man knew he would accept these appointments.

The King replied. "And know this, Puryn. As long as breath is in my lungs and my heart beats in my chest, I will defend you and yours with the full fury of Yslandeth. If anyone smites thee, I will wipe them from the face of the Ert,or be destroyed in the attempt. You are now one of the families, as are those you love. I will recognize you from this day forward as such." Falda's eyes glistened with tears at that statement. The King continued. "My sword." Sir Ontak handed the King his sword. "I dub thee, once, twice, and thrice." Then the King struck Puryn in the mouth, drawing blood. "Be that the final blow you receive without answer. Arise, Sir Puryn, Baron of Yslandeth."

Puryn stood. As Sir Ontak shook Puryn's hand, the soldiers erupted in a cheer. Puryn bowed to the King and stepped back. Adasser grabbed his left arm.

"Your Excellency," the King called.

"Yes, Your Majesty," Puryn answered.

"I found several old friends of yours who insisted they were assigned as Erynseere's first cabinet of scribes and advisors. I am not sure if you will want their services, but I told them I would allow you to decide. You can take them into the office over there and discuss the matters privately if you would like." The King motioned to a quiet room with some lighting and a table and chairs. "Oh, and stay tonight. It's too late to travel to your new lands, as tempting as that might sound!" He smiled and slapped Puryn on the back. "Go, form your household. Enjoy your first night home, my boy!"

Puryn motioned to the gaggle of young scribes, and they all filed into the room. Adasser sat next to her husband. The King made his way over to where Queen Falda was standing alone. She was crying quietly. The newly appointed Baron turned away to give them their privacy and got to the task at hand.

"Good evening, gentlemen. Why should I take you on as trusted members of my council and ministers?" The scribes all stared at Adasser, having never have met an Elf in person, let alone one as beautiful as she. Adasser ignored the looks and glanced at her husband with slight annoyance. Puryn eyed them and could not shake a familiar feeling he had regarding at least two of them. "Who are you, all of you? What is this?"

"Your Excellency, I am James, the tax collector. I was your training partner in the evenings at the monastery. I doubt you remember me after all these …"

"James! Oh, my Gods, No, it cannot be!" Puryn sprang to his feet and grabbed the young man, who was now much shorter and thinner than he remembered. He hugged him and laughed. "Oh, how I had wondered about my brothers at the towers. How did everyone else fare!?"

The other familiar man stepped forward. "Your Excellency, I am Donick, the herald. I was there in your ward during your …"

"Donick! The Gods are merciful! How I missed you, my oldest friend! I am so glad that life has treated you well! You all look so different. Has it been that long?" Puryn was elated that his two closest childhood friends were in the room. The three spent the next fifteen minutes catching up, and then they got down to business.

Donick introduced three other younger men, who were barely old enough but considered men in Yslandeth. "This is Willum, the botanist. This is Marst, the doctor. And finally, this is Bandu, the constable. We would consider it an honor to be counted worthy of starting up the barony with you. Erynseere has always struggled financially, but that was due to mismanagement and Sir Verdin skimming money from the traders who traveled North of our, er, I mean, your lands."

"Verdin? That scum. Is he still among the living?" Puryn spat the words out as if they actually tasted bitter on his tongue.

"Sadly, no. He died in battle against Hodan," Donick said sarcastically. "But to make matters worse, you will not guess who is running Korin now." Donick looked at Puryn's blank stare and realized that Puryn did not get his drift. "Athis."

"Athis!? That son of a whore is running a barony?!" Puryn slammed his fist on the table, startling Adasser. She had seen him angry like this only when a bad memory or an episode was about to erupt. The Baron collected himself as guards looked into the room. Puryn waved them off, and they went back to patrolling. "What cruel twist of the fates would reward that piece of filth with a barony?" The Draj was dismayed. He looked at Adasser, "I'm sorry, my love. He is the reason for the stripes on my back."

Adasser finally understood his rage and nodded sympathetically. She rubbed her husband's hand and mumbled something in Elfish to herself. Puryn smirked, having understood her curse, but not letting on what she had said. The scribes all stood expectantly.

"I shall take you all on as my ministers. Of course, we must recruit wisely, and we must make do with little in the beginning, but I think that with my Baroness by my side, and my friends around me, we will surely prosper soon!" Puryn called for a bottle of mead and some cups. They all sat in the room and drank together. "Pack tonight, for you shall travel with me tomorrow morning."

* * *

King Swyk and Queen Falda walked without saying more than a word or two between them. They ended up in the throne room, where Falda had heard the initial call for Arla's labor. Then, she remembered Wilda.

"Swyk, where is Wilda?"

"Here, My Queen," a quieter and frailer voice responded.

"My oldest friend!" Falda hugged the older woman and wept. She kissed her on the cheek, and Wilda cried openly.

"I missed you so much, My Queen! No more long vacations!" Wilda smiled. "I will fetch some wine and food for you both! Girls!" Wilda barked at two girls Falda did not recognize.

"Same old Wilda," Falda laughed through her sniffles. Then she turned to Swyk. "My King, do you still love me?" she asked plainly.

"Did you not read my missive, my love?" he responded seriously.

"I did, but things change, and feelings grow cold. Do you truly want me here?" The Queen stared at the rising moon outside her window.

"I want you more than my life, Falda. My life has been cold and lonely since you left. So many days, I wondered why I should get out of my bed, but alas, the damn Hodan kept my attention fixed on duty! This, while my love was buried, but not forgotten."

The Queen turned and faced him. She held his hands in hers and then abruptly reached up and kissed him hard, as if it was either for the first or the very last time. She wrapped her arms around his neck and held onto him, sobbing. He had tears running down his cheeks, too, as they held their embrace for some time. Finally, the Queen let go, and the King reached into a pouch, producing a ring with the largest diamond Falda had ever seen.

"I give you this, not to buy you back, but as a pledge that you are my first concern, forevermore. Please, do not leave me again. I will do better." The King slipped the ring on her finger. She looked at it in awe, then kissed him again.

"It was not your fault, my love. Politics and my own impetuosity laid the foundation for this travesty. Our marriage has survived a reign, separation, and war. We have earned a second honeymoon!"

"I am for that idea!" The King smiled and kissed his wife.

"Can we go to Erynseere and see the kids to their forest? I would love to see the trees again!" Queen Falda asked awkwardly, looking at Swyk's face as a grin stretched from ear to ear. He began to laugh.

"What?" Falda asked. "What's so funny?"

"The forest will never leave your blood, My Queen, nor should it. We shall ride to Erynseere and settle our new barony," Swyk agreed.

They hugged and then walked to the bathing area. After a nice long bath, both retired to the royal quarters. The guards were told that no one was to disturb them, "Unless Hodan is scaling the wall, and then call me when they reach the palace," as the King had forcefully stated. The guards did their jobs, and the King and his wife spent the night reacquainting themselves, one with the other, and starting their second honeymoon a night early.

* * *

As the sun rose, Falda found herself nude with her husband under red silken sheets and blankets. She felt as if this was her own wedding night. Everything seemed new between them and familiar at the same time. They had both changed in many ways, but remained the same in others. Time would tell if they would ever be as close as they once were.

Falda hoped she had not returned too late after all. This night together was a good start toward normalcy; however, the rest would be work. It would be determination and understanding that would save their marriage. She was ready to do what was necessary, and she felt that Swyk was also committed. However, time would tell.

The Barony of Erynseere

Falda rose and wrapped herself in a sheet. She grabbed for the pitcher of water on the nightstand, washed her face, and combed her hair. She braided it absentmindedly, as she had done for the past ten years in Torith. Swyk did not seem to mind as he walked up quietly behind her. She saw him in the reflection in the mirror. He was still a very handsome man, and she felt like an old maid, returning home.

"Good morning, My King. How did you sleep?" Falda asked, slipping on an under dress and walking to the armoire.

"Better than I have in an eon," the King replied, never taking his eyes off her. Falda felt awkward. She didn't know what he was staring at. Then he stood and hugged her in her silken slip, kissing her on her neck. "I have longed to feel your touch. I missed the smell of your hair … of your skin. I missed you in every way, My Lady." His embrace was firm and comforting. She took his hands and turned toward him.

"I feared I am too old for you to love me now. I cannot bear you sons. I am useless." Falda frowned and looked at the floor.

Swyk lifted her chin gently, and then, looking into her eyes, he kissed her. "It was not life without you. It has only become an existence worth continuing since you returned to me. Never believe that you are not precious, for if I die today, I die fulfilled. I can go to my grave, knowing my Falda came home, she loves me still, and I have known her as my wife once more. That is why I still breathe—for the chance to see your face. I love you more than anyone. I desire you more than all the riches and power this world has to offer. I wish I had gone to Torith with you, living where you are happiest, instead of living in these stone walls, alone, as a hermit."

Falda reached up and stroked his scratchy beard, then laid her head on his chest, hugging him as she smiled. "I am not worthy of such a love, but I will take it if you offer it, My King."

"Not true, My Queen. You are indeed worthy of all things, and the offer is only for you." They held each other for a long time before finally dressing and joining the rest of the party in the courtyard.

* * *

Puryn woke to the dawn, as usual. He slept well within the stone walls that once condemned him. Adasser slept quietly on the feather mattress. He could not help but sit and stare at his lovely bride. She was so beautiful, it hurt his heart to look at her, but when he remembered that she was truly his partner in this life and felt the same way about him, he smiled and thanked the Gods. He dressed in his undergarments, then put on a gambeson and chausses. As quietly as he could, he slid on his hauberk of Elfish mail. The jingling of the chain woke his sleeping wife.

"My love, why do you dress for battle?" Adasser asked sarcastically.

"We ride for Erynseere, my love, and I have no idea what to expect. I will not sit in that gilded carriage again and be of no use. I am a Baron, and I must show our people that I intend to lead from the front, by my example!" Puryn was very fervent in his speech. He was excited about this new opportunity, and he wanted to make a good first impression.

"As you wish, my love, but don't go stirring up the Hodan, if you don't mind. I wish to live in our home for a few days without barbarians coming for tea." She smirked and then slid out of bed. She was nude, and he noticed. She smiled at his reaction. Then, coyly, she asked, "Why do you look at me so, husband?"

"Is it not obvious? You are bewitching me with a spell! But I don't mind, please, keep doing it." He smiled and kissed his wife, but she pushed his hands away.

"Not now, sir, no! You are already in armor, and we are assuredly late for the departure! I will not be the reason we are later!" She turned, slipped on a silken under dress, and then put on the white sundress that Puryn first saw her in. He remembered falling off his horse and Master Gulsbane standing over him, chiding him for not paying attention. Puryn laughed.

"What is it, my love?" Adasser asked, knowing full well what he was thinking of.

"Oh nothing, just a memory," Puryn replied.

"Of falling off of Haystorm during drills, no doubt," Adasser said, giggling while walking out of the door in search of breakfast.

"Hey! You saw that!?" Puryn asked, embarrassed. Then he smiled, realizing she had been watching him, far before he thought she was. He left the room strutting confidently—helm, shield, and Elfish short-glaive in hand—looking for his Lady and some food of his own.

Arla and Durn were in the courtyard, wondering where everyone was. "Where are Their Majesties? Is everything all right?" Durn asked a guard.

"Unknown, My Lord. They do as they please. I find that I add two hours to any time anyone expects anything to happen around this place." He chuckled and went about the carts, checking the ropes and recounting the supplies.

"Well, I have no other place to be," Arla said as she hugged Durn.

Durn turned and kissed his Lady on the cheek. "It is a beautiful day. That it is, my love. That it is," Durn said, then he lit his pipe.

Eventually, somewhere around the third hour of the morning, all of the royals ended up in the courtyard. Falda and Swyk were fawning over each other like teenage lovers, as were the actual young lovers, Puryn and Adasser. Durn sighed. They were getting nowhere today, and fast. But, at least everything was already staged and ready to go. King Swyk, Queen Falda, and the new Barony of Erynseere sat on the carts near Arla and Durn.

"So, I have been thinking, Puryn," the King began. "You will not have the population from which to conscript an army anytime soon. I will transfer five-hundred reserve soldiers and their families directly to Erynseere by royal decree." The King looked sternly at Puryn. "You will be right above the Hodan hordes, my boy. I know you can fight. Whip them into an Elite force."

"Yes, Your Majesty. That will not be a major problem. Yslandeth forces are trained well enough. I can work with soldiers who know the basics." Puryn was encouraged by the gesture.

"Also, to bolster your population and bring craftsmen into your province without stealing talent from other nobles, I suggest you send emissaries to other kingdoms and baronies, asking for anyone who would like to immigrate to your barony. Of course, most will not want to part with their subjects, due to a particular skill-set or potential taxes, but you should attempt anyway."

"Your Majesty, if Elves and Dwarves choose to move to Erynseere and become subjects of Yslan, is that permissible?" Puryn asked hopefully.

"Puryn, due to your work in Torith and Glorin's diplomacy, Elves, Dwarves, and the Men of Yslandeth live in peace. Free trade across the borders now exists. Yes, by all means, if a Dwarf or Elf wishes to move here, they need only swear loyalty to you, and through you, to me."

"Excellent! We are excited for this chance, My King! Thank you for the faith you have placed in us. We shall not disappoint you." Puryn looked to Adasser, who was smiling contently, but still wary. So there was a forest of her own, and now she could bring Elves to her? She liked this idea more with every passing moment, but what was the catch?

"We should get moving," the King suggested. "I have taken the liberty of selecting the five-hundred families who will move to Erynseere. In addition, I have included a few tradesmen, a blacksmith, farmers, and laborers. In all, it totals somewhere around two-thousand souls."

Puryn's eyes opened wide with surprise, and the King smiled. "You will be thriving in no time."

The caravan left the main gate of Empyr and met a vast gathering of people. The mob consisted of men, women, and children. Many of the warriors were clad in make-shift armor or hand-me-downs. Their weapons mainly consisted of crude spears and hunting bows. There were plenty of wagons, but many women and children were also on foot. Puryn nodded and silently contemplated the work he saw before him.

The new Baron shouted while standing on top of a supply cart. "Pray attend, Pray attend!" Unfortunately, the crowd was much too large and disorganized to hear him. Erynseere's new herald, Donick, commanded a bugler to play. The horn played loudly as Donick took charge of the crowd.

"Pray attend! Pray attend! Shut up! All of you! Your Baron wishes to address his people. Show some respect!" Donick wore an intimidating scowl. The crowd buzzed, but then slowly died to a quiet murmur. "Thank you!" Donick yelled impatiently.

Puryn turned to Donick, smiling, but shaking his head. Donick held out his hand as if to say, *They are all yours,* and then he stepped back into the shadows.

"Thank you, Master Donick. I am Puryn, your new Baron. My Baroness is Her Excellency, Adasser, who is seated in the carriage at this time." The young leader heard someone say, "She's an Elf," but Puryn ignored the murmurs responding, "I see that many women and children among you are on foot. This is a long road, and it will take several days to reach the center of our new lands. Therefore, I ask those with space to grant those walking a place to sit upon your wagons. A kindness done now will reap a kinship for later, as we strive to build our lands together."

The soldiers took the Baron's words as an order. "You heard His Excellency! Everyone scoots over and allows a less fortunate member of our society to ride, too!" Soon no one but the foot soldiers was on foot.

"Thank you all for your kindness!" Puryn bowed to the crowd, and half of them cheered. He figured it was probably the half who were initially walking.

The new leader shrugged and joined his Lady in their carriage. He figured they would make about eight to ten miles per day. At best, they would arrive the day after next, at midday, but with such a significant contingent, delays were inevitable. It was early spring, and the temperatures were not yet reaching oppressive, but he still felt it in his armor. "Adasser, my love, forgive me, but I will ride with the soldiers, if it does not anger you."

"It will not … as long as you make it a point to come to check on me every couple of hours!" She kissed him. "Be safe, my love. See you later." She began knitting something as she watched her husband ride off on a warhorse King Swyk had gifted him for his Knighting. It was a beautiful white horse, but it was much larger and stronger than the Elfish breeds. However, in contrast to an Elfish steed, it was also much slower.

The caravan went out of the territory of Empyr and approached the Great White Wall. Puryn could see that the gate had been damaged by fire, and the "whiteness" of the wall had been tarnished by soot and trebuchet fire from the South.

Through the bars on the gate portcullis, Puryn could see the smoke of Hodan encampments or settlements. It was hard to tell from where he sat, but regardless of the source, the smoke was Hodan. The Great White Wall was at least twenty-five feet high and ten to fifteen feet wide. Soldiers wheeled ballista over its surface. Guard shacks were erected on top of the structure, allowing for command and control, and murder holes and embattlements were everywhere. Archers stood ready along the whole top of the wall.

After a long day of traveling, the King called for a halt. The soldiers set up the royal pavilions, and the fires were set. While building the camp, there was a disturbance in the distance. Several soldiers were attempting to detain someone, and a fight had ensued.

The new Baron rode over with purpose to see what the matter was about. There, he found that the guards had captured a girl dressed in black, who was armed with a sword. They had found her hiding and observing the procession from inside the wall on the Yslandeth side. She was Hodan.

"Who are you?" Puryn demanded.

"You should let me go, Yslan. My people will not stand for this." She scowled at him and struggled to free herself, but she was too small. Puryn figured she was maybe fourteen years old. One of Yslan's guards smacked her squarely in the mouth with the oak shaft of a long pole arm. She yelled and then recoiled, bleeding from her lips.

"Mind your mouth, vermin," the soldier growled. "This is a Baron of

Yslan. You should show a bit of courtesy."

"That will be enough of that, soldier," Puryn remarked, holding up his hand. The soldier bowed apologetically. "Why are you here, young one?" the Draj asked, sounding like an elder, to the amusement of Swyk, who stood just out of sight. "Why do you infiltrate our lands and risk an engagement?"

"Why do you move troops along our border, warmonger?" the girl snapped. Then, she sneered at the soldier with the pole arm.

"We are not moving soldiers. Well, yes, some, but we are relocating this populace to my barony in Erynseere. It is a place you should know well—a locale where the Hodan executed man, woman, and child. They left not even the livestock breathing. You speak of warmongering?" Puryn dismounted his horse and stood before her. He towered over the much smaller girl and leaned on his glaive.

The girl noticed that he was wearing Elfish mail, and it puzzled her. Then she asked, "Who are you, Your Excellency, who wears the chain of the Elf? What is your name?"

"I am Puryn, son of Durn, Baron of Erynseere … and you are?" The Draj warrior stared at the young girl's face as it lost some of its color at the sound of his name.

"You? You? You are Puryn of Torith? The Draj-Manot? He who stood with two-hundred against twenty-thousand, during the Battle of the People?" The girl's eyes were as big as goose eggs. She had obviously heard of him and was impressed. "Is it truly, you?"

Puryn closed his eyes and sighed at the number of twenty-thousand enemies.

"It is I, but who are you?" The warrior knelt to eye level with his captured spy. "Are you hungry?" He handed her some rations. She grabbed them greedily, eating so fast that she almost choked, needing a swig of water from Puryn's canteen. "I do not wish to harm you."

The girl looked at Puryn's face and could tell he was genuine. "I am Faylea, daughter of Chieftain Orus. He rules over the lands directly South of here." She looked at the wall. "He would not be pleased with me if he found out that I was caught, especially because he does not know I have left our village."

"He does not need to know. Just know this … I do not wish to fight the Hodan or harm your people in any way. I only wish to grow my own lands and to provide for my people. If Hodan can coexist with us, we will leave you alone." Puryn finished and looked at the pikeman. "Fetch the doctor."

"But Excellency, she an enemy and a spy. We should kill her and set her head on a spike," the pikeman gritted through his teeth. He was war-weary and obviously despised the Hodan.

"Enough. Do as I say," the Baron commanded forcefully.

"As you wish, Your Excellency." The soldier responded and went to the medical tent to fetch the doctor.

"Why do you care what happens to me, Hero of the Elves? You killed so many of my brethren at Torith …" She faded off in thought. "Your people massacred the Suden and killed more than half of the Hodan forces supporting the Dwarves at Torith—after the Elves treacherously destroyed peaceful logging camps that were not in the Elfish territory. You are all warmongering criminals to my people. We sought to liberate our allies. Now, those turncoats are friends of Elf and Yslan," she spat.

"You will find, young lady, that history and legend start in truth, but the color of the story is always determined by the victor, or by the defeated, while back at home, justifying incursions into sovereign lands. All sides were to blame for atrocities. No hands are clear of blood from this war." Puryn stared at her intently, remembering his own barbarity.

"Hodan was abandoned and left to rot and die by its allies. Yslandeth burned our crops and our stores. For more than three years now, we have been unable to recover, and half of my people starve or are hungry. My village took shelter in mud holes cut from the frozen ground, because our homes were razed and our possessions burned. But we are the evil ones?" She sat dejected on the ground. Her arms were now hugging her knees. Puryn thought she looked more like an Yslandeth school girl than a skilled Hodan scout.

"Again, I say that all are at fault for their contributions to the suffering. That is why I seek to build, not to tear down. I will seek friendship with your father and peace at the wall. I swear it."

King Swyk was standing still in the shadows, eavesdropping. His brow furrowed. He liked the sound of peace, but was unsure if Puryn knew who he was dealing with. Swyk decided to allow the boy enough rope to hang himself with. He would see if the Draj leader's peace aspirations bore any fruit. Still, in the event of failure, the King resolved to jerk the noose tight if Erynseere's soldiers were needed to protect Yslandeth. Puryn knew his duties, and Swyk had confidence in that. He trusted the boy.

"If you offer peace, it would be the first time in forever. But you are not the King. How can there be peace without his approval?" she responded, surprising Puryn with her astute observation.

"You are right. I will seek a mandate from His Majesty Swyk to seek peace along the border wall. We shall see what comes of it. If he agrees, I will need an emissary to your father. Are you interested?" The girl cocked her head with a look of confusion.

"You want me to deliver a message to my father concerning peace with Yslan?" Faylea asked incredulously.

"If the King agrees, yes, most definitely." Puryn offered his hand and helped her up. Adasser was now watching. The doctor arrived and cleaned Faylea's split lip. She complained and made a face, but ultimately thanked the Yslan medicus. When he was done, the doctor left them.

"If I am set free, I will let my father know that Puryn, the Hero of Torith, is moving into Erynseere. I will urge him to meet with you. You must have the authority of your King to make this happen, or it is all for nothing." Faylea looked hopeful. Her angry warrior façade began to fade and was replaced by the look of an optimistic child, who begged for a change in the status quo. King Swyk stepped out of the shadows. He was wearing his crown, and Faylea gasped, stumbling back in fear.

Swyk spoke. "I have listened to this parlay and have to say that I am impressed with the acumen of such a young warrior woman as you. Faylea, was it?" Swyk turned to Puryn. "I like this idea of negotiations and peace. You have my authority to sue for it with the Hodan, as long as we do not have to capitulate and agree to reparations. The war was an eye for an eye.

We will both walk away partially blinded by it."

Puryn looked at the Hodan girl. "You see? He grants it now! Let us see where we can go from here!" Puryn looked to the patrol. "Excellent job capturing this prisoner, gentlemen."

"Thank you, Your Excellency," the soldiers responded.

"Now, take her back to where you found her, and make sure she goes back to Hodan *in one piece!*" Puryn placed a strong emphasis on his last three words.

Swyk nodded at Puryn, saying nothing more, and then walked back to where Falda was waiting. He had other things to tend to, and Puryn had this.

The Baron said goodbye to his guest and spotted Adasser standing quietly, observing her husband's handling of a prisoner of war. She was impressed with his restraint. Knowing how his dreams and episodes made him, she feared he would open the girl's scalp with a gauntlet. But, instead, he fed her, healed her wounds, and then set her free to return to her home under an offer of peace. Not too bad for day one as a civilian leader.

* * *

"Good evening, wife," Puryn softly kissed Adasser's lips. She smiled at him.

"You are quite the ambassador, husband. I have never seen you that way. I am not disappointed that you have these qualities within you. Every day, I thank Haya that I chose you over all others. You truly are a hero, my love." Adasser brushed his face with the back of her hand, then led him back to camp and to some food.

Songs were played around the fire, and some people danced. Swyk and Falda turned in early, as did Puryn and Adasser. Durn and Arla danced and enjoyed the merriment. Eventually, all the activity died down, and the camp quieted. The watches were posted, and all others slept.

The morning arrived, and a quick breakfast was served around the various tents. Then, the soldiers called reveille and directed the orderly tear down of the entire encampment. By the third hour of the morning, the caravan was moving out, down the road. At midday, it reached the edge of Erynseere. The forest was a bit farther off, and they continued, pushing as hard as possible to reach their destination.

Along the route, Puryn saw the chaos of war, untouched by recovery. Hodan had killed everything in Erynseere. Bodies, some picked clean by the birds, were found in burned-out buildings and in the crop plots. The fields were fallow, and the char of fire raids still marked many of the bushes and trees. Yet, it was eerily quiet in the plains outside of the forest, as if the woods were foreboding, becoming an overgrown and dark entity. Adasser saw it differently.

"My love, may we talk?" Adasser asked.

"Of course! What is it?" Puryn answered.

"Would you permit me to speak to the trees and make us a home within them, such as in Torith?" Adasser looked at him expectantly.

"You can do that?" Puryn asked incredulously.

"I was chosen by the High Priestess to become a Priestess, but I declined it. Whether I like it or not, it is in my spirit to speak with the trees, as the old mothers did. I can and will talk to this forest. The Holy Mother taught me much while I was at my studies. I do not know all, but I think I know enough to get started on creating our own holy forest." She looked at his stunned face. "If that is what you want, my love."

"Yes, yes, please do this! Can I be in both places at once? My own forest in Yslandeth? True, Torith is surrounded by Yslan, but this will be our own private holy place! I cannot want this more. If this pleases you, my love, I am overjoyed to say, yes, please do!" Puryn held Adasser's hand. Her face almost glowed with happiness.

"I need a horse and a couple of archers," Adasser listed. Puryn called out and made it happen. "I will be gone for a bit, my love, but do not worry. I am a friend of all trees, and these will see our bond. I am sure." She kissed her Lord's hand and rode off to the nearest tree line to the North.

Puryn watched her go, but was unsure what his wife was talking about.

The young man wondered if his Lady could do what she thought she was able. But, even with his doubts, he knew never to put anything past the magic of an Elfish woman.

Gulsbane had taught Puryn years ago that all Elfish women possessed a magic gift from Haya. At puberty, it would manifest itself. His lessons also taught Puryn that the true power of the gift was revealed after the first child's birth. If Adasser could do this without children, Puryn wondered what would happen if they ever had a child. There was no downside to this, but he made a mental note to not anger Adasser without cause.

While the Baroness, flanked by her archers, introduced herself to the forest, the Baron called his council and set out a map of the lands. The barony was divided into parcels. Each lot of land was determined by how much farmable acreage was available on the property. Some parts of the region were hilly or rocky, so lots in those areas were granted larger borders, because less space in those places was farmable. Others were smaller, because of the fertile, flat lands they possessed.

"Gentlemen, our infrastructure is in disarray. I know this is not news to any of you. Our first order of business is to ensure our water supply is free of the disease and pollution of war. Form a group to scout out any places where disease seems rampant. Have them clear the water of death and debris. Second, we must recondition our roads. Have men drag large logs or stones down the roads to scrape them to a usable surface. We need teams to fill in large holes and remove any obstructions that make them impassable. Third, our agriculture minister Willum has determined a system of fair division of lands according to estimated crop yields. Most of our folks are farmers, not skilled guild members, so we need to start incentives somewhere. My plan is to offer land to those who aid us in rebuilding infrastructure." Puryn paused and looked around for anyone with any questions. All stood by and nodded, impressed with his generosity and organizational skills. The Baron continued. "Adasser wishes to build our main city within the forest proper." Some gasped.

"But, Your Excellency, it looks to be a foul and cursed place," one young apprentice remarked.

"To an Elf, all forests are the same," Puryn responded. "This one is just angry. She will soothe it and make it our friend." No one knew what he was going on about, but they all nodded and went along with the idea.

"We shall make a large road to the edge of the forest, for the time being, Your Excellency," Donick responded.

"Yes, that would be advisable. And if she asks for anything, do not hesitate to provide it for her." Puryn looked at Donick, who acknowledged and left to organize the teams.

"As for revenue, James, you will be my exchequer and my reeve. For the first two years of my rule, there will be no taxes or tithe of food to the barony. Understood?"

"But, Your Excellency, what will you do for food!?" James protested.

Puryn smiled. "I will grow my own! Besides, the King of the Elves and the King of Yslandeth have filled a supply cart with treasure to get me started. I think it will be sufficient to provide enough mutton and mead for two years!" Puryn chuckled and then whistled at the haul. "This money will be secured by a watch, night and day. Thievery from the treasury will be punishable by death. This money is not just to be used for my pleasure—it is what I will use to improve our lands for my people. I will use it to make everyone's lives better and bring prosperity to all in the end."

"Yes, Your Excellency," the remaining ministers replied in unison, leaving to set up the teams required to improve the lot of the barony. Lands were handed out to families who worked tirelessly. Most families settled away from the wall for security, but much of the baronial lands remained unsettled.

As ordered, master Willum directed most of the common folk to land reclamation. They cleaned up the remaining pollution, removed bodies and burned them on great pyres, cleaned out their wells, and fertilized the fields. Willum also noticed that large herds of wild horses ran free in the open fields. So he sent ranch hands out in groups to rope and capture as many horses as possible. The men were charged with breaking the broncos and making them rideable. Agriculture was easy for these people, but land reclamation took time, and horses were hard workers.

Master Bandu, the newly appointed security minister, directed the road resurfacing and the river reclamation. Soldiers who were not on duty were ordered to ride the length of the river, clearing it of pollution and debris. These efforts allowed the river to flush out the taint of death. The water eventually became potable over the next few weeks, without the requirement of boiling it first. The roads also took some time. After weeks of hard labor, the main roadways were reconditioned and passable by cart or horse.

Master Marst, the minister of health and welfare, monitored the progress of the barony and who was doing what. From a large tent city, where everyone still lived, the minister observed the populace. He determined which families contributed the most to the Baron's efforts by careful examination. Finally, after almost two months of living in canvas and out of carts, the people were ready to head out to whatever serfdom they were doomed to endure. They were surprised when Marst collected his data, formulated his plan, and finally addressed them.

"Per order of their most generous Excellencies, I have been authorized to bestow parcels of land to each family who has worked so hard to reclaim the lands of the Baron and Baroness. Each family, as they are called up, will be shown three parcels of land. The head of the family will choose one. This parcel will become your family homestead, to do with as you choose. It is still under the rule of the King and of the Baron, but the borders are your homes, unless stripped for actions against the crown, in compliance with Yslan law."

"What taxes are we forced to pay for this honor?" a faceless voice jeered from the back of the crowd. There was much laughter, and Marst stood still until they were finished mocking him.

"I am not sure of whom your last masters were, but be informed that Puryn the Hero is an honorable soul and will mete out justice for wrongdoing without blinking his eyes. However, in that same vein, he will reward good and faithful service with blessings and substance. His Excellency calls for a moratorium on taxes for two years. That is two full crops per year for every landed family, without taxes."

The crowd was silent for a moment as that sunk in. "Two years!? Is this a joke?" a voice screamed in disbelief.

"No, I am deadly serious. The Baron wants nothing from you other than your loyalty for the first two years, and will adjust the tax rate only after he sees recovery within the lands."

"Well, let me be the first to say that Puryn is the best Lord I've ever been called to serve under! Three cheers for free lands and no taxes for two years!" the voice screamed in elation.

There was a raucous cheer and roar from the camp. Puryn and Adasser were several miles off near a small grove. The young Baron looked up in concern.

Adasser laughed loudly. "Marst has told them of your grand tax schemes, no doubt!"

"Oh, that was today. I am rather glad not to be there!" Puryn bantered. "How goes it with the trees?" the Lord asked, but he knew it went well, because the trees looked healthier and less intimidating. There was also a feeling of peace around them, and birds were returning to their branches.

"It is a work in progress, my love, but I think they trust me now. Soon, we will be true friends, and they will love us as much as we love them." Adasser touched a tree trunk and said something in an ancient tongue that Puryn could not quite grasp. The idea it conjured in his head was, "peaceful soul, my friend." The tree groaned a bit, cracked, and then its leaves rustled briskly. Adasser answered plainly in Elfish.

"We shall speak again, ancient one." Then she turned to her husband. "We should go back."

* * *

Falda enjoyed the camping excursion, but Swyk was tired of the extended stay. It had been over two months, and he was ready to return to his maps and strategies. Falda knew this and hugged him from behind.

"Puryn has this with Adasser, and I know you tire of the field, My King. Perhaps we should ride back tomorrow morning and have a long bath together?" She winked at her husband.

The King turned, surprised. "Truly, my love? Would you return with me now? I long for my study." He smiled and laughed, and Falda laughed with him.

"I can visit another time, my love," she replied. "For a week maybe ... when they have buildings."

"When they have buildings ..." Swyk smiled, nodding, and they both went to get something to eat.

* * *

Swyk and Puryn both received reports that Hodan forces were detected several times on the wall and along the Erynseere River. The encounters were all without incident, but they were located on the edge of the Erynseere territory. Both Swyk and Puryn agreed this was more likely a reconnaissance and intelligence gathering action than an actual threat.

The Baron wondered if Faylea had ever told Orus of his offer. Then the young man had an idea. He would approach the border and see if he could make contact with the Hodan scouts again.

Before that could happen, Puryn knew he had to be seen as having a position of strength, which, unfortunately, his barony sorely lacked. Yslan would tolerate the probes from Hodan, as long as they were not violent or destructive. In the meantime, the Draj-Manot would build his infrastructure and logistics while training his own Draj units. The young warrior always hoped for peace as he looked to the South, but prepared for war as a contingency.

Renewal

Yslandeth, like most of the northern part of the continent, has two planting seasons. Below the Great White Wall, the weather remained a bit warmer in the winter months as one approached the lands of Sudenyag. However, for the most part, planting could happen twice a year in most places to the North.

Farmers planted spring and summer crops harvested in late summer, and early autumn crops harvested just before the first frosts. Erynseere had seen three such planting seasons, and the yields were far more than abundant. Food stores were bursting, and the farmers had enough to glean the silos of seed for growing in the spring.

Hodan had not been as fortunate. They struggled, suffering for the pride of their King. Still, the average Hodan folk were on edge, having endured just about enough of their leadership's policy of willful starvation. Many knew there was food in Erynseere, and out of desperation, hundreds were beginning to travel North to the edge of Hodan, camping in makeshift tents and hovels in the hopes of finding food for their starving families.

This did not sit well with the local warlords in Hodan, but they could not stop the mass exodus North. Puryn rode South to his border many times to assess the situation. He had not heard back from the Hodan Lord to the South of Erynseere and was becoming concerned this was a military buildup—until he saw them.

Emaciated women and children crouched, huddling together under canvas and rubble they had cobbled together from the ruins around them. Hodan's Elite seemed to eat well, as did their military, but the rest of their people made do on the scraps left behind.

Puryn sat in gleaming armor upon his white horse and looked at the dire scene. His heart was broken for the children as they ran to the border, crying out desperately for help. Yet, at the same time, Puryn's army of fifteen-hundred Draj repelled their advance at blade point.

"Stand down!" Puryn barked sternly. The men instinctively withdrew their weapons and stood at the ready. Fifty or more small, ragged skeletons stood at the borderline, staring at Puryn. Their faces were desperation and fear incarnate. Some were crying and begging for mercy, while others stood blankly staring off into the horizon, a gaze Puryn knew much too well.

The Baron of Erynseere called for James, his exchequer and tax collector. The minister arrived about an hour later on horseback. The Yslan leader met James, gesturing wildly at the children while he implored, "This will not do, James. I have sworn to protect and defend the innocent and weak. What are these children, if not in need of help?" Puryn turned his face toward the weeping crowd.

"Your Excellency, our barony is prosperous, that is true, but do you wish to ask the people to give up part of their bounty to feed their enemy's children? That is political *suicide!*" James stressed the last word. Then he shook his head as he witnessed the scene, understanding what his Lord was feeling, but afraid of what the man might do.

"Call a council meeting. Invite the family heads. We shall discuss this, and I will state my case. I will not force the people to provide from their self-earned wealth. I promised no taxes for two years, but that is coming to an end after this planting season. They have been a faithful people, but truthfully, they live quite well for common folks. While others starve and live in thatch roofs, our immigrants from Dornat al Ar provide us with technology to build stone homes with slate roofs and wooden floors for all. I hope my people have not forgotten wallowing in the mud and paying fifty percent to their other former Lords while living in thatched, mud huts. I will ask for much, but I want to aid our neighbors to the South, before they are forced by necessity to attempt to take what they need. They will not ask—at least their leaders will never ask. These children plead. I am not a monster, and I will not eat in front of a starving mob of children." Puryn's face was twisted. He was caught between his ideals and the reality of petty hatred and grudges. His people had a valid right to hate the Hodan, but these were women and children.

"Sir," James responded. "When our armies entered Hodan, and the enemy troops were here slaughtering this very barony, these same women and children rained the Underworld's fury upon the heads of our best sons. You do remember that every one of them is a warrior first, then a tradesman or craftsman? Those crying children would have stuck a dagger in your belly two years ago, rather than speak two words to you."

James had a point, and Puryn knew his words were valid, but that was then, and this was now. They were desperate. "All the more reason to show our good intentions, my brother," the leader said, softening his tone. "They need these things. It is not greed or want that drives them. They beg us for mercy. If we deny them, they will come and try to take what they need by force. It is inevitable, unless they choose to lie down and die where they stand. We both know that is not the Hodan way."

James nodded. "I will gather the council, brother. I hope you know what you are doing. I am always on your side, my old friend. We have seen much together, and you have never steered me wrong!"

Puryn smiled. "Thank you, and have my stewards send a wagon, no two, here from my stores. Bring grain, rice, root vegetables—filling foods—and bring a large keg of mead or ale."

James's eyes widened. "What of your needs, my friend?"

Puryn responded solemnly. "I have lived in a monastery and was well-fed. I lived before that on gruel and porridge. I will make it six months on twice as much as I have ever had in my life! This tribute will be an example to my people. I will not ask them to do what I will not do myself."

James smiled and saluted. "I love you, My Lord. You will always be my brother. You are the best man I know. I will execute your orders immediately." James bowed and rode toward the rising keep that had begun to show against the thickness of trees in the center of the horizon.

* * *

Puryn turned to his troops, exhorting their vigilance, but warned them against undue atrocities against civilians, friend or foe. The Commanders acknowledged and continued their defense of the southern borders. The Draj-Erynseere, as many—even those of Torith—had begun to call Puryn's force, dressed in blue and white tabards, covering silver mail armor of Elfish design and Dwarfish construct.

Puryn had commissioned several thousand suits of armor, one for each of his graduates, as well as Elfish glaives and bows. And, of course, the Elves gave freely to their comrades. Still, the Baron nearly depleted the treasury with his order from Dornat al Ar, figuring his economic recovery would replenish the treasury in due time.

His concerns were unfounded, for when he received his massive order of armor from the Dwarves, King Bogrol returned his treasure, plus ten percent, with a note to Puryn, written in the King's own hand:

Most honorable Baron and Protector of the Elves,

You honor me by offering payment for my wares, but let me give you these few things as a down payment against what I owe your people for your assistance in creating our alliance. I remember your people assisting mine in the feeding of our children while both our people still stung by the pain of loss in war. We will repay in peace.

You may directly call upon the Dwarves at any time, Your Highness. You are not only a Baron, but also a Prince of Torith. I do not forget my friends.

Be blessed favored one,

Bogrol, King of the Dwarves.

This grand gesture allowed money to be spent on stone from the quarries on the border of Cinnog. As a result, the mud huts of Puryn's people gave way to stone homes with cellars that could be used to secure women and children against an invading force. Their homes would not burn, and the stone provided protection similar to what Puryn's family enjoyed, minus the guards who were always on call.

The barony recovered rapidly, and the people were motivated by the good they saw in their leaders. Erynseere enjoyed prosperity unrivaled by any place North of Sudenyag. The people were overjoyed with the attention their Baron paid them. Now, Puryn hoped they would listen to his call for mercy.

The Baron rode somberly back to his castle.

His Lady was out talking to the trees again, and Puryn smiled at her peaceful visage. She touched the trunks as if patting an old friend on the shoulder. Adasser rode gently, trotting here and there, occasionally reaching down and stroking her belly, which now showed too full and round.

The young warrior was to be a father soon, and he loved Adasser more each day. Arla had become the companion of the pregnant Baroness, riding with her Lady on Haystorm, who had been gifted to her son by Glorin. Haystorm had adopted Puryn's mother as her new friend, and Arla loved the horse.

Durn was now the Senior Commander of the Draj-Erynseere. It felt odd having his own father serving under him, but Puryn worked it out as a partnership, vice a hierarchy. Durn still knew his position in life, but his son provided generously for the family. The older warrior was proud to faithfully serve his new lands, even as he grew gray. He taught the Draj swordsmanship, and Puryn learned the skill along the way.

The Baron trotted into the castle under a raised portcullis. The guards snapped to attention, and a crier announced his return. The Baroness was still off in the woods. Several pages and stable hands met their Lord at the central courtyard. They took Puryn's horse and equipment when he dismounted.

James was speaking to several of his men. They were preparing to depart to call the family heads to the court. He dispatched the riders and turned, bowing to Puryn, who waved him off. "Enough formalities, brother. What is going on?"

"I have dispatched the riders. The people will arrive after the evening meal. That is the fastest I could arrange things." The Baron nodded. "I have set up a shipment of two cartloads of foodstuffs and a keg of ale if that is acceptable?" The young nobleman nodded again. "We will depart early in the morning for the border, giving the crews time to load the provisions."

"Thank you, James." Puryn turned and called to a servant, and then the Baron left for his war room with a goblet of wine. There, in the war room waiting expectantly, was Durn.

"Father, how are you?" his son asked genuinely.

"I am well, my boy. James tells me you have been busy this morning!" Durn smiled and sipped from a mug of ale.

"I suppose you also are against feeding the Hodan?" Puryn complained with disappointment. "We must do something, Father, or there will be war. I can see the desperation on the faces of their youngest children, never mind what the full-grown adults are thinking."

"No, no, no, my son, you misunderstand my statement. I apologize for being sarcastic." Durn put his hand on Puryn's shoulder. "I am surprised by your charity."

Puryn looked at his father with pain in his eyes. "Their faces, Da. Their little eyes were so full of tears. They were little more than skeletons. We have so much. Why not help them and extend a hand in friendship? Can you imagine a world where Hodan and Yslandeth are friends? No one could stand against us in the Ert."

Durn smiled. "That is a wonderful dream, my son. It may be a bit too idealistic, but a great goal, indeed." Durn finished his drink. "We must convince the people. If we get their backing, your ideas may just become a reality." Durn got up to go back to his duties. "By your leave, Your Excellency," he declared, saluting his son.

Puryn snorted, waving at his father. "Stop it!" Then he stood and hugged him like an overwhelmed schoolboy. "Thank you for your counsel, Da. I am above my head right now, and I am afraid for the future."

"You have already made the wise and merciful decision. Haya will honor you for it. Now, we must get the angry Yslan to follow your lead. That is the challenge! We shall see, my son." Durn left the room and returned to his duties.

Puryn stood over a map, not unlike what Swyk did every morning. There were small carved wooden pieces on the map, signifying forces, units, and deployments. The young Draj-Manot felt a momentary wave of disgust as he saw the map as a nobleman's tabletop game. The only problem with this game was that real people suffered for any gains, and no one on the bottom ever truly seemed to win.

* * *

Adasser returned from the wild, a bit disheveled, as was the usual case. Her intense interactions with the forest left her scraped up by small branches or underbrush. Her long, beautiful mane of hair would frequently have leaves, flowers, and other natural items interwoven into it. This day was no different. Pine needles were her decoration of the day. Puryn smiled at her return, ignoring the pine needles.

The Baroness dismounted her horse with Puryn's assistance. She hugged her husband, kissing him quickly, rattling on about the elms on the hilltop being stubborn. The young man had learned to just nod and agree with whatever she was talking about.

"My love, are you listening to me?" Adasser asked, grabbing Puryn's spaulders. Truthfully, he had drifted off to the faces of starving children and had been nodding periodically, but not really listening.

"The elms, yes, my love," Puryn guessed.

Adasser smirked. "What is on your mind, husband?" She took his arm as they entered their throne room. Ladies-in-waiting skulked in the shadows with brushes and combs, waiting for their moment to pounce and make their Baroness presentable. Adasser sat down, and the preening began. Puryn tried not to laugh as he saw Adasser's facial expression of dismay and defeat. She sat and talked while rolling her eyes occasionally. *Human women could be such a pain,* she thought.

"I went to the southern border today. The scene is desperate. I am sending food from our plenty. I hope you do not mind." Puryn looked at his wife, who was becoming irritated with all of the brushing.

"Why would I mind, my love? You are not sending a tribute, are you?"

Puryn shook his head emphatically.

"Then feed them, my love. I know you have thought long and hard on peace and lost many hours of sleep over it. Your heart is true. We will manage."

The young man looked out of his castle window over the growing crops, and he saw bountiful plenty all the way to the horizon. "I will ask the families to contribute fifty-percent of their surplus."

Adasser's eyes widened. "That is a lot, my love."

"There are many to the South who die for lack of bread, My Lady." Puryn was staring off into space, remembering something. Adasser had a look of concern on her face. Puryn spoke Elfish, and since he returned to Yslandeth, he rarely broke into the language. He didn't appear to realize he was not speaking Etah.

The Baroness answered in kind, surprising Puryn, who realized he had been speaking in the foreign tongue. She replied, "It is well, my love. They will do as you ask."

After thirty minutes, the preening ended, and Adasser looked flawless once more. In her husband's opinion, her belly was unnaturally large, but he kept that to himself. Adasser would speak to her belly in Elfish all the time. Then, once in a while, when the child was feeling frisky, the expectant mother would place Puryn's hand on her belly, and her husband would feel the baby kick. This routine always made Puryn laugh, and Adasser loved his laugh.

In the mid-afternoon, the riders who James had dispatched returned. They had given the family heads no option. James had made it clear that this was not a suggestion or request. All were under orders to come. They would be at the court after the evening meal, or else.

The lead rider reported to James. "All families have been notified. All heads have been spoken with directly. They have been apprised of the serious nature of this meeting, but not given details, as ordered." The rider bowed.

"Very well. Thank you, rider," James replied.

* * *

As evening arrived, Puryn ate with Adasser in their castle. The Draj guard had just changed over as Puryn watched the border platoon march southward toward Hodan. He wondered if the people on the Hodan side had a mouthful of food among them.

He could smell the smoke of the far-off Hodan fires. It was starting to get colder in the evenings. Soon, the summer crops would be in the barns, and the early autumn planting would begin. The harvest looked plentiful again. But even with this plenty, he wondered just how vindictive the families would be. He was loath to break his word and demand a tithe before the two-year promise was fulfilled, but it would be too late for the Hodan if he waited any longer. It was now or never.

* * *

There were approximately five-hundred representatives in an outer court-yard when they all arrived. Many sat on makeshift benches or chairs they had brought with them. Puryn and Adasser entered the square on an elevated stone platform. The herald announced the baronial entry and called all to rise. The courtyard din subsided, and the Baron bade them all sit. Adasser sat on a small, but elaborate velvet chair, off to the side, and observed.

Haeldrun hid among the gathering family leadership, poisoning their minds with greed and malice. Most resisted, but some succumbed to the Underlord's suggestions. The Dark Lord worked the crowd as the meeting was ready to commence.

"Good evening," Puryn said with gravity. "I have called you all here at the end of the day to speak to you, not as an iron-fisted Lord, but as your leader and friend." Puryn looked around at many nodding heads. "Be that as it may, I am your Baron, and as such, I am required to provide for the defense, of not only Erynseere, but of Yslandeth proper. To the South, the Hodan starve and wallow in despair."

Many cheered and raised a fist into the air. The young leader was concerned.

Haeldrun goaded his select few.

"The war has been over for almost four years, my friends. It is time to mend our fences and forgive," Puryn continued forcefully.

The crowd murmured and began to get loud. Rabble rousers fanned the flames of hatred with their goading and malice. Master Donick stood and called for order with a surprisingly loud voice. "Pray attend to His Excellency. Respect the man who has granted you all you have. Shut your mouths!"

The crowd looked up at Donick, and some sneered. Donick stared them down.

Puryn raised an eyebrow. "Thank you, Master Donick. As I was saying …" Puryn cleared his throat. "Hodan has not posed a serious threat in more than two years. Their military posture is barely tenable and would collapse under the attack of a serious enemy, such as ourselves."

Again, Haeldrun's pawns cheered and goaded the crowd, warmed by the fire of the Conflict.

"Then we should attack and kill every one of them!" a random voice exclaimed. Donick searched the crowd, but did not see who said it. Instead, the courtyard erupted in cheers for war.

After several minutes, the chaos settled as Draj warriors surrounded the crowd. Puryn continued. "The Draj-Erynseere." He pointed to the men standing smartly to the left and right of the courtyard. "They are valiant warriors. I trained them myself. My father trained them in swordsmanship. They could very well kill the men, and then the women and children of

Hodan." Some cheered again.

Haya had taken notice of the evil that was present. Puryn was losing the crowd. They were so ungrateful and arrogant. She was not amused at this display. Haeldrun hid in the shadows, far from Haya's view.

Puryn was angered, shouting in a voice of a God. "But what of the honor of Yslan? What of the honor of our alliances with the Elves and Dwarves? Hodan dies between the snakes who prosper to their South and their rivals who prosper to their North. Surely, they have committed atrocities against our people, but we, for our part, returned the favor tenfold. Not many years ago, our own people lived in mud hovels cut from the ground and scraped by with moldy bread and rotten meat. You too lived in squalor due to the destruction brought about by wanton war."

Haya stood in anger behind her champion. Haeldrun grinned maliciously and remained hidden.

Adasser looked at Puryn with her head cocked slightly to the left. She was not sure if she was hallucinating or if she saw a halo appearing around the crown of her beloved. She initially discounted it as light playing upon the jewels, but now she also saw it on his person. She could smell the ozone in the air, and the hair began to stand up on her neck. Haya was here, and the fledgling Priestess was terrified. Adasser could feel the presence of her Goddess plainly. The Baroness scrambled, hiding behind her chair. Her ladies-in-waiting were concerned that the baby was in trouble. The eyes of their Baroness were wide as she waited, with bated breath, for what she feared was about to happen.

"Let the rats eat their own dung," a voice cried from the crowd. Many cheered in unison.

Puryn's fury was now focusing. Adasser screamed, and they all stopped in their tracks. Some of the crowd began to notice the glow on Puryn's person and murmured nervously.

"Speak carefully, your next words, my gentle people, for Puryn is a prophet, and his words hold the weight of the Gods," Adasser declared in old Elfish to the crowd, who did not understand her. They still called for Hodan blood.

"I have promised you lands. I collected no taxes for two years. I spent my treasury building stone homes, creating roads, cleaning the rivers, and opening trade with our neighbors. I simply ask that you give of your surplus to women and children in need, and I am greeted with barbarity and greed? Have my people become so selfish as to neglect the pain of even a child!?"

Adasser's eyes were wide and fixed on Puryn. She was trembling and praying in Elfish, asking for forgiveness for the people.

Haya was not listening. She had her hand on Puryn's shoulder as he spoke.

One leader stepped forward. "We will not feed the dogs that ripped our children from us. Instead, we will overthrow the man who demands this."

"May Haya judge your hearts appropriately," Puryn said in an ethereal voice.

Bolts of lightning struck five members in the crowd as the Baron called for judgment. The recipients died where they stood, burned beyond recognition. The mob panicked, shrieking in horror, now realizing that the Gods were indeed present, and they were being judged.

It was determined later that those who died that night had been conspiring to overthrow Puryn from the very start of things. However, the Goddess had remedied that situation. The crowd was now much more receptive to their Lord's demands, and they looked to the skies expectantly. Many were on their knees. Adasser was one of them. She was begging Haya for mercy.

Haya relented, but, in her judgment, she was still not pleased that violence was necessary to coerce mercy from these proud humans.

"I, Puryn, Baron of Erynseere, have promised that you shall pay me no taxes until the following season. The food you have gathered for yourselves, and the gold you make from its sale, is your own, as promised. I will exact a tax to feed our neighbors next season, but it will be too late for thousands who will die of malnutrition and disease. Think of the children, women, and even the men who want to provide for their families, but cannot. I will not order you to hand over your goods. Instead, I will ask every family to provide a sack of seed and a cartload of hearty vegetables for transport to Hodan in the morning. I am not asking you to impoverish your families, just to contribute to the cause of humanity. If we extend a hand now, we may create an atmosphere of peace and brotherhood for the future." Puryn's glow began to fade. The crowd was silent, except for the sniffling of those who were now crying. "I had hoped this would be an occasion for hope and love. Instead, it results in greed, hatred, and more death. I will send my wagonload down with the rest who see fit to show their better selves." Puryn turned to go, but a familiar voice stopped him.

A herald began announcing an arrival, but he was cut short by a person entering the crowd, waving a hand for the pompto cease. "Your Excellency, I say those words with utmost seriousness, for you are most excellent, Puryn, son of Durn, and I am but a worm and a cur."

Puryn spun around angrily, recognizing the voice. It was Athis. *What is he doing here?* Puryn thought, as he looked at the bowing robed figure. Athis's face was almost normal now. The Elfish healers reconstructed him as best they could.

Verdin spared no expense in repairing his heir. Athis still could not use his sword armor properly, no matter how many healing sessions were performed. Over the years, he learned to use his left arm for the sword, and his damaged one had a shield strapped to it. People called him Lord Athis, the Sinister—not inappropriate, by Puryn's standards.

"I come here humbly, Your Excellency, to offer my goods to your quest for peace. I, too, tire of war and destruction. I spent many years in the towers, learning the value of life. I agree that your proposition is the right way forward." Athis bowed again and walked into the crowd. The people recoiled in fear, and Athis frowned. No matter how much he tried to atone for his sins, people always recoiled in fear.

"Lord Athis," Puryn said, trying to sound hospitable. "This is an unexpected visit. How did you know of this meeting?"

"I have ears everywhere, as do all of the Lords of Yslan," Athis replied calmly. "I only wish to support your decision. There is no ulterior motive, although, considering our past, I would not blame you if you did not believe me." Athis looked at the floor, something uncharacteristic of the old Athis.

Puryn looked at this new man in wonder. Who was this new Athis? Or was this a trick? He still hated him in his heart for the death of Master

Elig, but swallowed his pride and continued the conversation. "How much do you have to offer, Lord Athis? Anything is better than nothing," Puryn taunted as he looked at his own people in disgust.

"You may not believe this, my old adversary, but during my days in the towers, Reti did something right. He sent many monks to tend to me and to my wounds. They were patient and kind. They did not judge me and even forgave me when I confessed my sins and weaknesses. I lament the day I slew Elig. If only he had gotten to me sooner, perhaps I could have lived my life in honor, vice the shame I now bear."

Puryn's demeanor changed. Adasser picked up on it and continued muttering incessantly to Haya in Elfish. The ladies-in-waiting surrounded their Baroness, who did not even know they were there.

"Puryn, son of Durn, you acted justly in response to my impetuous, nay, murderous outburst that day. I hold you blameless and wish I could bear the stripes you were unjustly awarded. I only hope that in my quest to atone for my sins, now as a Priest of Haya, I may earn your forgiveness as well. She was here. She was who guided me to this meeting, if you should know. Haya is a Goddess, but may take any form she wishes. The Goddess of Life and Light touched you tonight, my brother. Your words were backed by her power." Athis turned to Puryn's people. "Make no mistake, people of Erynseere, your Baron speaks truth and light. Haya has noticed. To oppose this man's will in this endeavor is to cut your own throats. Haya favors this Lord, and you all would be wise to heed his counsel. Adasser was true when she called him a prophet of the Goddess."

"A prophet? When did she say this?" an elder asked respectfully.

Haeldrun recoiled in anger at his turncoat minion. Once again, the Underlord attempted to poison Athis with words of despair, but his efforts received only silence, as Athis had learned to ignore his goads. Haeldrun fled to the Underworld, knowing he had lost the day. The Underlord would need to gather his allies, far from the prying eyes of Haya and her devoted.

"When she screamed in Elfish as Haya's light permeated Puryn's person. I am sorry. I forget that not all speak Elfish, as do I." Athis smiled genuinely and proceeded to the platform, where he knew Puryn stood, amazed at this turn of events.

"I will accept your apologies, Athis, but truly I say to you, it will be a lifetime before my heart forgets. I welcome your assistance and your support." Puryn extended his hand to Athis, and the two shook hands and bowed.

"I completely understand, Your Excellency. You have every right. I am thankful for this opportunity to serve the Goddess and prove my contrition. I will leave you now, brother, and return with a wagon train by sunrise. My caravan sits ready at the border of our lands." Athis turned to go.

"Athis," Puryn said awkwardly. "Thank you." Puryn saw tears now streamed from Athis's eyes.

"No, thank you," Athis said in a subdued tone. He and his guard left without incident and rode northwest to the border of the barony of Korin and Erynseere.

"And now, my people, this has been a much more taxing night than I had anticipated. It is late, and we all need to make our decisions for the morning. I hope to see you all here with whatever you feel you have to offer. I am not ordering,only asking, but if Athis is right in his assessment and the Goddess cares for the plans of men, you would do well to contribute as your heart leads you. You are dismissed." Puryn turned in disgust, approaching his Lady, who tentatively stood and greeted him. She kneeled before her husband, shaking. Puryn was alarmed.

"What is it, my love?" Puryn asked obliviously.

"Athis speaks truly, my husband. Haya was here, and she was upon you. She struck down those five, because they opposed you and threatened your life. I am afraid. The Gods are involved now. I have worshipped Haya all of my life, but never met her on the Ert." She touched his armor and sensed the holy presence was dissipating. Still, the connection was real. "You are her chosen Champion, my love. I am not worthy of you." Adasser was crying.

"Who is worthy of love? Who is worthy of compassion? Who is truly worthy of anything in this world?" Puryn replied, caressing her tear-stained face. "You chose me, because you saw something to love. I chose you, because you are the epitome of beauty, grace, and light. There is no one on this Ert who I would rather be joined to than you. Never doubt this. I will die your man. I will be joined to no other."

Adasser hugged her armored husband. They had both said the whole conversation in Elfish. The ladies-in-waiting had concerned looks on their faces, until Puryn kissed his wife and held her face gently in his mailed hands. Smiles appeared on the young girls' faces, and they giggled. Puryn smiled at their giddy twittering, and they laughed more.

Puryn and Adasser walked somberly to their sleeping chambers after the Baron set the watch. The remaining heads of households left the courtyard and the guard removed the bodies of the attempted coup. The Draj warrior slept well in his Lady's embrace—the best sleep he had experienced in a year.

* * *

The morning was brisk, and the smell of fireplaces filled the air. There was much noise outside of the castle, which woke Puryn. He washed quickly and dressed in clean clothing, putting his armor on. He was armed with a short glaive and carried a small metal shield. He kissed his exhausted, pregnant wife, who barely stirred in the bed, and then left for the courtyard.

His horse was readied for battle. Puryn looked like the holy warrior Athis claimed him to be, as he rode out dressed in white on his white horse. As the horse galloped to the road, people moved out of his way.

Upon arrival, the Draj warrior was overwhelmed with what he saw. As far as the eye could see on the roads, there were wagons covered with tarps, sent under the banners of every family. Athis was positioned at the rear of the caravan and had a small contingent of his army with him. Puryn was not concerned. The more he thought about what Athis said, the more he began to believe the story of change. He hoped it was true.

Athis rode up to Puryn. "Are we ready, brother?"

"I am," Puryn replied.

"Then let us go and do the work of the Goddess!" Athis exclaimed jubilantly. Puryn could not help but smile.

"As you say. Let us go." Puryn turned and barked orders to the changing guard, and they marched in front. The convoy departed at the first hour of the morning.

Late in the day, they arrived at the southern edge of Yslandeth. The Draj Commanders gave their reports, and the guard was changed. Puryn advanced to the front and saw that the numbers on his border had increased tenfold in the last few days. He had a rider affix a white flag to a lance.

Fifty Draj surrounded their Baron as Yslan officially invaded Hodan territory for the first time in four years. People cried out and begged for mercy as the pristine unit moved through the decimated Hodan people. Women fell to their knees prostrate on the ground, begging for their children. Puryn was appalled.

Then it happened—the Hodan military showed itself—one-thousand Hodan foot soldiers and two-hundred-fifty bowmen met Puryn's contingent, who rode under a flag of truce. The Hodan Commander rode to the front, accompanied by his Lieutenants and a young lady whom Puryn recognized. It was Faylea.

"Hail, Yslan. What is it you desire? Your death?" the Commander quipped. "I am Orus, King of Hodan, by right of arms. My proof is in this box."

A foot soldier opened a wooden box containing the head of a man. The face appeared to be that of the feared King, Jabir the Fierce. "I challenged him a week ago and defeated him in combat." King Orus was beating his chest in an attempt to make an appearance of ruthless power, but Faylea spoke up, cutting off her father, as many young maidens did in Hodan.

"He let them live," Faylea declared to Puryn.

"Who, Faylea? Who did he let live?" Puryn asked, focusing on the girl.

"Jabir's Queen and sons. My father is just. He seeks only to heal our land." Faylea looked at her father respectfully. He was shaking his head.

"Damn you, girl, hold your tongue," Orus snapped.

Puryn smiled. "So you, too, wish for your people to live?" Puryn was encouraged. "I have been blessed by the Goddess with an abundant crop for three seasons running. I have gathered our surplus and submit it to your people as a peace offering. I am authorized by King Swyk of Yslandeth to sue for peace, but not pay reparations. I do not consider feeding my neighbors to be payment, but instead an investment in future relations."

King Orus looked at his starving people and knew he had no choice but to accept Puryn's offer. Faylea had told her father the story of her encounter with Puryn and his offer of peace many times. She portrayed him as an honorable man, an accomplished warrior, and a great leader.

The Hodan leader was concerned the people would see him as weak, as he answered Yslandeth's offer. "I cannot accept charity." Many groaned. "But, I will fight you in a duel. The winner gets bragging rights and the food." The people perked up and listened intently.

"So, I cannot just give it to you, Your Majesty?" Puryn looked confounded and then smiled. "So be it. Let us fight, but not to the death, agreed?"

"Agreed. Hand to hand. No weapons. No armor," Orus replied.

Orus dismounted, disarmed, and removed his armor. Puryn did the same. Orus was a tall man, muscular and strong, but older than Puryn. He reminded the Draj warrior of a younger version of his own father. Thinking of his da, he remembered how deadly the old man could be with a sword. He would not take the Hodan King lightly.

A ring of men and women surrounded the two warriors. On the border, the remaining Draj were worried, but dared not enter Hodan, under Puryn's orders. So instead, they held their ground and waited patiently for their Baron's return.

Haya's obstinate sons, Runnir and Gunnir, watched the duel from Aeternum, betting on the outcome. Runnir chose Orus, and Gunnir chose Puryn. Aluia scowled in disgust and went to find her mother.

The fight started like any playground dispute. Orus popped Puryn square in the mouth, busting his lip. Puryn spat some blood on the ground, and side-stepped the Hodan King, delivering a kick to his solar plexus that garnered a loud "oof" from his adversary. The old warrior chuckled, sucking wind, and attempted to take the younger Draj to the ground, but the Yslan warrior sidestepped his opponent's attack, and instead instinctively slipped into his monk fighting style. This did not work on Orus, who had fought the monks many times before and still walked the Ert. Puryn ended up on his back.

The young God brothers cheered for their champions. This was a good bout!

From the ground, Puryn covered his head as Orus delivered a flurry of blows that bruised the younger man's arms, but did not hit their mark. The Draj warrior kicked his body upward, bridging his opponent off, then rolling over the Hodan warrior and delivering a crushing elbow to his enemy's chin. Orus, stunned, instinctively kneed Puryn in the groin. Both men lay on the ground, collecting themselves for a moment, and then stood. The fight continued, evolving into a boxing match. Both men tried to knock the other out. There was the occasional grab, but punches landed from both warriors. Puryn's white garments were now bloodied with his blood and the Hodan King's.

The older warrior was staggered, and his clothes torn. The Yslan Baron could see an open wound on the side of the Hodan King. Puryn assumed Orus had acquired it while taking a certain Jabir's head the week prior. The Draj warrior knew he had the upper hand, but the Hodan opponent was now bleeding from old and new wounds. He would fall and perhaps die if the fight continued. So, Puryn stepped in awkwardly, deliberately exposing himself. Orus, seeing his chance, took it, putting Puryn in a chokehold. As he won, Orus knew Puryn was conceding the fight purposefully, but was unsure why. Tapping furiously on Orus's arm, Puryn officially conceded the match. Orus released his grip, staggering back to Faylea, who immediately began applying pressure to her father's abdominal wounds.

Gunnir was not amused, storming off angrily while claiming that Orus cheated. Runnir smiled, having won the contest. Haya shook her head and watched as her plan unfolded.

Sitting, Orus reran the fight in his mind. He knew the Draj warrior was not being honest. Yet, despite his concerns, the Hodan people cheered in a crazed manner. Their King had won, and the food would be coming as a result. Orus motioned to his adversary, who looked no worse for wear aside from a fat lip and a black eye. Puryn approached him cautiously.

"You quit, Yslan," Orus whispered, as a matter of fact. Faylea's eyes widened, knowing it was true. "You let me win, but why?"

"You are an honorable man. You needed to win, to prove your strength to your people. We are an even match when you are healthy, Your Majesty, but that wound gives me an unfair advantage." Puryn smirked. "Perhaps when we are friends, we shall have a rematch in private and settle this properly?"

King Orus smiled. "You are wise beyond your years, young one." He shifted, sitting straight up, despite Faylea's protests. "I will take you up on that rematch, but for now, please, feed these people. I see a future where we are friends. I will work to convince my Lords of your worth as a warrior and your honor as a leader and man."

"I will send an Elfish healer if you will permit it," Puryn offered.

"If you wish, that would be greatly appreciated," the King replied weakly. He was sick and still fought like two regular men. Puryn called for the healers. The people stood and watched on as Puryn, the foe of the King, healed his wounds.

"Is it him?" some questioned quietly. "Is this Puryn, the one our prophets wrote about one-hundred years ago? Will peace finally be forged between Yslandeth and Hodan?" The murmur intensified. Puryn looked around at all of them in wonder.

One of the older Hodan women approached the Draj warrior and spoke to him. She was blind, robed in tattered rags, and was carrying a large leather-bound tome. Orus did not protest. Puryn assumed she was a mystic or oracle, and he was correct.

"Son of Yslan, hear my words!"

The people stopped cheering, listening to their holy woman.

"During Sana, the Dragon's child will be born unto Yslandeth. She will bear the uniter of the races, the peacemaker, and the leader who will show the way from death, oblivion, and darkness. By showing a true heart, a common man will assume the mantle, being chosen by the Goddess of the Elves and man. Her mantle will he keep. By her favor, will he wield justice and mercy. The forest will call him brother, and Yslan will call him

King. From nothing, he will come, and from nothingness, he will save us all. During the last day, he will stand upon the holy hill beneath the shadow of the mountains, beside the sacred forest. He will unite the people and resist the darkness. Fire will purge the enemy from our midst, and peace will reign for an age. Praise be unto the Goddess."

The old woman then took a vial of oil and drew a rune of protection on Puryn's forehead. Orus, in awe, smiled, because the Gods had seen fit to let him live to see this day.

Puryn stood confused, looking at the old woman, who smiled and laughed at his expression. She could not see it physically, but she could feel his discomfort with the whole incident. "Relax, my boy. Even when the truth is declared to you, you do not think highly of yourself. You are the true instrument of Haya's love. You are her sword of justice. You are a friend to all who possess honor and a terror to the coming darkness." The old woman left, praying quietly, using her staff and a young child as a guide back to an old mildewed tent as it began to rain.

Puryn declared loudly, "Your Majesty, I request permission to enter your Kingdom with a caravan of peace offerings. You have won them from me fairly, and I concede your well-fought victory."

Hodan cheered and congratulated their King with adulations. Orus smiled at Puryn. "I accept, under one condition. We will revisit our conversation privately, one day soon?"

Puryn smiled, extending his hand. "I accept this condition."

"Let them in! Guards control the crowds and distribute the goods equally to those in need. Save the seed, and allow the Elves to come South to assist in healing our fields." Orus looked at Puryn as he turned to go. "Will you drink with me, my new friend?" He produced a small cask of ale and poured two small cups. "To a new frontier, where no one can stand against us."

"To unity and peace, forever," Puryn responded. They both threw back their cups. Puryn bowed, and Orus saluted.

The caravans were unloaded, and the food was moved throughout Hodan. The people of Erynseere playfully taunted Puryn. They teased that he was finally defeated, but most conceded the realization that it took a battle-hardened Hodan King to do it. The Baron allowed this version of events to become the official story, but he and Orus knew the truth. They would settle things another day!

* * *

The Draj-Manot returned to his barony as a messenger from the castle arrived on horseback. Adasser was in labor, and Arla stood as the head midwife with several Elfish healers surrounding the Baroness. Puryn goaded the warhorse and lit off at a gallop toward home. The Draj did not relax their posture, but they did not provoke the Hodan.

On the Hodan side of the border, people were singing, drums played, and music filled the air. There was cheering and celebrations as far as the Draj could see. It was late afternoon, and the sun hung low on the horizon. A Draj Lieutenant watched as Hodan looked alive, and Empyr looked like a stone tomb on the horizon. He was glad to have been fortunate enough to be chosen to come to Erynseere with Puryn and his Lady.

The soldier thought to himself, *Puryn impressed everyone of importance and made peace without aggression. What a King this man would make!* Dismissing the thought, he prayed for King Swyk in repentance. For now, Puryn would best serve as the King's man, rather than the King himself. Haya saw it this way. Who was a common Draj to question her judgment?

Changes

Puryn arrived at his castle. The ladies were with Adasser, who, contrary to expectations, was not yelling as loudly as Puryn remembered human women yelling. At first, this concerned Puryn, but an Elfish midwife assured him that not only was Adasser Elfish, but she was also a Priestess who had things under control. The father-to-be had never thought about her as a Priestess, only his beloved.

The impatient husband decided to step out for fresh air while waiting on pins and needles. What he saw next took his breath away. The tree line now surrounded Castle Erynseere and its surrounding villages. The wooded barrier was thickening by the hour. Each tree leaned in toward the center of the clearing where the castle was located, as if it listened for its friend's call. Puryn looked in awe, knowing she had done it—they were her trees now. They waited for their Priestess, surrounding her in a protective ring while she was in need.

Inside, Adasser used her magic to dissipate the pain, aiding in the safe delivery of her first child. Arla made her comfortable by distractions, such as discussing possible names and future occupations for the child. The young Elfish mother appreciated her friend's distractions during labor. Finally, she cried out as the child passed from her body during birth. Puryn ran to the door with concern, seeing his father smoking his pipe.

"Stay out of there, my son!" he beckoned. "They are not finished. Soon. Soon. Sit by me, and let us talk about the future."

Puryn sat, but could not help looking at the door, while waiting impatiently for it to open.

The older man smiled sympathetically, saying, "My son, you will be a father very soon. Thanks to your efforts, the world this child will inherit appears to be on the road to eternal peace."

"It is not finished, Father. King Swyk must sign a proclamation and make the formal treaties first. All I did was feed women and children," Puryn dismissed nervously.

"I know Swyk. I have known him forever. He hates the Hodan, but a chance for peace … genuine peace … that is too good to pass up, my boy, and he gave you the authority to sue for it without admitting fault, which you executed perfectly. I do not see another option for the King. Yslan's people are tired, our forces are weary, the kingdom coffers are almost empty, and food remains a precious commodity on the Ert. It seems Erynseere and the lands of Athis run the food production for all of Yslandeth now."

"Athis. I often think of him now, Father. Do you think he is true or false? Is he setting me up for something evil, or is he truly reformed? I hope it is the latter, for if he betrays me after I forgave him for Elig, I will see his head on a spike, whether His Majesty approves or not." Puryn was deadly serious, and Durn knew Swyk would not challenge Puryn's claim of justice if he ever called in that marker.

"We shall see, my son. No one knows a man's heart, but Haya and that man himself," Durn sighed.

The door opened suddenly, and light entered the darkened waiting area where Puryn and his father sat. The younger father sprang to his feet and ran over to the midwife.

"She is fine, My Lord," the midwife said with a smile. "She is feeding your son as we speak." The midwife bowed and led Puryn to his wife and newborn son. Arla sat next to where Adasser lay and wiped the sweat from the Baroness's head.

"He is beautiful, my boy. Look at what you did!" Arla said, whispering with excitement.

The child was attached to his mother's breast, and Adasser was looking down at her new son, singing an Elfish lullaby, when she looked up to see her husband staring at them in shock.

Adasser spoke in a raspy voice, because she had been yelling at the end. "Come see our son, husband. He is beautiful." The new mother smiled. She was exhausted and just wished to sleep.

After the child had finished eating, a maiden took him. She cleaned him up, wrapping him in warm clothes and setting him in a bassinet beside the Baroness. Puryn drew close to his wife, who now slept. He stroked her black hair. Gently, he kissed her forehead and sat with her for a bit, but then his mother told him that he should let her rest.

"Goodnight, my love," Puryn said, stepping out of the room, but Adasser and his unnamed son were fast asleep.

Puryn walked out into the courtyard and staggered at what he beheld. The tree line was threefold thicker than a couple of hours ago, and even Adasser's pesky elms had joined the ring. To top it off, all of the trees were flowering at night and at the beginning of fall.

The townsfolk stared, gape-mouthed, pointing at the scene, wondering what the sign meant. Puryn knew. Her trees were celebrating her happiness and congratulating her on the birth of her son. Puryn smiled. Torith had arrived in Erynseere, and Adasser was a Priestess of the forest, whether she liked it or not.

* * *

A few days after these events had passed, the emissary from Erynseere reached the castle at Empyr. He was led by a guard to the war room, where King Swyk was poring over his maps and devising strategic responses to non-existent Hodan threats. The emissary waited for the King to acknowledge him and call him in.

"Yes, yes. Who are you?" the King demanded.

"I am Donick, of the Barony of Erynseere, Your Majesty. Baron Puryn and his Lady send greetings and well wishes." He bowed.

"Ah yes, Puryn's man. How goes the reconstruction?" the King asked absently, while looking at the pieces on his map.

"It is almost completed, Your Majesty. Baron Puryn has made contact with the Hodan to his South."

"Made contact! How many are dead? Did they invade? They invaded. That scum never stops!" the King paced.

"No, No! Your Majesty." The King looked at the herald with a puzzled expression. "He rode out to the field under a flag of truce and negotiated peace with the new King of Hodan."

"New King? Jabir is the King! He has been King for going on fifteen years!" Swyk looked at the herald with disdain. "How do you not know this?"

"Your Majesty, King Orus of Hodan defeated Jabir in mortal combat approximately twenty days ago. He showed Puryn Jabir's head in a box to prove it. Orus challenged his King, because Jabir's pride was killing Hodan, and the new ruler wanted to better the situation of his people. Therefore, Puryn and Orus made a tentative agreement of peace, and our Baron sent aid in the form of food, drink, and firewood to the people of Hodan. Many rejoiced. I genuinely think this man Orus is honorable."

"You know nothing of the Hodan. You are too young. You were not there." Swyk swatted the pieces from his map and pounded his fists on the table.

"Your Majesty, I only know that Puryn does what he thinks is best and Haya is with him. She manifested her glory on his person when he exhorted the people to donate goods. Five stood in opposition and sought to harm the baronial family. Lightning struck all five dead as they protested. It was terrifying."

Swyk turned to Donick with a look of concern on his face. "Haya? The Haya? The Goddess Haya interceded for Puryn at a meeting of the populace at his castle?"

"Your Majesty, there were more than five-hundred witnesses." Donick cleared his throat. "Except the five who perished. Even Lord Athis came down from his lands and offered material support. He is a Priest of Haya now, and he declared what we saw to be a true manifestation of Her Glory. I was a bit terrified to be in the presence of a Goddess."

Swyk weighed the story in his mind. It would have been nearly impossible to stage anything like this. The boy, from birth, was said to be a chosen warrior or priest. His wife, Queen Falda, went on about that nonstop when she was younger, before the separation. Swyk had never paid it any mind. He wrote it off as the ramblings of his beautiful wife, who dabbled in Elfish magic when she should have taken up needlepoint instead.

"Then, if all of this is true, and I believe it to be, the Goddess is setting a mandate for peace among the armies of the Ert. I never thought I would live to see Hodan and Yslandeth on the same side of a battlefield, or as trade partners." Swyk glanced at the old familiar map table and thought, *things will definitely be different from now on.*

Donick pulled a scroll from his satchel and handed it to the King. "We have written the conditions of peace down upon this scroll, My King. With your signature, it is binding. The Elves and Dwarves are elated to have Hodan on their side, vice against them. We all await your decision." The King looked at his trusted General Ontak, who sat at the end of the table, quietly listening as the story was told.

"What do you think of this, Ontak?" Swyk waved the scroll toward the Knight.

Ontak stood. "Hodan as a friend? Yes, we will keep our friends in plain sight and our enemies afraid. If what Master Donick says is true, this is a dream alliance. Peace and ultimate strength. What downside could there be? Edenyag will become autonomous, but was never truly tied to us. Cinnog is a useless ally and never comes when called, but they expect us to run to their aid whenever they bid us." Ontak sneered. "I say let them fend for themselves. But honestly, if Yslan, Hodan, Dornat al Ar, *and* Torith align under a common banner, who can stand against us? Cinnog and Edenyag, as well as those snakes in Sudenyag, would have to fight among themselves or risk annihilation. If Hodan reneges on its pledges, things simply revert to the old days. Take the chance, My King. I would do it if it were my choice."

"Very well! That settles my mind. We will have peace." Swyk called for a quill and wax for his signet. He signed the treaty and made Hodan his ally. This was the first time in history that both Yslandeth and Hodan stood together against the Ert. Swyk was uneasy. This would take some getting used to. He rolled up his maps and put away his carved figures.

"Have the tacticians draw up a new map—one that takes the new political landscape into account," the King commanded his scribes. They acknowledged and went off to make it so.

***

As expected, Edenyag sent a scroll of protest to Yslandeth, as did Cinnog. Both withdrew from their tenuous alliances with Yslan. The Dwarves secretly confided in the Elves of their concern for the addition of Hodan to the coalition. Still, they stayed put, for neither kingdom had the armies to defend their lands. Sudenyag went into a panic.

The Suden King, Yanat il Arnar, the Extravagant, called an emergency meeting of his council and Generals. Suden had also lost most of its armies and had turned its back on Hodan as an ally. Yslandeth had been keeping Hodan from looking South, and Swyk's rule kept Cinnog and Edenyag from looking for retribution for past war incursions. Yanat was concerned that the balance of power had been significantly altered. Suddenly, Sudenyag, with its lucrative trade routes, was left to fend for itself against two smaller rivals and one extremely large one.

Ironically, Edenyag's significant, yet unproven forces worried Yanat more than Cinnog, but the Suden King knew Yslandeth was civilized and would not allow an invasion of Sudenyag without provocation. Yanat was prepared to soothe the egos of the northern leadership and play compliant until such a time as he could assert his own claims to power. Now was not the time.

The Suden council was formed in the lavish throne room of Yanat il Arnar and his Queen Kilma, the loved. Several Generals, advisors, and ministers sat around an exceptionally long imported wooden table.

"Gentlemen, we have a serious problem developing to the North. The unexpected alliance of Hodan and Yslan leaves us exposed on all fronts. Edenyag has conscripted thousands, and Cinnog still possesses some might. Hodan has been leashed for the moment by Yslan, but that dog will bite the hand that feeds it in time, causing things to revert to their former condition. We must survive the current turmoil at all costs." The King paced to the back of the room and opened the door. Several hooded individuals, dressed in black, entered. "Our Offlander trading partners have seen this turn of events coming. Due to our extremely profitable arrangements, we have offered an alliance to stay any advance of our adversaries." The room murmured.

The hooded figures removed their head coverings to reveal a woman and two creatures who had not been seen in Sudenyag in hundreds of years. A Goblin and an Orc warrior stood behind the woman who spoke. She had many rings and chains that pierced her ears and nose. Some went places beneath her shirt. She appeared to be human, but her skin was darkened with markings and runes. The room gasped at the sight of them.

"You gasp, but you do not reject our payments. Do not judge us on the tales of others. We only seek to enrich our people and coexist in peace, as do you," the woman said with venom. She moved gracefully, almost floating, to where the King sat. "We have seen your threats, and they are real. We offer a solution that benefits all concerned."

"Indeed," the King chuckled. "The allies to the North do not know of this agreement. They will not know of its implementation, until it is too late to intervene. Yslandeth and its holier-than-thou attitude …" The King threw a knife, sticking it in the wall across from him, startling a servant. "I shall remind them where their borders lie, with the help of my new friends. Does anyone have anything they wish to add?"

The council knew better than to contradict the King. He was an unstable and unscrupulous man. He would have anyone killed in their sleep for looking at him crossly. "Then we are in agreement. Scribes, draw up the necessary treaties and documents. Servants, show our guests a good time!" The King nodded to the female emissary and walked out of the room.

The lady said something in an unknown guttural language to the Orc and Goblin.

Haeldrun smiled at the ease with which he turned Yanat's heart to the darkness. Yanat was a selfish fool and that, Haeldrun could work with. Quietly, without Haya's notice, Haeldrun would execute his plans to kill the life and light his wife so dearly loved above her own spouse. He would have his revenge upon the light, and Sudenyag would bring the darkness. The Underworld and all of its minions rejoiced in the catacombs. Haeldrun turned to his Offlander worshippers, coaxing them to action.

"This fool. I despise him. Our scouts have tallied that maybe twenty-five-thousand to forty-thousand total troops remain on this entire continent?" She laughed. "We will crush these fools and take these lands for our profit." The three Offlanders laughed. Those of the council who remained in the room were uncomfortable, feeling that they had missed the joke.

✳ ✳ ✳

The treaty was signed by Yanat. Shortly thereafter, the dark lady boarded a great black ship and handed the scroll to its captain. The ship sailed away, while another, which sat in the mist offshore, went undetected as it entered the harbor and disembarked more than one-thousand Offlander warriors. About ten-percent of them were Goblins and Orcs, and the rest were marked and runed men, much like the dark lady had been. The Suden people openly walked the streets, pointing and staring, wondering who these new soldiers were. Suden roads quickly cleared as people took their children indoors, unsure of what was happening.

✳ ✳ ✳

Upon the mountains of Oron Falmarindi, Glorin, King of the Elves, was happily surveying his new fortress. Three years ago, he had commissioned the Dwarves to create his underground stone fortress, which was built within the cliffsides of the mountainous plateau. The Dwarves agreed to do it. In return, the Elves continued to help their partners prosper with farming and other botanical sciences, including medicine and healing. The trade helped both sides.

"Bogrol, this fortress is amazing." Glorin smiled, shaking his Dwarfish counterpart's hand. "I hope we never have to use it. Maybe Swyk's new alliance will hold?"

Bogrol replied, "I do not pretend to know the future, but if Orus is anything like Jabir was, we are not long for this peace. Hodan can prove to be a fickle friend."

"Still, Puryn likes the man, and I trust his judgment. So far, it has led us to peace and prosperity, once again. I only wonder what Sudenyag is up to. My scouts have not returned from their observation posts. I fear they may have been compromised." Glorin frowned. He knew they were dead.

"Do not despair, my friend," Bogrol encouraged. "We have our defenses, and we have Yslan, and Yslan has Puryn. Our odds are good! Still, I hear reports of constant shipping traffic in and out of Sudenyag. They are most definitely up to no good … those snakes."

"I agree. Sudenyag is a pestilence, but I see no way to address it directly. Hopefully, the solution is found before it is too late." Glorin bid Bogrol farewell and then boarded his carriage, returning to Torith.

There, the Elfish King met a messenger, who told him he was a grandfather. Glorin rushed to tell his wife that her baby was a mother. Hansu shed tears of joy and resolved to visit, as soon as she had word that Adasser was up and about. She did not want to intrude on the new family's space. There was time to fret over the child, and she would enjoy all of it.

* * *

A week passed. Puryn became restless, waiting for Donick to return from Empyr. He was about to send a rescue team when the messenger was seen entering the villages below the forest ring. Donick could not believe how the forest had changed in a little over a week. It was now a dense ring, five miles in diameter, surrounding Castle Erynseere and its nearby villages. The trees were beautifully flowered. As Donick approached the end of the road, the trees parted and allowed him to pass, forming a path for him to traverse on horseback. The master was shocked. Puryn watched and waited on the other side of the trees.

"Come on, Donick, move it, before they change their minds!" Puryn laughed, as Donick trotted quickly through the wall of trees, which promptly closed behind him.

"What in the Ert is going on with these trees!?" The master was impressed, but unnerved.

"Nothing to worry about, my friend. This is what Adasser does on her outings. She befriends the trees, and they have formed a bond. Now they are her family." Puryn smiled and said something in Elfish to the trees. Leaves rustled, and a flower was dropped at Puryn's feet. He picked it up. "I will give it to her." The trees swayed as if a strong wind blew, but the air was still. Donick moved toward the castle. He was not sure what to make of all of this.

In the castle, Adasser was nursing the baby and walking around inside the feast hall. Donick entered the hall, turning and immediately averting his eyes.

"Thank you, Donick. I will cover with a blanket for your modesty."

"Thank you, Your Excellency." Donick turned, clearing his throat. "I return from Yslan with wonderful news. The King has accepted the peace and has signed the agreement and treaties."

"Outstanding!" Puryn exclaimed, frightening his infant son. The child began to wail. Adasser stared at Puryn with an annoyed face.

"Sorry, my love," he whispered.

Adasser went back to feeding the child, and he soon quieted.

"I will travel to the South and deliver this news personally," Donick replied.

"You should be here with your family."

"Thank you, my dear friend. Send Orus our regards. Tell him to visit when he wishes. He is always welcome in my home." Puryn was serious.

"I will tell him, Your Excellency. Er, Adasser, My Baroness?" Donick turned to Adasser.

"Yes, Master Donick, what is it?" Adasser asked, adjusting the wiggling little boy.

"Is there some manner of communication you have with the trees that you could inform them not to crush me when I leave or return?"

Adasser thought Donick was joking, but then realized the serious nature of his request. Then she laughed, and the baby cried again. "Shh, Shh. It is all right, boy, be silent." She looked to the skies, pleading for a break, and then remembered Donick's request. She smirked. "Are they being naughty? Master Donick, the trees will not harm any of our people. I have informed them that those of Erynseere are to be allowed to pass within and through them without molestation. As a forest, they know each and every one of us. You are one of us. You are safe. Not so for anyone else trying to sneak around the trees."

"Well, that is a relief. Did you see their foliage? It is wonderful!" Donick exclaimed and then cringed, remembering the sleeping child. Adasser looked at the boy with wide eyes, then sighed in relief. He was still asleep.

"Yes, it is wonderful! They are celebrating the birth of our new son, who I have named Ilari, son of Puryn. Ilari means 'cheerful,' for he brings us joy." Adasser kissed his tiny head. He whimpered in his sleep.

"Ilari. He will be a good man if he learns from the likes of you both!" Donick declared. "I must go and find King Orus. Peace depends upon it. Congratulations again, My Baron and Baroness."

* * *

The couple thanked their friend. Donick left, riding South, taking a stick with a white flag upon it, but found it was unnecessary. The people of Hodan cheered at the banner of Puryn when it appeared at the border, requesting an audience with King Orus.

The King granted the audience and was informed of King Swyk's decision to embark on a new alliance. Peace was official. Orus shouted out a battle cry of elation! Donick swallowed hard, expecting the end had come, but quickly realized by the man picking him up with a bear hug that this was an expression of happiness, not anger. The people responded to their King in kind. Then another serious party broke out.

Donick laid out the plan for aid with King Orus. The master then set up a schedule for teams to come and assist in reestablishing the farms. Dwarves were initially shunned, but eventually, the old wounds healed, old bonds were rekindled, and friendships renewed. So Yslan, Dornat al Ar, and Hodan set to rebuild Hodan's Kingdom. Finally, the people of every nation had hope, and all seemed right on the Ert. However, as with all things, nothing is ever as it seems.

Haya was pleased and blessed the new alliance. Peace had arrived. However, the Conflict was not pleased.

The Lull and the Forest Queen

Two years passed, and many things changed concerning the political landscape. In the beginning, the alliance between Yslandeth and Hodan brought both cheers and boos, depending upon who you asked. Still, over time, the populace of Yslandeth warmed up to the idea of peace that also provided a solid buffer to Sudenyag.

Hodan kept its part of the agreement, immediately withdrawing their forces from the borders, as the ink literally dried on the treaty. King Swyk was genuinely surprised at the ease with which all of this occurred. Even Swyk, with his well-known disdain for the Hodan, had become a vocal proponent of change and reconciliation. The Elves and Dwarves kept their opinions to themselves, letting the human nations determine their own way. Alliances remained intact, but Elves and Dwarves stayed as far from Hodan as they could, unless called there by an official function requiring their attendance.

King Orus was quite fond of Puryn and made it well-known that an attack on Erynseere was an attack on Hodan. Puryn and Orus had created a rivalry between Hodan and Erynseere. Every six or eight months, the two men would drink too much mead or ale and challenge each other to a rematch.

At last count, the decision was best three out of five, with Orus holding the advantage. Puryn disputed the count, but only in a joking manner. The two had grown quite close, and the people of Hodan and Erynseere traveled freely, becoming a close-knit community. Of course, some on either side still held their wartime grievances, but they knew better than to stir trouble where none was to be found.

Hodan recovered over the next couple of years, their fields producing more than ever before. Births were on the rise, as people no longer feared to bring children into the world. The warrior nation rebuilt its homes and roads. The smaller military was retooled and trained, but this time, all alliance members wore the new standard of the Northern Alliance.

Puryn and Orus conducted war drills between the Draj-Erynseere and Hodan Elites. The battles were fought with non-lethal weapons, but each side kept plenty of healers on hand, because neither side played nice when combat was involved. No one died during these practice sessions, but the injured, at times, numbered in the hundreds.

Other Commanders around Yslandeth laughed at the pair, shaking their heads. They were oblivious to the fact that Puryn and Orus were readying for the inevitable, which many who were paying attention felt may come out of Sudenyag. By training together, the armies became a well-oiled machine. Both leaders grew to know the other's thoughts and tactics before they thought of them. This made the pair a dangerous force to be reckoned with.

Athis made his way down, from time to time, to partake in the war games and to reaffirm his devotion to the alliance. His units were mainly cavalry and spearmen. Although the cavalry was not as well trained as those of Orus and Puryn, Athis wished to be a useful ally, but he made it known many times that he had lost the taste for killing long ago.

* * *

Commerce was booming, and food production was staggering, so much so that no one wanted for sustenance in any kingdom. This prosperity led to the common belief that lasting peace could be real. People thought of raising families, tending their farms, and less of war.

Puryn and Adasser were no exception. After the birth of their first son, Ilari, Puryn wasted no time in impregnating his young wife again, and this time she had twins. Ilari was barely walking when Adasser bore Puryn another son, who she named Altwidus, meaning "Old Forest," and a daughter, Elpis, meaning "Hope."

Adasser had her hands full with three children. She took them on her daily journeys to the trees. Ilari was walking, but she would take a small wagon to pull the children in most times. The children would ride near the trees, watching their mother talk with nature. Ilari always laughed when his mother made the trees do things by speaking to them. Almost daily, they would picnic near the edge of the trees, lying in their shade. Adasser would lay blankets down and let the children crawl around, while Ilari would look for butterflies or other bugs.

One such day, while sitting beneath a tree, Adasser set the usual picnic lunch out. Her younger children played on the blanket. Altwidus and Elpis were scarcely six months old and barely crawling. Adasser looked up at the sun and was concerned that the children would be burned, because they were so fair-skinned. She looked over at Ilari, who played twenty feet away in an open field by the trees. He was digging in the dirt. The young mother looked up at the elm above her and asked it to shield the children. The tree rustled and rearranged its leaves, providing shade as requested.

Adasser smiled, but suddenly her attention was drawn to Ilari, who was now talking to something in the woods. At first, she thought nothing of it, believing it to be just the boy playing. Then distinctly, she heard a low-throated growl. Ilari was laughing, not realizing the danger he was in, but Adasser was seized with immediate terror.

"Ilari! Get over here, now!" pleaded Adasser in Elfish, but Ilari was pointing at the growling beast, smiling innocently. Frozen in fear, Adasser felt the air cool around her. Her vision blurred, except for her focus on a silver wolf, stalking her son on the forest's edge. The young mother uttered something in a tongue she had never spoken before. It was a whisper. No one heard it but her.

Sensing its Queen's sudden terror, the forest responded to her call. Ilari had turned back to his digging as the wolf moved closer. Vines shot out of the thicket and wrapped around the wolf's throat. It yelped and struggled to break free, but the vines were too strong. More wrapped around the stalker by the second. Suddenly, as sure as if they were spears, branches thrust into the sides of the immobilized canine. There was a sharp yelp, then silence. Ilari looked up puzzled, but was none the wiser about what had happened. Ilari played as the wolf died. He simply waved to his mother, and said, "Mama!"

Adasser was shaken, and she bolted to her son, grabbing the others as she went. He was unharmed, but she scanned the area intently, because she knew wolves often hunted in packs. The trees rustled as if searching, but no threats were found. The young mother hugged her oldest son, kissing his face furiously. She laughed as he wiped his face, wet with her kisses and tears. He kept saying, "Mama! No! Mama! No!"

Adasser loaded the wagon quickly and left the area. No one had seen what happened. She was unsure if she had made the event occur, or if the trees had acted autonomously. Keeping the incident to herself, she made her way quickly back to the castle.

The incident with the wolf made Adasser think about what was happening to her. After the birth of Ilari, as was the way with Elfish women, her magical gift manifested and supposedly magnified tenfold. In Adasser's case, she figured it had magnified one-hundred-fold, and she was becoming concerned.

She did not want to accidentally use her power and end up killing someone without cause. She called for a servant and asked that they notify Puryn that she needed to speak with him. The servant bowed and found the Baron in the courtyard, looking at the formidable ring of trees encircling his home and the villages. His wife was putting the three young ones down for a nap after her eventful lunch outing when the Baron arrived in the sitting room. Adasser looked a bit shaken.

Puryn rose, hugging her, and asked, "What's wrong?"

"Please sit down, husband. I have something I need to tell you."

The Baron was concerned. "Is there someone I need to talk to, my love?"

Puryn looked at his wife with a dire face. "I will go 'talk' to them immediately if …"

Adasser cut in. "I killed a wolf. I mean, I think I killed a wolf. But, no, I'm sure I was the cause of the wolf's death." Adasser was looking at the ceiling and taking a deep breath.

"What are you saying, my love? Did you shoot it with an arrow? I did not think there were any wolves South of the northern plains or mountains." The worried husband looked at his trembling wife. Her hands were shaking.

"Puryn, do not be angry. I went to the edge of the forest to sit in the shade with the children. I set out the picnic, as usual, and Ilari wandered off ten, maybe twenty feet. He sat digging and playing, as always, looking for bugs." She brushed her hair from her face. Puryn could see her eyes were red from crying. She had her arms crossed and was hugging herself.

"Go on, my love, I will not be angry with you. You are a wonderful mother. Why would I be angered?" Puryn held her hand, and she cracked a small smile while looking at her shoes. "Please look at me, my love. No one is dead. We are all fine. You did nothing wrong!"

"But he could have died! That damned wolf appeared from nowhere, and I was too far from the boy to react. I was guarding the other two, frozen in fear for my oldest son. The next things are foggy, and I only partially know what truly happened and what did not." The Baroness was becoming frantic.

Puryn could see the guilt on her face. "It wasn't your fault, my love. You are a good mother. But, how did YOU kill the wolf? I do not understand what you are telling me." Puryn looked at his Lady reassuringly, wondering if she needed some time to rest.

"All I can recall was the terror I felt when I heard its growl … his little face was oblivious to the danger. He kept digging and flinging the dirt." She wiped her eyes. "Then I don't remember anything, but focusing on the wolf. I uttered some words."

"What words?" Puryn asked.

"I don't know what they were, but all I felt was fear and anger. I was focused, and then *they* acted." Adasser looked at a branch peeking in a leaf or two through an open window. Adasser wondered if it was listening like a child, wondering if it was in trouble. She could not help but giggle. Then she spoke to it in Elfish, and it moved out of the window. Puryn looked over his shoulder, not seeing the branch before it left. He looked at Adasser with concern.

"I am not mad, husband! The trees, the trees acted! They wrapped it in vines and then stabbed it to death with their thicker branches. It yelped then lay on the ground dying for a few minutes. I watched the light leave its eyes. But I was not sorry. It wished to harm our baby. Better it than he." Adasser's look startled her listening husband, because her eyes burned red as coals as she remembered. Her whole eye turned red as forge coal, not just around the eyes. Then it immediately subsided. "I have never seen a tree kill before."

"Nor I," Puryn responded, thinking. "Please do not be offended, but Elf women get special powers after having a child, correct?"

Adasser raised an eyebrow, wondering where he was going with this and unsure if she liked his tone.

"You have had three. Do you think you got three times the usual ration?"

Adasser thought about it. "I don't think it works that way, husband, but I do not know for sure. Stranger things have happened. Perhaps we should travel to Torith and visit. I can speak with the Holy Mother and find out what is going on. Oh, and another thing, the ring gets thicker by the day, and I do not know where the trees are coming from. I have all of Erynseere's assembled." She looked at Puryn. "How do they hear me?"

"Those are good questions. We will leave in the morning, my love. Perhaps you should reassure your trees that they are not in trouble. I fear they may wonder why you are so upset, my dearest," Puryn suggested.

"Good idea, my love. I will do that immediately, and then I will go to bed and rest. The twins will be hungry in a few hours. Perhaps we can take the carriage, and I can sleep on the way?" Adasser batted her eyes playfully at her husband.

"Of course, My Lady, we shall ride in the carriage." Puryn kissed her forehead.

Adasser sipped some wine and then gulped down the entire tankard. She rose and walked outside, tentatively, staring at the forest surrounding her. It was thicker than ever. She shook her head and thought, *Where in the Underworld are they coming from, and how?*

Adasser approached the most prominent tree. It shuddered, and she felt as if it was recoiling in fear. Calmly, she spoke in Elfish. "What is wrong, my friends? I am not angry with you in the least, nor did you hurt me in any way. Much the opposite, my heroes. You saved my child, and for that, I am eternally grateful!" The tree's leaves rustled, as if exhaling in relief. "I only ask that you respect all life. Please do not kill, unless it is the last option." The forest swayed in unison, leaves rustling melodically, as if a strong wind blew where the air was still. They were relieved. She could feel it. "I love you all. May you live forever, my forest."

Adasser's tears returned as she hugged the elm tree before her. Eventually, she let go and touched its trunk after kissing her hand. She walked back inside smiling. They would protect her. They loved her, and she loved them. She had three half-Elfish children, but thousands of others. Finally, Adasser went to bed and slept well.

* * *

The first hour of the morning came early. Adasser was up and had the children packed and ready. They were waiting on Puryn. He was in the training hall, performing his morning routine. First, he did his monastery forms, then his Draj martial arts, and finally worked the pell for a bit. This routine helped to keep his demons at bay, so the Baroness said nothing. Besides, it was still quite early when Puryn finished up. He washed and dressed in a nice tunic.

They both wore Yslandeth baronial coronets, but carried the Elfish crowns in a chest on the back of the carriage. The pair would change into them when they arrived at Torith. The ride took ten days. The Baron and Baroness had their close attendants and a couple of guards, but the peace had made guards a bit of overkill for those days. Puryn did not care. He and four Draj were enough to quell any highwaymen. However, despite the precautions, there were no incidents along the way.

Upon arriving in Torith, Puryn and Adasser immediately noticed that the ring of trees had thinned significantly.

"What is wrong with Torith?" Puryn asked, squinting as if he might not be seeing correctly.

"I do not know. Wait! Oh my Gods!" Adasser's eyes were wide.

Puryn interrupted. "Oh, NO! Do you think they came to Erynseere!?"

"Maybe," the Baroness replied sheepishly. "I didn't tell them to! Father is going to kill me!"

"It's not your fault. We need to talk to the Holy Mother, and soon!" her husband replied, putting his hands on top of his head. Ilari was sitting on Adasser's lap and copying him. The boy began laughing, and then his father laughed also. Adasser shook her head, smiling, but was unsure what was going on.

After entering Torith and visiting with her parents, Princess Adasser and Prince Puryn made for the temple. The Holy Mother was praying and talking to the trees when they arrived.

"I have words for Adasser alone, young Prince. I mean no offense, but I wish to converse with her privately." The Holy Mother looked older and frailer than the Prince remembered.

"I will go by Master Gulsbane's house, my love. Meet me at the palace around evening meal?" Puryn asked.

"If I do not show up, I will be tied up here, husband. So please do not be offended," Adasser replied.

"Never. I will simply catch up with Gulsbane and your parents. I hope you get your answers." He kissed her and bowed to the Holy Mother. The Holy Mother bowed in return. Then, the Prince departed in the direction of his old master's house.

"Come in, My Princess. I think I know what brings you to the temple today." The old woman grinned, as if she already knew the answer to a novice's question.

Haya had a look of amused satisfaction on her face. The prodigal daughter had returned to her.

"Yes, Mother, I have serious questions about what is happening to me and my forest." She looked at the trees around her. She felt as if they were listening and watching her intently. She was right, and she suddenly felt uncomfortable in her old home.

"Go on, girl," the old woman prodded.

Haya listened intently, amused at the situation that unfolded before her.

"My forest thickens beyond the count of our trees. I did not know from whence they came, but upon reaching Torith and seeing the ring..." Adasser trailed off. "What have I done?"

"You have no control over what trees will answer your call, young lady," the old woman answered. "You rejected training as a Priestess. Your gifts are strong, but you do not know the full potential they possess."

"Mother, I spent over a year making friends with my local thickets and copses. I went to the lone clumps of trees and spoke to them as well. Eventually, they followed me to Erynseere and encircled my castle. Then, Ilari was born, and they became VERY attentive." Adasser chose her words wisely.

"Attentive." The old woman snorted, as if she knew Adasser was understating the situation. "You are saying they listen to you constantly now, don't they? As if they hang on your every word?" The old woman looked at Princess as sarcasm dripped from her lips.

Haya smirked.

"Yes, exactly," Adasser said. She cleared her throat and continued, thinking of how to phrase the statement, but instead, the Princess decided to just blurt it out. "My child was in danger, and I panicked. The forest killed a wolf without my conscious order, but I am not sure if I did anything to command it."

"How are you not sure?" the Priestess replied. "Did you tell them to do it or not?"

"I am not sure." Adasser related the events of her focus on the wolf and the unknown words she spoke.

The old woman was gravely concerned. All of the jovial banter drained from her countenance. She became deadly serious. "You spoke power words without knowing them?"

Haya stood silently beside a statue of her Elfish representation.

The old woman looked at the statue of Haya, asking, "Do you realize what you are doing, My Goddess?" Then she turned, as if she realized her folly. "You are a Goddess, of course you do!" The old woman sighed. "Sit down, Adasser." She pointed to a padded blue velvet chair. Adasser sat quietly, looking at the Holy Mother with a worried face.

Haya was laughing at both of them.

"Child, when you were young, did I not tell you that you were the Priestess of the Wood? Did I not plead with you to train with me and become my successor?" The Mother was irritated with the memory. "But no! You pursued folly and boys!"

Adasser interjected, "But …"

"No buts, young Lady! I told you that your gift was special, but you would not have any of it!" She bent over, eye to eye with Adasser, scolding her. "A Priestess never marries! She trains her gift, and when the first tree becomes her follower, her magic is released, as if she was its mother. But you!" The Mother stood up quickly, startling the edgy Adasser. The Priestess threw her hands up in the air, cursing, then asking for forgiveness.

Haya, amused, forgave her Priestess, waiting for her to continue.

"You. You married, and not even an Elf—you married a human!" the old woman lamented.

"I cannot help who I love, Mother! That is not fair!" Adasser retorted angrily.

"Yes, but logic and discipline dictate that you must make the hard decisions. But, alas, it is too late for that now." The Priestess looked at the statue of Haya, shaking her head. "If I only knew what Haya had planned. But then I would be the Goddess, now, wouldn't I? Suffice it to say, you changed the dynamic of the Priesthood."

Haya agreed, thinking, "For the better, My Priestess."

"But I am not a Priestess, Mother," Adasser retorted, confused.

"The trees do not care, Adasser. I fade, and they look for a new Mother among the Elves. There is none such as you! You would have been a perfect successor, but now you are 'the one,' perfect or flawed."

Adasser's face became pale. "I am not a Priestess."

"I am not a Priestess … I am not a Priestess," the old woman mocked in a childish tone. "Repeat that until the Underworld collapses, but it doesn't matter. You are, and I will explain now what is happening to you and to our forests."

Adasser sat up with a concerned look on her face. The old woman pulled out an ancient tome and opened it to a marked page. She read, explaining passages to Adasser, which affirmed what she was telling her. "I am not making this up or playing 'I told you, so,' Princess, but 'I told you so'!" The old woman grinned. She was missing teeth.

Adasser pursed her lips and crossed her arms. "What is going on?"

"You married and had children, causing your magic to manifest differently. Trees will not cause a mother's maternal instinct. A child will. Three … well, wow. Mothers will kill to protect their children. Trees do not evoke such emotion. So, you have three children and a very protective streak. You started out simply talking to the trees; now your voice is their beacon, due to your children. The children made your gift stronger and, in some ways, aggressive. Hence, the wolf's demise. The trees consider you their Queen."

Adasser stood, and her head cocked to the left. "Their Queen? I am no one's Queen, Mother! Of what do you speak?"

"I do not know why they consider you their Queen. Ask them, but rest assured that anyone who threatens their Queen, or anyone she loves or cares for, will incur the wrath of the forests. All of them." The Priestess closed the book for emphasis and handed it to Adasser. "Read it. Heed it. Learn it, because I fade now, and you are gaining strength. Whether you want it or not, you will be the High Mother."

Adasser gasped. She looked at the book, caressing the rune-covered case. She didn't know if she was High Priestess material.

"Do not doubt yourself, Priestess," the old woman chuckled. "Learn quickly, though! And be careful and respectful with my children. They love the Elves, too much, I fear, for their own good."

"Mother, what of Torith?" Adasser looked out of the window at the thinning trees. "If you return, they will also. If not, Erynseere will become the new Torith," the old woman said plainly. "It will take some time, probably fifty or so years, for the full transition. I may be in Aeternum by then. Will you preside from Yslandeth or come home?"

"I will stay with my husband until the end, Mother. After that, I do not know." Adasser was suddenly saddened, realizing that in fifty years, she would probably have no husband to stand by. She shook it off and closed her eyes, focusing on the conversation at hand.

"Remember, child … they follow your lead. You must control your emotions or let them know to look for a cue to act. Perhaps a power word or command word. Pick something that cannot be mistaken. I did that when this happened to me, but I did not possess the aggressive power you do."

"How do they know to come? Who tells them?" Adasser asked.

"The forest communicates by its roots. All plants are connected to the soil. You are heralded by proxy to all of nature. But, quite frankly, your power may not stop at trees. I do not know where your limits lie. I pray you are careful and respect this new power, young Lady. You can destroy entire cities with it." The old woman patted Adasser on her shoulder and guided her to the door. "He is waiting for you. Love is never bad, my young replacement. Be sure you preserve the trees, as well as your children. For make no mistake, the trees are also your children."

* * *

Adasser left with the book in her hand. She walked her familiar streets. Some folks waved and called out, bowing to the Princess they knew and loved. She smiled, strolling down memory lane, ending up at the palace. The guards saluted and allowed her to pass without blinking. She walked to where she heard laughing and music. Her father, mother, and Puryn were sipping mead and playing with the babies. Grandmother and grandfather were pinching cheeks and spoiling the children rotten.

Puryn smiled as he saw Adasser. "So? What did the Holy Mother say?"

Adasser smiled and hugged her father and mother. "Well, she said I have a special gift and gave me this book to read about it. She said I needed to work out what my limits are and that the trees are becoming part of our family. Part of my increasing power is the result of having children."

"Well, that is normal, I hear," Puryn said, hanging Ilari upside down by his feet. The boy laughed hysterically. Adasser glared at her husband, so Puryn put him down gingerly.

"What about the tree loss, Adasser?" Glorin looked at her knowingly. She was already found out.

"Yes, Father. For some Gods-forsaken reason, they are coming to me without me calling them! I am so sorry! I wish I could give them back, but she says they will follow me. I cannot leave my lands right now." The young Priestess frowned.

"It is well, my child. Do not fret. I will miss them, though. Let me have some, would you!?" he smirked and then laughed. "Our brothers, the Dwarves, have carved out a fortress at Oron Falmarindi for us, so the loss of the trees, however sad, is not a tactical issue. We will plant more. Stop poaching my trees, young Lady." He messed up her hair, and she laughed, hugging him.

"Oh, Da, I missed you so much!" Adasser said gleefully. "And you also, Mother!" They hugged as a trio, and Puryn remembered when he proposed, and they had done the same thing. He smiled quietly and kissed Elpis on her little forehead as she grabbed at his chin hairs. Life was good. He wanted it to stay that way. He would support his reluctant Priestess.

After the children were asleep, grandmother and grandfather went to bed in the same room, watching the young ones and allowing the parents a moment of privacy. Puryn walked in the moonlight with his Princess once again. The Prince walked to the well where they once hid their love from his Lady's father. He hugged his Lady close and kissed the top of her head.

She nuzzled in close, putting her head on his chest. He was a large man now, not a skinny boy, and she felt safe and loved.

"I often cursed my luck and wondered if Haya truly cared a lick about me when I first got here. Then, I met my master, saw the Elves for the first time, and learned their ways. I thought that was enough, until I saw you." Puryn looked at his wife earnestly. "You confirmed that Haya loves me. When she gave you to me, I realized that all my suffering was payment for a chance to be your man. Now, you bear me beautiful children, and I find out that you are a chosen Priestess of your own people. This honor is against your will?" Puryn chuckled softly. "And you dared once to say that you do not deserve me?" He raised her face to his and kissed her. "We are where the Goddess wants us. We know not what the fate we share is, nor of the affairs of Gods, but I know that I am here now with you, and I love you more each day. You are the perfect wife and friend, a perfect mother, and a trusted ally in my life. I would be nothing without you."

Haya rejoiced in their display of love. She was delighted with her choice of Champion and Priestess. Their relationship was all the things she had always wished her own to be. The Goddess was saddened by her failure with Haeldrun, but encouraged for the future, leaving the two with a blessing before returning to Aeternum, where her two boys were disgusted with all of the kissing. Aluia was tearing up with emotion.

Adasser smiled. "You are too kind, my love, but I know you were this man before me and would be him, with or without me. You are the chosen Champion of Haya. I know it. I fear terrible things await us, husband, for with powers such as these come tests and trials. I will be ready for my part, as I know you are always ready. We must endure for the sake of our children, the people, and our forests. I love you."

They walked back to the castle and slept. The family remained in Torith, returning to Erynseere at the week's end, to the protests of Queen Hansu. Adasser promised they would return soon. As she left Torith, she asked the carriage rider to stop at the forest ring.

The Priestess walked to the most significant, oldest tree and spoke. "Old one, ancient friend, please hear my plea. I realize you all travel to Erynseere to be with me, and I am honored, but Torith needs its trees, and I beg of you not to leave my family. You have stood for many thousands of years as protectors of the Elves. Please continue. I promise to visit you here if you hear my words. Torith is loved by all Elves; it would be selfish of me to steal all of you for my forest! Perhaps, you can trade off on occasion between the two rings? For if you can move to Erynseere, you can surely come back to Torith! That is the answer! Visit me and return here to my people. That is my decision. Please honor it." Adasser hugged the tree and smiled. A solution had been found. The trees swayed as if a strong wind blew once again, acknowledging Adasser's command.

The Holy Mother smiled, witnessing the swaying of the ancient trees. "She doesn't know it yet, Haya, but her husband will not be the only one sung of in lore when your plans are achieved. I know something is afoot, My Goddess. That girl is going to shake things up around here!" The old woman cackled and poured a drink, leaving one on the altar for Haya. It instantly dissipated. She smiled and refilled the cup. "It seems we all need a bit of wine today, My Goddess. Thank you for your blessings."

The old woman lit some incense and sat on a mat meditating. She was tired, and her time was getting short. Soon, she would drink wine with Haya in Aeternum, but now was not that time. So she meditated peacefully, knowing the Gods had chosen for her a powerful replacement.

II

Part Two

The Rebuttal of the Underlord
"Look at how a single candle can both defy and define the
darkness."
—Anne Frank

The Offlander Threat

From the beginning, Haeldrun reviled the light and held great animosity toward the family he abandoned in Aeternum. For a time, the God sat alone in the darkness of his own creation. He was lonely in his solitude, so he created beings of death and darkness to worship him and be his companions. These creatures are known to those of the Ert as the Denir or the Keepers of the Gates of the Underworld—doers of mischief to any soul unfortunate enough to enter their realm.

The Denir may take physical form, but it was not so from the beginning. Even with the power to exist in the physical world, they preferred to remain spirits capable of concealment in the dark corners of any abode. This preference is the reason for the chill that runs down a victim's spine when an unsuspecting soul crosses their path during their daily routine.

The Denir are devoted servants of the Underlord Haeldrun. They serve his desire to subjugate, dominate and destroy the light. They are bringers of pestilence, violence, death, and ruin to any place where they are allowed to remain. These servants tend to migrate to any locale where hearts are focused on the darkness, self-interest, or show a rebellion toward the light. The Denir consider anyone who has this predisposition as fair game, working to pervert the victim's desires to suit their master's will.

After Haeldrun created his darkness and his followers, he looked outside of his realm at all of the light and life Haya had made. He realized the abundance that was allowed to flourish in his absence. The more light and life that existed, the angrier he became. Surveying the entire Ert until he found a barren and miserable wasteland, the Underlord decided to create his own perversion of Haya's world. He named the place the Wargyrn, fashioning it into a locale of suffering and despair.

Haeldrun used his Denir to protect the secrecy of his new domain. The demonic spirits were sent out to confuse the few sailing vessels that happened to stray toward the Wargyrn's shores. Then the God cast a spell of protection over the land, creating a great shield of darkness, which would not allow anyone from Aeternum to detect the presence of his new endeavor.

Haya and the children did not notice Haeldrun's evil intentions, because ironically, even when Haeldrun *didn't* influence the affairs of the light, mortals always found a reason to bicker and kill each other. This carnage pleased the God of the Underworld, and although these petty conflicts never entirely extinguished the light, they kept Haya occupied and focused elsewhere. Her intervention saved her precious life and hid the coming darkness.

* * *

As Haya's light grew, so did her power. She became confident and complacent. Haeldrun watched from his darkness as his former love became blinded. He smiled when she began to doubt that he was interested in creating much mischief. The jilted God maintained a low profile, strengthening his wife's belief that all was well, while he continued his plans from the shadows.

While Haya tended to her mortal children, Haeldrun launched his plans. His first order of business was to create his own army of abominations. He chose to pervert the races of the Ert, starting with mankind.

In contrast to Haya's use of two elements, Haeldrun created these mortals from fire alone. His men and women were belligerent, warlike, suspicious, and prone to violence. He made them lust after one another, and they procreated, multiplying throughout Wargyrn. Eventually, these beings fought, killing each other over the meager resources that their God had provided to support life.

Haeldrun named these beings the Todessen. The Todessen evolved into fierce warriors over time, bickering over mates, land, resources, and power. There was no end to their debauchery, and Haeldrun fed this new evil with all of the strife and despair that Wargyrn provided. Later, it would be rumored by Eden scribes that the Todessen were even habitual eaters of their own kind. This creation quickly became the favorite pastime of Haeldrun, and he loved them in his own vile way.

Next, Haeldrun perverted the Elves, naming them the Harkyl. They were vaguely Elf-like and pale-skinned, with oversized eyes meant for seeing better in the darkness of catacombs and dark places. The Underlord's Harkyl hated forests and growing things, unless they were provided as food or drink by the God of the Underworld.

The God gave them several rows of short, sharp teeth and claws with which to rip living things apart. Harkyl enjoyed eating their prey alive, never feeling remorse for killing any living thing. They harvested the few trees of Wargyrn, burning them for warmth, and never gave a thought to the needs of tomorrow. These beings preferred to dwell within canyons, feeding upon anything foolish enough to wander into their territory.

Finally, the Underlord perverted the race of the Dwarves by creating the Kvern. The God made the Kvern much like the Dwarves of the Ert, except they were hairless, wrinkly-skinned, and pale. They, too, had huge eyes, but none of the sharp teeth of the Harkyl. The Kvern instead possessed the most strength and durability of any of the races of Wargyrn.

Haeldrun placed his Kvern in caves and underground tunnels located within the mountains of his dark continent. There, they scavenged food from what they could find, killing unsuspecting wildlife or an occasional unfortunate passer-by. The Kvern were secretive and preferred dark places. This pleased Haeldrun, and he increased their numbers one-hundred-fold.

Finally, Haeldrun ensured that his creations could communicate freely with the tribes of the Ert by endowing them with a knowledge of the language of Etah. This made communication easier with potential future allies or captured slaves, by allowing the knowledge of the most common tongue of the Ert.

The kingdoms of Ert were not even in Haya's dreams during the Wargyrn's development. Most tribes of the Ert were barely established, and wars were still rare in Haya's realm, due to the abundance of land and resources. However, this was not so on Wargyrn. Haeldrun had created his lands to be a crucible used to purify his creations. He sought to create "the army to end all light," and his plans were done as a God would prefer—gradually, with intention and over the long run.

* * *

In the desolation that was the Wargyrn, desperate beings fought over every scrap of food, drop of water, and piece of territory. Haeldrun kept them at each other's throats by providing only enough resources for half of those whom he had created. The urgency of this shortfall forced all life to provide for its own needs by violence and coercion. It kept the Underlord's whole world on edge and in a constant state of conflict. Haeldrun was pleased, because this chaos honed the lethality and cruelty of all of his creations. Still, he was not completely satisfied with what the end result was becoming.

Over time, the Todessen developed martial arts that rivaled all others. They were as proficient in killing with an open hand as with any implement or weapon. Todessen were fierce warriors who fought in large bands. They were prone to use superior numbers to overpower better-equipped enemies through escalating violence and brute force.

The Harkyl built small sailing vessels, eventually developing larger ships. They were formidable foes in their own right, but preferred to skulk around in the shadows, stealing what they could find. This tribe chose to engage the weaker stragglers from any of the opposing tribes of the Wargyrn. The Harkyl were considered cowards by the other factions of the dark lands, but in reality, they were of the highest intelligence and knew when to fight and when to flee. Their descendants would eventually discover how to navigate by use of the stars when Haeldrun finally allowed the skies to be seen by his creations, much later.

The Kvern became miners and blacksmiths. They created the first metal weapons and were the first to tame the advances of the Todessen. The Kvern were an even match for the Todessen, due to their incredible strength and skill with superior weaponry. Eventually, the Todessen learned to avoid the Kvern warrior class or bring more significant numbers, due to their enemy's proficiency in warfare and martial combat. The Kvern eventually invented the first body armor, dominating the Wargyrn through its use.

Haeldrun looked upon what he had created and was still not satisfied. He wanted the darkness to be more formidable. Although his former love's world was a place of light, the prowess of the Yslandeth, Hodan, Torith, and Dornat al Ar still concerned the Dark Lord. Eons had passed, and the Ert's kingdoms were starting to strengthen. He knew he needed to push his plan a little further to be successful. That is when he thought about using his Denir.

At this time, Haeldrun first gave the Denir their ability to take physical form in the mortal world. The Denir were already masters of reading the innermost needs and desires of any mortal being. They would then use this knowledge to manipulate and coerce the living into doing things they would not normally be willing to do. Haeldrun counted on their abilities.

The Todessen were resistant to the coercion of the Denir. Haeldrun surmised that it had something to do with their anger and depravity. Their default disposition made the people unable to care about temptation or offers of emotional bribes. They already took whatever they wanted. Moreover, their fire elemental souls burned too hot and angry to interest the Denir, so the deceivers went on to the other races and found much easier candidates for perversion. Haeldrun chuckled when he heard the reports of his demons, and figured that at least one of his races was apparently ready.

The Denir went to the Harkyl first, promising strength and prowess. The deceivers came to the dark Elves as beautiful creatures. They seduced them into unnatural relationships and created offspring with many of the Harkyl.

The bastardization of the race created the first Orcs on the Wargyrn. At first, the Harkyl were appalled at what they had done, but eventually, they changed their minds completely when the first generation of Orcs came of age.

The resulting Orcs were seven to eight feet tall. This was taller than any race seen on the Wargyrn. The Orcs also had the strength of two Kvern and were of average intelligence. Soon, eligible Harkyl sought out the Denir impostors for mates, hoping to create children who would elevate their tribe to dominance, and the Orcs thrived for a time.

The Denir also went to the Kvern and did very similarly. The Kvern were also duped into taking the Denir impostors as mates, creating their own hybrid generation of children. The result of a Kvern and Denir union produced the first Goblin races of the Wargyrn. Goblins were wiry, but very muscular, four to six feet tall, and fast. The new race of people was not quite as strong as the Orcs or the Kvern, but they made up for their inadequacies with speed and agility.

An Orc and Goblin encounter often ended with both sides dead. Goblins, although smaller and weaker, had already learned to even the odds through the use of swords or spears and by adopting the practice of wearing body armor. Through technology, they became the equals of their rivals, the Orcs.

* * *

Haeldrun watched from his Underworld as the Ert took up arms again against its brothers. The early kingdoms finally established their borders, and a tentative peace reigned for many years, save for the occasional skirmish or battle that marred the silence and harmony.

Simultaneously, the Underlord watched as the Wargyrn writhed in discord and suffering. The new races slowly dominated and extinguished the ancestral lines of the Kvern and Harkyl. Very few remained. The only remaining original people were the Todessen, and they were as evil as ever.

Haeldrun finally intervened, increasing the provisions found within the misery he had created. Next, the God ordered his Denir, who had long ago returned to being hidden spirits, to coerce the remaining peoples of the Wargyrn.

The Denir sought to have all races put aside their former differences and form bonds of friendship and alliance. Crops grew, resources flourished, and every race prospered in peace over the next few millennia. The Denir influenced the Orcs and Goblins to create new military technologies and great ships for exploration. In their hearts, all the races of the Wargyrn desired to find a new place to conquer and dominate, and with this shared vision, they united as one army. Death was part of their souls, and now they were of one, dangerously lethal mind.

So, Haeldrun looked upon his creation and was satisfied that he had finally created the massive, lethal army, capable of wiping out all light on the Ert. He pushed to move his plan along. After making his races, uniting his clans, and enhancing their technology and weaponry, the Underlord finally revealed the stars to the Goblin sailors. The descendant of the Harkyl created instruments by which they could navigate the open seas and sail far from their own shores. The races of the Wargyrn built massive black ships with which to cross the open seas. They brought provisions for themselves and cages for future prisoners, setting off to unknown places for the sole purpose of war.

Haeldrun first directed his forces to unknown islands inhabited by primitive followers of Haya. Most were humans and Elves who were unknown to the races of the Ert. These tribes were isolated and ill-prepared for the onslaught that came their way. Haeldrun had watched over the eons and knew of the location of Haya's expansions. He saw all of her attempts to expand the light and her sphere of influence. The God had been watching and cataloging these smaller continents, determining which would give his followers the years of necessary practice, before finally deciding to reveal the location of his ultimate prize—the Ert.

When the Underlord finally allowed his creations to find the Ert, he figured they had sufficient numbers and experience to accomplish his will. Haeldrun was, however, worried that the Ert may prove too well defended to just barge in with a full-force frontal attack. On the God's behalf, the Denir spoke quietly to the leadership of the Orcs and Goblins, imploring them to use subterfuge and quietly invade. They quietly allied with the humans of the South, so as to not awaken the warriors of this immense new island they had just found.

Scouts were also dropped off in other remote locations. Their reports stated they had never seen anything like the advanced civilizations of Yslandeth, Cinnog, Edenyag, Sudenyag, or Hodan. Haeldrun knew that the Ert did not have had seafaring vessels. Still, the God was concerned at the potential might that Hodan or Yslandeth was capable of projecting on his forces in as little as a few days. The God prepared his armies for an invasion, but he was unaware that during this distraction, the entire Ert had just concluded a major war among all of the peoples. His fears of vast numbers were unfounded.

Haeldrun's minions befriended the Sudenyag crown with the help of the Denir. While trading with the fools of Sudenyag, Haeldrun's spies did a reconnaissance. This survey of the continent told the Dark Lord's Commanders that the Ert was virtually defenseless, compared to their invading forces.

The Underlord was emboldened by these reports and pushed his creation into Sudenyag, confident of victory. But in his arrogance, he hadn't noticed that Haya had heard the cries of her conquered people outside of the Ert. Quietly, years prior, she had made her own plans to intervene and save her devoted.

While Haeldrun was known for his subterfuge, Haya was now showing him up at his own game. Where the Dark Lord saw only numbers and strength, the Goddess of Light saw covert opportunities to respond to her husband's incursions into her realm. Haeldrun, in his anger and jealousy, had seemingly forgotten who he was dealing with.

So, Haeldrun fed the Suden fears of invasion, allowing his children to infiltrate the Sudenyag capital. He relished the fact that he no longer had to work to cultivate the Suden fear of being conquered by the northern nations. Sudenyag had willingly allowed its conquerors to walk in from the sea. The Underlord loved the fearful Suden faces and tears of regret.

The southern kingdom had not always been wise, but they were still Haya's children. What Haeldrun failed to realize was that the Goddess had been lying in wait for him. It was unclear of the end game of this encounter, but she would give her estranged husband all he could handle and more.

Trouble from the South

Sudenyag was effectively saturated with the Offlander forces. The King pretended to be the sovereign, but knew he had lost control months ago. Peace had now reigned for six years, but Yanat knew it was only a matter of time before all of that changed. The people of Sudenyag turned a blind eye to the gradual invasion of their lands, because their occupiers had, up until now, allowed them to continue life as usual, and their businesses were booming. Suden was enriched in all things. The kingdom's wealth was the envy of all the Ert.

Some, however, thought privately that this might be the fattening before their slaughter. Thousands slipped to the Northwest, hiding in the forested mountains on the Hodan/Cinnog border, in efforts to form a secret underground. There, they used their contacts within the Port of Valent and its surrounding areas to appropriate supplies and weapons. This rebellion boasted some of the best leaders in Suden, who trained their meager forces to the best of their abilities. Still, they were an ill-equipped, poorly prepared force, which was low on supplies.

The rebellion set up a system of nomadic units to thwart detection by their adversary. Splitting into several smaller groups, they sought to avoid their entire force being captured at once. The tactics were sound, but their worries proved unfounded. The people of Sudenyag were more concerned about internal affairs. The majority of the populace scarcely acknowledged the forces in the mountains, and those who did, kept it to themselves, hoping that perhaps the rebels would prove to be their saviors.

King Yanat sat on his throne, fiddling with a large, ruby-encrusted ring on his finger. He wondered for the future. The Offlanders brought a large contingent of "peacekeepers" to his lands, including a leader known as Magrut the Conqueror, who had begun to assert his political power in the palace.

* * *

"Yanat, we will need more food and shelter for my soldiers. You will provide homes or shelter in homes, immediately." The Conqueror spoke with authority. He was no longer asking.

"I have no homes to spare, My Lord, but I can arrange for my stewards to provide as many tents as our military supplies contain, if it pleases you." Yanat nodded as if he was doing the Orc a favor. However, the Orc was not impressed.

"Beware, little human. I have no use for your platitudes and trickery. I care not where the homes come from, but they will be provided by nightfall, or I will take this castle from beneath your ass." The Orc approached the King, and two Suden spearmen pointed spears at the Orc's throat. Chuckling, Magrut sneered. He let out a war cry, and the spearmen backed up in fear.

"Such pathetic warriors. We chose a perfect point with which to set our beachhead!" One of the Orc's advisors shook his head, looking at the Orc, and made a "quiet!" sign with his hand. The Orc rolled his eyes. "Do you think this one is that stupid, Goolog? He has been posturing and calculating our strength for over a year. He knows he has lost. This is all for show. Why do we play this game?"

Goolog whispered in his ear, and Magrut sighed. "You have become soft, brother. These humans are pathetic. This whole continent is ripe for the taking." Magrut eyed a tapestry, which showed the kingdoms of the Ert, while smiling an evil grin.

Goolog only nodded and then padded away in his well-worn leather boots. The two had killed so many as a team that they thought of victories in terms of nations, vice people and money. To them, it was a foregone conclusion that the Erthad already lost.

* * *

The Suden citizenry protested the invasion of their homes. Anyone who stood up to the Offlanders was executed on the spot. Yanat sat in fear and wondered when his turn would come. Resistance forces lurked just out of plain sight on the edge of the capital, where they gathered intelligence for their units in the hills. There, they witnessed the carnage of the *peacekeepers* first-hand. In an effort to pass on the intelligence they had gathered, the rebel scouts scurried northwest to one of their preset rally points. There, they found a large contingent of their forces camping. There were approximately five-hundred spearmen and one-hundred archers.

"Captain Harun, they are murdering civilians, and Yanat sits and trembles in his own piss," the scout leader reported.

"It figures. That man is not worth the horse dung on my shoe," Harun spat. "This cannot stand."

"There are too many, my Captain," the scout replied, looking at the many angry faces before him.

The scout knew he was not going to win this fight. Many of these men had fought Yslandeth and Edenyag in the last war, surviving to tell the tale. Yanat had left them to fend for themselves on both occasions. One or two claimed to have survived Ontak's charge on the Arondayre almost eight years ago. No one could confirm their stories, because there were no other survivors. These men desired blood for the deaths of their countrymen, and knew King Yanat would simply roll over to his keepers, like the coward he was.

* * *

The Offlander forces were overconfident. They did not set a watch over the city walls, so the rebels used the night as cover to sneak in undetected. Moving swiftly over familiar terrain, they were able to enter the palace courtyard without detection. The entire unit crept stealthily to the palace doors. The invaders became confident, thinking their enemy was foolishly dismissing their abilities, and began moving at will along the borders of Sudenyag. That is when things changed drastically.

A Goblin guard detected the unit in the open. It was obvious, because the rebels were not trying to hide with much effort. Instead, they focused on speed and surprise. The Offlander sentry sounded the alarm, bringing the evening guard of twenty Orc warriors to the yard. This response was a challenge to the unproven Suden rebels, even though they outnumbered the Orcs thirty to one.

Many of the rebels had never held a weapon in combat. Some fled, and others froze. Captain Harun il Armat barked out orders to his remaining soldiers as they were baptized in battle, successfully destroying their first enemy unit. Rebel casualties were light, and they made their way to the throne room unopposed. They were greeted by the scene of Commander Magrut and Goolog taunting their King.

Harun led his rebels into the chamber. The Captain immediately charged forward, swinging his glaive in a wide arc. "Die, you abominable scum!" As Goolog turned to respond, his head was neatly severed from his shoulders, having been caught by surprise by the human.

Magrut was enraged. "No! Goolog, my brother! You human filth!"

Magrut charged the Captain, throwing him into the nearest wall. Wooden shelves splintered as Harun fell to the floor. Magrut turned, focusing on the human, who was trying to collect himself and stand. The Orc roared loudly to the chirping response of thousands off in the distance. Several hundred Suden spearmen now crowded the ten-foot-wide entryway to the throne room in preparation for the thousands of Offlanders who they knew were pouring in from every corner of the capital.

On the other side of the large room, twenty rebels attacked Magrut. The Orc disemboweled one of the men while toying with the rest, who dared to face him in combat. Angered by the lack of chivalry and decency, Harun struck again with his glaive while the Orc was distracted. The Orc's head hit the floor with the sound of an overripe cantaloupe.

The rebels cheered halfheartedly, and some now angrily stared at their King. "Wait now, men. I am still your King. Put down your arms. We must negotiate with them. They are too strong, and you cannot win. I will … guttt …" The King was stopped mid-sentence by a glaive blade to the throat. The Captain looked at him in disgust.

"Sudenyag falls for your lust and greed. We are ruined, and our families are forfeited for your selfish ambitions. Die, and go to the Underworld, never to see Aeternum, you pile of dung."

Shortly thereafter, the rebels also executed their Queen by decapitation while she begged for her life. Their mission was an apparent success.

Outside, deep-toned horns blew. The castle was quickly being surrounded by a sea of Offlanders.

"Quickly, take the heads of the Orcs. He must be the Commander, and the other, he was a minister or aide. We need proof to take to Hodan. This is going to end badly." The Captain looked at his men. Some frowned, some were crying, but everyone stood their ground now, knowing there was no place left to run.

One of the survivors of the Arondayre stepped forward and spoke. "Run, Sir, run and get free of here. Take the evidence. Our people will suffer dearly for what we have done, but it was necessary. Do not squander their deaths."

"I will not forget this day until I enter Aeternum. Save a place for me at the hero's table, my brother." The Captain's voice wavered as he turned to find an open, darkened passage in the nearby sleeping quarters of the King. It led outside the walls. Harun hoped there were no guards.

"I will pour a cup of the finest ale for you, Sir!" the soldier waved and then turned to meet his doom.

Within minutes, the battle was over, but the Captain successfully escaped out of the castle walls and into the forest with his grisly prize of two bloody Offlander heads. Making his way back and forth in the trees, until he was sure he was not followed, he maneuvered to another predetermined meeting place high in the mountains. Looking over his shoulder as he ran, Harun saw Sudenyag in flames, the sound of distant screams emanating from every corner of the city. He wondered if he had made the right decision, but knew it was too late to go back and change things now.

Up in the mountains, the rebel units were on high alert. Harun approached an edgy guard on the perimeter of the camp, who nearly ran him through.

"Hold there, soldier, it is I!" the Captain yelled.

The soldier stood down. "Sorry, Sir! With all of the fire and smoke, I was unsure of what was happening!"

"It is the worst, my boy. We accomplished the objective, but were discovered and, in the process, we killed a couple of important enemy leaders. Unfortunately, the enemy is razing our city in retaliation. I am sure many Suden are losing their lives. We must leave for Hodan immediately!" The Captain looked over the mountains at the glowing horizon. They were coming now, and no one was safe. The Ert needed to know.

The small army packed their meager belongings, headed northwest toward the Alabaster Sands Canyon, and then changed direction North as they marched directly into Hodan territory. Not long after passing the border, they were challenged and captured by the Hodan military. Hodan put the three-hundred remaining Suden warriors in chains, except for the Suden Captain. The army awaited the arrival of King Orus, who would be notified of the situation.

The Legion Commander questioned the Suden Captain. "Why are you here, Suden dog?"

"I come with a warning from Sudenyag. We must alert the Northern Alliance to the coming onslaught!" The Captain was frantic. "I have proof, Hodan, if you will allow it?" He reached for his bag.

The Hodan Commander drew his sword. "Carefully and slowly, Suden. Or you will be run through where you stand."

"Agreed," Harun said, putting his hands up, and then he undid the twine on the top of the burlap sack, dropping the heads at the Hodan Commander's feet. The Hodan man did not flinch, but did do a double-take when he saw the faces on those heads.

"Are those … Orcs?" he questioned.

"Yes, Commander, they are," the Captain responded emphatically.

"How did you come by these heads, Suden?" the Commander asked suspiciously.

"I collected them personally," Harun said smugly.

"What is going on in Sudenyag, dog? Tell me now!" The Hodan Commander grabbed the Captain forcefully and pulled him close to his face. "Start talking, or I will make you talk."

Harun scowled and pushed the Commander's hands away. "There is no need for that. We came to you. I will tell you." The Hodan Commander then relaxed his stance and listened.

"For a year, maybe two, our illustrious former King made an alliance with the Offlanders to counter the Northern Alliance."

The Commander picked up on the fact that the Suden Captain referred to King Yanat in the past tense.

The Suden man went on. "Yanat sold us out to save his own skin, because he feared the wrath of Hodan and its allies. So he made a deal with the evil you see before you. Over the past two years, ships have come and deposited thousands of these vermin on our land. They move in, take our homes and enslave our people. Yanat tolerated these atrocities, because the invaders allowed him and his whore to sit upon the thrones of Suden, playing royalty, while the Offlander armies took what they pleased from the rest of us," the Captain spat. "We sought to scout the area and see how bad the infiltration and abuses had become, but our mission evolved into a coup when we witnessed civilian executions. In the process, we succeeded in killing two of the Offlander leaders. Apparently, they were well-liked, or at least well-connected, because my unit perished, holding off the hordes, so I could return to our base. So I took these heads as proof. The armies of these two ravage the Port of Valent, taking whatever, or whoever, they please." He looked at the heads on the ground. "We are begging for your help and wish to warn of their coming. They will not stop at Sudenyag.

You can be assured of that."

"An interesting story. We shall see what King Orus thinks of it. Put your heads back in the bag, and set them somewhere for safe-keeping. They may save your life yet." The Hodan Commander turned, calling for the watch.

The watch Commander set a perimeter around the encampment, using the Legion at his disposal. Still, the Commander kept his remaining forces vigilant, not giving in to a false sense of security. The night was moonless, cold, and damp. The guards were uneasy. Most believed the Suden Captain's story, which did not bode well for the Ert.

* * *

The Hodan woke to smoke and hazy conditions. Many experienced older warriors recognized the unmistakable smell of a burning village or town. It wasn't a clean wood smell, but the smell of civilization on fire.

Even though this generation had never fought a true enemy, the Hodan Legion was well-trained and prepared for battle. The Commander knew it would be days before their King returned, if at all, so he ordered his men to set embattlements as best they could, and the men all dug in for defense. Watching the smoke rise, they waited for their King or the enemy to arrive, whichever came first.

* * *

The Suden lived in terror. The Offlanders assumed control of the palace and burned entire neighborhoods in the affluent sections of the capital port city. Rape, murder, and mayhem were rampant, as Offlanders wantonly abused the population, stealing any material wealth they desired. In some extreme cases, there were reports of cannibalization. Orcs and Goblins considered human flesh a delicacy, and the Todessen would eat anyone and anything, according to rumors.

The enemy army erected large iron cages in the city square where they imprisoned people who they randomly selected to join their slave labor pool. Anyone resisting or protesting would result in an on-the-spot execution. Except for the port, Sudenyag was in ruins.

Thousands of troops now freely disembarked from countless ships at the piers, while waiting vessels stretched off into the horizon. People hid their children in root cellars, praying for mercy, but apparently, Haya was busy elsewhere.

Haeldrun rubbed his hands together in anticipation. All of his long preparation was about to make his dream of extinguishing the light true. He would revel in the resulting death and despair.

The rebellion that was left behind in Suden totaled maybe one-hundred-fifty souls. They snuck back into the city, making contact in clandestine locations with anyone who could be trusted. A network of agents was created with a mission to quietly smuggle women and children out of the kingdom. Their plan worked, but with their limited resources, very few made it out alive. The network saved as many as it could.

A new Offlander Commander arrived with his cohort of young, eager Lieutenants on the pier. They seemed naïve in the ways of war and were very idealistic. They were not jaded like Goolog and Magrut were.

"Soldier, come here," the new Commander called.

"Yes, Sir!" the young Orc answered. "How may I be of service?"

"Get the slaves to unload our supplies and a slave crew to clean up this mess! Tell these idiots that we strive to take this land, not raze it to the ground. Stop burning the buildings! Imbeciles."

"I will relate this to the Captain, Sir," the soldier replied respectfully.

"You do that. Where is the Captain, Orc?" the Commander growled.

"He is in the castle, Sir. Upon the hill." The soldier pointed to a large, beautiful, and elaborate stone building.

The new Commander and his cohort traveled up to the palace and found the newly commissioned Captain. He was having his way with one of the ladies-in-waiting to the former Queen, and his actions were not consensual. She was crying and begging for him to stop. So he did, killing her with his bare hands for good measure.

Getting up, the Orc saw the new Commander. "Oh well, plenty more where that one came from," he chuckled. "Sir, the city is secured."

"I can see that, Captain. What of the continent?" The Commander seemed impatient.

"Sir, we gather the forces and logistics required for the main offensive. It will be a week or so before it can begin." The Captain looked at the new Commander as if he should already know how this went.

"Do not attempt to lecture me, or I will take your head next!" The impetuous leader leaned forward and attempted to impose his authority, but the Orc Captain was clearly not impressed.

"As you wish, Sir," the larger Orc replied to the Todessen man, walking away and calling for his aides.

The leaders discussed logistics and plans. Finally, after about an hour, the aides left their Captain to carry out his orders.

The Orc leader returned to the throne room, where the Commander was now guzzling ale directly out of a small keg. "The plans have been related to the leadership, Sir. My cohort is dispatching the orders and arranging for the deployment of our forces."

"Very good," the Commander droned, waving him off as if shooing a fly. Then, visibly annoyed, the Captain sneered and left the room.

"We shall utterly defeat these weaklings, and they shall serve us as slaves or lose their lives. Humans are so weak." The Commander's cohort laughed as they celebrated on King Yanat's stores. Yanat's body was still on the floor, barely cold.

* * *

It had been three days, and the Hodan encampment now resembled a battlefield emplacement. The Legion closely monitored the hanging smoke and haze wafting toward them from the southwest. Within the waning morning hours, the sentries saw the first intruders making their way up the mountainsides toward the Hodan position.

"Hold your fire, Hodan!" the Suden Captain begged. "They are refugees, not soldiers!"

The Legion still stood on full alert. They did not trust the Suden, and it was difficult to tell who was coming through the haze. Eventually, a small girl and her family materialized into full view of the front lines. The refugees were in shock, looking as if they had passed through a war zone, but the patrols still gruffly took them into custody.

As they arrested the first arrivals, a vast mob of souls began to show up, from nowhere, out of the smoke. Within no time, the field was filled with civilians carrying what they could put on their backs. Children wept quietly, grasping dolls or small pets. Their clothes were ragged and filthy, and many looked as if they had walked for several days without sleep. The refugees were not trained for the long hike through the rough, mountainous terrain. Even hardened Hodan warriors stopped and looked at their Commander.

"Set up the canvas. Get the children under cover. Distribute aid as best we can. Get the water wagon over here!" the Commander yelled, directing traffic.

"Thank you for your kindness, Commander." Captain Harun choked, fighting back tears, as he saw the stunned children's faces. Some said nothing, but their blank stares screamed very loudly.

"We know what it is to be desperate, Suden," the Commander said sadly, thinking of his own family, who had braved three winters on sawdust and grass soups. He remembered eating his own horse after the first snows. The Suden Captain was taken aback by the expression of sympathy on the Hodan face.

While settling the seemingly endless flow of refugees, another disturbance was announced by the northern watch, but this one was expected. Orus, King of Hodan, had arrived with the messenger who had summoned him. The Commander ran to greet his King.

He bowed, saluting. "Hail Orus, King of Hodan! May fortune meet you, and may your enemies be crushed before you."

The King saluted in return, dismounting his horse. "What is it that brings me this far South, Commander?"

"Sudenyag, Your Majesty. It burns, and according to reports, the Offlanders bring an army that threatens us all. This is the report of a Suden Captain. He brought with him proof within his burlap sack—the heads of two Offlander Commanders, which his rebels killed on a mission that ended the reign of King Yanat il Arnar." The Commander crossed his arms. "They were quite busy, Your Majesty, but they riled a wasp's nest in the process."

"Who are these civilians?" the King asked in dismay. "Suden?"

"Yes, Sire. Refugees, escaping atrocities at the hands of Orcs and Goblins."

"Orcs? Has anyone seen an Orc or a Goblin in one-thousand years?" The King was not convinced. He continued. "Next, you will tell me that you have found a Dragon." Orus chuckled, stopping abruptly, realizing his Commander was not joking. "Show me," the King said.

The two walked over to the Suden Captain, where Orus then demanded to see the Offlander heads. The Captain produced them as ordered.

"My Gods! They are Orc heads! At least, I think they are. My father's father spoke of their evil. They have not been seen on the Ert for at least one-thousand, maybe fifteen-hundred years. Where did they come from?"

"Ships, Your Majesty," the Suden Captain replied. "They have been invading our kingdom for almost two years now. We are inundated with their kind. We sought to topple our King and inspire our populace to fight back, but it did not go as planned. Instead, the people hid, and the enemy razed our city and did Gods know what to those who resisted." The Captain looked physically ill. "Look at all of these children. Where are their parents?"

The King surveyed the tactical situation. "We cannot stay here. This area is indefensible. We are exposed. How many of the enemy soldiers are there? Estimate, man!" He looked to Harun for an answer.

"Truly, I cannot count that many, Your Majesty. Perhaps hundreds of thousands, and some report that ships are coming with more soldiers as we sit here. The ships wait to dock at the port. The line extends until one cannot see them." Harun was worried.

After a couple of days, the stream of refugees stopped. The Suden Captain figured the resistance had been discovered or betrayed by someone selling them out to save their own skin. This number was all his men would save. All that was left of Suden were two-thousand men, women, and children. None of the old made it over the hills. The majority of the survivors were children without parents.

* * *

"It is late, and we brought supplies. Send out hunters for deer or elk. We will feed these people and meet up with Puryn to devise a plan. I do not know what kind of plan there is to devise, but devise one we will. We will not lie down and die without a fight. We will set a wagon train and march the Suden to Erynseere. I am sure it will take several days, but what else can we do?" Orus called the Commander over. "Release these Suden warriors. They will stand watch over their own. They have proved their worth."

"Thank you, Your Majesty," Harun bowed.

"Make no mistake, Captain. I am a fair man, but if even one of your men threatens or attacks a man, woman, or child of Hodan, I will execute ten at random. Do we understand each other?" The King lowered his gaze, so he was eye to eye with the shorter Captain.

"Clearly understood, Your Majesty." Harun blinked, swallowing hard.

"Good. Then get up and take control of your army, Captain. We have work to do." The Hodan King stood, and everyone rose. Orus left their company to speak with his Commanders alone. They were displeased that there were armed Suden within their encampment, but none dared to question the King's judgment. He was fierce, but fair, and the men loved him for it. For the first time in many reigns, they would ensure he would die of old age before anyone challenged the throne.

The morning came, and the Hodan removed their embattlements, packing up their war supplies and setting the wagons at the front and rear of the ragged group marching North. Surprisingly, the Suden did not complain. But still, the Hodan made sure to stop frequently, to allow for rest and water. Supplies were rationed due to the slower pace of travel and the fact that Hodan had only planned for one-thousand troops. Orus used hunters, who were regularly dispatched to augment the food supply. He sent a rider to Erynseere, calling to Puryn for immediate aid and wagons.

After three days, the messenger arrived in Erynseere. Puryn ordered the logistics wagons to be loaded without delay, and then he activated the Draj-Erynseere. The procession marched southeast toward the last known position of the refugees and the Hodan Legion. Yslandeth was met by Hodan forces near a small village, one or two days' ride from the northern Hodan border.

"About time, Yslan!" Orus called out, mocking.

"We got lost!" Puryn joked. "Someone gave me bad directions!"

The Hodan scout looked at his King in fear.

The King shook his head. He said to his scout, "Relax, boy, he is jesting!" The guard let out a slow relieved sigh, saluted his King, and returned to his unit.

Orus rode up to Puryn and hugged him like his kin. "Thank you for coming, my brother," Orus said seriously. "This is bad."

The Yslan warrior looked at the bloodied faces of the women and children. The Draj-Manot was disgusted. He turned to his comrade, asking, "Who did this, Orus, and why? Gods know that Edenyag could not do this, and King Lorus in Cinnog would never do such a thing."

"Orcs, boy. Orcs," the King said with a straight face.

Puryn laughed and mocked. "And dancing Unicorns burned their villages."

"No, I am serious." He showed his brother the bag, and the young man's face went pale with the revelation.

"Where did they come from?" the young Baron asked, instantly worried about Adasser and his children.

"Ships from the Offlands. Swyk warned Yanat, that damned fool. He died for his foolishness, and now his people burn or are enslaved. I fear they come for us next," the weathered Hodan warrior sighed audibly.

"Donick!" Puryn shouted.

The minister rode up quickly. "What is it, My Baron?"

"Take this down and seal the scrolls with the signet. Send one to Edenyag, Cinnog, King Swyk, Torith, and Dornat al Ar." Donick nodded. Puryn dictated, "Sudenyag in flames. Orc invaders found. Many dead and injured. Refugees traveling to Erynseere for asylum. Request immediate military aid. There is no time for negotiations. They will come soon. We need to be ready. We are mustering our forces at the Hodan capital. King Orus is in agreement." Puryn looked at Orus, and the King nodded solemnly.

"I hope those doddering fools don't try to talk for a month before acting. I fear things will escalate quickly. Gods help us if they have as many armies as the Suden Captain estimated." Orus sighed again, looking southeast.

Puryn nodded silently, wishing he could warn Adasser. He scrawled a note and handed it to a Squire. "Go to the Baroness and give this to her. Hurry, and do not stop until you arrive at her door!" The boy saluted and rode away at a gallop.

Puryn looked to the South and saw the smoke off in the distance. He imagined a horde of evil moving North toward his wife and children. His nightmares had shown this to him repeatedly. The Draj-Manot was genuinely afraid of the enemy for the first time in his life.

In his reoccurring premonition, Puryn stood on a hill against a nameless black. His army, which was decimated, had made its last stand. Hopelessness and despair were palpable. Still, Puryn resolved to stand for the people, even if it meant his army would all die in the attempt. Later in the visions, Puryn saw Adasser fighting in her own way. Her eyes were as coals as she defended her trees, while the children cowered with Puryn's mother in the castle's stone cellar. The young Baron never saw the result of the events, but every time he woke from the dream, he was drenched in sweat and felt impending doom. Now, he saw the manifestation of his worst fear while awake. It was coming, and now the warrior knew the blackness was them.

* * *

After a restless sleep, King Orus led the people northward to the Barony of Erynseere. Puryn left a detachment of fifteen-hundred Draj-Erynseere at the border to augment the Hodan forces. The Yslan Baron rode North and waited for reinforcements from King Swyk.

While the two brothers united forces, a third arrived in Erynseere with three-thousand cavalry. Athis had come. It was unexpected. "Going to war without me, gentlemen?"

Truthfully, Puryn had not thought of Athis. "You are most welcome to help defend against invasion, Baron Athis." Puryn bowed.

"No need for that, Puryn. Please, never bow to me." Athis frowned remembering his past. The Baron of Korin gave the order, and his unit went to the border to augment the Hodan.

It looked as if Hodan was shaping up to have a decent deterrent, but the numbers, by all reports, were still much too skewed in favor of the Offlanders. Puryn and Orus doubted there were enough people on the Ert to conscript an army sufficient to deal with what they reckoned to be the emerging threat.

"We may not be able to defeat them, brother," Orus admitted quietly, "but we Hodan will die trying. We will bleed the field red or black with their evil blood."

"I agree, brother. My life is forfeit for the safety of my family and for my people. I will not rest until they are safe, even if it means my demise." Puryn looked off to the North and could barely make out his castle's outline on the horizon. His father, Durn, now commanded the Draj-Erynseere, who remained behind with Adasser. Puryn had left about two-thousand there to defend his home.

Hodan had seventy-five hundred soldiers. The Hodan King sent riders to the four winds. They lit the signal fires and rode hard to every Commander in the kingdom. By week's end, most had joined their leader at his home in the small town of Warrior Crossing, where the Northern Alliance was born. There were three-thousand Korinian horsemen from the lands of Athis, fifteen-hundred Draj from Erynseere—five-hundred of which were bowmen—and five-hundred Suden rebels, armed with what they could find.

For the nations of the Ert, this was a formidable force, but not an adequate response to the armies attacking from the Offlands. So King Orus prayed to Runnir and Gunnir, asking them to rain the fire of the Underworld on the invaders. He also begged quietly for help in saving his people. However, the weathered warrior remembered the horrors of many battles and doubted that anyone listened to his pleas.

In spite of his doubts, in Aeternum, the two brothers did listen and were intrigued by the lost cause Hodan was about to embark on. Runnir chose Orus as his champion, and Gunnir chose Puryn. The two brothers blessed their champions with the strength of several men and Godlike endurance.

Both men immediately felt ready for anything, but both were afraid their deterrent would not be up to the task.

The riders from Puryn reached their destinations. As expected, Cinnog pulled into the citadel and bolstered its own defenses. It responded to Puryn's pleas with a simple one-line response: "Not interested in spending the lives of Cinnog on Suden dogs."

Puryn spat when he read the response. "Cowards."

Orus shook his head, muttering, "I figured as much."

Yslandeth had the most soldiers of any kingdom, but King Swyk over-thought the whole endeavor, spreading his troops thinly along his Great White Wall. He then dispatched two-thousand troops to Edenyag and sent another seven thousand to Puryn, holding back seventeen-thousand-five-hundred to protect his capital city. Puryn shook his head in disbelief. The King of Yslandeth expected to hold Empyr with seventeen-thousand-five-hundred troops against hundreds of thousands of invaders.

Sir Ontak had better be on the ball, Puryn thought sarcastically, shaking his head. *Still, seven-thousand is better than nothing.*

The riders arrived in Edenyag too late. Swyk's two-thousand reserves lay dead on the field, and Edenyag burned. The Orcs swarmed over Edenyag, and the Eden who could run headed North as quickly as possible. Draj runners took notes from their surveillance, avoided the Orc patrols, and then rode hard to Hodan to pass the news of Edenyag's fall.

* * *

King Swyk called an emergency meeting of his Generals. Sir Ontak suggested evacuating the city of all non-essential personnel. Swyk agreed, sending criers to pass an edict that his people should flee to the North as best they could, or attempt to make it to Oron Falmarindi. Swyk hoped Glorin would have room for his people. He knew if he did, Glorin would never turn away Yslandeth. Swyk then secretly called his Queen to his planning room, where he hurriedly tried to devise a viable plan to defeat the new threat. Unfortunately, nothing was coming to him.

The Queen entered the room. "Yes, husband, what is it?" the Queen asked, though she knew.

"Falda, my sweet," Swyk said, lowering his voice. "There are two guards and a fast chariot at the ready in the courtyard. Go to Puryn, or run to Torith! Get out of here. Sudenyag is in ashes, and Edenyag burns now. We cannot win this war. Live, my love. Please do as I say." He looked haggard. He hadn't slept in days and had been drinking. Falda knew this was the fulfillment of her visions. It had all come to pass, just as she had seen countless times before in her sleep.

"I will go to Erynseere, My King. I will aid Princess Adasser. She will need my healing if there is war." The Queen teared up. "What of you, my love? What will you do?" She already knew. She had seen his death. She had begged Haya to let this pass unfulfilled, but she now knew that was not the will of the Goddess.

301

"I will stand with my men. I must protect my kingdom." His eyes watered. He never thought it would come to this. Then, with shaking hands, he touched Falda's face, knowing it was for the last time. "My love, you have always been my heart. I will wait for you in Aeternum." At that moment, Swyk knew he would not gaze upon her face again, for this battle was suicide.

Falda hugged him and sobbed. Then, knowing it was their last hug, she kissed him as if for all of eternity. "Until we meet again, my love. Whether it be in this life or in the presence of the Goddess." Falda turned and did not look back. Swyk watched her go.

She would be safer with Adasser. The castle was a prime target, and they could not hold it with what they had, against what the intelligence cited. Swyk prayed.

* * *

As Eden burned, the amassed allied army relocated South of Erynseere, where the soldiers sat and waited. Some began to question if the enemy was ever coming. It had been over two weeks since Sudenyag had been razed. The general consensus was, "If the enemy had so many soldiers, what was taking them so long?"

Puryn was in no hurry. He was about to ride to his castle and check the preparations for the one-hundredth time, when a rider burst into camp at full gallop. Jumping off his horse, he handed the scrolls to Puryn and almost collapsed from exhaustion. A servant brought the Squire some water while Puryn broke the seal and read it. Orus waited for him to speak. With mixed despair and disgust, Puryn handed the scroll to Orus.

Orus read. "Your Excellency, I regret to inform you that, upon reaching the borderlands North of Edenyag, we witnessed great plumes of smoke rising from the villages and towns. People were seen fleeing the kingdom for Dornat al Ar and Torith. Our scouts were able to determine that the invaders were indeed as described. Dark clothed humans, Orcs, and Goblins. By my estimate, there were at least fifty-thousand enemies on the ground in Eden. Edenyag has fallen to the enemy. No word on the condition of the royal family there. The situation is dire."

Orus shook his head, and then he looked at Puryn. "This may be our finest hour, my young brother, or at least our most trying." Orus laughed, handing Puryn a flask. Puryn took a swig and grimaced. It was Hodan whiskey. They loved it, but it was as harsh a drink as they were as a people.

"We have no choice. We are warriors. We serve the King, and, in your case, you serve your people. Therefore, we shall maintain our honor and pray for mercy from the Gods." Puryn looked to the trees. "Haya, please hear me."

It was not Haya who heard, but Runnir and Gunnir. They listened intently, rubbing their mischievous hands together. The God-brothers loved a good fight, and this one was shaping up to be an epic battle. The pair maintained their blessings on their champions. These two humans promised to be very entertaining warriors. Haya was preoccupied with another who had called for her attention, and the Goddess was not watching her sons.

* * *

In Erynseere, the people battened down their homes. They moved the livestock indoors and set up provisions in their cellars. The villagers tried to set up a militia, but Puryn would have none of it. He forbade anyone to throw away their lives. He knew men would need to survive, in order to carry on after this mess had resolved itself.

* * *

Over several years, in the castle at Erynseere, the Baroness had been reading her book and practicing her arts. She became adept at controlling not only her emotions, but also her family of trees. When she heard of the impending attack, she called to the tree leaders, asking them to position themselves strategically in the path of where the enemy was likely to advance. The trees complied, lying in wait.

While learning how to be the Holy Mother, Adasser had spent many hours in meditation and prayer, so much so that her five-year-old son, Ilari, would often sit on his own and pray to the Goddess, which tickled Haya to no end. The three-year-old twins were busy chewing on things they were not supposed to and getting into everything. Arla managed them while Adasser tried to master her arts. Grandma did not mind. She loved to be around her grandchildren.

Adasser had quietly grown in power. The only people who knew what she was truly capable of were Puryn, Arla, Durn, and Ilari, but none had seen everything. She tried to keep her arts to herself, but Ilari followed her everywhere, always asking questions. She could not be annoyed, because he was adorable and wanted to be helpful. He learned her ways as she practiced with her son by her side.

During her studies, Adasser learned to speak to the trees and how to have them relay messages to their comrades anywhere on the Ert. In this way, she could make a connection and "see" what was going on through the perspective of the forest at any location on the Ert.

A side effect of meditation was that she became more attached to nature. She progressed from talking solely with trees to having a strange understanding with all of the animal life within her direct vicinity. Often, birds would perch on her while she meditated, or they would sit on a windowsill listening to her voice. At times, this ability unnerved Puryn, because Adasser had once attracted a giant snake and some very creepy-looking insects.

The animals and the forest could sense Adasser's mood and her will. Of course, the forest would unquestioningly do her bidding. Still, the animals could be a bit less predictable in their actions. Sometimes, they listened and helped; other times, they would do as they pleased.

Adasser had an idea. She would be helpful. She decided to aid her husband, even if he didn't see it coming. As the horde approached, the trees looked more menacing than usual. More vines and jagged branches seemed to be appearing. Adasser's army had formed right under Puryn's nose, and he hadn't noticed.

The Priestess wasn't going to tell him, because she knew her husband would only try to stop her. He would figure it out soon enough, but it would be too late to stop her by then.

The Queen of Nature

The sudden destruction of two southern kingdoms concerned King Swyk. Fearing for the Dwarves and Elves to the East, he sent riders to warn them. Glorin and Bogrol had seen the smoke and sent their own scouts earlier, so they were fully aware of the dangers lurking on their southern borders.

The Elfish King declared a state of emergency, ordering all Elves within Torith to withdraw to the underground fortress at Oron Falmarindi. It was an orderly migration. The enemy was still a ways off, and the Elves were not yet in a panic. However, the forest was thin, the tree ring was barren, and it would not provide adequate protection. Moreover, the Holy Mother's health was failing, and she was becoming too frail to hold the trees in her presence. They were migrating to Erynseere against Adasser's wishes, but the Mother knew it had to be so.

The High Priestess addressed her last remaining trees. "My loves, I depart you soon. Grant an old Elf a final wish before we say goodbye, will you?" The trees rustled, some groaning. They were not pleased with her words. "Be still, my trusted family, all that lives, must end. I am no different. She is your Queen now, and I must diminish. I would ask that you relay the message that I will not see the morrow, for my time is full. Haya calls me home, and I am ready."

The trees dropped flowers from their branches all around the Holy Mother. She bent down, picking one up, smelling its fragrance one last time. "She will lead you well, my children, for she is greater than I. She wields all the forms and does not know her true potential. See to it that she survives and preserves the people she loves, if you are able. She is a good girl, but foolish and strong-willed." She smiled. "But she also possesses a true heart and a sharp mind. So respect her, as you did me."

The old woman hugged a tree and bowed. Glorin watched as the old woman removed her headdress and looked to the sky with her hands up and outstretched. "Holy Mother of all that lives, I am ready." There was a bright flash of lightning and a clap of thunder where the old woman once stood. The ground was not scorched, nor was there a crater, but she was gone.

Glorin looked to the sky and waved goodbye to his old friend and teacher. She was home. Then, he looked out over to the Raven's Pass, toward Yslandeth, wondering what his daughter was up to. He had an idea of her intentions and prayed to Haya to protect her from the enemy and from herself. Then, the Elfish King departed with the remainder of his people to the underground fortress. The Draj remained behind, within the remaining trees. They set up a defensive perimeter and awaited their doom. None of them expected to survive the engagement.

The Dwarves did similarly, moving their farmers and as much of the harvest as they could gather into Dornat al Ar. Then, Bogrol set his meager Dwarfish armies outside the city's immense granite doors. The Dwarf King ordered his men to defend the populace to their last breaths and wished them luck.

He, too, asked for the blessings of Haya, but felt a cold chill run down his spine, as he realized he was sealing the fates of all those young soldiers by closing the great doors behind them. Frowning, he walked solemnly to where the refugees were gathering and constructing their makeshift campsite. The King then spoke a few words of encouragement to his people before leaving to join his family. There was no celebrating by the crowds, only quiet talking and a nervous, dark mood. The Dwarves were sick of war.

Yslandeth manned its Great White Wall and set troops at key points within the city of Empyr. Swyk attempted to come up with a viable defensive plan to save the capital, but the best he could come up with was an evacuation plan, and ways to delay the inevitable. He was not optimistic, nor was Sir Ontak, who was leading their forces. The King took solace in the fact that his love was in Erynseere with his most trusted Baron, surrounded by Hodan and Athis, who had become a key player in the defense of Yslandeth. Unfortunately, all the preparations seemed too little and too late.

Swyk called for Master Reti, and they prayed together in the monastery. The King burned offerings and begged Haya for mercy, then left to armor up. He rode out with Ontak, joining the men who were readying to die. They all resolved to meet their fates head-on, vice trying to hide. He smiled, imagining how Falda would have screamed at him for his *foolish pride*. He would make their deaths worth it. Something good would come of this sacrifice.

Now the waiting began. The defenses were as good as they were going to get.

* * *

In Erynseere, the trees had become so thick that they appeared as a tightly made picket fence thirty feet wide. The gaps were so small that even a sword could not stab through the alignment. The forest had formed a circle five miles across, with the castle situated in its center. Adasser's tree emplacements, which she had directed along the enemy's likely travel route, appeared to those unaware as small, wooded glens. The enemy would not suspect anything. Her minions were silently lying in wait.

While the reluctant Priestess was preparing for war, she received a message through her link to the trees. "No, she did not …" Adasser trailed off, frowning, then nodded. "She's gone. Am I the Holy Mother by default? Oh my Gods. I am not ready! I am not worthy!" She turned to the trees. They cowered in her presence, because they could feel her displeasure. "Is it true, my friends?" They affirmed her thoughts. "Then so be it," she relented. "We must prepare."

While speaking to her trees, a commotion occurred at the edge of her forest. The Draj were there to intercept the invaders. Adasser saw them—they were more bloodied men, women, and children. They were running from the southwest. Then she saw the smoke past the canyons, realizing these were Cinnog's people.

A woman hysterically cried out for her child, who ran through the crowd to her. Scooping him up, she hugged him tightly while she wept, shaking. Adasser put her hand on the woman's shoulder, and she immediately calmed.

"Who are you? What has happened?" Adasser asked, knowing full well what the woman was about to say.

"The evil ones. They brought down the citadel with siege engines. There were so many of them. We ran through the rubble. So many are dead." The woman began shaking and crying. Adasser had heard enough.

"Trees, scout for me. Where are the evil ones?" she asked calmly.

The trees looked over the plains and saw that the enemy was moving northwest from Sudenyag, toward the location of Puryn and Orus. The Offlanders were also moving up the West side of the canyon, directly toward Korin and Erynseere. Adasser knew that Puryn would be cut off and surrounded. Panicking, the Baroness called for her ministers. Donick and the others had returned from the field long ago and were busy organizing supplies.

Donick ran to his Baroness. "What is it, Your Excellency?" he asked and bowed.

"Until this is over, dispense with the formalities, my dearest friends. We do not have time for pleasantries. My tree scouts tell me the enemy moves on the East and West of the canyon. This means Puryn and Orus will be cut off and surrounded. We must send word immediately. The refugees I have spoken with, and my trees estimate …," Adasser looked at the tree, and it answered her, "… eight hours until impact. Eight hours. Assemble the Draj. Send one-thousand to Puryn and leave one-thousand here with me."

"My Lady, that leaves you without adequate protection," Donick protested.

"Trust me, my friend, I have all I need." Adasser looked at the ring. The forest was getting busy now. The wolves had come down in their packs and patrolled freely within the trees. Lions came down from the mountains bringing their prides and did similarly. Birds of prey circled high over the ring, perching where they pleased. Erynseere was full of life in all of its menacing forms.

No one saw Haya as she stood within the center of the ring, watching her Priestess with interest. The Goddess smiled. Once again, she knew she had chosen wisely.

Adasser ran into her castle after the Draj left toward Puryn. She did not know how far they were or if the reinforcements would reach their Baron in time, but the warriors were needed outside the ring, not within it.

Adasser found Arla. "My dearest companion and constant friend, please guard my children with your life. Take them below ground into the fortress that my wise husband built while others laughed at him. Provisions have been moved within the fortifications. Do not come out, for any reason, until all is calm. I fear the end may be near, but I am confident Haya will make a show of it. Best case, we all feast tomorrow in the forest green! Worst case, I will see you all at the gates."

Haya was impressed by the Elf's bravery and resolve.

"Do not joke about such things, daughter," Arla said as she choked back her tears. Adasser lifted Ilari and kissed him. Then she did the same with Altwidus and Elpis. The two younger children had no idea what was going on, but Ilari was as sensitive to the spiritual as was his mother.

"Momma, the evil comes. I wish to fight." His little face twisted, and he picked up a stick. He was his father's son, but his mother's also.

"You will do no such thing, young man!" Adasser scolded. "Go with your grandmother. Now!"

Ilari cried and protested. "I want to see Haya, Momma. You are going to bring her here, aren't you?"

Adasser turned, stunned. He saw. He had the sight. She hoped she could talk to his little soul about what he saw when this was all over if they survived. "You can watch from a window, but not too close to the opening.

Things may get out of hand, My Little Priest." Adasser stooped and kissed him on his tiny lips. "Mother loves you, my big boy. You are your father's son! Go, now. Move!"

Arla swept up the kicking and screaming Ilari and the other two children, ushering them within the fortress made by the Dwarves of six-foot-thick granite. Adasser turned and swallowed hard, trying to focus. She had less than eight hours before the end, but she was ready.

* * *

The Priestess's rider found the Korinian cavalry riding Southwest toward the smoke. The scouts had cut across the Erynseere and ran parallel to the river on the Hodan border. Athis was leading his men into the canyon in an attempt to cut off the enemy as it moved North toward his lands. It seemed that Puryn and Orus had the same idea, as they all met at the Cinnog border. Hordes of the enemy could be seen as far as the horizon, and the Scourge moved North toward Yslandeth.

"My Lords. Well, the Baroness sought to warn you of the fall of Cinnog, but apparently, you are aware," the Squire said sarcastically, looking over the field of the endless enemy. "Cinnog's refugees are holed up in Erynseere. There were very few survivors."

Puryn and Orus nodded grimly.

"We must move North to counter their threat, brother," Orus said to Puryn.

"How do we leave without exposing this approach?" the Draj asked.

As this was said, a Goblin scout yelled something unintelligible, and the marching stopped. The Goblin was pointing toward the alliance position, but Puryn didn't think they had seen them yet. "They have discovered this path. We must move back and allow them to come in, but we must not allow them to cut us off and limit our movement."

Athis rode up between the two. "Puryn, allow me to take the point." The

Baron of Korin had thousands of cavalry in the canyon. They would be effective, but not ideal. Then, the Suden Captain approached.

"We shall set a wall. Lord Athis can run the flanks. It is not ideal, but it will allow your forces to regroup on the other side, toward Erynseere and Korin. If all else fails, it buys you time to come up with a better plan." Harun spoke to his Lieutenant, splitting his forces, leaving three-hundred to Athis, and taking two-hundred to support Puryn and Orus.

"Athis, you do not need to do this," Puryn stated.

"But I do, my friend. I must atone to Haya for my misdeeds and sins. I will aid her chosen in his purpose. She will honor my sacrifice. I will see you in Aeternum, at the table of heroes. We shall sup and drink wine forever. I will save you a seat and one for your Lady. I fear being an Elf, we may have to wait upon her." He looked at Puryn with a childish grin. He was happy. This was the chance he had waited for, for almost twenty years.

Haya nodded, smiling at the man Athis had become. She called for his seat to be readied at her table, and Aluia made the preparations.

Puryn looked sadly at Athis. He had hated him for so long. Now this man was an honest soul, a good man, and he was heading off to die. "We shall break bread in Aeternum. Let it be known in your heart that I forgive you for that day, and with his final breath, Master Elig also forgave you. I ask for your forgiveness for holding my hatred for so long. You will redeem not only yourself, but also your family name, and if I live, I will celebrate this day, and so will my people."

Athis wiped a misty tear, smiling. "Until we meet in paradise, gentlemen."

Orus and Puryn solemnly saluted Athis, then turning quickly, they had their Commanders quietly pass the word to move North through the canyon to Erynseere. The Draj looked up at the canyon top. Trees had appeared in small groups here and there. Smiling, the Baron wondered if they were up to something.

Witnesses reported that Athis held his ground for three days, before falling in battle, to his wounds. His men killed ten times their number, as the enemy's movement was badgered by ill-tempered trees. Offlander Commanders could not understand why they could not flank their opponents or control the higher ground, because everywhere they went, trees were in the way. Some Orcs and Goblins reported strange things happening when their units entered the glens on the canyon ridges. Chariots were caught in vines, and mysterious deaths occurred.

It was general chaos, but despite the best efforts of the forest, the enemy eventually entered the canyon and made a straight line toward Hodan and the Erynseere. Puryn and Orus decided to make their way to the castle in Erynseere, but when they reached the edge of the open field around the ring of trees, they saw the enemy had taken the advantage. There were too many.

Knowing they could not engage them directly, Puryn and Orus instead chose to push toward the Grand Gate of the Great White Wall, in an attempt to circumnavigate the barony and come out on the northeastern corner of it. Puryn was encouraged by how the trees held the line and hurried his men to cover the open distance required. It took two days before the alliance was able to get into position.

Meanwhile, Adasser was dealing out chaos of her own creation.

In the tree circle, Adasser stood with her one-thousand remaining Draj. The one-thousand who had left her walked right into the onslaught that came to her doorstep. The fields were black with the enemy as they engulfed the land surrounding the trees. The forest of Erynseere reported there were Orcs and Goblins, as far as the eye could see. The Priestess inquired of her friends as to the whereabouts of her husband, and two hawks informed her that approximately ten-thousand remaining Draj and Hodan forces had just arrived northeast of the barony. Puryn was leading them with Orus.

She knew it. "Those fools! What are they thinking? Glory and honor in a pig's ass!" Adasser spat. "These damn men and their delusions of glory. He will not be happy until my father is right! That son of a mule!" Adasser was working herself up, but she did not care. She ordered trees to Puryn's location, and then the world slowed down for her, and in the moment, the Priestess had no idea what was happening.

Ilari pointed out a window and shouted to his mother. "She is here, Mother! She is you, and you are her!" Ilari smiled with a glint of red in his tiny eyes. His mother's eyes were burning coals, and her hair began to float as if in water. Then, absentmindedly, as if this was just an everyday moment, she smiled and waved to her son, calling to him in a strange voice.

"Hide," Adasser said in an ancient tongue.

"Yes, Momma. The Goddess watches you," Ilari replied in kind.

Adasser smiled wide, laughing, which unnerved her already wary soldiers. They had no idea what was going on.

The Elfish woman walked calmly to the center of her tree circle, where Haya waited, observing.

Static popped between the Druid's locks, which were now a silvery-white. She looked out over her men with blazing red eyes, spying the Orcs who came for her babies. The trees awaited her command. Their lines stood tightly wound, and the Orcs tried to chop at them with axes and burn them with fire.

With an angry tone, she shouted to her trees. "Ilari!" was all she said.

The trees pulsed, much like a shield wall charge of Puryn's men. They thrust out thirty feet, engulfing the 1st rank, shredding the enemy instantly within the branches and vines. The 2nd through the 5th ranks of the enemy were crushed by the impact with the tree trunks, and the 6th through 10th ranks were thrown fifty feet, many dying when they hit the ground.

Adasser's head was now lowered, and she was looking at the enemy's front rank through the eyes of the trees. The Scourge were now turtling up and locking their shields. They looked around with bewildered faces, wondering what sort of magic had just hit them.

Adasser yelled her second power word, shouting with authority, "Elpis!"

Her daughter's name brought a hail of birds of prey. The sky was filled with them. They swooped down, tearing at the enemy with relentless fury. From within the forest, bull-moose, elk, bear, lions, and wolves waded into the enemy ranks, crushing or tearing to shreds anything that stood in their path. The attack lasted twenty minutes, with the enemy losing another five ranks of troops. The dead totaled in the tens of thousands within thirty minutes of engaging the Erynseere, with another half of that number injured. However, the enemy had plenty more in reserve.

The Offlanders counter-attacked with catapults and a full shield wall charge. The ring adjusted as trees were knocked down, filling in the holes in its defenses, just as in Torith. Then, the enemy began to stack their own dead, climbing over them in an attempt to move over the trees, vice through them. While mildly successful, most who made it over were immediately destroyed by Draj, while Adasser attacked for the third time.

She cried to the forest, "Altwidus!" The old forest groaned and cracked. Vines shot out and grabbed the enemy forces as they advanced, dragging them into the trees, where they were cut to shreds by spear-like branches. The enemies who were still scaling their dead were impaled as they climbed. The evil withdrew, but some had made it over the tree ring. Three eventually made it to where Adasser stood.

"My Lady!" the Commander shouted at Adasser, but she was not listening.

An Orc shot an arrow that found a young girl, who had wandered out of the keep. Motionless, the girl fell to the ground, and Adasser's eyes turned from red to black as coal. She saw her daughter's face in the girl. "This will not do," the Elf said.

The same Orc charged at the distracted Baroness. Her Draj protectors were too far to intervene. As if she was dealing with a common pest, Adasser raised a hand, suspending the Orc in mid-air. He clutched his throat and gurgled as if he was being choked. There was an audible snap as Adasser swept her hand toward the trees, and the enemy flew through the air, where he was grabbed by waiting vines, never to be seen again. The two remaining Orcs looked at each other fearfully.

"This Witch is too powerful, brother. We should run," one said to the other.

Adasser bent down and pulled the arrow from the child's neck, prayed quietly, and the wound closed. "Wake, young one," she said, cradling the girl's tiny face. Adasser guessed she was only five or six years old.

The Orcs sat paralyzed with fear, deciding what to do. The Draj were coming.

The little girl woke as if from a dream, smiling, and hugged Adasser, whose eyes had returned to a golden red. "I saw the gates, My Lady," she said in a tiny voice. "They are beautiful. Mum and Da are there now!"

Adasser teared up. "Well, they will wait for you, young lady!" Adasser saw that Ilari was standing outside, and she was not amused. In an irritated voice, she ordered, "Go with my stubborn son and seek Arla. Go now!"

Ilari ran up and kissed his mother, then ran away. Adasser stood, turning back toward the Orcs with a bored expression on her face. "You shall die now, pigs." She thrust an open hand out, and one of the Orcs flew backward until he impacted a well. He had a sizeable hand-like impression on his chest when he fell limp on the ground, and his innards burst by the force of impact.

Adasser glared at the other Orc, who was now looking for a place to run. "There is no place to go. You came to me, fool!" Adasser hissed. She put her hands together and then opened them forcefully. The Orc exploded instantly as if he was torn in half like parchment.

Adasser walked through the carnage she had caused, looking to her trees, which were standing by for her orders. "My loves, kill at will, anything not of my people. Protect my fool of a husband and his idiot friend, please?" The trees swayed in acknowledgment of their orders and began killing everything within their grasp. The ground was blackened by Orc and Goblin blood.

Adasser, now surveying the situation, was distracted by the chaos of her Draj, who were directly engaging an additional one-hundred or so Orcs, who had somehow survived the wall of trees and animals, only to regroup in front of Adasser's defenses. Adasser ordered the Draj to hold the portcullis, stepping to the front of her lines.

"But, My Lady, I cannot leave you alone with these animals!" Durn pleaded. He would not betray his son's wife.

Smiling, Adasser touched her Commander's shoulder. "As you wish, my protector. Send your men, but you may stay."

Durn sent his unit to the portcullis. They closed it and stood guard inside. Adasser stood in front of the one-hundred or more Orcs, as many laughed at her. They were not privy to who was controlling the trees or what had happened near the well. Durn knew they were overconfident. Smirking, he wondered how his son's wife would dispatch this brood.

"How dare you come to my home and threaten my family, pigs," Adasser said in an ancient tone. The trees were in a fury, the frenzy of killing was at a peak, and they were as deadly as they were beautiful. So was their Queen.

"Inkindus furiar culmenar!" Adasser spoke words she did not know, but knew in her heart. She made a fist above her head and pulled it down before her face. Fire rained down from thin air above the Orcs. A sulfurous stench filled the air as Orcs tried to run in all directions, but they were consumed by the heat of the fire. Adasser opened her hand, and the fire dissipated, leaving a circular reminder that it had happened. One-hundred or so sets of Orc bones were found laid in formation, in memoriam. Adasser chuckled. She was starting to have fun, but she had pushed too hard.

The Priestess swooned after the fire attack, and Durn knew something was wrong. He reached out and caught her before she fell. Her hair was still white, but slowly regained its natural black color. The red was fading from her eyes, and she had a far-off look on her face. The Baroness did not seem completely coherent.

"I guess, perhaps, I overdid it for my first time, my protector." Adasser produced a weak smile, and Durn, her Draj Commander, carried her to a shaded area near a tree, which had moved itself to the center of the yard. He called for some water, and a Draj brought a canteen.

"Thank you, gentlemen. I shall be all right." The Draj soldier also handed the Baroness a wedge of cheese and a small loaf of bread from his pack. She ate. "That is much better. Thank you." The Priestess rested. All was quiet for the moment, and the Offlanders were in disarray. Durn looked around at the carnage in disbelief. The Goddess was definitely with Adasser. The older warrior would never look at a tree in the same light.

* * *

The Orcs and Goblins had no answer for the trees, and the Witch was handing them a sound defeat. No number of troops seemed to matter. Initial estimates by the Offlander Commander stated that the Witch, her trees, and swarms of animals had killed at least sixty-five-thousand soldiers and wounded another fifty-five-thousand. Many would not recover from their wounds. The dead would increase by a large margin by morning.

One spy stated that all he could see was one Elfish Witch and a Legion of Elfish warriors holding back the glorious forces of the Offlander King. The High Commander was livid and had his Senior Field Captain executed for dereliction of duty. He then promoted the next Lieutenant in line, with a stern warning that failure would not be tolerated. Still, the General realized that the Witch was a formidable foe, for which they had not planned.

The Todessen General worried that he was losing too many of his men on this small patch of land. He knew the Scourge had plenty of troops. Still, these humans had put up a decent fight, killing close to a combined hundred-thousand soldiers, between the meager forces of their three southern kingdoms. He knew the northern kingdom was the largest, and spies reported that the humans in the North possessed three times the troops they had encountered to the South. If the northern kingdom killed at the same rate as the other three southern kingdoms, the General worried that he would be facing the warriors of Torith and Dornat al Ar with scarcely one-hundred-fifty-thousand men remaining. He knew with this number, it was not inconceivable to lose.

Erynseere had bloodied the nose of its enemy and bled them dearly. The Offlander intelligence could not determine how many warriors awaited them under the two mountain fortresses of the Elves and Dwarves. The Todessen leadership had to be conservative now. There was still much land to cover and many people to conquer.

"This Elfish Witch is more than we had bargained for, Sir," the new Commander said plainly. "If we continue down this path, we will be severely weakened and unable to complete our mission. Reinforcements will take years to acquire, Sir. We must think of a way into the tree wall or go around."

"Go around. That is a sound idea. We shall go around them to the northwest. We are sure to encounter pockets of resistance, but if these armies are foolish enough to engage us in the open field, we will crush them. Their Commanders will know this. Look for them at choke points and avoid giving them an advantage. First, we must rout the remaining resistance. Once we have secured the lands, we shall revisit this Elfish bitch. I will use her as my concubine until I tire of her, and then I will put her body on a stake, decorating the entrance to her castle. She will pay," the General growled angrily.

The Orc and Goblin Commanders called out in a guttural language to their units. Then, they formed up, marching away from the tree line to a distance at which they felt was safe.

Adasser saw their retreat from her seat near the tree, smiling with satisfaction. "I will make you bleed again if you come within reach of my family—child, husband, or tree kind."

The Draj helped their Baroness as she staggered into the portcullis. She was weakened, seeming more like a frail Princess than the force of nature she had been an hour before. None of her men died, because of her ferocity in battle, and Adasser's trees were none the worse for wear. The animals patrolled in herds, packs, and prides. A new ally arrived in with the dark. The fields outside of the forest were filled with biting insects and snakes.

Adasser laughed, speaking to her trees. "Excellent job, my loves. Please protect my husband and his band. Form a protective circle where they lie. Let him know I love him and think about him. Give him a tree lily from his Lady." The trees swayed again as it began to rain. "Ah, thank you, Aluia! Goddess, please give the enemy a muddy, bug-ridden bed in which to wallow in tonight!"

"Sleep, My Lady," Donick said, bringing a lantern to his Baroness. "Please come inside and get warm. Rest. Tomorrow is another day. I fear they will still be there when we wake."

"You are correct, master Donick. I will sleep now. Commander, you have the watch," Adasser said, sounding much like her husband.

Durn smiled at his daughter-in-law. He saluted. "Yes, Your Excellency! Sleep well."

The Draj used Elfish camouflage and hid within the friendly trees, knowing that there, they would be ten times more effective and privy to things humans could not see in the dark. Trees did not need eyes to see.

***

To the northeast, the Orcs dispatched a scout unit that had come around to check out the route toward Empyr. Hodan cut off their escape, killing any stragglers on sight. None, to their knowledge, made it back to enemy lines. Orus and Puryn split their forces, setting up a cold camp on either side of the farm road leading toward the capital. The men all went to sleep in the open within the tall grass, waking to their surprise, in a small copse of trees maybe a quarter-mile in diameter. No one remembered trees in the area at sundown the night before. Orus rubbed his eyes in confusion, unnerved at the instantly appearing forest.

"Puryn! Wake up! Dark magic is upon us!" Orus yelled across the road.

"Shh, Orus! They will hear you, you oaf! What are you yammering … on … about?" Puryn woke disoriented and covered in tree lilies. They were Adasser's favorite flower. He picked one up and breathed in its fragrance with a deep breath. Smiling, he knew it was her.

"What in the Underworld is going on? Why do you smile?" Orus questioned.

Puryn rolled over, brushing off the flowers gently and then putting his hand on a tree. "Good morning," he said calmly to the tree. "Please tell my love that I am fine and thank her for the flowers. Also, thank you for coming, my friends." Puryn talked to the trees, and they swayed. On the other end, the trees were elated when Adasser giggled and hugged the ancient elm she often spoke with. It had just passed Puryn's message.

"My beloved idiot is still alive. We shall have our hands full with that one, elm. He's a hero, and he is a man. Unfortunately, they tend to do stupid things. Thank you for your vigilance." The Baroness stood and walked over to the guard. They were working on a half night's sleep, but there was no sign of an Orc, Goblin, or Todessen incursion since the carnage of the day prior.

The old elm spoke to Adasser, informing her that the evil ones appeared to be withdrawing and moving to the Northwest, clockwise toward where her beloved was. Adasser thanked the elm and informed the Draj. She found an old Elfish scout who had immigrated from Torith and asked him to find Puryn and warn him. He agreed without hesitation.

"Remember, brother, you have no time. They will be upon him within two days. Take a horse and ride hard to the copse in the middle of the open field. I think they are there." She turned to the elm, who confirmed. "Yes, it is sure they are there."

"I will let them know, or die in the attempt, Holy Mother," the Elf replied. Adasser's eyes widened. She had forgotten who she was now. She was the spiritual leader of Elves, by default. They looked at her as the direct representative of nature and the Goddess. After yesterday's display, no one doubted her. They knew who she was without a formal introduction.

The rider reached Puryn half a day before the enemy arrived. He and Orus rested their soldiers in the cover and protection of the woods. The copse thickened up around the edge, making it hard to see anything within the trees. The Orcs approached unaware, avoiding trees, and considering the field as open and without resistance. They did not see Puryn and Orus, and the two liked it that way. Their unwanted guests would see them soon enough.

The Battle of Arondayre

unnir and Gunnir whispered as they watched the battles unfold on the Ert below. Haya was concerned that the darkness was gaining too much ground. She looked to her two rival sons to alter the heroes to the advantage of the people of the Ert.

Runnir watched as Puryn weakened from sickness and exhaustion. His hero's valiant armies were pushed back repeatedly by the hordes of Offlanders. The God set out to intervene, healing the hero's wounds and bolstering his endurance. To Puryn's surprise, he felt invigorated and extremely strong after a short nap.

Not to be outdone, Gunnir did the same for Orus, who was also waning. The two men had been fighting for almost ten days when the brothers chose, once again, to intervene. Concerned for the light, both Gods blessed the remaining armies of their champions. Secretly, the two wondered what their mother was up to. Things looked bleak for her side.

There were lulls in the fighting, but the enemy's advance was relentless. The black army stretched as far as the eye could see. Puryn, Orus, and their men slept and ate when and where they could. Combat was so constant and spontaneous that many did not even have the time to defecate or urinate properly. The men stunk of piss and human waste, having had to relieve themselves within their armor, while on the march and while striking down the enemy as best as they could. Sickness was rampant, not only because of unsanitary field conditions, but also because the enemy had begun to poison their own weapons by coating their blades in their own waste.

The Orcs and Goblins pushed northeast through Empyr toward Raven's Pass and Torith. Puryn was determined to give Adasser's people their best chance by directing the remaining soldiers at his disposal as effectively as possible. With Runnir's blessing, Puryn's men spread terror, uncertainty, and death within the black army's ranks.

* * *

Empyr fell, but not without a fight. King Swyk had set up a formidable defense. If the King possessed the army he had before the Great War of the People, Swyk would have defeated the invaders handily, but that was a pipe dream since his numbers were only ten-percent compared to in those days. His men held at the choke points and from the top of the wall, but the sheer numbers of the darkness were too much for Yslan. Yslandeth fell with a great crash.

The enemy deployed siege engines again. They tore the walls of the castle down, one by one, and then toppled the great towers of the monastery. Puryn stood in the breach with Orus and Swyk. Yslandeth and Hodan made them bleed in the courtyard as the stone fell down around them. Swyk and Ontak became separated from Puryn's forces as the battle raged on.

As it became evident that the battle was unwinnable, Puryn called to Orus and their remaining men to regroup on the edge of the forest, near the lands of Clan Gur and Torith. The men slipped into the woods, gaining a few dozen Yslandeth regulars, and licked their wounds. The army was picking up military forces from every locale they passed through. Still, every time Puryn or Orus seemed to grow their numbers, a battle would claim those new souls, negating any gains.

In the forest, Puryn looked at the remaining men and sighed. "Orus, how many Hodan Elites remain?" The Draj warrior wiped the filth from his face with an equally filthy piece of linen he had torn off a corpse. He needed to see, and his face was covered with Orc blood and Goblin innards. Puryn handed the rag to Orus, who declined it.

"I counted one-hundred-fifty Hodan warriors remaining." The Hodan King looked defeated and as if he wanted to cry. This was the first time Puryn had ever seen him so unsure of himself. "We have killed so many of them. How many more can there be, brother?"

The Draj frowned, scowling. "I think the Underworld is empty at the moment."

Orus smiled widely at the sarcasm and nodded in agreement. "It is a surety that the catacombs have been purged, and this filth came out. I think we need to return them to their home." Orus regained heart and made a defiant gesture of profanity into the distance, sitting down. The Hodan King ate some hardtack and drank a shot of Yslan whiskey he had salvaged from the rubble of the castle. He offered the flask to his brother-in-arms, who declined. Puryn instead laid down beneath a tree and tried to take a nap.

The two warriors rested momentarily while their armies bound their wounds and ate. While many tried to slumber, a messenger ran into the forest unmolested. It was sure the lad was one of theirs, or the trees would have mutilated the boy upon entry.

"Where is the champion, Puryn?" the boy gasped, trying to catch his breath.

Puryn moaned and rolled over, glaring at the boy. "What is it now? Where have they advanced to? Can I not sleep for five minutes?"

"It is not that, Sir." The boy was trembling and starting to cry. He was scarcely twelve years old. Puryn felt terrible for his outburst and sat up.

"I'm sorry, son. What have you got to tell me?" The Baron stood, towering over the boy.

"His Majesty is dead. So is Sir Ontak." The boy looked to the ground, tears freely streaming from his eyes. Puryn noticed that the tabard the boy wore was Ontak's. He must have been his Squire or page.

"What!?" Puryn cried. "How? When? What do you mean Swyk is dead?! Sir Ontak? No!" Puryn grabbed the boy's shoulders and demanded answers.

The boy looked up with reddened eyes. "An hour ago, Your Excellency. The filthy bastards captured the King and Sir Ontak. They took them to the Great White Wall and threw them off its top after publicly ridiculing them. They died from the fall. They were made an example of for resisting. The people are fleeing to the North, and Empyr is no more. Yslandeth is conquered."

Orus looked up seriously and, with a clear head, inquired stoically, "Why is this surprising, Squire?" He put his hand firmly on the boy's shoulder. The Squire stopped crying and stood up straight. "My homeland of Hodan fell several days ago. We watched it from the Great White Wall, while trying to hold Empyr. We ravage their lines, but they reinforce without effort. I fear there is no end to these vermin."

Puryn gave the Squire something to drink and sat down wearily. He wasn't tired anymore. In fact, he felt strangely invigorated. He wouldn't be able to sleep. He had watched as his old order was eradicated in their monastery as they fought to protect the wounded. Master Reti killed many, but he could not kill them all. His King and the Commanding General Ontak were also now dead.

Sudenyag, Cinnog, Hodan, and Yslandeth were reduced to the soldiers left in these woods. The only thing left to do was meet the enemy on the Arondayre in one last push or surrender.

Puryn wondered if perhaps they could scrape up a regiment of Edenyag regulars or a few Draj or Dwarf Legionnaires. The young leader was not encouraged, but he would not surrender. The Draj felt defeated, as did his brother, Orus. Puryn could see it on his face. There was an aura of silence and failure in the forest as if all there waited for death to come and snatch them away.

Puryn stood and shrugged. "We may as well die standing, my brothers," he said to Orus and the men around him.

The Draj leader thought about the situation. The only logical choice was to cut through this forest and try to protect Torith and Dornat al Ar. Puryn knew if those kingdoms were lost, nothing else they did would matter. The enemy would possess all of the lands, and no one would be left to resist.

The young Baron wondered what had become of the Erynseere. He shuddered, remembering how the rest of the Ert had fared. Puryn only hoped the Gods were with them in the forest. Then, the Draj-Manot called to his unit. King Orus brought in his one-hundred-fifty men and women.

"Rest up, my faithful warriors. We will cut through the woods and come out North of the Raven's Pass. We will try to stop them at Torith. Make your peace with the Gods. This will be our final stand."

* * *

In Erynseere, Falda worked on the wounded and the sick. When Swyk died, she screamed and fell to the floor crying. She said he had appeared to her in golden robes. He was a shimmering visage, which quickly faded away.

"Goodbye, my love. I will wait for you at the gates as promised," the spirit whispered as he went.

Falda was inconsolable for days. She instead drank a small keg of whiskey, raising a fist to the sky in defiance. Then, staggering over to her charge, Falda wiped Adasser's forehead, focusing on her work in a feeble effort to forget. The Baroness had been sleeping on and off for many days after the initial display of her powers.

"Curse the Gods, and curse these wretched pieces of cow dung. You motherless serpents! You filthy pigs' asses! Die, all of you, die!" Falda's face dared someone to tell her to calm down. No one did. "This Princess will not die, Haya! You sit upon your throne and watch us suffer. Where are you!?"

Just then, Ilari waddled into the room. He looked at the Queen with a puzzled little face. "Miss Falda? She is there. The Goddess is there." Ilari pointed to his mother.

"That is your momma, child, not Haya," the Queen slurred. "She may be a Priestess, but she is not the Goddess. That one sits in Aeternum and laughs as we burn."

"Not so, My Queen," the little boy answered, with a serious look on his tiny face. "She weeps for us and sends us aid against the Underworld.

Mother is her friend, and she visits with Mother freely. When they are together, I cannot tell where Mother ends and Haya begins. She is the Goddess, and the Goddess is Momma." Ilari touched the Queen's tears and hugged her.

The Queen cried, moaning while hugging the small boy. "He's gone, my boy. My love is no longer here. What shall I do now? Why does she hate me so?"

"He is not gone, My Queen. He simply is above us all! He sits and watches. To him, it will be a blink of an eye before you join him, but I'm sad to say, for you, it will be some time." He kissed her cheek. The Queen brushed his hair aside. He looked like his father, and that made the Queen smile.

"You are too wise for a five-year-old boy. Go play, and do not seek to grow old before your time!" The Queen hugged him and noticed that Adasser had opened her eyes. Falda brought her water and juice. When she was ready, the servants brought Adasser a more substantial repast. Regaining most of her strength within another day, Adasser again spoke with the trees.

"Where is my dearest, my loves?" Adasser asked in a raspy voice.

The trees answered that he was North of the Raven's Pass in the forest. The remaining armies were heading toward Torith to apparently meet the enemy head-on. Adasser moaned.

"This will not do, my loves. He is doomed. Set a corridor of trees in front of the enemy and force them to move in an enclosed space. Kill them when they are trapped in the corridor. Thin the herd for my husband. Haya, please help them. They are all we have left. Do you desire that we should all perish? What is the purpose for all of this suffering?" Adasser screamed at the sky until her voice cracked.

Durn ran into the room and saw Adasser was upset and awake.

Haya nodded and reassured her Priestess. However, Adasser still felt as if the end was near.

"Are you all right, My Baroness?" the Commander asked.

"As well as can be expected," she said, losing her voice. She turned to the trees. "My loves, look in all places, even those beyond our sight. Find friends to stand against the foes of the light. Stir them and bring them to our side. We are in need of a miracle!" The trees swayed and sent out a search to all corners of Ert.

Haya smiled smugly as she saw her beloved openly mocking her, laughing at her expense. Haeldrun stopped laughing and wondered what his former spouse was so calm about. She was up to no good. The God suddenly felt unsure of his victory. The Underlord enraged his armies further, increasing their bloodlust and depravity to levels unseen in the history of the Ert. The Scourge moved in to finish the job.

* * *

Over in the forest, Puryn was concerned. The trees were thinning as they moved East. He didn't know what Adasser was up to, but they were losing their cover, and fast. The ragtag, bloodied, and exhausted forces hurried out into the Arondayre, North of the Raven's Pass, and regrouped. Puryn looked at what he had left. About two-hundred Suden remained, including Captain Harun. Cinnog had around two-hundred-fifty pike men left, Yslandeth had three-hundred of Puryn's Draj-Erynseere, and Hodan was represented by the orneriest one-hundred-fifty warriors Puryn had ever had the pleasure of fighting beside.

Torith appeared to be deserted. To the South, the farms on the Altyr were abandoned. Puryn figured they were all underground in Dornat al Ar. Who could blame them? This was a suicide mission. The Yslan warrior sent out his scouts while Orus inspected the armor and weapons. The reconnaissance teams reported that everything was coming their way.

The warrior who reported didn't even guess the number of enemies, but told Puryn that the entire northern plains were covered in squares of troops moving past the great lake toward Torith. The Draj-Manot grimaced, setting his jaw, knowing it was time to die. He held a wilted tree lily from the forest and smelled it one more time. He would miss his family, but it would be worth it all if somehow his sacrifice allowed them to continue living. The trees set up as a massive corridor.

The Draj leader shook his head and snickered. "She is still up to her tricks," he muttered. Then the younger man hollered over toward Orus. "Brother, look at this development." He pointed northwest at the tree line and the corridor.

"So? Trees," Orus responded.

"Yes, but there have not been trees on this part of the Arondayre in a couple of hundred years, because they were over-logged or moved to Torith. These are new, like 'today new,'" Puryn emphasized, raising his eyebrows.

"Your Lady again? I like her tactics," Orus laughed. "We should set up at the mouth of the corridor and draw them in. I am sure her forest will be hungry for more Orc-flesh."

Orus winked at Puryn, who smiled. "Yes, they shall have their fill, and we will make those remaining pay dearly until our final breaths." The brothers-in-arms hugged and set off to give the orders.

Runnir and Gunnir were now standing. They blessed their warriors again. Never had the two seen such courage on the Ert. The God-brothers were saddened as they contemplated the deaths of Puryn and Orus. They liked these humans.

Puryn's visions flashed before his eyes. The pine trees. A pine cone. Pine needles. The smell of pine. The rustling of the wind, then flames. He shook his head and focused on his task. The final hour had come, and he freely accepted that he was ordained to die. All of Adasser's aid was for naught, but he welcomed the additional forces. He wanted to bleed the blackness as much as possible before having to depart for Aeternum. It was time.

* * *

While men lost hope and readied for death, and most of the forest gave up looking for a savior, a lone pine, high upon a frozen mountain, stood beside a cave, where an ancient being slept. So terrible and fierce was this creature that she had once been thought a Goddess herself, but the Dragon knew better than that.

Maradwynne, Mother of Dragon-kind, slept for several years, having moved her head out of her foul-smelling cave to enjoy the brisk, clean air. These times, to the ancients, were dull, and Dragons had lost interest in watching over mankind, Elves, and Dwarves. The Dragon slept to pass the boredom, but her naps sometimes lasted for decades. This had been a long, restful vacation from the Ert.

The pine tree first shed its needles, dropping them upon Maradwynne's face, but the Dragon shooed them away, thinking them to be a housefly or some other such nuisance. So, the tree tried harder, depositing several pine cones on the head of the Dragon, which garnered the same result.

Maradwynne was an Ancient. She was not only thousands of years old, but she was also thousands of years big. She was one of the full-grown matriarchs of Dragon-kind. Her head was the size of a large Dwarfish carriage. Her neck was as wide as five tavern barrels of ale, and she stood from head to tip of her tail, almost as long as one of the towers that used to stand in the monastery at Yslandeth. She was immense.

The pine, deciding to give it all it had, threw subtlety to the wind. It shed three pine cones with expert aim, dropping them straight into Maradwynne's exposed right nostril. The Dragon woke immediately, sneezing and blowing fire out of her nose.

What in the fires of the Underworld was that all about? thought the Dragon as she sat up, looking around, but nothing was there, save the wind, some snow, and one lone pine that she did not remember being around when she had laid down for her nap.

Recalling that there was a sapling near the cave entrance when she laid down, she sighed. "Oh dear, I did it again. How long have I slept this time!?" While pondering her answer, she was alerted to distant screams and the sound of crashing armor and steel. Annoyed, she moved to the cliff edge, stretching out her enormous golden wings. She sat up, looking down at the Ert below. She was intrigued by a small patch of light, which seemed to diminish as overpowering darkness threatened to overtake it.

"What is this?" the Dragon wondered aloud. "I missed everything. I must really stop taking naps." She leaned forward, looking closer with Godlike vision, seeing how the light was now a pinprick compared to the darkness surrounding it. There, in the middle of the black, she spied a tiny armored creature. Sitting upon a white horse, he prepared to face certain death at the hand of an overwhelming enemy. The human rallied his band and exhorted them for their bravery. Listening intently, she sensed his aura. He who was the light had unmatched pureness of heart, as if he was Haya's own. Then the Dragon realized that he was.

Maradwynne listened from her perch to this tiny figure's final words as he gave his exhortation, wondering what the human was thinking and what his epitaph would be.

The shining figure shouted into the face of death:

"Stand tall, young and old.

Yslan, with your sons so bold,

Raise high the sword and shield,

Cut them down to bleed and yield.

Stand strong, men of Hodan,

Ride your steeds this field today,

Send the evil ones to Haeldrun,

With their lives do make them pay.

Stand strong, men of Cinnog,

Raise your pike and lance to bear,

Run them through, as if a parchment,

Rain death upon their icy stare.

Stand strong, men of Suden,

Hold the evil beasts at bay,

With your swords and shields locked tight,

Let our archers have their way.

Stand strong, men of Eden,

Your valor saw their corpses rot,

Your loss was heavy but ne'er for naught,

For love and honor have you fought."

"This cannot be! I have failed them in the hour of their need. Haya, forgive your servant." The Dragon mother sprang from her cliff, roaring angrily. "He shall not die, if I have anything to say about it. I will preserve this light, even if it is but a candle in the wilderness."

The Dragon tucked her wings, diving at incredible speeds toward a hill on the Arondayre. Off in the distance, Maradwynne heard the roaring of her many children. She was pleased as they answered their mother's call of fury.

"They come. Good, my children. We will purge this evil from the fields of Arondayre and save this puny human who dares to be a God. I like him!" The Dragon smiled as Dragons do.

* * *

Puryn's men headed for the opening of the forest. They were surprised to find a single Legion of Elfish Draj already standing in the breach with a single Legion of Dwarves by their side. Puryn advanced to the Elves, who were on horseback. One horse looked familiar; it had come home when the carnage began. It was Haystorm. Puryn smiled and petted her on the brown spot on her nose. She was old and frail, but ever loyal. The Draj riding her recognized Puryn and Orus. He dismounted and handed Haystorm's reins to the returning Elfish Prince, and Puryn took them, thanking the young Draj. The rider saluted and then called his unit to attention.

"Stand tall, men and women of the Draj. The Hero of the Elves returns. Draj-Manot Puryn is among us!" the Draj cheered with enthusiasm.

"Good to see you still breathe, my student," a familiar voice said from the front of the Draj unit.

"Indeed, master. Haya, be with you," Puryn responded, knowing it was Master Gulsbane who led this charge.

"We are here to die for Torith, Puryn. What brings you here? You have a land to die for," Gulsbane quipped flippantly.

"I am between two lands, my dearest brother. I will fight here for the both of them. Adasser does well for my people. I fear I do not fare as well as she." Puryn looked to the west and sighed.

"You are correct, My Prince. She has grown to immeasurable power. She is the Holy Mother. You are married to our High Priestess."

Puryn was staggered by the proclamation. He now understood how she ran the trees at will. He smiled, remembering her face.

"She has augmented my forces for almost two weeks now. We have fought with short naps and breaks in the trees she has provided. We are weary and ready for Haya to do as she wishes." Puryn looked to the sky and searched for a sign, but there was none to be had.

The Draj leader spoke to Gulsbane and suggested they quickly reallocate the forces and the equipment to where they would do the most good. Hodan was given horses and spears; some of the riders were given bows. Puryn knew Orus was most deadly when his forces were armed and mobile. Yslan's Draj-Erynseere armed themselves with sword and shield.

Cinnog grabbed one-hundred-fifty pikes, and Suden was given any leftover swords and shields they could find. Finally, Edenyag arrived on the field with one-hundred-fifty men carrying their own standard nine-foot spears. This was all that was left.

Puryn and Orus counted about one-thousand total warriors from all of humankind, one-thousand Torith Draj for the Elfish people, and one-thousand Dwarfish Legionnaires for the Dwarves. Finally, all of the Commanders set their armies in place, as everyone in the ranks hugged their friends and said their final goodbyes.

Puryn commanded in a subdued tone. "Shields to the front, gentlemen, pikes to the rear, horses to the flanks. If we had some archers, I would tell them to hit the higher ground or the trees." This evoked laughter from the men of all nations. "I am proud to call you all my brothers and sisters. May Haya grant you all a seat at her table."

"Huzzah, Draj!" the Hodan shouted.

"Huzzah, Hodan!" both Torith and Erynseere shouted.

"Huzzah, Cinnog!" Suden cheered.

"Huzzah, Suden!" the Cinnog returned.

"Huzzah, Eden!" the Dwarves celebrated loudly.

"Huzzah, Dornat al Ar!" the Eden spearmen bellowed enthusiastically.

Then they were silent. The armies could hear the rancor of metal rattling as hundreds of thousands of the remaining Offlander threat advanced toward the Arondayre.

Puryn steeled his gaze, commanding in the voice of a God. "Ready … LOCK!"

In a single motion, the Draj locked shields. The Dwarves did the same. Then, Puryn mounted his horse and drew his sword.

"Spears … preeeeeeeesent!" The spears shot forward like the quills of a porcupine between the shieldmen, and a loud "HA!" echoed in the tree line. "Commander, harass and kill them all. I love you, brother. See you on the other side." Puryn saluted Orus.

Orus's eyes were red as he choked on his words. "Let's make them bleed so badly, they leave and go back to the Underworld from whence they came."

"Agreed." Puryn smiled as he watched the enemy funnel into the tree corridor. The Baron of Erynseere shouted sarcastically toward the oncoming horde. "Let me introduce you to my extended family, Orcs. The trees are on my wife's side."

Orus chuckled. The remnant watched as the trees ripped at the flanks of the evil, making a sizable dent in the oncoming darkness, but unfortunately, it was not enough to change their odds of success.

The enemy's advance through Adasser's gauntlet took several hours, but the Offlanders eventually reached their objective. The Priestess was doing her worst, but after several minutes on the lines, Orus and Puryn realized it was no use trying to fight the hordes in the open field.

Puryn called to Orus. "Orus, regroup and reform on the hill behind us! We need higher ground!"

"Go, boy!" Gulsbane shouted. "We will hold them here. Retire to the hill and kill them there! This is a lost cause!"

"You must come with us, master!" Puryn begged.

Gulsbane turned, smiling like in the old days. "You know that is impossible, you fool! Run, save yourselves, and find a way to save the Ert! You said it earlier. We shall meet up on the other side!"

The Offlanders were raging and pushing against the Draj, but the Draj remained impressive. They moved with expert precision, as if they were one cutting machine. The blades of their weapons whizzed in a circular motion, shields moving expertly, covering the next comrade as they executed an attack. It looked like a wave pulsing through the shield wall—all at once, as the enemy crashed upon the Draj blades, and they died in a grisly heap.

The Dwarves were doing their share of damage as well. However, the Dwarf Legionnaires relied more upon their superior armor to take the brunt of missed blocks. Their movements were not as pretty as the movements of the Elves, but they hit like mules and crushed everything that opposed them.

Despite the initial success, Puryn retired to the hill, knowing that without Adasser's trees, the enemy would have engulfed Gulsbane and his forces, ending this battle within minutes. As it stood, the trees were losing to waves of suicide attacks, and attrition had begun on the Draj shield wall. Despite the valor of the warriors, they were dying, and Gulsbane was bleeding, but still fighting.

"Run fool, run!" he shouted as the Orcs overran his position.

Tears streamed down Puryn's face. He shouted as he retreated, "I will never forget, master! Never!"

The last five-hundred warriors of men rode, ran, or limped the one-thousand yards to the hill on the Arondayre. The rest were torn to shreds as the blackness swept them away.

Puryn looked at Torith and imagined the King and Queen of the Elves, looking out of their windows at the carnage and praying for the people. He was not wrong, because as the men bled, the Elves stood vigil, knowing the standard of Yslan and Hodan.

Glorin wept as he saw the battle coming, fearing this would end his valiant son-in-law's life. Grieving for him, he also wept for Adasser and the children. There was nothing Glorin could do. Torith was helpless now. All of his armies were spent, and Puryn and Orus were all that was left.

Haystorm stood upon the hill with her boy on her back. She was terrified by all of the commotion, but happy to have him back. She trotted wearily in place, wanting to run, wondering why she had run here in the first place, but the mare knew there was no place to go and figured she would spend her last moments with her boy. Men crowded around her boy, and other horses were charging here and there. A large man ran interference with one-hundred other horses and boys. Puryn gave his speech, which was later etched in stone, to be read on Puryn's Day for generations to come.

* * *

It was all a muffled blur to the exhausted and emotionally numb Puryn. He was so torn and tired that he could not hurt anymore. The men cheered after his speech, but he did not remember saying any of it. He figured it was Runnir, Gunnir, or Haya—one of them must have channeled their speech through him, but it was only him, speaking from his heart. Praying to Haya in silence, he waited for his death to free him from his torment.

"Have mercy on us all. Please spare Adasser, the children, Father, Mother, and the poor widowed Queen." Puryn looked around him as he snapped out of his daze. The men of all nations crowded around him. Each one looked at him for answers. The faces were somber and resolved as they waited for the end.

Then it happened. A roar came from the sky. The cry was so intense and powerful that everything stopped on the battlefield. Many Offlanders instinctively turned, running, knowing something big had made that sound. Puryn looked up into the blinding sun, unable to see anything. Then there were more roars.

"Oh damn, this already? What new evil have these bastards unleashed?! Will Haya never respond?" Puryn bellowed angrily to the sky.

The Draj-Manot was livid and fed up. He just wanted it to be over with already. The warrior twitched in his saddle and screamed in the voice of

Runnir. "Come on, you filthy wretches, come to your death or bring me mine!"

Then everyone on that hill saw them flying in from all angles—gold, silver, copper, and bronze—for starters, and then every metal imaginable. Some were big, some were small. Some were long and snakelike, while others looked like the Thunder Lizards described in the old stories. However, all of them flew, and they were making a beeline toward the hill where Puryn sat in his saddle.

Landing with a massive crash squarely on the Offlander front lines, Maradwynne made her grand entrance. Puryn looked up and was not afraid. A seventy-foot-tall golden Dragon crushed several platoons of the Scourge under her massive body and then roared again. Puryn's men instinctively covered in a dome of shields, some cowering in fear, but the Draj-Manot stood straight in his saddle. He did not care anymore. The Dragon would eat him. It would be over, but he would fight her. Then, the unexpected occurred. The Dragon turned to Puryn and nodded.

The Draj's jaw dropped in disbelief. When Puryn finally realized that the Dragon was his ally, he roared loudly to the sky, raising his sword. This was Haya's answer. The Dragon jumped and lifted off, turning toward the scrambling Offlander army, which now ran in all directions. Maradwynne lit the killing fields on fire.

Adasser's trees quickly withdrew to a safe distance as the Dragon Mother roared angrily, spraying Dragon's fire up and down the enemy ranks and all around the hill where Puryn and his men now stood safely. The men on the hill could smell the burning hair and flesh and hear the squealing cries of the dying Offlanders. Orus and most of his men barely escaped to the hill, but some Hodan were caught in the fray. Orus was gravely wounded from battle, but remained in good spirits.

"Looks as if we have found a way somehow, brother. Or should I say, Haya or your Lady blesses us?" Orus held his hand over a severe gash on his side. He could see Puryn's concern. "Just a scratch, brother! Jabir gave me worse when I cut his bloody head off." Orus laughed, but grimaced in pain. "Regardless, I think this may be what we needed. This will turn the tide." Orus pointed to the sky as hundreds of Dragons arrived. "Welcome, my scaly friends! Fry them all!"

Haya stared stoically at Haeldrun, who angrily retired to the Underworld. He had failed, but promised to return.

Puryn smiled for the first time in a couple of days. He rode over and hugged Orus. "Don't you dare die, you old goat!" Puryn chided. "I've lost too many who were dear to me today. I cannot bear another."

"Oh, quit with your crying, boy!" Orus chuckled, and then he slapped Puryn on the spaulder.

The aerial battle raged for almost two days. By the time all of the Dragons had arrived, they numbered in the hundreds. Offlanders were torn to shreds by tooth and claw—crushed by tails and, of course, burned to ash by Dragon fire. The Dragons decimated the Offlander army, hunting them to the ends of the Ert.

When the Scourge had all been laid asunder, and the Dragons had burned many of the remaining ships in the Suden port, Maradwynne tallied her dead. Two-thirds of her kin had perished. Many simply left the battle when they had had their fill of Orc flesh and destruction, but Maradwynne returned to the hill where the tiny human still remained. A few of her children circled in the air above them all, searching for stragglers.

The Dragon Mother saw them on the hill in a makeshift camp. They were resting and healing. Puryn stood the watch alone. His army had collapsed from exhaustion, disease, and malnutrition. The Draj-Manot treated Orus's wound the best he could, but knew his brother needed professional attention. The Dragon swooped in quietly, but landed with authority. It was as if the towers had dropped in front of the hill and planted themselves before Puryn.

Puryn rose, realizing this was no ordinary Dragon. She was definitely an Ancient. He knew they were brilliant, some rivaling the wisest of the Elves.

The hero bowed and saluted, sheathing his weapon. "Hail, Dragon. I thank you for your rescue. You are truly a magnificent savior."

The Dragon understood him, but could not respond to his words by the use of spoken words. Instead, she spoke to Puryn through his thoughts.

"You are the reason I came. You, and an accursed pine tree and its damned cones."

"Pine tree?" Puryn asked with curiosity.

"That is a story for another time. Suffice it to say, Dragons have been the keepers of the Ert in times past. I was asleep, but I woke to see your plight and was compelled to act. Many of my kind died to purge this continent of the evil that sought to kill your light. Be sure to tell your people that Dragons may look fierce, but we are not to be feared—unless, of course, you seek to kill the light. That will never be tolerated."

Puryn nodded. "You are always welcome in my lands. Thank you, er, I do not know your name."

"I am Maradwynne, Mother of the Dragon-kind," she growled quietly.

Puryn gasped, remembering his lore from the monastery. "The Maradwynne who helped to purge the ancient Scourge of the demons? The Maradwynne who sided with the founders of Yslandeth during the clan wars? The …"

"Yes, the …," she replied with embarrassment. "I am she. Your stories are always better than the truth, human!"

Puryn bowed. "I can never repay you for saving all I love."

"You can by leading these fools to unity," Maradwynne insisted. "I think you will have a mandate after this near apocalypse. So many innocents …"

Maradwynne roared, but the men slept on. They were used to it after two days. "I must return to my home above the clouds, but remember your obligations, and remember the Goddess. Peace and glory, Puryn, the Hero. We shall meet again. I shall speak with you again in this way from my home, if you would not be opposed. Do not be alarmed. I will identify myself." Puryn thought he saw the Dragon smile.

The warrior snorted. "Thank you. I would not like to wonder if it was you or if I was going mad!"

Maradwynne roared, laughing the way Dragons do at times, and then she jumped into the air, flapping her massive wings. She lifted up into the sky, climbing so high that try as he might, Puryn could not make out where the Dragon came from. So he gave up his attempts, and instead began to pray to Haya. The hero realized he was still breathing, while so many others were not as lucky.

The Goddess Aluia sent the rain. It rained for almost two weeks straight when all was said and done. The water was welcome, because it put out the random fires that raged here and there on the Ert. It also washed away the filth of death and the ashes of the fallen Offlander army.

While it rained, Puryn roused his army. "Let's go to Oron Falmarindi. I know healers are there. We can get food, too. Then, we sleep and find our way back to what is left of our homes."

The men groaned, waking from the first real rest they had enjoyed in a couple of weeks, and then began walking a day to Torith. The forest had burned to the ground. Puryn frowned as he remembered his childhood with Gulsbane. It was completely gone. The men walked another day until they reached the foot of the mountains, where they were met by citizen guardsmen. None of them were trained warriors. They were primarily hunters and farmers.

"Who goes there?" one guard challenged.

"I am Draj-Manot Puryn, Prince of Torith and Baron of Erynseere, and this is my entourage. We were just passing by and saw the light in the window." Puryn's men began to laugh. Orus was reminded of Sir Ontak's sarcastic humor. The man who stood before him was not a young boy any longer. Puryn was a hero and his brother. The guard dropped to his knees, prostrate on the ground, but Puryn bid him stand. "Please, there has been enough groveling for one century. May we please see your healers and get a meal?"

"At once, Your Highness," the guard called back, and several men ran out with gurneys and a horse-drawn cart. The survivors, totaling around five-hundred, rode, walked, or were carried into Oron Falmarindi, where they were treated as heroes.

King Glorin hugged his son-in-law, thanking Haya and her children for their mercy. Then, the Elfish King told Hansu, who wept joyfully, running to the nearest tree and ensuring the good word got to Adasser in Erynseere immediately.

Adasser, upon hearing the report from her mother, began crying tears of relief. She could not thank the Goddess enough, hugging her three children and kissing them repeatedly, telling them, "Daddy is alive and will be home soon!"

Ilari said plainly, "I knew he would win. Haya is on our side, Momma. You are her, and she is you, and Daddy is her favorite warrior. How could we lose?" He kissed his mother on the nose and ran off to play with the other children. Adasser watched him go.

That one will be interesting when he gets a bit older, she thought in amazement. The boy was too young and cute to be taken seriously right now, but he spoke as if he was ten years older, which made the Priestess a bit uneasy. Shrugging it off, she remembered that she once tore an Orc in half with her will. Adasser knew more study was needed. However, there was no doubt in her mind that he would tag along.

* * *

In Hodan, Faylea, daughter of Orus, was organizing the survivors who dug out the remains of Hodan. She waited for word from her father, but figured Orus must be dead. Stoic in public, she cried in private, hoping the King still lived. Too many were killed. She did not want to burn her father, too.

The word of Puryn and his Dragon friend spread like a fire. As stories go, this one was no different, growing with each retelling. The legend grew, and Yslan began to call for its addition to the Books of Lore.

Yslandeth knew the King was gone, but their Queen still remained. They petitioned Falda for direction, but she was in no mood for life at the moment. Widowed, she no longer wished to rule alone and hid in Erynseere.

Two weeks later, when the rains finally stopped, Falda eventually traveled to Empyr to live in the rubble that was once her home. Every stone was a memory. The Queen decided she would never live in a stone building again. Instead, she resolved to abdicate her throne and move to Torith once the monarchy was settled. Yslan's Queen was ready to retire and live out the rest of her life with her beloved Elves. No one could blame her, although many tried.

The Return of the Champions

T he legends grew throughout the Ert, with people naming Puryn the Champion of the Golden Queen. Those who remained thanked Haya for their deliverance, attributing the destruction of the enemy hordes to the courage and prowess of both of their saviors, Puryn and Orus.

However, as with all rivalries, Yslandeth leaned toward Puryn, crediting him with possessing such pureness of heart that the Dragon Queen was inspired to intervene, securing victory for humankind. (They were not wrong.)

No one knew of the feats of Adasser, and the Priestess was fine with that. She did not want the throngs of the helpless bowing to her, as some had begun to do with Orus and Puryn. Adasser saw this as worship and blasphemy toward her Goddess. She knew, more than anyone, that Puryn was indeed a hero, but still a man.

Those hiding in remote locations eventually heard of the victory through riders dispatched by all of the kingdoms. The horsemen rode in all directions, seeking survivors, calling them to travel to the capital city of Empyr.

Large masses of humans, Elves, and Dwarves, traveling from all corners of the Ert, hoped to get a glimpse of the new heroes and sought them out as the representatives of the Goddess. Many strove to touch them as they passed, thinking if Haya had graced them, they could touch the Goddess through the gesture. It was a silly superstition, but to desperate folk, the hope promised by a ragtag remnant of the Ert's glorious warriors was too bright to ignore.

Empyr became a refugee camp for all of the races of the Ert. The people who once despised each other, so much so that they swore oaths promising to kill their rivals and their families, now camped shoulder to shoulder, sharing their food and medicine.

Gone were the grand notions of nationalism and borders. It was all burned and crushed under the boots of the Underworld. No one was of any tribe or kingdom—they were all simply survivors of the Ert. Haya looked down on the devastation, shedding a tear of regret, but resolved that all was now as it always should have been.

Haya watched from the heavens as her plans came together below her. "My children, it is completed. The mortals have seen their end and fended it off through the use of light, love, and selflessness. In the blackness of extinction, I forced my creation to reconcile its differences and cast aside its prejudice. No longer are there factions that war and burn the innocents. The people are one, and they now see each other as souls striving to survive; each now assists one another as brothers and sisters. The Heroes will return. The people will worship them and perhaps the Dragon. I will not smite them if this brings them comfort and promotes peace. The remnant remains, and they will rise again from the rubble."

Haya's children bowed respectfully and went about doing whatever it is that the Gods go off to do when mankind is dull and peaceful. Haya smiled contently for the moment.

Aluia hugged her mother and prophesied to her in the heavens. "Your Champion will unite the people and rule for one-hundred years. Hodan and Sudenyag will unite and take to the seas, becoming a great and powerful nation. Edenyag will return to its scrolls, documenting things of importance and restoring art and the sciences. Cinnog will build defenses on the shores of the Ert. The Dwarves will once again move out of their mountains and into the light, and the Elves will greet them as brothers. The forests will return to Torith, growing over the ashes, and the fields will produce a bounty, blessing all who toil therein. There will be peace and prosperity for an age under the rule of your Champion and his sons."

Haya smiled and hugged her daughter back. "May all things be as you have said!"

* * *

In Torith, the Elves came out of their fortress under Oron Falmarindi. They cried silently at what they beheld. Torith was no more. All that remained was a blackened ring of trees and a pile of rubble where a beautiful Elfish city once stood. Glorin wept publicly at the destruction, as did his Queen. Puryn stood silently in thought.

Standing in the fields where his master once taught him, the Champion remembered the times of his childhood. The prophecy, the vision, whatever it indeed was, had come to pass, and he was in mourning for the place his heart had come to call home. The towers in Empyr were toppled, and his forest was burned, but still, the people remained, and this encouraged him.

Puryn muttered with a knot in his throat, "It can all be rebuilt if the people remain."

Kneeling in the burned-out tree line, Puryn wept for his master and Torith. Orus let him be. He would make no bantering calls to "toughen up" today. His throat tightened, remembering Hodan's greatness and how far they had fallen. He wondered how his girl had fared in the flames of the end as he looked around at his fifty remaining warriors. The tears began to fall from his eyes, too.

Sympathizing for his brother-in-arms, Orus walked to Puryn and knelt beside him. Puryn didn't notice. Instead, Puryn stared off at a nondescript hill on the Arondayre, still weeping. Everything that had occurred rushed over the Draj-Manot within minutes, overwhelming his soul. He was just a man, but now everyone was looking for the hero to lead this remnant out of the darkness.

Puryn hoped Haya still loved him and would hear his cries. But, after all he had endured and all that was lost, he was unsure. "It is a long road to Empyr from here, brother. It never seemed that long during a battle or when the rolling pastures met my horse's hooves all those years ago on the way to Dornat al Ar. It will be difficult to look at everything we ignored to get here, stand, and live to see this day."

Orus wiped his own tears, then steeled his gaze toward the hill. "They did not die for naught. They better not have, brother. There is still work to do. We do not have the luxury of grief or mourning. Let the people do that. But, in the meantime, you must help them. You must lead them back to the light."

Puryn looked at his brother-in-arms, pouncing on him. He hugged him in a firm embrace as the two wept harder, remembering all who dared to stand with them against the darkness.

"The Goddess could not have given me a better brother, Orus. You are a hero and a champion of no peer. I am here, because of you, because of my lady's trees, and because of the favor of the Goddess. Who am I to lead these people? Who do I dare to pretend to be?" Puryn released his friend, and Orus smiled.

"You are the Champion of the Golden Queen," Orus said seriously. "You are the only one fit to wear the crown. You are the only one who they will follow. This is your destiny."

"King? I am no King. I am a boy who has never been a child, always trying to prove myself a man and never seeming to attain the level I seek while ever striving to reach that mark. I will never make it to the end. I will never reach the goal. Why would they follow me? Why should they?" Puryn sighed and stood up. "Who in the Underworld am I to assume I will ever fill the shoes of Swyk or any of the great Kings before? I am nothing."

"That is why you are the one. You will never settle, and you are always growing. You do not see the great feats you have accomplished, but everyone else with eyes does. You are loved and respected, son. You are the only one who will succeed." Orus stood and put his hand on Puryn's shoulder. "We must leave this place. We must travel to Empyr and there, claim your throne."

Puryn reluctantly agreed, walking out to where the ring once stood. He remembered his masters, Elig and Gulsbane, and all they taught him. Taking a deep breath while trying to let his hatred and anger go, he prayed to Haya.

"Holy Goddess, I know not what you see in me or why you have seen fit to elevate me to this lofty position. I pray that my beloved masters both sit and feast at your table, and I ask that you tell them that I miss their solid and wise counsel. I wish they were here now, so I could ask them many things. Please grant me wisdom and affirm to me with a sign if you desire me to assume the crown of Yslandeth. If not, please forgive my assumption."

Puryn finished praying. Opening his eyes, he saw the sign he sought after within the charred remains of Torith's trees. He now stood in a field of wildflowers in full bloom. But, within the flowers, he saw something else. Bending down to shoo the petals to the side, he touched the first of many sprouting acorns and pine cones. Torith was in renewal, and the Goddess had granted Puryn his sign. He turned toward the King and Queen of the Elves.

The dumbfounded warrior shouted, "Your Majesties! Your Majesties! Come quickly! It is wonderful!" Puryn was smiling wide. He was pointing to a curious ring of wildflowers that Their Majesties had not noticed while in tears, lamenting the loss of their trees. They rushed over to see what the matter was. There, they saw their son-in-law pointing down toward a tiny sapling. Puryn jumped back.

"That was a seedling moments ago, Your Majesties. Magic is afoot here, and Haya has blessed our wood again."

Their Majesties cheered and thanked the Gods. Elves in the area wondered why everyone was so happy all of a sudden. Then they slowly filtered out toward the ring, seeing the young trees growing all around them. The Elves shouted loudly to the sky, thanking Haya, singing, and dancing in their open field. Soon, they would rebuild. Soon, Torith would stand again.

* * *

Several weeks after everything calmed, the Dwarves within the mountain sent scouts to look around. Human riders were seen in the area, but the Dwarves hid quietly, waiting and watching to see if the coast was clear.

When the Dwarfish riders had determined that the enemy was nowhere to be seen, King Bogrol ordered the gates of Dornat al Ar to be opened, and the surface dwellers re-inhabit their homes above ground.

The Dwarves were no worse for wear, but they were totally defenseless, save for a small police force that patrolled the city under the mountain. Their farms were desolate and destroyed. The hill Dwarves, as they had become known once more, remade their homes and plowed their fields, cleaning up the residual filth of the enemy, burning it at the foot of the mountain. Within weeks, farmers were planting seeds and watering. It was late in the season to grow for the spring, but meager crops were better than none.

The Elves eventually arrived at Dornat al Ar, rekindling their friendships with their neighbors and helping them with their fields. It would be a short season, but this was not the first time either race had tightened their belts and rationed their food. The alliance could not see defeat, as it worked together as a family. Within six months, food was scarce, but not a dire concern in the lands of Dwarves and Elves.

Edenyag once again wept for their lost tomes and scrolls. They sifted through their cities' remains and found all of the remaining knowledge, art, and lore they could gather. It was a considerable amount, but much was lost to time forever, only to be remembered by spoken word or in song or tradition. Edenyag strove to rebuild their libraries and galleries and then set upon the task of building a viable defense.

The Eden also built great fisheries and planted for the autumn harvest. Food became normalized within a year. This was not an easy task, because, like the rest of the nations of the Ert, Edenyag had scarcely one-hundred men to stand watch. As a result, many of the nation traveled to Empyr in search of guidance and protection.

Cinnog rebuilt over time. The great citadel was torn down by the Scourge, but the castle remained. Cinnog took to building small outpost fortresses on the shorelines of the entire Ert after gaining permission from Puryn and his war ministers.

Cinnog collaborated with Eden mages for assistance with technology, while engaging the Dwarves to manufacture precision machinery. The Eden scientists introduced Thunder Powder to the Ert. Their Dwarfish counterparts devised a precision cylindrical tube, capped on one end and open on the other.

They put the Eden Thunder Powder in one end of the cylinder. After packing it in tightly, they tamped a sizeable smooth stone on top of the charge within the chamber. Then, the Eden mages lit the powder by using a small hole drilled in the chamber that was holding the powder. Unfortunately, the first few tests resulted in severe injuries, because the large tube crushed several Dwarves standing behind it as it blasted backward against a stone wall.

Although the initial tests were dangerous, the researchers could eventually jettison a stone almost seven hundred yards away. Eden scientists and Dwarfish engineers decided later that the second generation of the weapon would be secured to a stone slab. The improvement provided an anchor to counter the tremendous force of the Thunder Powder explosion. It proved successful, as the new weapon threw a twenty-five-pound spherical rock more than one-thousand yards with ease. There were no casualties to the research team this time.

Eden then set to figuring out the science of ballistics, and when they did, the Dwarves created reliable sights. A new powerful weapon was born. Cinnog commissioned hundreds of Thunder Ballista, setting them in their small stone embattlements to protect the entire continent. No ship would enter the Ert's waters again without permission—not without fear of being sunk where they anchored off-shore.

Orus and his Hodan eventually went South to Sudenyag, finding a few salvageable ships in the harbor at Port Valent. Suden had no complaints when the Hodan took a couple of barges to the vessels to investigate these floating marvels.

Inside the large ships, they found more than they had bargained for. Orus found cages with men, women, and children locked inside them. Some were starving, and many had already died from dehydration or malnutrition. The prisoners sat looking as if they were waiting for death when Orus opened their cages, freeing more than one-hundred souls.

Later, the Hodan King estimated that more than a thousand had perished in these cruel conditions. He did not venture a guess as to how many more may have been on the ships that the Dragons burned and sank during the war. So the King sought out the Edenyag scientists, and together they figured out how to operate the vessels. The Eden sages took notes, writing down specifications, in hopes of duplicating and improving upon the enemy's design.

One of Eden's sages consulted the Dwarves, seeking to make a smaller version of Cinnog's new defensive siege weapons. Eden and Dornat al Ar created smaller guns, outfitting one ship with five. The new miniature version only had a range of five-hundred yards with a projectile of ten pounds. Still, when tested on a derelict, listing in the harbor, Orus was pleased that he was able to sink the vessel from four-hundred yards away.

This marked the beginning of the naval forces of the Ert. With captured enemy maps and navigation instruments, Orus decided he would track down other peoples who had been subjugated under Offlander rule. Hodan's amphibious assaults became the stuff of legends, and Orus was considered like a God of the seas until his supposed demise, while reportedly fighting on the high seas in defense of women and children of a foreign continent.

Faylea, daughter of Orus, stayed behind and led the rebuilding of the Hodan nation. She became the first female Hodan Chieftain by choice of the people. Faylea was so loved for her bravery and compassion that no one dared to challenge her rule, and she became an icon in Hodan lore and like a Goddess in her own right.

* * *

Empyr, before the reclamation, was a pile of rubble with thousands camped in squalor. Disease and hunger were commonplace, but the people of all races and kingdoms shared whatever little they had. Puryn and Orus—before the latter left on his own adventures—rode with their five-hundred survivors through the Raven's Pass. It was eerily silent as they traveled. The only sound heard was that of the clopping of horse hooves. Even the wind was quiet, and the birds had no song.

Soon, the heroes reached the river to the East of Empyr, but the bridge was burned, so the band traveled North for a day to find a usable ford from which to cross. Puryn was still riding old Haystorm. Her steps were still sure and strong, but she was old and ready to relax and eat grass in her old pastures. The old horse was near the end of her life, but would stay with her boy and see him home.

The tired Draj stroked her mane as he rode, his mind drifting to his master and learning to ride. Resisting the urge to feel sorry for himself, the hero refocused on the journey ahead, looking at the devastation as he rode at a trot through the remains of Yslan. Soon, the band of men could see the ruins of Empyr in the distance.

To the South, the Great White Wall had collapsed in several places, and the guard towers were all burned out and blackened. The steel gates were broken and twisted, and the roads were marked by catapult shot. Puryn frowned, looking at the mess he would be inheriting.

Entering Empyr's lower villages and shires, the Draj-Manot looked at all of the dirty, crying faces. He remembered how, in years prior, his father had ridden these villages as their constable. As a child, he lived within what was once a great castle, under the care of a great King and a loving Queen. Looking to where the towers had fallen, the Baron sighed wistfully.

"Oh, Elig, I have failed you. Gulsbane, you put your faith in a fool," Puryn mumbled, but as he said this, the young man was startled by a loud, strong cheer. Muddy faces stood at the tree line. Thousands were looking at his shining silver armor and torn standard, knowing this was Erynseere.

The Champion of the Golden Queen approached. It was Puryn, Haya's chosen, and these were his heroes. They had come, just as the people had hoped and prayed. A little girl in a filthy dress ran with a buttercup in her tiny hand. She held it up to Puryn, who looked down at her and swallowed hard, lifting the waif up onto his saddle. He hugged her looking to the sky. "Gods help me," he whispered.

The little girl smiled. "They are, My King. They are." The girl's parents were beside themselves in embarrassment. They begged Puryn for his forgiveness for their child's audacity.

Puryn responded. "There is no need for forgiveness, my people. She honors me more than you know." He let the girl down gently, and she ran to her mother and father, waving and cheering for her new hero. Puryn rode away with a broken heart; he was numb.

Much to his dismay, the scene was only getting worse. The word spread, and the streets were now lined with tens of thousands of muddy, soot-covered faces. They all stood in rags and were exhausted. They came from every place on the Ert to stand and wait for Puryn, who didn't know how to begin. But, then, things began without him.

It was Donick who instigated the whole thing. "People of the Ert, behold the cohort of the Golden Queen and her Champion, Puryn. Three cheers for our saviors."

The people erupted as one in a thunderous roar. The cheering went on loudly for about another hour. The crowds had engulfed the five-hundred warriors. Puryn sat on Haystorm. He again felt like the boy of Torith, as the weight of rule began to sink into his head.

He would need a miracle to rule the whole of the Ert. But, then, Puryn remembered Donick and looked to where he sat, in the old courtyard, upon the platform where Swyk had called his father in from the wall on his day of birth. There, he spied his family sitting on old crates. Adasser looked older and tired.

Ilari was waving, jumping up and down. "He is screaming at the top of his lungs, no doubt. Adasser is going to kill me," Puryn said offhandedly.

Orus heard him and laughed loudly. "Go to her, my brother. If they will let you!"

"Make way for the Champion! Make way!" Orus shouted forcefully. The crowd parted, allowing the cohort to enter the courtyard. Then, as quickly as they could, thousands drew close to witness history. Puryn cared not for the crowds, nor Yslan, nor the Ert, for that matter.

He ran across the stage to his Lady, sweeping her up in his arms and off of her feet. She wrapped her legs around his waist, as she had done the last time he had gone to war, weeping again, all over his face. He looked like that same hurt puppy dog, except now his locks were graying, his face bore the scars of war, and wrinkles had formed at the corners of his mouth and eyes. She kissed him as hard as she could.

Embracing her love, the Elfish High Priestess made her decision, praying: *Haya, it is my right as a Priestess and as an Elf to give my life to others as I see fit. I give freely and am privileged to do so. I thank you for your gifts. Please bless this man with longevity. I will not truly live without his light.*

The Goddess nodded, "As you wish, My Priestess."

Puryn jerked back from her kiss as if it slapped him in the face, not knowing what had just hit him. He felt invigorated and happy for the first time in forever. His wife smiled as the gray hair faded and returned to blond in most places, and Puryn's wrinkles faded. The returning warrior hugged his wife for a few more minutes, knowing he had to answer an overzealous swarm of his children. Ilari, Altwidus, and Elpis now hugged their father's legs and were all calling for his attention.

Adasser released him and smiled. "Talk to them before they explode, hero. We will reacquaint ourselves later this evening. You will have no other plans." She was not asking.

"No plans, my love. I only want to lie with you tonight and love you until my final breath." Puryn turned to his bouncing children, who were all smiles. They rattled on about the Orcs and their mother's feats. Ilari was particularly eloquent in his detailed description. Puryn looked at his wife in awe with a knowing smile.

Adasser heard them, playing it off until she saw her husband staring at her. Then, he rose and bowed. "Do not bow to me, husband. You bled on the fields until you had no more blood to give. You ran to save my family when no one else came. I owe you my life, as do my people."

"Not the entire story, my love, and you know this. We fought as hard as we could. Hodan, Suden, Eden, Cinnog, and even Torith and Dornat al Ar stood with me at the end. I know Erynseere was there, too. The trees and animals gave us an edge when we needed them. The Dragon spoke of pine cones waking her and bringing her brood to our aid. Your doing? If so, you saved us all, but I get the credit." Puryn smiled at his wife.

She looked at the ground, and then replied, "I was the anvil, and you were the hammer. How it was at the beginning of this journey is how the end played out. Now, the people look for a hero, but I am a Priestess, not a ruler. Take your place among your people, my husband. Rule." Adasser sat.

"Queen Falda is the ruler of Yslandeth. Where is she?" Puryn replied as he noticed a cloaked figure dressed in funeral robes striding with purpose toward him from out of the corner of the courtyard.

The figure removed her hood and walked confidently over to Puryn. "I am here." She knelt before him.

"No! Rise, Your Majesty. You shall never kneel before me!" Puryn protested, pulling her up by her hands, but she would not stand.

"I am Queen by marriage. I have done nothing to deserve this position. My love is dead. The kingdom is in ruins. I sit upon its ashes and cry through my nights. I am alone, Puryn. Without my Swyk, my heart grows cold." The young man could see it in her eyes. Falda was worn out. "I want to return to Torith. I want to serve the Elves as a healer and a teacher. They will need me there."

"But what of Yslandeth? What of your people?" Puryn gestured over toward the mob, who listened silently, dejected and exhausted. They wanted Puryn, and Falda knew this. She was not opposed to it. It was her vision, after all. He would save them and then lead them out of darkness.

Falda replied. "Puryn, son of Durn, the Courageous. I stood by and watched you grow from the cutest little boy, into the strongest man I have ever known. You are not assuming, and you never think yourself better than another. Your chivalry is unblemished, and your peers find you of impeccable reputation. You have learned all there is to know about Yslandeth—the lore, the martial combat styles, the politics, and power struggles. You have also learned much of what it is to be an Elf, and strangely to this day, you and I are kindred in that our souls both yearn for the trees and Torith. We even shared the same master, who is now passed into Aeternum and sits with the Goddess." She turned to the people who were listening to her speak. "Who better than you to stand here today and assume the throne of the Light of Yslandeth, the Beacon of the Ert? Who else has managed to claim the title of noble, become a Prince of the Elves, and win the hand of the Holy Mother of the Forest?"

The people gasped, looking at the Elfish Princess. They did not know this about Adasser. Falda continued, speaking to the crowd. "Puryn became an Elite protector of the forest and is the last living Draj-Manot, and from what I have gathered, perhaps one of twenty Draj who still walk the Ert. He came back to his home among men at the request of his King and assumed rule over a decimated barony. He took men, women, children, Elves, and Dwarves and built an empire that fed the kingdom when food was scarce. He was so blessed in his endeavors that by his mercy and love, he sent aid to those who were considered our enemies, also saving their people from desolation and starvation."

Orus had found Faylea with Adasser earlier. He had not ceased hugging his daughter from the moment he found her. The pair nodded in unison, affirming the report.

"Hodan is now our friend for the first time in history, and by Puryn's leadership and wisdom, he fashioned an army from the remains of our combined greatness, most of which perished upon the Arondayre before the Dragon Queen chose this hero as her Champion, and burned the Scourge to ash, preserving not only his life, but all who stand here today."

The people began to cheer. There were whistles and drums. The crowd erupted in a jubilant display of thanks. Puryn blushed with embarrassment, looking only at his wife.

"Go. Be their King," Adasser said plainly. Then, she kissed each of her children and bestowed longevity on each of them as well, without anyone's knowledge. It removed years from her own life, but she was determined to have them with her, or to leave the Ert as soon as possible, so she could rejoin them. What were a few decades to an Elf who didn't want to live after her loved ones passed?

"Are you sure, My Princess?" Puryn asked, envisioning her as the young lass in a white dress. He teared up again and cursed his eyes.

His Lady smiled. "I am. It is what you were born to do, husband."

Falda looked more powerful than she had ever been. She turned to Puryn and said in Elfish, "Are you ready to assume your rightful place, my son?

"I am, my dawn," he replied. "You are my second mother, and I love you. I am sorry for your loss. I loved him also." Puryn sniffled again. Tears fell from Falda's eyes freely as she kissed Puryn's face.

"Step up to the front. This will be the simplest coronation in history!" She smiled as if a weight was lifted from her soul and knew Swyk cheered from Aeternum. "People of the Ert, I salute your tenacious loyalty and perseverance. I submit that King Swyk now lies in a tomb, along with my heart. I have nothing more to give this kingdom. I wish to return to my trees in Torith and resolve to do this as soon as possible. I also submit to you that Puryn is the Champion of the Golden Queen, the Draj-Manot of Erynseere, the Baron, the Prince, the Protector, and the chosen of Haya. Who better to lead you out of darkness than he? What says ye, Yslandeth, what says ye, Ert? Shall Puryn be your King, and Adasser your Queen?"

Adasser sat up startled, forgetting that she would be part of the package. She sat straight up and shushed Ilari and the other two children, trying hard to listen. Arla and Durn appeared, as if from nowhere, whisking up their grandchildren.

"Go be with your King," Arla and Durn said solemnly.

"I will go, Parents of the Chosen. You are blessed. Thank you." Adasser stood and walked to her husband and took his hand.

The crowd erupted in cheers, affirming their desire for Puryn to assume the throne. Puryn stared blankly out over the sea of suffering faces. He saw everything as a blur. Falda raised her hand for quiet. The crowd noise quieted to a murmur. Grabbing two velvet pouches from her pack, Falda turned toward Puryn and Adasser.

"Kneel," Falda commanded.

The two knelt in the stone courtyard, looking up at their Queen expectantly. Falda opened the two velvet bags, producing two golden crowns. They were the very crowns that Swyk and Falda wore as they ruled together for thirty-plus years.

"Puryn, son of Durn, and Adasser, daughter of Glorin, you by right of arms and chivalry have shown your true qualities. You have shown your love for the people of the Ert and your love of the Goddess." Falda wiped away tears as she looked at the crowns, her life with Swyk flashing before her eyes.

"My Queen, are you all right?" Puryn asked, concerned.

"I am. These bloody memories break my heart, my beautiful son," Falda replied, smiling through her tears. She cleared her throat, handing the smaller crown to Donick, who stood stoically watching the whole affair. "Puryn, son of Durn, do you swear to protect the people? Do you swear to uphold justice and mercy? Do you swear to defend her to the death?" Falda broke down and then composed herself.

Many in the crowd cried along with her, remembering her husband's just rule and the Queen's constant concern for the people. But those days were gone, and a new day was dawning.

"I do, My Queen, and I swear by my children that you are always a Queen in my eyes and welcome in this castle. I swear this until the end of my days. You will always have shelter, food, and clothing. You shall never want. If ever in need, all you need to do is send word from Torith."

Puryn bowed his head, and Falda set the crown upon his head. It fit as if it was made for him. She smiled. "Of course, it fits."

Puryn rose.

Falda shouted as a proud mother. "Hear me, Yslan! Raise your voices! All hail Your King. King Puryn, the Champion of the Golden Queen. Three cheers for your new King!"

The crowd cheered their new crown and settled down quickly, knowing this was not over yet. Orus could not stop smiling, watching the boy he met a few years prior truly become his peer. This King was already his brother in his book, but now they were true equals.

Falda handed the other crown to Puryn, who turned awkwardly and saw his Princess on her knees before him, smiling as tears streamed down her face. To Adasser, her husband towered to the sky, looking like a giant from the lore of old. The sun was behind him, and his golden locks flew wildly in the winter breeze. The Priestess saw him standing in his Elfish chain, shining in the sunlight, a ragged tabard of Erynseere fluttering like a flag around him. Smiling, she thanked the Goddess.

"Adasser, the only woman—Elf, human, or Dwarf—who has ever ruled my heart, I ask you to be my Queen. Humbly, I beg of you to sit beside me and guide my hand with your wisdom. For I am but a man, and without your temperance, I will fail and fall into folly. You are my light and my guide. You have been my partner throughout this mess, and I know I would not be here to offer you this shiny piece of metal without your intervention. It is only a symbol of our position. Gold and silver have their places. Gems and stones are beautiful to gaze upon, but without you, they are just as useless as rocks of the fields and rusted iron implements to me. You know the value of life. Our people are the treasure. We will increase our wealth by increasing our people." Puryn looked at his wife as if he beheld the Goddess herself, placing the crown upon her head.

Adasser sprang to her feet and hugged Puryn tightly around the neck. Then, picking her up, he spun her around. There was no decorum to this ceremony, and the people in attendance did not seem to care. Falda laughed and clapped for the new monarchs. As they presented themselves, the birds returned to the trees. Some of them perched on Adasser's shoulders. A column of light now encircled the new King and Queen as they looked at each other in disbelief.

"The Goddess approves," Falda said smugly. "Who would have thought?" *Haya laughed at Falda's sarcasm.*

Puryn picked up on her sarcasm, then looked to the skies. With a fist in the air, he thanked the Gods. The new King would set his cabinet tomorrow, but he had one final thing to do tonight. He would send Swyk and Ontak to Aeternum in proper Yslan fashion. Stone tombs were not for the men of the Ert. A pyre was the only proper warrior funeral. Falda nodded and sent for the bodies to be retrieved. Both had been dead for weeks, but strangely, they were preserved. No signs of decay were found on either hero's body.

Puryn smiled, knowing this was the Goddess's hand once again.

* * *

Donick was appointed as the new master of the Order of the Sect of Haya. He performed a traditional funeral rite for King Swyk and for Sir Ontak. Throughout the ceremony, Puryn held Falda as she wept. She was inconsolable, and Puryn was beside himself with his own grief.

Puryn ordered the ashes of the two to be collected and stored in two large barrels. They were remembered where they fell in battle, at the foot of what remained of the Great White Wall. Over both sites, memorials were eventually created by King Bogrol's masons. The Dwarves created a twenty-foot-tall statue of King Swyk, the Warrior, and another of Sir Ontak, the Champion of Yslan. They stand in remembrance with great tablets, exhorting the great deeds and sacrifices of the two men. The new King visited them often throughout his life.

When Puryn ordered the monastery to be rebuilt, he had memorials created for Master Elig of the Order; Draj-Manot Master Gulsbane of Torith, and finally, a monument to his former nemesis, but a brother in the end, Athis, the Redeemed. The lore of Athis was often taught as a lesson in redemption—a story of how anyone who sought redemption with a genuine and contrite heart would find it in the end.

* * *

The day after the coronation, Falda mounted Haystorm, heading East for Torith. She arrived a week later, without escort. Puryn had offered, but she declined. The King set Falda up with provisions, clothing, food, and plenty of gold and jewels. She arrived at Torith and was welcomed by the Elfish people with open arms.

Falda became a mistress of the Order of Haya within Torith. She taught many Elfish children the ways of nature and healing. She lived to a ripe old age of sixty years old. Although she would never see Yslandeth rebuilt, she was content that Torith grew a ring again and was happy within the trees. The Elves and Dwarves always seemed to recover without much effort. Nature took care of her followers.

Puryn and Adasser ruled from Erynseere for twenty years, while the Dwarves and humans rebuilt the capital of Empyr. Puryn was forty-five years old when the monastery and the towers were finally finished. Finally, at fifty years old, he saw the castle reopened. Then, with Adasser, he officially moved the government back to the traditional location.

Puryn left Ilari in charge of Erynseere. He had become a holy man, much like his mother, and was the head of the local Elfish clergy. In his time, he grew strong and made his own legends.

Altwidus was given the plains, mountains, and forests North of his brother, taking over where Athis left off at the Barony of Korin. Altwidus brought great wealth to his people through agriculture and the breeding of horses. Cross-breeding Elfish horses with warhorses of Yslan produced the fastest, most agile, and bruising steeds the Ert had ever known. His father would adopt their use in his slowly recovering cavalry.

Elpis went to Edenyag to study science and magic. She became a well-known mage and scholar. There, she met a young noble. A few years later, they were married. She eventually became a Baroness and a scholar in Edenyag. She successfully petitioned her father to fund education for the common people.

The King created a Learning Ministry, assigning Donick as minister. Teachers were trained at the monastery in Empyr and sent out to the surrounding lands. The resulting literacy led to a more efficient economy and a proliferation of new authors and poets. No longer did the Elves and Edenyag have a claim to all of the poetry. Mankind had begun to write their odes and their songs. Peace reigned for sixty-five years upon the Ert.

* * *

The time of Kings and paupers is measured, and as with all good things, the end finally came. Puryn passed into Aeternum with Adasser and his three children by his side. He died of old age, but he did not pass in pain or suffering. Durn and Arla had long passed before him, as had Falda and Puryn's friends and ministers Donick, James, Willum, Marst, and Bandu. Orus was lost on the seas.

Adasser saw that with each passing soul, Puryn saddened a bit more. She understood his pain all too well, as she feared the day when she would burn his body, sending him to the Goddess.

That day occurred in the 803rd year of the Age of the Nations, and Adasser burned Puryn's pyre with her children present. Shortly thereafter, Adasser abdicated her throne, feeling it inappropriate for an Elf to lead mankind. In her mind, her sons were at least half-human, so Ilari was made King by the line of succession, ruling well for another one-hundred years. He died at the age of two-hundred-and-twelve years, and Adasser sent his soul to the Goddess with Elpis by her side.

Altwidus became King for a very short duration, dying a few years after assuming the throne. He lived for two-hundred-and-fifteen years, but he was only two years younger than his older brother. He was already an old man when he sat upon the throne. Elpis passed within a year of both of her siblings, leaving Adasser alone. They had left her no grandchildren.

Adasser, with half of her life still before her, was now alone and in dire sadness. She prayed to the Goddess for guidance, deciding she needed to be with the Elfish people.

Yslandeth had formed a council to determine who would be King after the line of Puryn died out, but Adasser no longer cared who sat upon the throne. Her heart was thoroughly broken, and she resolved to return to Torith, knowing her parents were not far from leaving the Ert themselves.

Within fifty years of her return to Torith, Adasser sent both of her parents to Aeternum. Her sister, Adenya, assumed the rule of Torith with her husband, Feli, but Adasser's sorrow was now complete. The High Priestess decided at that time to commune only with her forest and serve the Elves and her Goddess. She was not often seen in public, preferring her privacy and trees to mortals. The woods were eternal and would never leave her.

Writers wrote long poems and songs as the musicians played merry tunes. Yslandeth worked out its political system, and the Alliance held for a time. But all things come full circle under the sun, and all things pass into Aeternum.

Mankind eventually forgot their brotherhood pacts over petty nonsense as weak men climbed to power, leading the people astray over petty gain and personal pride. Adasser cursed their utter stupidity, turning her back on mankind permanently.

* * *

In Torith, under the great tree of the temple, sits a carved stone tribute with King Puryn's ashes beneath it. His children are all buried around him. A tablet sits beneath the statue of a proud Draj, surrounded by three playing children who tug at his tabard, looking for his love. Torith honors its favorite man unto this day.

The tablet reads:

"From *'The Reckoning of the Age of the First War of the People.'* A passage from the Ancient Books of Lore from the lands of Yslandeth and of Her Exalted Holiness, Maradwynne, Champion of the Skies, Savior of Men.

The Battle of Arondayre

"Once, when time was young, and man was without malice, all lived as one within a single land. But as with all good things, this too passed in the tide of the years, and man grew restless. His desire and ambition became fuel for the fire of self-promotion and advancement.

"Heroes arose from masses of men, calling forth great armies of followers—some to peace, but others to conquest. Thus were the days preceding the great darkness, in the days before the great purging of mankind, in the first war of men. The lands became separated by imaginary lines of demarcation.

"Clan territories and allegiances were formed. Nations rose and fell as borders between neighbors were established, creating another rallying cry for war. Peace was scarce for a time, and mankind seemingly could find no use for life, save to end another's existence until the first Great War against that unspeakable evil.

"The evil came in the night. Some say man's bloodlust brought the plague of doom upon the people. The evil had no preference; it hated no one more than the other. Ages of strife among men became a distant memory. These same foes, who had in days prior, sought to slay the others' sons, now strived for peace and alliance against a common threat. The demonic forces of evil and darkness crushed army upon army, leaving strong men to ponder their choice of profession and many a man to flee to the hills. But alas, there was no safe haven, and the enemy showed no quarter and no mercy.

"The Orc and Goblin swords, poisoned with the vilest potions, spread disease and death throughout the land until a final Yslan Legion, cobbled together from the remains of all feuding mankind, made a final stand before the plains of Arondayre, at the foot of the Altyr Mountains. There, the hero Puryn and his men stood bravely, their banners flowing in the cool autumn breeze, the sound of horses whinnying and armor rattling. A prudent band would have run for their lives as the black mass approached the open field, with odds of one-hundred of them to one.

"There, Maradwynne, Mother of the Dragon-kind, and future Goddess of the Yslan, did see the mortal, Puryn, give his final address to his men. Her gaze fixed upon the wonder of this tiny armored creature seated upon his horse. Maradwynne gazed into his soul and saw it bright as metal, pulled straight from a fiery forge. She saw his heart was pure and honest and that he was prepared to die to defend those who could not defend themselves.

"Puryn then exhorted his men as thus:

> 'Stand tall, young and old.

Yslan, with your sons so bold,
Raise high the sword and shield,
Cut them down to bleed and yield.
Stand strong, men of Hodan,
Ride your steeds this field today,
Send the evil ones to Haeldrun,
With their lives do make them pay.
Stand strong, men of Cinnog,
Raise your pike and lance to bear,
Run them through as if a parchment,
Rain death upon their icy stare.
Stand strong, men of Suden,
Hold the evil beasts at bay,
With your swords and shields locked tight,
Let our archers have their way.
Stand strong, men of Eden,
Your valor saw their corpses rot,
Your loss was heavy but ne'er for naught,
For Love and Honor have you fought.'

"Maradwynne, so inspired by this final act of bravery and courage, left her cave within the mountain that touches the sky, rearing back with a roar that pierced all upon the field that day. So fierce was her shout that the demons themselves stopped in their tracks to see what had made such a sound. Upon that moment, and at that predetermined time, when Maradwynne did roar thusly, a return roar came from a distant mountain in the North, then the South, then the East, and finally the West.

"Within moments of her cry, men shielded their eyes from the sun to see a sky filled with Dragon-kind of all ages on the horizon. These same Dragons rained fire and misery upon the evil ones on that field of Arondayre, sparing the small band of humans, who were preparing that day to die.

"The exchange of blows went on for a full day and night. In the end, Maradwynne and her band of Dragons prevailed, but none of her kind survived, save she. Many Dragons lay dead upon the ground in a grisly heap of Orc, Goblin, and demons. Maradwynne only smiled and said in her native tongue, 'Who truly desires to live for eternity, rest well, my family,' but her words fell upon deaf ears, and no one heard a word, but instead, a roar.

"The people cheered and cried out to the Dragon. Some swore their allegiance, some their worship. And as with all good legends and stories, the truth became skewed and faded by time's hand and foggy recollection. Dragons became Gods of men, and men, once again, became the enemy of man.

"For it is a truth of all things, that all things return in a circle, and all things have their season under the sky. Thus ended the glorious victory of Maradwynne, our Savior, and of the hero, Puryn, her chosen. May she reign above forever."

* * *

Adasser often sat at Puryn's feet and read the words, remembering her loves and their lives. Three-hundred years later, she left the world of the Ert and joined her family in Aeternum. She was reported to smile with her last breath. Her final words were recorded as, "At last, My Love, I see you. I come to you."

Her people burned her, as is the custom of the Elves and men. They placed her ashes beside her love's and within her family's circle. There, they planted a pine tree, which grows to this day. It is now a natural memorial, which towers over the statue of her husband and is visible from the outside of Torith, from as far as the Raven's Pass.

At the foot of her memorial is a plaque that simply states, "Holy Mother of the Forest, High Priestess of Haya, Queen of Yslandeth, Princess of Torith, wife of the Champion and Mother of Kings and nobles. Rest well in Aeternum, sister."

When Adasser and Puryn were reunited, it is said that twin stars, adjacent to each other, burst into view. Navigators call these stars the Lovers or the Heroes, depending upon who you ask, and they are used to guide sailors home safely unto this day.

* * *

In Aeternum, Haya rewarded her heroes and her faithful with an unimaginable paradise. The Goddess personally greeted Adasser upon her arrival, with Puryn and her loved ones all around. They all sat together at eternity's table, feasting and catching up on lost time. The family and friends walked the flowered fields and forests of the afterlife, basking within the light of eternity, secure within the knowledge that they would never again suffer or cry for death or separation from a loved one. They were eternally home and together forever, having fulfilled their parts in the Conflict of eternity.

Haya comforted herself in the knowledge that they were happy beyond their wildest dreams, but still felt a bit of guilt for all they had experienced on the Ert. Nevertheless, the Goddess knew there was a reason for all events under the sun and that nothing happened without the knowledge and permission of the Gods. Knowing these truths, she left her new arrivals to their happy reunion, redirecting her attention to the renewing cycle of things. It was only a matter of time.

Epilogue

After an age of lesser leadership and suspect devotion to peace, the Ert gradually returned to its old ways. The lands healed and their scars covered. Eventually, time erased all memories of the events that had transpired and forced the races together as brothers and sisters.

Mankind became complacent and petty once again. The stories of the heroes were never forgotten, but the horrors of those days faded with many plentiful harvests. They were replaced by arguments over power and wealth.

Haya lamented her creation's return to foolishness, and sat back to see if man would need another reminder of its true priorities. She hoped for a change in the eternal cycle, but wondered if mankind was truly capable of retaining any lessons of the past. She began to doubt it. They always seemed to revert to their baser selves. Haeldrun never seemed to repent. She wondered if he would ever come home.

It has been written and proven, time and time again, through trials of man and Gods, that all things return in a circle, and all things have their season under the sky. Great deeds tend to turn into dusty scrolls that sit on a darkened shelf in some great library, when fools forget their past, and are doomed to repeat its folly.

About the Author

Austin Belanger is a retired United States Marine and graduate of American Intercontinental University. He is a poet and author who has published many poems and short tales in various online writing communities. Austin has been married to his wife, Karen, for over 30 years. He is a father to three grown men, one growing boy, and eight grandchildren. "The Champion of the Golden Quee" is his first formally published work and is the first book in a collection of stories entitled "The Tales of the Ert."
Email: bardofthesand.publishing@gmail.com

You can connect with me on:
f https://www.facebook.com/BardoftheSandPublishingLLC

Also by Austin S. Belanger

In the Shadow of the Great White Wall (Book 2)
The Goddess has won her battle, but her love, the Dark Lord, continues in his struggle for dominion. Puryn wrestles with gaining control of his ravaged and lawless lands. New smaller wars simmer in all locales around his borders as vile pretenders rise with claims of title and rights to foreign thrones. Civil war and strife threaten to derail the fragile peace of neighboring kingdoms. Evil seemingly survives and pushes to bring their Lord to the Ert to exact his revenge.

A new band of heroes is called to action as the new generation takes up the mantle of their elders. Theirs is the task of bringing the King's vision to pass. The teams are young, but they are the best that Yslan has to offer. A tenuous future rests in the hands of the unproven few.

"The Ert was a smoky, charred mess of disorder, chaos, and violence, and despite the gilded words of a victor's Scribes and Heralds, real people suffered in those first few years after the great reckoning of the Goddess. The official truth is always skewed, and seldom bears a resemblance to the reality of what happened. Humankind is known to tell a good tale when the drink is good, or the lady listening is fair, or when the truth is too ugly to remember. Many times, a scribe takes poetic license with the events of man, washing facts with cleansing waters of prose and legend. More often than not, fairy-tales are not written for the children of men, but instead for adults seeking comfort in better memories of their past deeds. These prettier versions of the truth soothe the guilt of many past indiscretions. This tale is not one of those stories. This account is of what happened next."
—The Ancient Tome of Lore

The Long Run to Redemption (Book 3)

King Orus of Hodan is an aging Champion. His warrior Kingdom is well known throughout the Ert for its prowess in battle and thirst for glory. The old King knows full well that those who cannot defend their throne when the challenge comes end up dead, and their defeat takes their families with them.

Orus knows his people. Their memory for the glory of the past is short and their patience shorter. Political strife within his own borders combined with problems with alliances push the old warrior to decide; stay and die a disgrace in the eyes of his people or leave for places unknown in search of a glorious legacy. As the grumbling of his people continues to increase and with no wars left to fight, he is left with little choice.